# WAVE DANCER

## DAUGHTER OF VANRIS
## BOOK ONE

NIKKI McCORMACK

•

*To everyone who has supported me along this journey, from friends and family to my amazing readers, I offer a heartfelt thank you.*

•

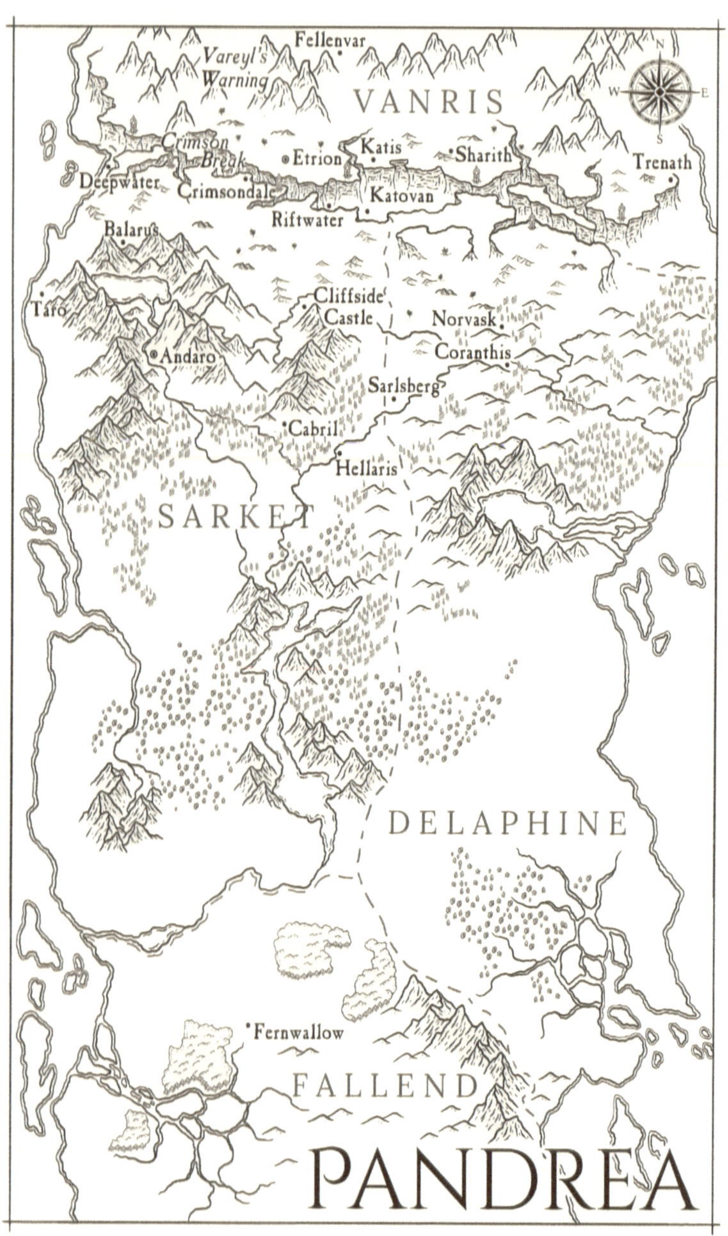

Fellenvar
Vareyl's Warning
VANRIS
Crimson Break
Etrion
Katis
Sharith
Trenath
Deepwater
Crimsondale
Katovan
Riftwater
Balarus
Cliffside Castle
Norvask
Taro
Coranthis
Andaro
Sarlsberg
Cabril
Hellaris
SARKET
DELAPHINE
Fernwallow
FALLEND
PANDREA

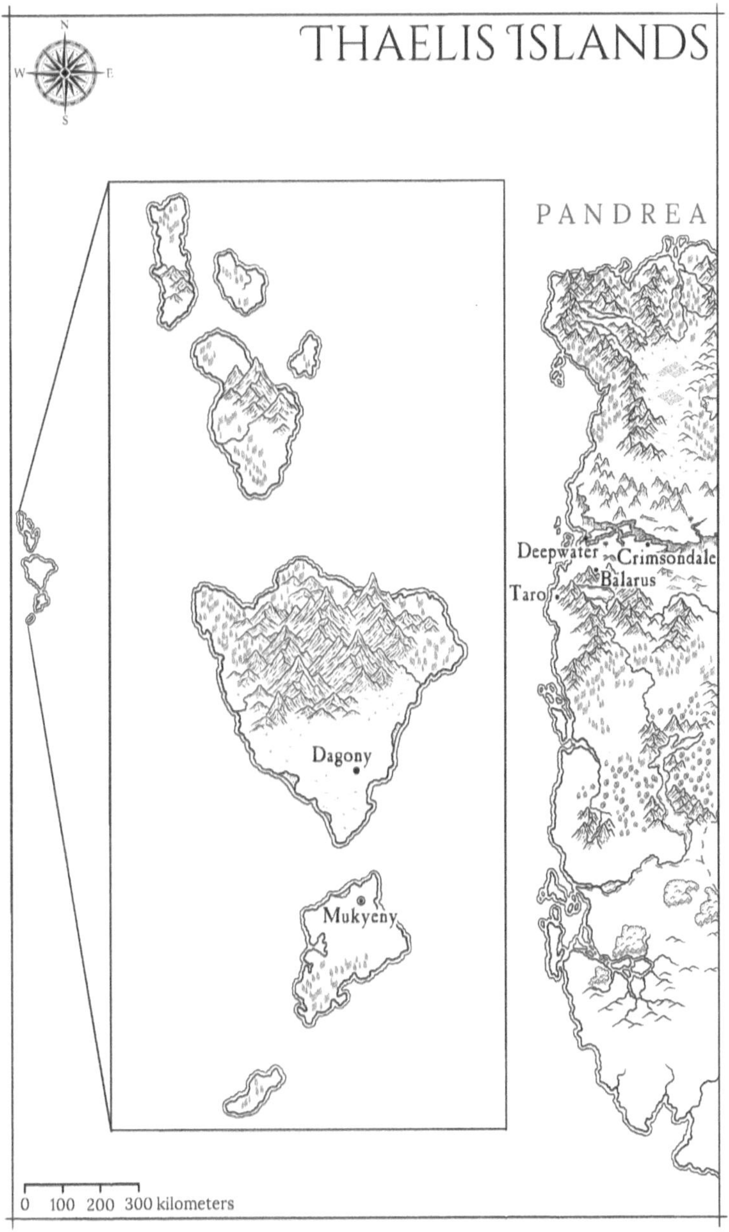

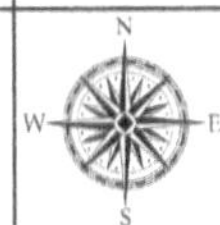

THAELIS ISLANDS
N
W E
S
PANDREA
Deepwater
Crimsondale
Balarus
Taro
Dagony
Mukyeny
0 100 200 300 kilometers

Veyl crouched on the edge of the black-tiled rooftop of one of the academy buildings, peering out toward the towering black gates that marked the main entrance to the desert city of Etrion. This academy had some of the tallest structures in the city, overshadowed only by the central tower of the mind-crafter academy and a few sections of the palace. She and the two boys with her were almost high enough up now to get a good view of the entourage arriving soon.

Two Feral mind-crafters were providing an escort mounted on their massive kanodraks. The vaguely feline, scaled predators were reason enough to seek a good vantage. Not that she didn't get to see her father's kanodrak quite often, but the revered beasts never failed to impress. The entourage they were escorting carried her maternal grandparents, arriving from the northern capital of Doran to be there for her Trial day and accompanying celebration. Now that she was thirteen, she could go through the Trial to awaken her mind-crafting ability, assuming she had one, which she obviously would as the first-born child from two powerful mind-crafter bloodlines.

She had to.

Fresh apprehension coiled like a serpent in Veyl's gut. To distract from it, she focused on the familiar inner yearning that pulled her west. The best views in Etrion would never satisfy the feeling that something far beyond the walls of the city called to her. A manifestation of her imagination no doubt, always needing to believe more awaited her, as if being the future ruler of the most powerful kingdom on Pandrea wasn't enough. She hadn't spoken of that yearning in a while, not since Gannon had teasingly called it her 'fish sense,' since the most notable thing to the west was the ocean.

She dragged her attention back to the task at hand, shifting into position to help the two boys behind her if they needed it.

"You know we're just going to get in trouble for this." Despite his remark, Jaysen prepared to climb up after her.

She glanced down at him. Sarket's future king brushed a lock of dark auburn hair out of his face, gazing up at her with eyes the same vivid blue as his mother's. His hair needed trimming again, at least by the standards of his kingdom, but Veyl liked how he had let it grow longer in the Vanrian style. It hid his odd, rounded ears and complemented the strong jaw that was becoming more defined as he got older. He was fourteen now. In a year, he would return to his homeland.

She ignored the tightening in her chest and smirked down at him. "Then why did you agree to come up here, *Crown Prince* Jaysen?" She emphasized his title with a touch of biting sarcasm.

"Because you wanted to, *Khesran* Veyl." He gave her title the same treatment, though a grin cracked his features, undermining the attempted insult in it.

Veyl tried to suppress a smile with limited success and offered a hand down to him, the other resting on black tiles that were cool to the touch despite the blazing sunshine thanks to some unique property of the substance they were made from. She didn't understand how it worked, but it made clambering around on the black rooftops in the desert heat easier.

"I'm sure Mother and Father are going to love that logic," Tavin grumbled, the faintest nervous tremor in his voice.

Veyl's good humor faltered. Her gaze moved to her little brother crouched a few feet behind Jaysen, his stance and wide eyes speaking to his discomfort as he stared down at the distant ground. Then Jaysen took her hand, pulling her attention back to him. The prince's grip was firm and confident, his trust in her spreading a flush of warmth through her chest.

Looking past Jaysen at her brother, she said, "I told you not to follow us, Tav. You shouldn't be up here."

Tavin's green eyes narrowed in a fierce glare. "Neither should you two."

Veyl ignored the remark, focusing her attention on helping Jaysen to the next level.

As soon as he was securely situated beside her, he turned and smiled smugly at Tavin. "Your parents are going to love your logic as well."

Glowering, Tavin reached up for a small statue of a sitting tethdrak—hound-like reptilian beasts that Feral mind-crafters used for hunting and combat—affixed to the rounded corner of the eave. He smacked away the hand Jaysen offered him. "I don't need your help."

Jaysen shrugged and moved away to give him space.

"Tav, don't be like that. You'll just get hurt." Veyl inched closer, shifting discreetly into position to assist if he needed it.

Tavin pulled himself up with the hand wrapped around the front legs of the tethdrak fixture, getting one knee up onto the next roof level. Some of his long red hair fell into his face. Veyl had warned him to braid the sides back as she had done with hers if he insisted on coming, but he hadn't listened to her about that either. He reached out, seeking purchase on the smooth tiles that made up the academy rooftop. When it looked like he was going to make it, she started moving away, searching for the best route to the vantage point she wanted. They would have a decent view from this level, but a flatter area she had spotted around the front might provide a more secure place to settle and watch.

Scrabbling and a startled cry snapped her attention to Tavin as he began sliding back over the eave, a thirty-foot drop from the lower roof to the ground looming a mere ten feet behind him. If he fell, he would have a hard time arresting his momentum before going over that next lip. He had let go of the statue, perhaps thinking himself secure enough not to need it.

Veyl shifted her weight, balancing on the balls of her feet, and skidded down to him, stopping at the edge of the eave by leaning back onto the less slippery heels of her boots. She grabbed his wrist, her position precariously close to the drop. His weight pulled her off balance, but before she could fall with him, Jaysen caught hold of her arm, sitting down to use his rear and feet for traction against the roof.

Veyl leaned back to counterbalance her brother, struggling to keep him from going over, her heart beating triple-time. "Grab the statue!"

"Don't let go!" Tavin's eyes were wide, tears rising in them.

"Just grab it!"

He pulled against her, straining their chain of support. Her feet slipped a fraction. Then he caught hold of the statue's legs and some of the weight eased. When he started hauling himself up, she lost the leverage in her current position.

"Jaysen, help him."

"I'm not letting go of you," Jaysen countered.

"I'm fine. Help him up."

She checked her balance as Jaysen's hold slowly loosened, then disappeared. He grabbed her brother's hand. When he nodded, she let go, allowing him to take over. With Jaysen's help, Tavin finally clambered the rest of the way up. He scrambled away from the eave, one foot slipping as he hurried past her. Veyl felt his boot collide with her ankle and knock her leg out over the edge. She pushed forward with the other foot, panic sending a jolt through her as she made a desperate lunge for the stone tethdrak Tavin had just moved away from. One hand closed on the back of the statue, sliding down as her arm pulled taut, the ridges along the beast's spine slicing into her palm.

Veyl cried out, tears springing to her eyes. She fought the impulse to let go of the object that was wounding her. It hurt, the pain so intense that she could barely think past it. Only the threat of that long drop behind her kept her holding on while she sought purchase with her other hand. She swung her arm up, reaching for the statue, feeling the palm of her wounded hand slipping from the slickness of her own blood. Then Jaysen caught her wrist, his grip crushingly tight, though she wasn't about to complain.

"Get your leg up." Jaysen grunted with effort, leaning back onto his heels and rear again to keep from slipping down with her.

Veyl met his eyes. He would never forgive himself if she fell now. She couldn't let him live with that. Tears streaming down her cheeks, she pulled on the statue and Jaysen pulled on her. She could feel the serrations on the tethdrak's spine cutting deeper. Nothing appealed more than the idea of taking her hand away from the source of that pain, but she held fast, heaving one knee up to gain what leverage she could with it. Then, all at once, she was on the rooftop, half laying on Jaysen, her hand blazing with agony.

She rolled off onto her back, clutching the wrist of the wounded appendage to her chest. Jaysen lay next to her, drawing in a deep, shaking breath.

"Let's not ever do that again, all ri—" He cut off when he looked over at her and rolled up onto his knees. "Havaad's fires, you're bleeding."

"I noticed," she answered through clenched teeth.

"Veyl." Tavin's trembling voice drew her attention. He was staring at the blood streaming from her hand with wide, tear-filled eyes, the color draining from his face.

"I'm fine, Tav." She forced the words out, wrestling back her own tears despite how desperately she wanted to wallow in her misery. If her little brother broke down completely, they would never get out of this mess.

Jaysen yanked off his tunic and shirt. He ungraciously grabbed the dagger she had at her belt and used it to cut one sleeve off. Leaning closer, he said, "This is going to hurt, but we need to control the bleeding. Can you hold it up for me?"

She nodded and raised her palm.

He looked at the long, gushing wound, then cut the other sleeve off. This, he folded and pressed over the gash. She hissed, fighting the powerful impulse to jerk her hand away.

Jaysen's brows pinched. "Sorry. I need you to hold that there."

She placed a finger over the makeshift pad while he started wrapping the other sleeve tightly around her wounded hand. A few hot tears spilled down her cheeks, but she kept the hand steady, pulling her finger out when the bandage was secure. He tied it in place, then started inching toward the corner with the tethdrak statue, its spine now painted red with her blood.

"Where are you going?"

He met her eyes. "You can't safely climb with your

hand like that. I'm going to get help."

"Then Father will find out, and he'll kill me."

Jaysen took hold of the front legs of the tethdrak. "I doubt that. He thinks you're the reason the sun rises. Stay put."

Tavin started following him. "I'll come with you."

"No!" Jaysen pinned them each with a fierce gaze. "If either of you moves from this spot before I return, I will never speak to you again." When they both stayed where they were, he nodded and inched back to the edge of the eave.

"Jaysen."

He froze, staring at his hand that gripped the legs of the statue. "What?"

"Thank you for not letting go of me."

He met her eyes, something changing in his expression. "I would never let go of you, Veyl."

Her breath caught as he dropped over the side. She didn't breathe again until she saw him inching out toward the edge of the lower eave where they had come up a tricky climb from the top of a wall enclosing the academy grounds. Tavin, seeming calmer now, also stared after Jaysen as he made his way down. Veyl gripped her wounded hand and brought it to her chest, hissing through her teeth at the pain.

After a few seconds, her little brother gave her a contemplative look. "I don't think he meant that the same way you did."

"Meant what?" she snapped, her focus on not screaming or crying. Blood was already soaking through the fabric of Jaysen's ruined shirt. He was right. She wouldn't be able to climb with the injury.

"The part about letting go of you."

Veyl's attention returned to Jaysen as he moved into position to lower himself over the next eave, the wiry muscles in his bare torso taut, his tanned skin picking up a warm glow in the sunlight. Her cheeks grew hot. "Shut up, Tav. Jaysen and I are best friends. That's all."

"Too bad he's not Vanrian."

Veyl sucked in a breath at a particularly intense stab of pain. Did she have it in her to reprimand him right now if he said something insensitive? "Why?"

"He would be a good tehnaak for you."

Veyl closed her eyes and laid her head back on the roof.

Everyone in Vanris had a spirit sibling—a tehnaak—bonded to them at a young age. The pairings did nearly everything together, their families sharing in the process of raising them, which had the added benefit of providing a second home for children orphaned during times of war. It meant they always had someone they could turn to. Someone with whom they shared a bond deep enough to create an awareness of each other's emotions and needs so subtle it was easy to confuse them with one's own. Veyl had been without that since her tehnaak's death many years ago, but she had found a best friend in Jaysen.

For once, she agreed with her brother.

It took what felt like an eternity of pain for Jaysen to return with help. Veyl's father Kasiel, who ruled as khemron of Vanris alongside her mother, had ridden his kanodrak out to greet the approaching party. At least, that was his claimed intent when he departed that morning. They all knew he would take any excuse for a run through the desert on the magnificent beast. Her mother Velara, the khevarin of Vanris, was somewhere within the palace hastily ensuring everything was ready for their visitors, as if a greater amount of preparation would somehow deflect the scathing judgment of Veyl's grandmother.

With her parents otherwise occupied, Jaysen brought Avris and Merrin, two of the officers they did combat training under, to retrieve her and Tavin. He had also found Healer Nerith, who waited to tend her injury once she was on the ground.

He had made good choices in that she trusted the three capable women to handle the situation, but they were also members of her father's tehsheyn—his bonded spirit family—which meant she would never convince them to lie to him about how she had injured herself. Merrin scrambled up, making the climb look easy, and did most of the work of getting them down. As an accomplished soldier and former assassin, the woman had exceptional skills in navigating complicated situations.

Once they had Veyl and Tavin secure on the ground, Nerith, her long silvery hair pulled into braids behind her pointed ears, unwrapped Veyl's hand and frowned at the still-bleeding wound. "I'm afraid this needs stitching." Veyl winced when she pressed the bandage back over it. "Come. I'll take care of it at the healer's building. Keep pressure on it until we get there."

Avris put a hand on Jaysen's and Tavin's shoulders. A sparkle of amusement lit her pale green eyes and brought a faint smirk to her lips. "The rest of us will go wait for your father. He'll be delighted to hear about your latest adventure."

"You don't have to tell him how it happened." Tavin had to know the plaintive whine in his voice would earn no pity from them, but he was apparently desperate enough to try.

Merrin pinned him with a firm gaze. The warrior's braids weaving her white-blond hair against the sides of her head above her pointed ears enhanced the severity of the expression. "Your parents deserve to know the truth about how your sister got injured. You ought to be offering to tell them yourself."

Apparently missing the intended lesson in her words, Tavin scuffed his feet and cast a sullen look at Veyl. "She was the only one hurt. You don't have to tell them we were all up there."

Avris barked a laugh. "Watch your back, Veyl. Sounds like your brother would happily throw you to the desert cats to save his hide if it came to that."

The intense agony of the wound made it hard for Veyl to pay attention to their exchange. She looked up into Nerith's soft lavender eyes, desperate for the empathy that warmed them. "Can we hurry to the healer's building? It really hurts."

Merrin stepped in front of Veyl. "I have told you before, have I not…"

Remembering the dozens of bruises and minor injuries she had suffered over the years in the sparring ring, Veyl nodded. "Pain is a lesson."

"Do you know what it is teaching you?"

"Don't climb on the academy rooftop?" Veyl offered tentatively, holding her hand to her chest and wishing for the lecture to end quickly.

Nerith cleared her throat. "She's injured, Merrin."

Merrin touched Veyl's cheek and smiled with a deep affection that made the pain a little less somehow. "Good enough for now. Go with Nerith."

By the time Nerith finished stitching and bandaging the wound, Veyl's father had returned, and she had missed the arrival of the company from Doran that had inspired the whole debacle. Merrin would undoubtedly say there was a lesson in that, too. A set of guards escorted her, along with Jaysen and Tavin, to the palace to face the judgment of her parents. It was moments like this that she wished she had been born into an ordinary family.

If it had only been her and Tavin involved, the conversation would have occurred in the sitting room of her parents' private quarters. Because Jaysen was with them, the guards brought them to a small audience chamber within the palace. Though he had lived with them for six years as part of their family, he was still the future king of Sarket, so they maintained a level of formality for certain dealings. Particularly those requiring disciplinary action.

This room was simpler than many of the larger audience chambers, with a floor made of the polished black stone used in so much of their construction because of its abundance in the region. A thin line of dark metal divided the main floor from a border about a foot wide along walls of cream and gray marble, with strips of black stone worked in at intervals around the perimeter.

Two ornate thrones in black and purple with silver accents, the colors of Vanris, sat upon a low dais.

Her parents waited before that dais. They rarely made use of the thrones in any of the audience chambers that she had seen. Their father had one side of his red hair, a little darker than Tavin's, braided against his scalp, unashamed to let the world see the scar from having the tops of his pointed ears cut off as a child. The red lines of a small portion of his ke'hanoath tattoo, his Vanrian identity, framed a scar on the exposed cheek. His gray-green eyes were a few shades darker than Veyl's. Next to him, her lips pressed into a thin, disapproving line, stood their mother, Velara. Her hair, the same dark, blood red as Veyl's, had braids on both sides today, woven through with delicate strands of silver. A dark metal and silver tiara rested light upon her brow over the pale tattooed symbols of her ke'hanoath.

Tavin and Jaysen stood before them with her, Tavin squirming in his spot as if he might wriggle away somehow.

Her mother frowned, the expression tugging at scars that made a sideways V on her cheek, one line continuing across the bridge of her nose. Scars acquired during what was supposed to be a diplomatic mission near the end of the war between Vanris and the three southern kingdoms that ended before Veyl was born. A stark reminder that leadership came with substantial risks. She took a step forward, stopping when Kasiel's hand lightly touched her arm.

"What were you thinking?" she demanded.

They were both looking at Veyl, not the prince or her brother. Somehow, they always knew when it was her fault. Possibly because it usually was. Her mother's silver eyes now had tears welling up in them, making it less uncomfortable to focus on her father.

Jaysen advanced a few strides and bowed, his manner

and tone respectfully formal. "I apologize, Khevarin Velara, Khemron Kasiel. It was my idea to go up and watch the entourage from Doran enter the city."

Veyl cast a startled glance his way. She realized her error when her father shook his head, giving her a hard look before facing Jaysen.

"While I appreciate your devotion to our daughter, Prince Jaysen, I know this is her fault. It is written all over her face. Lying to us will not help her situation or yours. However, as you are the eldest, I have to say that I would have expected better judgment from you."

"Not when Veyl's involved," Tavin piped up.

Her mother stepped forward, pinning her little brother with an icy stare. "Don't look smug, Tavin. Just because this wasn't your idea doesn't mean you are not in trouble."

Tavin snapped his mouth shut and shrank back. Somehow, their mother's anger and disappointment were always more disturbing than their father's. Her parents exchanged a solemn look that stirred a twisting of guilt in Veyl's chest. Her hand throbbed, some of the feeling returning to it now as the numbing agent gradually wore off.

Her father met Jaysen's eyes when he spoke again and Veyl admired that the young prince stood steady before that gaze. "It seems Sarket's regent and Royal Council were right when they decided to delay your ascension to the throne until your eighteenth birthday. You have a great deal of growing up to do still."

"Father!" Veyl stepped forward, defensive anger flowing through her when Jaysen lowered his eyes. She could practically feel the shame that rose red in his cheeks.

His molten gaze turned on her then. "Don't start." The sudden softness of his tone warned her he was balancing on the edge of powerful anger.

The change in his posture brought to mind his kanodrak, Niskenya, when she was about to make a kill, the association sending a chill through her. She retreated a few steps, also lowering her gaze. "I'm sorry. I made a mistake."

"You did, one that could have gotten any of you killed. One that permanently marked you. Let that serve as a reminder next time you consider doing something this reckless." He stalked to her and raised one hand. Though he had never once struck her, she jerked back reflexively. He was faster, catching her chin in his fingers—his grip secure, though not painful—and lifting to make her look at him. "Do you understand what it would do to us to lose you or your brother?"

Her chest squeezed unpleasantly, tears springing to her eyes. "I'm sorry," she whispered, her throat suddenly too tight for her to raise her voice.

Her father kissed her on the forehead, then stepped back. His gaze shifted to the guards behind her. "Escort Khesran Veyl and her cohort to their rooms. They will all be spending the remainder of the afternoon in quiet contemplation." He looked down at her again. "Since you injured your dominant hand, you will practice sparring with me right-handed after your Trial. This doesn't get you out of training."

"Yes, Father."

He put a hand on her shoulder and turned her toward the waiting guards. "If you all need something to do while you consider your choices, you can study for classes or clean your rooms."

"But it's a free day," Tavin objected.

"Not anymore, it isn't," her mother answered.

Veyl hesitated, glancing over her shoulder at her mother. "What about grandmother and—"

"You will see them at dinner," she interrupted, pointing toward the door.

As she was turning away, Veyl saw her mother step into her father's embrace, wiping at a sudden blossoming of tears. "By the Break, Kas, they could have been killed," she murmured.

"I know," he answered soberly, then his tone picked up a hint of jesting. "See what happens when I don't use my beasts to spy on them?"

A soft, frustrated exhale accompanied the sound of her mother smacking him on the shoulder or chest. "You're terrible."

Veyl was almost glad they were leaving now. Next would come the kissing, something her parents did a lot of. She didn't want to watch that. Deliberately not looking at Tavin or Jaysen, she hung her head and walked out with the guards.

*

Less than an hour later, Veyl reclined on the couch in the sitting area of her rooms, trying to ignore the ever-present westward call and focus on a book about the different mind-crafting powers. Once her ability awakened, she would transfer from the main academy to the mind-crafter academy next to the palace, where they would add classes on using her ability to her regular curriculum and the extra political studies she and Tavin were required to take as heirs to the kingdom. Maybe she would be a Feral, like her father, and work with the minds of beasts, a Charmer, like her mother, or an Enkindler like her grandmother, capable of manipulating emotions. Or perhaps something more potent, like an Evoker or Dampener. There were plenty of options, and only one she didn't want, though it brought a twinge of guilt knowing her grandfather on her father's side had that ability. Most people feared him for his Frightener power. She didn't want that.

Her father knocked once as he opened the door and walked in with his cliff cat, Irith. The big predator's back came up to his waist, a little higher if you counted the ridge of blue-gray fur that ran along his spine. His brilliant blue eyes locked on Veyl the moment they entered, and he bounded across the sitting room to her. It felt like a trap of some kind, though she couldn't resist the cat's affection when he headbutted her in the chest, the rumble of his purr filling the room. Her father sat in a chair next to the couch, a fond smile curving his lips when she wrapped her arms around Irith's neck in a brief hug.

Her mother would be speaking with Tavin now. Her parents always alternated when they needed to have serious talks with the two of them, and it was his turn to deal with her. For Jaysen, however, it was almost always her father who spoke with him. That was partly because Jaysen's father was dead, killed by hers in the battle that brought an end to the war, and somehow that translated to the crown prince holding him in the highest esteem. Veyl found it odd that he didn't resent her father for depriving him of ever having the chance to meet his, but Sarket was a strange country, and settling disputes through combat was an honored tradition there.

"He does adore you." Her father rested his elbows on his knees and considered them both.

Sinking the fingers of her uninjured hand in the big cat's thick blue-gray coat, she dared a glance at her father. The crushing realization that she had frightened her parents enough to move her mother to tears made it difficult to find her voice. "I love him too," she murmured.

"What led you to think climbing on the academy rooftops was a good idea?"

She sat back on the couch. "I just wanted to see the entourage from Doran ride in. When I tried to figure out where we could get the best view from, I remembered a story Uncle Nakhul told me about him and mother climbing on the palace rooftop in Doran to watch the festival dancing in the main square."

"And you thought that sounded like a clever way to break your neck and maybe kill off your brother and Sarket's future king in the process?"

"Father!"

He stared calmly at her, his eyes two daggers that easily pierced into her soul. "I'm being serious. Somewhere inside, you got that sensation in your gut that told you it was a bad idea, didn't you?"

She lowered her gaze, staring into Irith's bright eyes.

"Why didn't you listen to it?"

"I don't know. I just... I wanted to... Ugh!" She threw herself against the back of the couch, wincing when a stab of pain shot through her hand.

"Impress Jaysen?"

Her cheeks warmed. "What? No."

Her father shifted further forward on the seat, his expression still solemn. "You know Jaysen is heir to the throne of Sarket. In less than a year, he will return home to begin preparations for his ascension to the throne."

She stared at her wounded hand, remembering how carefully Jaysen had wrapped it, and began picking at the edge of the bandage. "So? I've always known that."

"You shouldn't depend on him so much for company. Why don't you include the other children in your adventures more? The twins, Ahrin and Gannon, and their tehnaaks. Your brother's tehnaak, Ellaris."

She frowned at him. "You want me to get them killed too?"

He gave her a flat stare.

She focused on smoothing a patch of hair on Irith's head. "Ellaris can rarely escape her parents, and the others pick on Jaysen for his ears. Gannon especially. They call him earless and things like that. He jokes along with them sometimes, but I can tell it gets to him. It makes him feel like he doesn't belong, and it makes me angry." Certainly, he would understand, having been on the receiving end of such teasing himself once because of his cut ears.

He only nodded and stood, Irith hurrying to his side. "Don't forget to wear something nice for dinner. You start preparations for your Trial tomorrow. You may wish to make the most of tonight's meal."

Brow furrowing, she watched him walk to the door. The conversation felt incomplete, words hanging in the room unspoken, and yet, he was clearly leaving. She considered asking him if that was all, but perhaps things left unsaid should stay that way.

"And don't pick at the bandage," he added as he walked out.

She stuck her tongue out at the closing door.

## CHAPTER THREE

When it came time for dinner, Veyl donned a split-skirted dress like the ones her mother favored. This one was black with silver embroidery over a set of fitted ivory pants with shiny black beads worked in patterns on the lower part of the legs. It had long sleeves and a modest, rounded collar. She donned a woven silver and dark metal necklace with a deep red stone in the center. She liked to imagine it was a string of tattooed symbols, like the ones that formed a chain around her father's neck. Her story—her ke'hanoath—inked permanently in her skin. She had the symbols representing her family and her tehnaak's family tattooed on the back of her head, hidden by her hair in the Vanrian tradition. Her tehnaak was gone now, the tattoo altered to reflect that awful truth. Soon, after her Trial, she would get the true start of her ke'hanoath.

Lanis, her primary attendant, worked a few delicate braids into Veyl's hair, winding strands of silver through them. Then she slid the sides of a slender silver and dark metal tiara with a red gemstone in the center through the braids to rest lightly on her brow. It felt like too much for a family dinner, but her family was unusual. A long line of royalty on her mother's side. Military nobility on her father's. And yet, members of the unit her father led during the war, who became bonded as tehsheyn back then, would also be at the table tonight. Her "uncles" and "aunts" as she called them. None of them were upper society except for Jethan, who was her father's tehnaak and her mother's cousin. She much preferred dressing down to their stations as they did most nights, rather than having them dress up to that of her family.

"Don't pick at the bandage," Lanis chastised gently.

Veyl dropped her right hand to her side, raising the left a little higher. It throbbed more when she lowered it. "Do you think I'll have a tehnaak again someday?"

Lanis glanced at Veyl's reflection in the mirror, her smile full of affection. "I am certain of it. There aren't many unpaired children in Etrion around your age, but I know there is someone out there, a spirit brother or sister, whose heart will soar with joy, just as yours will, when you finally find each other."

Veyl frowned at her reflection.

Most of Vanris's population resided north of Vareyl's Warning, a black crag formation that created a natural separation between the rest of the country and the more arid region bordering the Crimson Break—a stretch of desert dividing Vanris from the southern kingdoms. During the war, people living in Etrion and other military cities south of Vareyl's Warning weren't permitted to have children. In the fourteen years since its end, that had changed, but it was a slow process. Many children lived in Etrion now, but she was one of a relatively small number born in the early years of that transition, and the rest were all part of existing tehnaak pairings.

With a sigh that earned her soft chuckle from Lanis, she turned from the mirror. "I'm ready enough."

Lanis gave her a patient smile. "I hope you know you are every bit as exceptional as your parents." Placing a hand on Veyl's shoulder, she turned and guided her out.

Veyl was the last to arrive in the formal dining room. The other dinner guests sat at a large, square table, its polished black surface inlaid with silver and dark metal accents. Everyone rose when she entered. Her newly arrived grandparents, Genyith and Seylin, smiled their welcomes, though her grandmother's was more reserved.

With all eyes on her, Veyl longed to run to her chair and fall into the comfortable space between her father's tehnaak and Jaysen. At large gatherings like this, she sat at the corner to the left of her parents and their tehnaaks because of her left-handedness. Aware of them all watching—her grandmother in particular—and judging every step, she forced a measured stride, the spark of pride in her parents' regard making it worth the effort.

Once they were all seated again, the kitchen staff swarmed the room, removing the covers from a grand array of aromatic foods. The dinner guests turned to light conversation while they filled their plates. Seylin was quick to engage in her usual pastime of finding something to be displeased with in her daughter's household.

"Khesran Veyl still has not taken a new tehnaak, I see. I find it troubling that you allow her to spend so much of her time with a southerner when she has yet to make that essential connection among her own kind." The word *southerner* fell off her tongue like a rotten bite of food she was expelling.

Next to Veyl, Jaysen's face reddened, his hand clenching around the handle of his fork. Her parents had stopped eating and were staring at the former khevarin. An uncomfortable silence rippled along the table, but Seylin forged ahead as if unaware of the effect of her words. Or perhaps she relished the attention.

"It has been what, at least six years since that girl died, has it not? It is well past time to move on, dear." Her pale blue eyes penetrated through to the pain that still lingered in Veyl.

Veyl stared at her plate, the food losing its appeal. It had been a little over six years. Her tehnaak, Jethan and his wife's firstborn child, died from the complications of a lung condition she had most likely been born with. Under the table, Jethan took Veyl's hand and gave it a gentle squeeze. When she glanced his way, she spotted his wife looking at her from her seat on the far side of her mother. Despite the sorrow in her eyes, she offered Veyl a supportive smile.

"Mother," Velara's tone was sharp when she spoke, "*that girl's* name was Minya, and if you say one more thing to upset someone at this table, I will have you removed from the room."

Seylin met her eyes, a challenge flashing between the two. "That does seem like something you would do, darling." A cutting reference to the fact that her mother had helped force her to abdicate the throne.

"Has anyone else tried this quail?" Avris's loud query broke the tension. She raised her fork with a piece of tender meat speared upon its tines. "It's quite remarkable."

Merrin agreed with her, and the table gradually returned to dining and casual chatter. Someone had pre-prepared Veyl's plate with food already cut to accommodate her injured hand. As much as she appreciated not having to struggle or ask someone for help, a flush of shame rose in her cheeks whenever anyone glanced at it curiously.

It was her grandfather, Genyith, who finally asked the inevitable question. "Khesran Veyl, whatever happened to your hand?"

She took a deep breath. It would be better to get the complete explanation out of the way as quickly as possible. Maybe confessing her mistake in front of everyone now would help to smooth things over with her parents.

As she opened her mouth to speak, her father said, "She fell and cut her palm. We've all had our share of minor accidents growing up. It's taken care of."

Jaysen looked at his plate, lips pressed tightly together. Tavin stared at Veyl with his mouth slightly open as if he couldn't fathom how she had gotten off so easily. Her mother took her father's hand where it rested by his plate and gave it a small squeeze, her warm smile making it clear she approved of his decision to brush aside the matter.

Farther down the table, the twins' father Darro, another member of her father's original unit, winked at Veyl. The gesture confirmed that her father's tehsheyn knew the truth, but she could trust that they would keep anything a secret if he asked them to.

She gave a tiny shrug, and Darro grinned before turning back to his dinner.

When she started to look away, she caught Gannon staring at her from his spot next to his twin brother, Ahrin. The two weren't identical, though they didn't miss it by much. They had the same slender features and build, but Ahrin had hazel eyes and brown hair with a hint of auburn to it, while Gannon had lighter, dusty brown hair that matched their father's, and eyes of a brighter blue. After a long moment, Gannon turned back to his brother, who was chattering on about something, oblivious to his distraction.

"Still developing." Genyith regarded Veyl thoughtfully, the deep scars along the left side of his jaw and neck tugging down that corner of his mouth when he offered her an understanding smile. "It can take a while to grow out of that youthful awkwardness. Judging from your composure when you joined us, however, it will not be long before you are as graceful as Velara." He finished with a fond smile for her mother.

"For her sake, I hope you are not as headstrong." Seylin's frosty gaze flickered to the head of the table as she took a sip of her wine. When she put her glass down, her attention settled on Jaysen again. "Veyl is already filling out into quite a beautiful young woman, would you not agree, your highness?"

"Mother." An edge of renewed warning darkened her mother's tone, her silver eyes boring into the former khevarin who pointedly ignored her.

Jaysen raised his head and looked directly at Seylin. "Khesran Veyl has always shared the gift of her mother's beauty, Lady Markanis," he answered with calm conviction.

Her mother breathed a soft laugh and graced him with a warm smile. "And you, Prince Jaysen, are developing quite the Charmer's tongue. Perhaps you are spending too much time around my husband's tehnaak."

Jaysen bowed his head respectfully, a hint of flush coloring his cheeks. "Thank you, Khevarin Velara."

Jethan chuckled. "I didn't realize you thought me so eloquent, cousin."

Her mother smirked at him, wrapping one delicate hand around the stem of her wine goblet. "Don't let it go to your head."

When the adults moved on to discussing other things, Veyl leaned closer to Jaysen. "Did my father speak to you earlier?"

"A little." He poked at some sautéed mushrooms with a sauce made of wine and black evalis fruit drizzled over them.

"What did he say?"

Jaysen glanced toward the head of the table, his brows pinching. "Not much about what happened today, other than restating his disappointment that I didn't argue against going up there. He also thanked me for not letting you fall and for going to get help. Then he asked if I was looking forward to going back to Sarket next year."

Veyl's appetite fully abandoned her. She took a sip of the small splash of mead her parents had allowed the older children before asking, "Are you?"

"Veyl." Her mother's voice made her jump. "Please let Crown Prince Jaysen eat his meal. And you should consider doing the same. Your Trial preparation starts tomorrow."

"Yes, Mother." She turned her attention back to her plate, forcing herself to eat despite the roiling unease in her gut. Preparation for the Trial involved a few days of a fasting diet, so she would undoubtedly regret it if she didn't eat well tonight.

A short time later, they excused the children to go entertain themselves while the adults prepared to move to one of the sitting rooms. Tavin and Ellaris sprinted off with an attendant hurrying after them. As Veyl got up to leave with Jaysen, she noticed Seylin approaching her mother and busied herself folding her napkin so she could hang back to listen.

"Velara, I am quite serious about my granddaughter. You know how important a strong pairing is. If there are no appropriate options here, then send her back to Doran with us."

Her mother's expression darkened. "Mother, I will not send my daughter with you and allow you the opportunity to get into her head."

Seylin rolled her eyes. "I am not the evil crone you have made me out to be, but if you are so concerned, come with her. Wait until that boy is gone if you must, then come spend some time in Doran with the rest of your family and we will find a pairing for her. The Break has been peaceful for years. I am certain Kasiel can handle things here for a few months without you."

Her mother's expression turned thoughtful. "Let us get through her Trial. Once we know the outcome of that, I will consider it."

A touch on Veyl's arm pulled her attention to Lanis. "Are you coming, Khesran?"

She nodded and followed the woman out. They had

barely stepped into the hall when Gannon and Ahrin approached.

"So, what did you really do to your hand?" Gannon asked.

Ahrin groaned. "Gannon, Mother said to let it go."

Jaysen stepped up close beside her as if to shield her. "She fell. How it happened doesn't matter, does it? Like Khemron Kasiel said, we all have accidents."

Gannon's eyes narrowed. "Veyl doesn't need some earless southerner coming to her rescue. She's perfectly capable of speaking for herself."

A flare of anger ignited in her core. "I don't need a rude calloch like you trying to speak for me either," she snapped.

"You are all in significant danger of being sent to separate rooms for the rest of the evening," the male attendant with Gannon and Ahrin warned, the severity of his tone making it clear they had already pushed too far by his estimation.

Ahrin inclined his head to the man in a show of respect. "Apologies. It won't happen again."

Jaysen mirrored the gesture, and Veyl followed suit. After a moment, Gannon did the same.

The attendants escorted them to one of the palace's many drawing rooms. A favorite space for their group, the room was one of the few with wood paneling on the walls, stained a brown so dark as to be virtually black, the sconces casting a warm glow that drew out the underlying color. The game tables were the same color as the paneling, set out on ivory carpets with silver, gray, and purple patterning. Comfortable chairs and couches carried up the purple from the carpet, with ivory and black accents. Paintings depicting the beasts of Vanris and their Feral handlers decorated the walls. A suitable backdrop for one of the more popular games played within that space.

Tavin and Ellaris were already engaged in a stacking game, giggling as they attempted to sabotage one another. Veyl envied her brother his tehnaak, but that didn't lessen the pleasure she got from seeing them having fun together.

Gannon strode to a cupboard against one wall and pulled out two Feral's Folly decks, tossing one to Ahrin, who caught it deftly. "Me and Veyl. You and Jaysen. The losers and winners of each match can pair off for the second round."

Veyl nodded. She caught Jaysen's eyes as Gannon went to claim a table for them. When his attention was on her, she glanced down and to the right, suggesting that he should throw the game.

He answered with an almost imperceptible nod.

Satisfied that she would get her chance to speak with him, she went and sat down across a small table from Gannon. He shuffled the deck and dealt it out between them.

Each player got half of the deck. Every card had a numerical value along with the value of the suit, with kanodraks being the highest, followed by tethdraks, then cliff cats, and hounds at the bottom. They both pulled a hand of six cards from the top of their respective decks. The object was for each player to put out individual cards or allowed combinations of cards from their hand on their turn. They could use the cards to defeat individual cards or combinations on their opponent's side or to fortify their own line in the hope of drawing something to create a more powerful combination in a later turn. At the end of their turn, the active player could draw back up to six cards from their half of the deck. When they defeated an opponent's card or combination with a stronger card or combination, they put it in their victory pile. The first to reach thirty-seven points or more worth of cards in their victory pile won the game.

There was an element of luck to the cards a player ended up with in their deck and in their hand on each draw. Because of that, deliberately throwing a game took almost as much strategy as winning did. Veyl and Jaysen played a lot of Feral's Folly, however, so she was confident they could pull it off. It might have been more satisfying to defeat Gannon, but tonight, all she really wanted was to talk to Jaysen about his conversation with her father.

Jaysen and Ahrin sat down to their own game at a table in the opposite corner of the room. The two got on well enough and were already chatting and taunting one another good-naturedly.

Gannon eyed her critically as she skimmed over her hand. "Why do you spend so much time with him?"

"He's fostering with my family. Why wouldn't I spend time with him?" She moved her cards around, investigating her options. She needed to keep from winning, but if she didn't play a few stronger hands, he would suspect she was doing it on purpose.

"He's southern."

"So? It's not like we've been at war with the southern kingdoms in our lifetimes. Besides, part of the point of him fostering here is to have a king on the throne in Sarket who's sympathetic to the Vanrian people. I don't think my ignoring him is going to help accomplish that." She placed a potent combination of two high-value tethdraks. "Why do you dislike him so much?"

"I don't," he countered, setting down a respectable lineup of beasts. He took her tethdrak pair with the sacrifice of a top-level kanodrak. "Can we just focus on the game?"

"You're the one who asked." Veyl shrugged and took down his kanodrak with a decent run of high-level cliff cats.

A group of three or more gained an extra one-point bonus per beast for attacking as a pack. She played the game strategically, taking advantage of some of her better cards to put up a reasonable fight, making certain he wouldn't suspect she was trying to lose.

Gannon looked at her bandaged hand often, undoubtedly noting how little she used it, though he resisted asking her about it again. It hurt a lot, but she did her best not to let it show. If she did, Lanis would summon a healer to give her something for the pain, and then her evening would be over. She needed to talk to Jaysen before that happened.

When Gannon finally won, he was smug for about a minute, until Ahrin won the other match and strolled over to take Veyl's spot. Then his sour temper rose again. He slapped the deck down between himself and his brother.

"You shuffle," he demanded, sitting back with his arms across his chest to glower at the table.

She joined Jaysen at the far table, leaning close to whisper, "I can't believe he wanted to play you that badly."

Jaysen shifted closer, matching her volume. "I think he just didn't want you to play me. It's obvious he has feelings for you."

"If that's what's going on, jealousy looks like shit on him," she snapped, a flare of anger spinning wildly through her.

"Khesran Veyl, mind your language," Lanis said, not looking up from the book she was reading in a nearby chair.

The woman had sharp ears.

"Sorry."

Lanis merely nodded.

Jaysen began shuffling the deck. "You were every bit the image of a true princess tonight."

Veyl wanted to embrace the warmth that would normally accompany such flattery, but his word choice stood in the way. When she tried to catch his eyes, he evaded her, staring down at the cards in his hands, and started dealing them out.

"Princess?"

"Sorry, I'm just practicing."

"For what?" It was a stupid question. That serpent coiling in her gut again told her what.

"I go back to Sarket in less than a year, Veyl. Here, if I call a khesran a princess or a dhomen a general, I get corrected and maybe teased a little, but it gets dismissed because I'm southern. There, any word or action that even whispers of my time here in Vanris will be noted and turned against me by my opposition. And I do have opposition. As my mother likes to remind me in her letters, the Sarketi people have more pride than sense. The idea of a youth ascending to the throne who was partially raised in Vanris—by the very mind-crafter who killed the former king, no less—is insulting to them. The Royal Council is postponing my coronation for three years, hoping it will give them time to prove that I'm not some Vanrian thrall. I can't make any mistakes there."

"Jaysen." Her throat tightened. "I didn't realize it would be that bad for you. Maybe we could start using the Sarketi terms for things for the next year when it's just the two of us. We could even speak the language in private. I know it well enough, and the practice would be good for me."

He shook his head. "No, I'm sorry. I shouldn't be making it your burden. I'm just…"

"Scared?"

He started to shake his head again, then he met her eyes and nodded. "Yes."

Veyl reached out and put a hand over his, giving it a

squeeze. "Helping you is never a burden."

At the other table, Gannon snapped to his feet, threw down his cards, and stormed from the room. The attendant supervising the twins jumped up and rushed after him, gesturing for Ahrin to follow. On his way out, Ahrin gave them an apologetic shrug and a small wave that Veyl and Jaysen returned.

Jaysen faced her and arched one brow. "That was definitely jealousy."

Veyl groaned. "Can I go with you to Sarket?"

"There's nothing I'd like more." He smiled, though the sorrow in his eyes undermined the expression. "Let's play. I believe I owe you a sound Feral's Folly thrashing."

Veyl grinned, though, between the upcoming Trial, Jaysen's looming departure, her throbbing hand, and now Gannon's apparently volatile infatuation, the expression required effort. "Your optimism is cute, if misplaced."

He gave an exaggerated wince. "So cruel."

The day was bright and hot. Veyl strolled with her brother along the top of a slot canyon in the Crimson Break. She spotted a lizard darting about, the reptile freezing still when the shadow of a sandhawk passed over it. During the war, no civilians would have dared to wander in the desert beyond the southern border. Even in these times of peace, scouts from the bordering countries kept a close eye on things in the unclaimed swath of arid land that divided them. Still, it struck her as odd that they were out there on their own. Their father must be nearby, most likely watching them through the eyes of the sandhawk as he often did.

"Aren't you afraid of becoming khevarin and being responsible for all of Vanris?" Tavin asked, kicking a pebble into the canyon.

Veyl shrugged, though he wouldn't see the gesture while walking in front of her. "Why would I be? It's my home."

"What if Sarket seeks revenge someday for the death of King Lodmund?"

She snorted. "That was fourteen years ago, Tav."

"They still hate us." He moved closer to the edge and kicked a larger stone over the side, his balance wavering for an instant.

Veyl might have ignored his risky behavior another

time, but given that she had recently gotten in trouble for putting his life in danger, she couldn't let it go today. "Tav, stop it. You'll fall over the edge."

He looked back and rolled his eyes at her. "Yes, Mother."

Veyl scowled at him. It would serve him right if he did fall.

As he faced forward again, his foot on the cliff side slipped on a loose rock and her heart stuttered, a flash of panic racing through her like wildfire. She lunged toward the edge, hoping to catch him before he could go over. The flood of relief that swept in on the heels of that panic left her feeling weak and shaky when he simply fell back on his ass, staring at the drop with wide eyes. One near miss this week was more than enough.

"Get away from the edge. Now."

"You too," he snapped back.

"I wouldn't be this close if you—"

The ground beneath her right foot disappeared, breaking free of the edge, and suddenly she was plunging toward the slot canyon floor, hard-packed sand and stone racing up to meet her.

*

Veyl awoke in darkness. Her first instinct was to try moving, but she couldn't. Nothing restrained her, but her body refused to respond to her will. Something was wrong. She remembered falling and the taste of fear spread metallic across her tongue. A fog filled her mind, resisting her efforts to orient herself. Was she alone here? Where was Tavin? Hadn't he been with her?

"Veyl?" A small, frightened voice cut through the darkness.

*Tavin?*

She tried calling out to him, but the strange paralysis

extended to her vocal cords. Was she dying?

Images gradually emerged from the darkness. Rock walls, one of which she was leaning up against, became visible around her. As more light revealed her surroundings, she saw a canyon passage in front of her that opened upon a larger space a few yards in. Tavin stood in the center of that space, his wide, fear-filled eyes staring at something outside of her range of vision. He started shaking his head as in denial, tears spilling down his cheeks. He hadn't seen her yet, and whatever he did see, terrified him.

Veyl cursed her inability to move. She couldn't do anything, not even turn her head or call out to him.

*Look this way, Tav! I'm here!*

No matter how she willed it, he wouldn't look her way, not that she could do anything to help him in her current state. He started backing toward the passage that would take him away from her location and three figures in dark, tattered clothes strode into view on the right, hoods hiding their faces. The one in the front was holding a longsword, its point dragging along the ground, hissing through the sand as it created a runnel behind him. The other two had weapons drawn as well, a mace and a double-bladed axe.

"You'll never get away, little khesran," the man in the lead taunted, speaking Sarketi. "We'll kill your family while you watch, then we'll feed you to your father's kanodrak one little piece at a time."

"No!" Tavin screamed.

He tripped and fell, catching himself with his hands. The way he pulled them to his chest when he got to his feet told her he had hurt them in the fall. He turned and broke into a run, only to stop abruptly, staring in horror at a thick wall of roiling dust advancing along the canyon passage toward him. Lightning flickered through the ominous front and Veyl realized, as Tavin also appeared to, that it would kill him if he entered it as surely as the men behind him threatened to.

He let out an incoherent wail, sinking to his knees. His shoulders heaved with despairing sobs that tore through her. She needed to help him. She was his big sister, but she could do nothing, say nothing. And when the strangers realized she was here too, helpless to flee or fight, what would happen to her then?

"Nowhere to go now," the man with the sword gloated. Raising his weapon, he stepped up behind Tavin.

*No! Tav!*

The scream only sounded in her head. Her chest seized, horror making it hard to breathe as her useless body trembled. Tears streamed down her cheeks now, too. Stupid, worthless tears that wouldn't save her brother.

When the sword started swinging down, a presence reached out to her, faint, but warm and comforting. She grabbed onto it, weeping and screaming in the prison of her own mind as the blade descended.

*

Something brushed Veyl's upper lip and a sharp smell assailed her nostrils, stinging through them. The fog in her head dispersed instantly, and her limbs tingled to life. She sat up on a bed in an unfamiliar room, though it had the familiar decor of chambers in the palace. Tears streamed down her cheeks. Arhk, her grandfather on her father's side and the dhomvalen of Vanris, head of their country's military, sat on the bed next to her. He pulled her into a reassuring embrace, and she broke into sobs.

"My Trial…" she eventually choked out.

"Yes. That is all it was," he murmured, stroking her hair. "You are all right, Veyl."

He was wrong. She wasn't all right. The terror of the experience still clung to her. On top of that, she knew enough about the Trial to know that hers hadn't worked. There had been no dark snap. No mind-crafting ability had awakened.

"I failed. Tavin died because I'm useless."

Arhk pushed her back, setting a hand on either side of her face and brushing away some of her tears with his thumbs. He smiled, an expression that always looked out of place on his austere, elegant features. "Tavin is in the next room, unharmed. You did not fail, and you are anything but useless. You are one of the most remarkable young women I have ever known."

She sat back, pulling away from him, and roughly wiped at her tears. "Why are you here?"

He gave her a look that said she shouldn't need to ask, then took her injured hand and pulled it close to inspect the fresh spot of blood seeping through the bandage over her palm. Turning, he met the eyes of his Evoker, Zafyr, who waited next to the door. Evokers could read surface thoughts and images, and whatever unspoken message she got from him in that moment, she responded with a firm nod before ducking out the door.

Veyl narrowed her eyes when he faced her again. "You made all that happen."

"Zafyr did some of the work, but a Frightener, if one is available, often takes part in the Trial. It provides us with a way to access your deepest fears and ensure a greater chance of success without risking injury to those involved. I insisted on handling your Trial myself because I do not trust anyone else with my granddaughter."

"It didn't happen, though. I'm not a mind-crafter." More tears spilled down her cheeks. She wiped furiously at them.

The door opened then, and her father and Jethan

walked in. Arhk stood and moved away, letting her father come to the bedside and sit in his place. He drew Veyl into a hug.

"Are you all right?"

She clung to him for a moment, comforted by that embrace, until she remembered that he too was a mind-crafter. One of the most powerful Ferals Vanris had ever known, able to not only connect with and control the minds of beasts, but to hear and see through them as well. Everyone in the room was a mind-crafter, except for her. Arhk a Frightener, her father a Feral, and Jethan a Charmer like her mother. All fundamentally something more than she would ever be.

She pulled away and stared down at the spot of blood seeping through her bandage. "I'm nothing," she muttered.

"Veyl." He reached for her chin as he often did to try making her look at him, but she jerked away, and he lowered his hand. "Everyone in my tehsheyn has accomplished amazing things and only two of us are mind-crafters. Having an ability is not a measure of your worth."

She wanted to believe him, but his words sounded empty, like the hollow in her chest. "What happened... It felt so real," she muttered. It had, in fact, been convincing enough that she had to ask, "Is Tavin really all right?"

"Yes. Your mother's with him. He's a little shaken but recovering."

"If he's the one with an ability, shouldn't it have awakened?" She stared harder at her hand, trying not to resent her little brother for what he might be.

"Awakenings are almost never triggered by a sense of self-preservation. When his Trial comes, it will be Ellaris who shares that experience with him." His hand shifted, as if he wanted to reach out to her, but he refrained this time.

Someone knocked on the door and Jethan opened it, letting Nerith in. Her father moved out of the way, going to stand with his father and his tehnaak while the healer came and started removing the bandage from her hand. As soon as she began the process, the pain finally speared through Veyl's distress over the Trial and its disappointing outcome. She sucked in a sharp breath.

Nerith tucked a strand of silver hair behind one pointed ear to get it out of the way. She gave Veyl a gentle smile, her lavender eyes full of that genuine caring that made her one of Veyl's favorite people. "You've had a bit of a rough morning, haven't you?"

"I don't remember coming in here." The last thing Veyl could recall was going to bed thinking of all the food she longed to eat after a few days of the pre-Trial restricted diet and… Had someone woken her up during the night? "I remember being brought something to drink in the middle of the night, although I don't remember who brought it."

Nerith finished removing the bandage and began carefully cleaning around the wound to check the stitches, earning a hiss of pain from Veyl. "That was only a few hours ago. You've got an excellent memory. Most people forget that part." She let go of the hand and reached into her satchel, drawing out a small vial. "Take a sip of this. It'll put you to sleep, but it shouldn't last more than an hour. I need to fix a couple of stitches you pulled, and you could probably use a little proper rest after all this excitement."

Veyl took a sip and lay down at Nerith's direction. She closed her eyes, her mind focusing on the hushed conversation by the door as the elixir began taking effect.

Arhk was still in the room. She could hear him speaking in a low voice. "You should know that your son harbors a deep fear of retaliation from Sarket for the death of King Lodmund."

"I'll talk to him about it," her father replied. "Out of curiosity, what does Veyl fear?"

"Being helpless to protect those she loves," Arhk answered softly. "And losing her tehnaak again."

"She doesn't have a tehnaak to lose." Her father sounded puzzled. Enough so that she could see the furrowing of his brow in her mind.

The elixir started dragging her under, but their words inspired her to cling to consciousness. Something in Arhk's soft voice when he spoke again demanded attention.

"When a Frightener runs a Trial, they are in the heads of their subjects longer than usual. In all my experiences, I have felt the tehnaak bond flare stronger before the dark snap happens. Veyl may not have had an awakening, but I felt something like that right before we brought her out. An external influence from somewhere."

She was having trouble staying with the conversation now, the pull of the elixir beckoning her down into that deep darkness.

"That's not possible," her father argued. "Her tehnaak is gone. For her to have a new one, a Bondmaker would have had to create that connection."

Jethan cleared his throat. "Kas, it might be possible."

Silence drew out as she tried to fight off the darkness. The door opened and swift footsteps left the room, her father's voice in the hall calling for someone to find a Bondmaker. Then she sank into sleep.

When Veyl woke again, she was in her own bedroom. She opened her eyes, blinking in sunshine that beamed through the many windows behind her bed. An unfamiliar woman with the symbol of the healers tattooed under one eye sat in a chair beside the bed. She touched Veyl's shoulder, a gesture meant to offer comfort, before getting up and walking out into the adjacent sitting room.

"Khemron, Khevarin, your daughter is awake now."

Veyl considered pretending to fall asleep again. Why were her parents here? She struggled through the thick fog left by the elixir, trying to recall the conversation she had overheard as she was drifting off before. It had been important; she was certain of that.

She struggled upright as her parents entered the room. Irith padded in after them and leapt up on the bed, his weight making the wooden frame creak. Her father raised a brow at the big predator, but Irith ignored him, flopping down and resting his heavy head upon her thighs. The weight was uncomfortable, but his presence was welcome, so she sank her fingers into his thick fur and encouraged him to stay.

Her mother settled on the edge of the bed, her gaze sinking to the bandaged hand before she met Veyl's eyes. "How are you feeling?"

"Worthless," she muttered.

Her mother glanced up at her father, a faint tightening around her silver eyes. "Veyl, there is nothing wrong with not being a mind-crafter. It skipped the first-born in my family too."

"And he resented you enough to try having you assassinated," she snapped back. Guilt twisted in her gut when her mother reflexively reached for the scars on her face. Veyl lowered her gaze. "I'm sorry, Mother. I shouldn't have said that."

"You merely spoke the truth. But most people are not mind-crafters." Her mother's hand moved away from her face and her father caught it in his, winning an affectionate smile from her. "Besides, being a mind-crafter isn't always a good thing."

"Yes," her father agreed. "Frighteners like your grandfather, for instance, aren't very popular in times of peace."

"Frighteners aren't well-liked in times of war either, I'm afraid. Nor are Charmers and Evokers especially well-trusted." Her mother pressed a kiss to the back of his hand.

Veyl rolled her eyes. "Would you like me to leave you two alone?"

Her parents laughed as if they thought she had made a joke. Irith got up suddenly, hopping down from the bed, undoubtedly responding to a mental prompt from her father.

He smiled at her, though the reservation in his expression hinted at some deeper unease. "Jaysen has been asking about you. We thought the four of us might have a pleasant lunch together if you're ready for a proper meal."

Her grumbling stomach answered for her.

Her father and Irith started for the door and her mother stood. "I'll help you get cleaned up and dressed."

For a while, Veyl let herself get lost in the process of bathing and getting prepared with her mother's assistance. It wasn't often the khevarin had enough free time during the day to spend some on such mundane activities. With her hand injured, Veyl needed help, but Lanis or another attendant could have managed it. Having her mother there, however, kept her from dwelling on the disappointment of the morning. Knowing she would see Jaysen soon also provided some comfort. She needed him there. As a southerner, the concepts of mind-crafting and the Trial were strange to him, but somehow, he would understand her heartbreak and help her face it.

Her mother walked her to a small, private dining room in the palace, appropriate for more intimate meals. When Veyl entered, her gaze locked with Jaysen's, and he got up from his chair, hurrying to meet her halfway across the room. She willed herself not to cry. Decorum held them apart for a heartbeat. Then he took a step forward and hugged her. The tears burst forth and she clung to him, the knowledge that her parents were watching urging her to pull away. Instead, she held on tighter.

When the tears slowed, Jaysen said, "Now you're just normal like me, huh?"

She broke free and shoved him halfheartedly. "As if you're normal."

Jaysen chuckled. "You'll never be normal either, Veyl. You're far too exceptional for that." He handed her a soft kerchief he had been carrying.

As she wiped her face and nose, she realized there was a fifth person in the room. An older woman with long blond hair braided back to expose her pointed ears stood with her back to them, facing her father on the other side of a modest dining table burdened with an array of mouthwatering dishes. The two conversed in hushed voices, then her parents locked eyes across the room, and her father nodded.

Her mother came forward and placed a hand on each of their shoulders. "Come. We have some things to discuss with you two, but first, I imagine Veyl is famished."

The strange woman bowed to each of her parents, never looking at Veyl or Jaysen. "Your majesties."

"Thank you for your time," her father said, politely dismissing her. When she was gone, he gestured to the table, offering them a somewhat strained smile. "Please, sit. This is an informal meal."

Her parents took seats across from each other, leaving Veyl and Jaysen to do the same on opposite sides of the small table. Anxiety from the discomfort that hung over her parents wasn't enough to quell her appetite. She served herself a slice of savory roast with some rich smelling wine sauce slathered over it and grabbed a piece of the braided loaf of fresh-baked bread. Next, she reached for a delicate medley of imported vegetables from Delaphine. A welcome abundance after a few days of eating tiny portions of the blandest foods in preparation for her Trial—her failure.

Her hand sank back to her side, empty this time.

"Veyl, darling, do you need something? The meat should be quite tender, but if you need help cutting…" Her mother trailed off when Veyl shook her head.

"It's fine. I'm just not as hungry as I thought I was."

"You had better eat," Jaysen said, a hint of taunting in his tone. "I plan to challenge you to a duel later. You'll have to fight right-handed. I'm not missing this opportunity to thrash you soundly."

Veyl fought the urge to stick her tongue out at him and began dishing herself up some vegetables. "Don't expect it to be easy, *Crown Prince* Jaysen."

He grinned. "We shall see, *Khesran* Veyl."

They relaxed into the meal from there, her parents expertly fielding the conversation to keep Veyl's from dwelling on the things that upset her. It wasn't until they finished that the sense of discomfort crept back in.

Her father stood, gesturing toward four chairs set around an oval table before the crackling fire. The stone of the fireplace in this room was white with traces of gray and black minerals throughout, the cozy chairs upholstered in a soft gray that unified those colors into one.

Her nerves lighting up, Veyl took a seat next to Jaysen, facing her parents. Maybe they meant to remove her from the line of succession now that they knew she wasn't a mind-crafter. But then, wouldn't they have Tavin at the dinner instead of Jaysen for that? In fact, wasn't it odd that her brother hadn't joined them? Maybe what they had to say only affected the two of them. Could they be sending Jaysen home early?

A prickling sensation raced up the back of her neck, and her chest tightened. Then what she had heard Arhk telling her father as she was succumbing to the elixir returned to her. She met his eyes, suddenly certain this had something to do with that.

He pinned them each with a steady gaze before he spoke. "We have a problem to discuss, but first, you need a brief explanation. You remember how my unit made our tehsheyn bond official before we went to find Queen Astrid, your mother," he added with a considerate nod to Jaysen, "near the end of the war?"

Veyl nodded. It was one of her favorite stories, partly because of how much she enjoyed watching her father and his spirit family together, delighting in the easy rapport they shared, and the way they anticipated one another's needs or finished each other's sentences almost like tehnaak. She especially loved it when Nerith told it, often sitting hand in hand with her mother. Nerith and her father had been romantically involved for a time after he first came to Vanris, and traces of that bond still existed, apparent in the smiles they shared and the way they interacted. Yet, somehow, it didn't spark jealousy in her mother, who considered Nerith one of her best friends, or in Nerith's partner, who joined them for larger gatherings when he wasn't out on patrol.

"There is an element to that experience that we rarely talk about, but that appears to be relevant here," her father continued. "After the bonding was complete, the Bondmaker told us that some of the work connecting the threads between us had already been done. Niskenya had been gradually weaving those threads together."

"Your kanodrak is a Bondmaker?" Jaysen exclaimed.

"The connection Vanrians built with kanodraks on our original homeland is part of how the creation of tehnaak and other bonds came into practice to begin with. That's a history lesson for another time, however. Right now, this is important–"

"Because Niskenya made us tehnaak." Giddy joy burst through Veyl's chest as she declared it. She absently reached out to find Jaysen's hand already waiting for hers. She had asked two years ago to take Jaysen as her tehnaak, but her father had refused. His kanodrak had apparently seen fit to override that decision.

Her parents looked much less pleased. It was her mother's sad smile that sparked a pinprick of dread in Veyl's happiness.

"Don't you have to be Vanrian for that to work?" Jaysen asked.

Her father shook his head. "The threads that our Bondmakers weave together exist in most living things. Vanrians are just the only ones who have mind-crafters that can manipulate them in this way."

"Veyl, Jaysen," her mother began, sympathy softening her gaze, "in less than a year, you two will have to part ways. That separation is going to be made far more difficult by this. Not to mention, this was a choice we had no right to make without input from your family in Sarket, Jaysen. Unfortunately, Niske doesn't understand all of that. She must have seen the strength of the friendship between the two of you and Veyl's lack of a tehnaak and addressed it in a way that made sense to her."

Her father spoke again, taking her mother's hand as he did so. "I discussed it with the Bondmaker. To sever the bond now would feel to both of you as if your tehnaak had died, an experience Veyl has already suffered through once. And so long as you are around one another, she said the connection would likely regenerate on its own now that it has been established. The obvious solution is to keep this quiet until you leave, Jaysen, and sever it then."

"What?" Veyl sat up straighter. "Why is that the obvious solution? Why can't we just leave it as is?"

Jaysen squeezed her hand before pulling his away. She looked over at him, a sinking feeling in her gut when he drew a deep breath and let it out, a hint of moisture rising in his eyes.

"If word got out in Sarket that I have a tehnaak connection with a Vanrian, it could send my country into full rebellion against my mother and I." His apologetic smile cut through her. "My people don't understand your bonds and your abilities. Many of them still believe we should be trying to destroy you because of your mind-crafters. Besides, with me as your tehnaak, you would be unable to form that bond with someone else after I'm gone. The khemron and khevarin are right. It needs to be severed when I leave."

Veyl stared at him, the room closing in around her. She could feel her parents watching her. Jaysen watching her. Already today, she had failed Tavin and proven herself something less than her parents were. Now, the spark of joy that had blossomed with realizing Jaysen was her tehnaak was being snuffed out by them and by Jaysen himself. She would lose her tehnaak again. Not to death this time, but to politics, and it would be just as crushing.

Veyl jumped up and sprinted from the room, ignoring their voices calling after her.

She couldn't escape to her rooms. They would look for her there first. And if she went somewhere outside of the palace, people would see the sorrow written upon her face. Everyone in the city knew who she was. She would also end up with guards accompanying her, which would undermine her desire to be alone. Making a quick decision, she ran to a reading room near her parents' personal chambers. It seemed unlikely that they would expect to find her in the spaces they normally frequented.

Her father had overseen the decoration of this room, which explained why it looked much different from most of the place in warm reds and browns with sparing splashes of gold and plenty of polished dark wood. Not the typical color selection for Vanris, but then, he had not grown up in Vanris. Jethan had helped him procure most of the books that lined the many shelves from every kingdom on Pandrea.

Wiping tears from her eyes, she walked up to an elegantly simple display case that stood centered at the front of the rows of bookcases. Within, on a bed of purple silk, lay a single tethdrak claw, easily as big as one of her hands. The lethal claw had belonged to her father's first companion beast, one of the large reptilian creatures used by Vanrian Ferals in battle. That tethdrak, Sylaryth her father had called him, died protecting him during the war. A story others told, but one that he himself rarely brought up.

She still stood there, tracing the shape of the claw on the glass above it with one finger and recalling happier stories her father told her about the beast, when the door to the room opened with a click.

Veyl heaved a sigh, not turning around. "How did you find me so fast?"

"I asked Jaysen where he thought you would go. He is your tehnaak, after all." The door clicked shut and her father walked up behind her, his reflection joining hers in the now thoroughly fingerprinted glass of the case. "Sylaryth was an extraordinary companion."

"Did he really save your life the day you killed Jaysen's father?"

Her father cleared his throat uncomfortably. "It sounds less like something to be proud of when you put it that way."

"Because he was Jaysen's father?" She didn't wait for an answer. "He was also an awful man based on what his mother told him."

"I'll leave such judgments to those like Queen Astrid, who knew him far better than I did." He set a hand on her shoulder. "But it is true that neither of us would be here now without that tethdrak."

"Maybe that would be better."

"This world would be much less bright without you in it." The tightness in his voice told her she had struck a sensitive chord.

A smile tugged at her lips, recalling what Jaysen had said on the rooftop about her father thinking she was the reason the sun rose. She turned to him, letting him wrap his arms around her. She didn't cry this time, merely accepted the support he offered.

"It has been a strenuous day for you. I wish I could make it better, but, if you'll let me offer a bit of advice that someone gave me once…"

She shifted back to look up at him and nodded.

"You know your tehnaak pairing with Jaysen has an end, and that isn't fair, but it is necessary. You can still choose to make the most of it for as long as it lasts. I know how strong the bond between you is. Make sure that your memories of this time aren't full of regret because you were busy dreading the future when you could have been embracing the present."

"That sounds like something Uncle Jethan would say." She settled back into his arms. With her cheek against his chest, she could feel him chuckle.

"It was." He kissed her head, letting her linger there. "Do you want to put off seeing the Heartsmith until tomorrow?"

"Can Jaysen go with me?"

He didn't answer for several seconds, during which she closed her eyes and counted his heartbeats, letting the rhythm soothe her. Eventually, he moved her out of his arms and met her eyes, a hint of reservation in his smile.

"He is your tehnaak. Spirit siblings typically support each other through starting their ke'hanoath. I think he should be there, unless he has an issue with the sight of blood."

She held up her bandaged hand. "I think we already know that's not a problem."

"Good point."

"I want to do it today," she stated firmly. Her ke'hanoath would show that she wasn't a mind-crafter, but no amount of delaying it was going to change that. In a way, her Trial wouldn't truly be complete until she had met with the Heartsmith and had the start of her identity, her personal story, tattooed upon her skin.

"You're certain?"

"Mm-hmm."

He pushed her away with his hands on her shoulders and held her facing him again. "You may not be in a place to accept this right now, but I am very proud of you, Veyl."

He was correct about that. Just hearing him say it made her want to lash out at him, but she swallowed back against the tempest still twisting deep inside her and nodded. "I won't let you down, Father."

He breathed a soft laugh. "There's no way you could."

She found a playful grin for him. "Am I your favorite?"

He kissed her forehead once more before letting go of her shoulders. "I'm going to pretend you didn't ask that."

"I knew it!"

A smile tugged at his lips. "You have an hour before you're due to visit the Heartsmith. Is there anything you would like to do?"

"Yes. Can we get Jaysen and go see Niskenya?"

He took her hand and turned toward the door. "We can. I'd like to have a word with her myself."

When they collected Jaysen from his rooms, he wouldn't meet Veyl's eyes. They had to pass through the front of the tethdrak habitat to get to the kanodrak area, so her father led them through the expansive, enclosed garden alongside the palace to a tunnel passage that sloped down to the base of the tethdrak canyon in uncomfortable silence. He stopped at the entrance to light a lantern, then handed it to Veyl.

"I forgot something. You two can head on down and wait for me outside the tethdrak enclosure. I'll be right there."

Veyl took the lantern in her good hand, gripping it tightly. "All right."

Her father gestured to the cool, dark passage, and she resolutely walked into the tunnel. Jaysen followed. The thunk of the heavy door behind them let them know they were alone. They hadn't gone ten feet before

Jaysen spoke.

"I'm sorry I upset you earlier. It was never my intention."

Veyl kept walking, holding onto her silence. It wasn't him that upset her so much as the situation, but the emotions were still raw.

He tried again after a few strides. "I hope you know that, if things were different, I would never let them sever that bond. Getting to be your tehnaak is an honor greater than anything I could have ever wished for."

She stopped and faced him, frustration rushing to the surface. "Then don't give up so easily."

"We can't keep this, Veyl. Not when I am destined for Sarket's throne. My people won't stand for it. You must realize that."

Veyl lowered her gaze to the lantern, staring into that bright flame as if it held the answers. Like it or not, he was right. Her own people wouldn't appreciate their leader being bonded to someone from Sarket either, though she suspected they might be less hostile about it than his, or at least she hoped they would.

"I know." The stone passage amplified her quiet words. "I just wish it could be different. My father said we should make the most of our bond while we have it, or something like that. Will you come to the Heartsmith with me after this?" When she looked up, a broad, toothy smile had blossomed on his face.

"I would love that. Watching you squirm as they pound ink into your delicate royal skin. Sounds delightful." His eyes brightened with glee at getting to tease her.

"I won't squirm, and I'm not delicate." She drew back her left hand, intending to punch him in the arm, but making a fist reminded her painfully of the wound there. She frowned. "You're lucky I'm injured."

His expression sobered. "I'm just glad it wasn't worse."

"Thanks to you." A different kind of awkwardness moved in with the way he looked at her then. She turned down the passage and started walking, avoiding that feeling. "Let's get to the enclosure."

When they exited the dark tunnel, coming out under the rock overhang in front of that part of the tethdrak enclosure, her father was already there, having apparently come down via the main entrance. His appearance there made it obvious he had left them alone, not because he forgot something, but to give them a chance to talk things out. Now he led them past the bars at the front of the tethdrak habitat to another tunnel passage that would take them to the front of the expansive kanodrak canyon.

Niskenya waited at the front. Because of her bond with Kasiel, she always knew when he was coming to visit. When they stepped through the door, she began kneading the ground like a cat, her enormous claws digging deep gouges in the hard-packed, reddish dirt. Her silvery-gray scaled hide picking up a soft glow in the sunlight. She pushed her face to the bars, one of the elongated canines that dipped below her lower jaw clanging against the metal. Her father put a hand through, letting her press the bone armor that protected her head into his palm. Her milky white eyes closed for a moment, a deep purr rumbling in her chest. Then she drew back and looked from him to the gate expectantly.

"In a minute. First..." He gestured to Veyl and Jaysen, who were cautiously walking up to the bars a little farther down. "You did this? You made them tehnaak?"

The hint of scolding in his tone didn't appear to impress the massive predator. She huffed in his face through the bars, then walked over to where Veyl and Jaysen were, lowering her head so they could reach her in a rare offer of affection for someone other than Kasiel.

"Thanks, Niske." Veyl gave her father a smug smile. "I don't think she's sorry."

He shook his head at the beast. "I don't suppose that should surprise me."

Making the most of their time together did nothing to slow its passage. The year raced by, and Jaysen's last day in Vanris arrived too soon. They waited together now for the entourage carrying his mother that would take him back to Sarket. Veyl could feel a faint prickling under her hair on the back of her head where the tattoo of Jaysen's family crest was hidden from sight. It was a subtle sensation, akin to the slight sting in one's eyes when tears first threatened. She hated it. She hated this.

Jaysen stood next to her at the top of the palace steps. His right hand twitched now and then, as if he wanted to reach out and take hers. As her tehnaak, such contact wouldn't normally be considered inappropriate, but for them, that bond remained a carefully guarded secret.

They had trimmed his dark auburn hair to a more southern style to help ease his acceptance back in his homeland. It still hung loose and longer on the top, with the sides and back now cropped shorter than she was used to seeing on him, though not short enough to expose the symbol of her family tattooed on the back of his head. Something the Heartsmith had done without consulting her parents first on the day of her Trial, when he had given Veyl the start of her ke'hanoath.

That was when she learned how much autonomy the blind Heartsmiths had.

A Heartsmith tattooed the story dictated by the threads of a person's life upon their skin. Like a Bondmaker, they could read those threads, only in a deeper way, but without the ability to manipulate them. Her father had allowed Jaysen to sit with her for the process, and the blind Heartsmith had responded to the tehnaak connection between them. Her parents could only get so upset about that, though it was still probably preferable that they never found out.

The fresh haircut looked good on Jaysen, even if it did make his round ears more visible. Over the last year, he had lost even more of that youthful softness and ungainliness. Veyl recently celebrated her fourteenth birthday. In a week, he would have his fifteenth. He would turn fifteen, and she would miss it. His mother had requested to bring him home to Andaro, the capital of Sarket, a week early, so they might throw a public celebration for his birthday and homecoming together to try casting a positive light upon his return. It was a request her parents couldn't, in good conscience, refuse.

Veyl stared hard ahead, tears stinging her eyes now.

Without looking her way, Jaysen whispered, "It'll be all right."

It wouldn't. When he left this time, he might never come back. Once they coronated him as king, they might encounter one another at political meetings, but it wouldn't be the same. They would never again get to be the best friends they had become over the last seven years. They would no longer be tehnaak. At least she had convinced her father not to have the Bondmaker sever that connection until they had a few months to get used to being apart. It wasn't necessary to have them both present for the process. They could break the bond from her end.

Thinking of that made her chest tighten and the threat of tears grew more imminent. Then her mother's hand came to rest on her shoulder, a gesture of support, but also a prearranged signal to the Enkindler waiting off to one side among the guards. A feeling of calm and comfort moved through Veyl, easing the painful sorrow enough that she could blink back the moisture in her eyes. Next to her, Jaysen breathed a soft sigh, apparently feeling the Enkindler's influence as well.

When the entourage rode into view, her father and Adnar, the Feral Ahndhomen who had once been her father's commanding officer and instructor, rode escort near the front on their massive kanodraks. The vaguely feline beasts were easily a foot taller at the shoulder than the biggest horses among the group. The Sarketi horses all displayed that unnatural calmness about them that told her either her father or Adnar was influencing them to keep them from panicking around the large predators.

An elegant carriage in the center of the entourage continued to the foot of the steps below them, where it slowed to a stop. Six Sarketi guards dismounted and came forward. Her father swung off Niskenya, pressing a hand to the hard bone plating over her lowered head to show respect to their bond before he walked to the front. Irith loped up the steps, coming around to push in between Veyl and Jaysen. The cliff cat had little interest in propriety, and her father allowed him to do as he pleased within reason. They both reached down to scratch his head, their fingers touching. After a moment, Jaysen moved his hand away.

Queen Astrid emerged from the carriage, accepting the assistance an attendant offered. She wore a deep blue dress the same color as her eyes, with a wide skirt that squished considerably coming through the door. Generous swirls of silver embroidery made the garment sparkle in the sunlight. A jeweled tiara rested on her brow with sheer blue fabric draping from the sides and back over her warm brunette locks. She had a softness about her that Veyl found both beautiful and unsettling. In southern Vanris, even after many years of peace, everyone still learned to fight, regardless of gender. Sarket had never allowed women to train for combat. Women could be mothers and decorations on the arms of their husbands and not much more. Even the queen had little genuine power. The king regent was the one who truly ruled Sarket until Jaysen assumed the throne, which he would do once he turned eighteen. Maybe he would change things.

Her mother walked down to meet her halfway up the steps, and the two women embraced. "You look beautiful, Queen Astrid. It is a pleasure to welcome you to Etrion again."

Astrid smiled, though the expression faltered when her hesitant gaze moved to Jaysen. "Thank you, Khevarin Velara. I wish our capitals were closer, so we might visit more often."

"As do I." Her mother slid one hand up under Astrid's as she turned and guided her to them. "I believe the children would agree."

Veyl managed a passable southern-style curtsy as Jaysen bowed to his mother. Tavin, who stood to the other side of where Velara had been, also bowed. His tehnaak, Ellaris, started to do the same, catching herself partway down and changing it into an awkward curtsy. Her cheeks turned a warm shade of pink.

Astrid's smile was tremulous as she approached her son, full of a raw vulnerability that made Veyl feel sorry for her. Jaysen, despite his youth, somehow managed to better conceal his unease, though she knew him well enough to spot it in the stiffness of his posture and his restrained smile.

"Crown Prince Jaysen." Astrid drew a tremulous

breath. "Look how you've grown."

"Queen Astrid," he responded, tentatively adding, "Mother."

The two acted almost like strangers. That was Veyl's family's fault. When Sarket surrendered after her father killed King Lodmund, one condition of that surrender was that the heir to Sarket's throne would live in Vanris and learn their ways for seven years, starting at the age of eight. They had done it in an effort to ensure Sarket's next ruler would have a better understanding of and empathy for the Vanrian people than previous generations. Astrid visited once every year on his birthday, but that wasn't enough to keep the familial bond from weakening. Veyl feared the same thing would happen to the bond of friendship between her and Jaysen in time.

Mother and son shared a brief, uncomfortable hug. Then the queen cleared her throat softly and turned to Veyl. "And look at you, Khesran Veyl. You are every bit as beautiful as your mother. I understand you have started your ke'hanoath."

Veyl flushed, but she turned obligingly, letting Astrid see the symbols of her ke'hanoath on the side she had her hair braided back on. The Heartsmith used an expert blending of soft and sharp lines in their styling, running the symbols down both sides of the back of her neck. They tapered in size as they descended between her shoulder blades with branches sweeping left and right that stretched out halfway along to her shoulders. She had been undecided on color, so the Heartsmith recommended the blue of a storm-tossed sea, the color her deceased grandmother on her father's side had used, saying it embodied the majesty and underlying strength of her spirit.

"It suits you." Astrid took her hands, leaning in to place a kiss on her cheek. She lingered a moment before letting go, a sadness in her smile that made tears sting

Veyl's eyes again.

The attentive Enkindler sent another boost out, a gentle nudge of contentment.

"Come, let us go inside," her mother said. She cast a glance at Kasiel. "Don't forget to join us once you have returned Niskenya to her enclosure."

His grin said he recognized she was leaving him the opportunity to go for a quick run with the kanodrak before he came inside. "Of course, my love."

Veyl watched him place a gentle kiss on her mother's lips, somehow infusing it with tenderness despite the brevity of the gesture. An unfamiliar twist of envy arose in place of the embarrassment she often felt when they did such things in front of everyone. What was it like to love and be loved that deeply?

Feasting filled the day from there, along with frequent efforts by Astrid to reconnect with her son, enabled by the khevarin and khemron. Veyl resented it, given that Jaysen's mother would have years to get to know him again, while she had only today to say her final goodbyes. The frequent looks he cast her direction told her he shared her frustration.

"We could play a few rounds of Feral's Folly."

Ahrin's suggestion drew Veyl's attention away from Astrid and Jaysen sitting on the drawing room couch where the queen had trapped him in a conversation regarding his studies in Vanris. They would have a multi-day journey back to Andaro, the capital of Sarket. Couldn't she ask him about those things then?

"All right," she muttered, unable to muster genuine interest.

When she faced Ahrin, guilt twisted in her chest at the defeat in his eyes. He was trying to help, unlike Gannon, who had the same pleased grin now that he had worn throughout supper. The expression made her feel unwell. His obvious delight at Jaysen's pending departure was part of the reason she had spent the evening meal pushing food around her plate to make it look as if she had eaten something. She had noticed Jaysen doing the same.

"Actually, I'm tired." She stood. "I think I'll retire a little early tonight."

Her movement toward the door caught the attention of others in the room. Her parents both shifted as if to get up, but after they shared some exchange through a silent glance, it was her mother who stood and walked over to Veyl.

"Are you all right?" she asked in a whisper.

She met her mother's eyes, fighting the sting of tears yet again. They all knew she wasn't.

Without waiting for an answer, her mother kissed her forehead and set a supportive hand on her shoulder while she made her excuses, giving it a gentle squeeze before she left the room. Veyl caught Jaysen's eye as she walked out and held her hand by her leg, the index finger straight, the one next to it slightly bent. He answered with a subtle nod. In an hour and a half, they would meet. By then, everyone would be in bed or, for the adults, retired to a more private room to talk and drink later into the night.

Veyl busied herself with studies until their chosen time arrived. Then she discarded the split skirt she wore over her fitted pants and crept carefully out a window next to her bed. The ledge was narrow, but this was far from the first time she had used it this way. The entrances to their bedrooms were in different hallways, but the rooms themselves backed up to each other and shared the same exterior wall. She and Jaysen discovered early on that they could use the windows to visit each other in secret. They didn't do it often. If anyone came to check on them, whoever made the risky traverse had no expedient way to sneak back to their own room. But occasionally, they took the chance. Tonight seemed like a most appropriate time to do so.

She crept to his window quickly and carefully, not looking down. The drop was significant enough that she didn't like to dwell on how it might end if she slipped. The window stood open, awaiting her arrival. When she reached it, he was there to take her hands and help her inside. He didn't let go of them right away, as he typically did.

"Promise me you'll never do that again once I'm gone."

Veyl noted the intensity in his blue eyes and the firm grip of his hands on hers. "I won't have a reason to." She averted her gaze and extracted her hands, moving further into the room. Her gaze fell upon the Sarketi clothes her mother had brought for him, draped over the back of a chair in a room full of Vanrian items he had accumulated over the years. He couldn't arrive in Sarket dressed as a Vanrian. "What do you want to do on our last night?" she asked, struggling to keep her voice steady.

"I want to stay here with you."

"We are here." She forced a smile when she faced him, deliberately misreading the intent behind his words.

He didn't smile. "Not just for tonight."

Tears broke through in response to his words, accompanied by a flash of anger. She hadn't wanted to spend her last night with them both bawling like children. She tried to spin away, but he caught her and pulled her into his arms. Veyl clung to him, burying her face against his chest, sobs shaking her shoulders. He squeezed her close to him, as though afraid she might disappear if he let go, but she wasn't the one disappearing.

"I'm sorry. I didn't mean to make you cry." The strain in his voice told her he wasn't faring much better.

"But you did," she managed through her sniffles.

"I did," he murmured.

When those tears finally ran out, they went to sit on his bed, leaning back against the headboard, a stack of silken handkerchiefs between them for the drying of tears that snuck up periodically without warning. They spent most of an hour talking about anything that didn't immediately set off more sobbing. She asked him about the things he looked forward to in Andaro; foods he liked, places he was eager to revisit now that he was older, and people he was excited to see after so many years away. Eventually, the words ran out. Veyl leaned forward, wrapping her arms around her legs, and rested her head on her knees.

"I wish I belonged here," he murmured. "I wish I had pointed ears and a ke'hanoath."

He reached up to brush aside her braids and lightly traced one finger down the back of her neck along the tattoo there. The sensation sent a shiver through her, and her parents' kiss on the steps came to mind.

"Crown Prince Jaysen?" She couldn't quite put the usual sarcasm into his title. Not now, when it represented a future she could not be part of.

"Khesran Veyl?" he queried softly.

She smiled to herself, and turned around to face him. "Have you ever kissed anyone?"

His look soured. "No. I'm an earless southerner. Who here would kiss me?"

Her pulse quickened, a fluttering sensation spreading through her chest. "I would."

Jaysen scoffed and rolled his eyes, but when her expression remained sincere, a flicker of something else lit his features. "You mean that?"

Veyl nodded. "Yes." She managed a teasing grin. "You are quite handsome for an earless southerner." The grin faded. "You're also my best friend and tehnaak. I trust you. I love you. That sounds like a perfect recipe for a first kiss."

He searched her eyes for a moment, as if looking for the joke, then he leaned forward a fraction. One hand came up, stopping a few inches from her cheek. "Can I… kiss you?"

The ability to form words suddenly vanished. A sense of hopeful anticipation filled her that she suspected was at least partly his, strong enough to be felt through their bond. She settled for a nod, leaning in a little. His hand continued its path, sliding along the line of her jaw and into her hair. She savored the sensation, closing her eyes as he closed the remaining distance. His lips touched hers. Careful. Gentle. Sweet. The contact lasted a long moment, during which time itself seemed to stop. Perhaps, if they stayed this way, he would never have to leave.

Then he drew back, and she opened her eyes. For a few heartbeats, his gaze lingered on her lips, and she thought he might kiss her again. Instead, he met her eyes and settled against the headboard.

"Thank you," he murmured, looking away.

Veyl faced the foot of the bed and shifted closer, leaning against him. He slid an arm around her shoulders. Though they had sat alone like this countless times in her room or his, it felt different now. Such an innocent, experimental kiss wasn't supposed to change anything between them. She hadn't meant for it to, but somehow it had. Given his imminent departure, maybe that didn't matter.

He slid his other hand down her left arm and took her hand, turning it palm up, then brushed his thumb over the scar from their rooftop debacle almost a year ago now.

"Khesran Veyl." He spoke in a whisper.

"Crown Prince Jaysen?" she responded in kind.

"I love you."
"I had a feeling." She picked up a handkerchief.

ind rattling the latch on Jaysen's open window woke Veyl the next morning. She lay with her head on Jaysen's shoulder, both of them still on top of the covers in clothes they had worn to dinner. When she looked through the nearest window, she saw dark storm clouds threatening on the northern horizon. An appropriate reflection of the inner tempest she would have to keep hidden all day behind a forced smile. When her gaze drifted to the window they had left open, she let out a groan.

Jaysen woke at the sound. "What is it?" he mumbled, half awake.

She sat up, staring at her father's black and silver nightstar eagle, Akyla, where he sat in the frame, almost as big as the window itself. The wind ruffled his feathers, and he appeared exceptionally annoyed, though she couldn't think of a time when Akyla didn't look somewhat irritable. Unfortunately, unlike most Ferals, her father could see and hear through the beasts he worked with, which meant he knew exactly where she was.

"We should probably get up. My father will be here any minute."

That sent Jaysen jolting upright. He looked in the direction she was staring, and a groan quite like hers escaped him. "Shit. Getting yelled at by the khemron for sleeping with his daughter really wasn't my plan for my last morning here."

"At least we were only sleeping." She watched him hurry off the bed, knowing no amount of haste was going to help the situation.

He glanced around at her. "What else would…" Red rising in his cheeks, he turned away and went to pull a brush through his mussed hair.

Veyl followed him, borrowing his brush to do the same with hers. Her braids were still tidy enough that she left them alone. Akyla launched from the window and flew off. The door swung open a few seconds later as she was running her hands over her rumpled clothes to smooth them. Her father entered the room, looking far less upset than she would have expected. Irith padded over to her, bumping her hand with his head to demand her attention. She met her father's eyes for a second, then lowered her gaze to the cliff cat, scratching behind his ear.

Jaysen hurried forward and sank to one knee. "Khemron, I…" he trailed off when her father held up a hand.

"Given the circumstances, we will not be discussing your inappropriate sleepover or how many times the two of you may have risked your lives sneaking into each other's rooms before this. I have only one question—"

"We haven't done…" Veyl felt her cheeks warm, remembering the brief kiss she had a sudden itch to try again. She didn't want more than friendship with Jaysen, but there had been something inexplicably captivating about the experience. "We haven't done anything improper."

Her father arched a brow at her. "Other than spending time together unsupervised in each other's rooms at night?"

"You know what I mean, Father."

"I do. Prince Jaysen is fortunate to be leaving this morning. You and I will discuss this later. I suggest you not take my leniency in this moment as permission to attempt any similar antics with anyone else in the future, unless you want me to feed them to the kanodraks." He held up one hand again to stay any further comments and gestured to the couch with the other.

When they had both taken a seat, he pulled a small vial out of his pocket and held it up before Jaysen. "We need to discuss the tehnaak situation. When the time comes, we will send you a missive sharing the cheerful news that Veyl may have found a new tehnaak. That will be your warning that we are going to sever the bond within the month, so you have time to prepare yourself. Even with that, it will be devastating. There is no way around that. More so for you, since you will only have your mother to support you through the loss of that bond."

Jaysen's eyes widened. "You told her?"

"A decision we made so that you wouldn't have to go through the grief with no one to turn to. This tincture will also help. A few drops will dull your emotions and deaden some of the pain of the loss. It's made from ingredients that are difficult to come by, so there isn't much of it. I recommend reserving it for times when you need to be functional in public."

"Thank you." With a look of dread, Jaysen took the vial and tucked it in his packs. He pulled something else out and turned to Veyl, holding an ornate dagger and sheath his mother had given him on his thirteenth birthday. "I almost forgot. I wanted you to have this." He held it out to her.

She took it and stared down at it, her vision blurring. A drop of moisture landed on his family crest inset in silver in the sheath. "Thank you," she said in a small voice.

The rest of the morning, after a formal breakfast, was taken up by efforts to ensure all Jaysen's things made it into the carriage, followed by tearful goodbyes. He left many of the clothes tailored for him in Vanris behind. Most weren't appropriate colors or styles for Sarketi royalty. The khevarin and khemron gave him one of the finer horses in the palace stables. A mount suitable for a king. A gift that lacked any visible ties to a specific kingdom, so he might not get harassed over it going forward.

The Sarketi entourage was ready to leave a little before noon. A steady rain was falling by then. Veyl welcomed the cool drops of water on her face that helped mask the hot tears coming from her eyes. When they said their last goodbye, she slipped Jaysen a fine braided lock of her hair that she had cut from underneath. Their hands had touched, staying that way longer than appropriate, and he stared down at them, roughly brushing a tear from his cheek with the other.

"You keep my heart," he murmured.

"And you mine," she whispered back.

When he was gone, Veyl retreated to her rooms and didn't come out again that day.

*

Veyl blocked Gannon's strike and leapt back, giving herself a second to consider what she had learned in the fight up to that point. She hadn't sparred with him in a while, so it took a few minutes to get used to his style again. Ever-present sorrow clouded her focus, feeding the dark anger that flowed through her like poison. It fueled an urge to hurt someone, him especially because of how he had always treated Jaysen. His delighted smile the day Jaysen left remained etched in her mind.

Gannon charged in again. Veyl blocked his swing,

but this time she spun out, swapping her blade to her dominant left hand and striking him in the back of his hand with her pommel. He dropped his practice sword with a hiss of pain, pulling the injured appendage to his chest as he retreated.

"Veyl!" Merrin's stern tone sent a brief pang of regret through her, less because she had hurt Gannon than because she had been reckless enough to do it in front of their instructor. "We're here to learn, not to cripple one another." Merrin beckoned Gannon over with a quick gesture and reached out for his arm to check the injury. "You can break someone's hand that way. You know that."

"So," Veyl snapped, "he should learn to defend better."

"I'll take the next round."

Veyl winced inwardly as she glanced around to see her father ducking under the fence into the ring, his dark look telling her he had arrived in time to witness her risky disarming and the attitude she had given Merrin. Merrin nodded her appreciation to him when he picked up Gannon's practice sword and squared off against Veyl. He held the blade in his left hand. Because of an injury to his right forearm during the war, he had learned to fight left-handed, though he could use both rather adeptly now and had trained her to do the same.

Veyl faced him, matching his stance.

Still holding his hand to his chest, Gannon moved outside the ring to watch with his brother and their tehnaaks, Lorek and Iyvalin. Her father's tehnaak, Jethan, and his cliff cat were watching now, having apparently arrived with him. The group also included the twins' father, Darro, who went to look at Gannon's hand, and Darro's sharp-tempered tehnaak, Kince.

Veyl focused on her father. She couldn't fight him while angry. It always turned out poorly when she tried. But anger was all she had to shield her from the sorrow that had plagued her constantly since Jaysen's departure. It had been a mere three days. The gaping hollow within would shrink, given time. It had to. She couldn't imagine living this way forever, but it would get worse again when they severed the tehnaak connection. The pain had eventually eased after Minya's death, although a lot of that had to do with the friendship she built with the crown prince. Who could she turn to when they cut her bond to Jaysen?

Her father attacked, and she darted to the side. Her speed and agility were her greatest assets, given that she didn't have substantial reach or power. All her instructors trained her to use those to her advantage, though none with as much persistence as her grandfather, Dhomvalen Arhk. But her father, particularly when he let his kanodrak's instincts guide him, was uncannily quick and almost impossible to predict. Given how effortlessly he tracked her through her dodge and struck out again, it was clear he had no intention of going easy on her.

A swing came, followed instantly by another, and another. Before she had time to consider a strategy, he had her trapped on the defensive, desperately trying to fend off his attacks. He offered no mercy, driving her back toward the edge of the ring. In seconds, everything—her sorrow, resentment, and anger—vanished before the frantic need to avoid getting hit by one of those powerful, lightning-quick strikes.

Then she remembered the move he had shown her that he used to defeat one of his strongest opponents in the war. Taking a chance, she lunged into his next swing and dropped under it, skidding on one knee and making an abrupt turn. But when she followed through to strike at the back of his leg, he was already coming around. His practice sword caught hers and twisted it from her grasp, sending it flying across the ring. The tip of his blade came to a stop, pointing down at her.

Veyl lowered her head, breathing hard. Her father's hand moved into her line of sight, and she accepted it, letting him pull her to her feet. When she dared to look up at him, his fond smile caught her by surprise.

"Are you all right?"

She nodded, still trying to catch her breath.

"That was very good. You used your size and agility to your advantage, like we've been teaching you."

"And you still won."

He grinned. "Did you honestly expect me not to?"

Veyl shrugged. "Someday."

"I think that may be true, but not today." He brushed a strand of hair away from her face and peered into her eyes. "How's your temper?"

"Burned out for the moment," she answered honestly, knowing it wouldn't take long to rekindle.

"Good. Are you up for dinner with my tehsheyn?"

"She ought to be," Gannon blurted. "She's been sulking over her Sarketi boyfriend long enough."

The scathing look her father gave him was almost as severe as Veyl's own. She took some comfort from that. Irith got up and growled at Gannon, reacting to her father's anger.

Darro placed a hand on Gannon's shoulder, squeezing tightly enough that he flinched. "Don't worry, Khesran Veyl. Gannon won't be joining us tonight."

"What?" Gannon stared up at his father, indignation flashing in his eyes.

"We'll talk about it at home. See you at dinner, Kas." Darro steered his still-complaining son away from the ring.

With a smirk, Kince ushered Ahrin and the twins' tehnaaks to follow.

Jethan stayed behind with Irith, but the departing group didn't get far before two guards and a scout came running up, their flushed features and labored breathing enough to make it clear they had run hard to get there. Darro's group turned back to wait as her father hurried to the edge of the ring and ducked through the fence, Veyl chasing after him.

The breathless trio knelt before him, three voices offering a respectful greeting. "Khemron Kasiel."

Tension crackled in the air as he made an abrupt gesture for them to rise. "What's happened?"

The scout stepped forward, her brows pinching. "The crown prince's entourage was attacked a few miles south of the Sarketi border—"

"Jaysen!" Veyl blurted.

The scout hesitated, glancing at her, then back at her father.

He nodded for the woman to continue.

"The crown prince suffered injuries, but his guards got him away from the fighting. They said he will recover. Queen Astrid was killed in the attack, along with many of their royal guards."

Veyl couldn't draw a breath until her father's arm wrapped around her shoulders, and he pulled her against his side. She turned in, closing her eyes and pressing her cheek to his chest. This couldn't be happening.

"Who attacked them?" he demanded.

"By all accounts, the assailants appear to have been Vanrian, Majesty."

Veyl drew a sharp inhale. The ground felt as though it was falling out from under her feet.

Her father's arm around her tightened a fraction. "Find the Khevarin and the rest of the council and have them meet me in the war room." She felt him turn slightly toward where Darro and Kince were standing. "Gather the unit and one of the other Ferals to join us and send word to Adnar to prepare some tethdraks for me. Jethan, I need you with me."

"I can take the kids to the palace," Merrin offered, walking up behind them.

He kissed Veyl's forehead. "It'll be all right," he murmured, giving her a gentle push toward where Merrin waited. "Thank you, Merrin. Meet us in the war room when you're done."

Merrin took hold of Veyl's arm in a light grip, guiding her toward the building. "You four, come with me," she called, glancing back at the others.

Veyl stumbled along with her, wishing someone would pinch her and wake her from this nightmare. Merrin took them to a drawing room near the war room, snagging a few attendants and two guards along the way to stay with them. Before leaving them, she took Veyl by the shoulders and met her eyes.

"We will handle this."

Veyl nodded, though she wasn't sure it was going to help. Jaysen had to leave his tehnaak and best friend behind, and now he had lost his mother as well. He had been wounded, physically and in a far more damaging way, emotionally, by her own people. She stared at the door for several seconds after it closed. When she was about to turn away, another guard arrived escorting Tavin and Ellaris, both of whom hurried to her.

"What's going on?" Tavin asked, staring at her with too much trust in his wide eyes.

She forced a smile, not wanting to disappoint him. "Just a minor incident Father needs to investigate. It'll be all right." Those last words echoed in her head in her father's voice. Had he been lying to her when he said that the way she felt like she was lying to Tavin? She mussed her brother's hair and gave Ellaris a quick hug before turning away.

Gannon was off to one side of the room with Lorek and Iyvalin, busy pulling out a few sets of dice. For once, he had the decency not to make any inflammatory comments, though his gaze flickered her way for an instant, his expression guarded.

Ahrin, who had been waiting patiently next to her took a step closer now, speaking in a low voice. "Do you need anything?"

She met his eyes. He had pretty eyes, though they weren't as rich a blue as Jaysen's. "Paper. And a quill."

Ahrin nodded and hurried away. A few minutes later, he had collected the items and delivered them to the drawing table she settled at in the far corner. Tavin and Ellaris joined the other three, all of them sitting in a circle on the floor to play an elaborate dice game.

"Thank you." Veyl caught Ahrin's arm before he walked away. "Not just for this, but for being... you, I guess."

"You don't have to thank me for that." He gave her a gentle smile before going to join the others.

Veyl spread out the paper in front of her, dipped the quill in the ink, and began writing.

*Crown Prince Jaysen,*

*I heard what happened, and I am desperately sorry for the tragic loss of your mother, Queen Astrid. I realize how alone you must feel right now. Please know my heart is with you. Somehow, I will find a way to visit you in person as soon as it is possible. I may have to wait until my father has tracked down the ones responsible for this atrocity, but I promise you, I will come.*

A tear hit the page, and her blurred vision made it impossible to continue, so she simply signed it and folded it. Somehow, she would go to him. He was her tehnaak, and he needed her. Her parents were going to have to understand that it was necessary.

*

They didn't understand, though. They refused to allow her to visit Sarket in the wake of the attack on Jaysen and his mother. In the months that followed, her father and Arhk coordinated and sometimes led Vanrian forces trying to hunt down the group responsible for the attack, while her mother managed communications to maintain peace with Sarket and keep their allies in the kingdoms of Delaphine and Fallend apprised of the situation. The guilty parties evaded discovery, even with Evokers helping to run interrogations.

After a few months, Dhomvalen Arhk took full control, moving search efforts farther north. Some rumors placed the blame at the feet of a known insurgent group that protested the peace with Sarket, claiming they couldn't resist an opportunity to try taking out the crown prince and his mother in one strike. Others suggested the rising anti-mind-crafter movement within Vanris was responsible, though it seemed odd that they would strike out at leaders from another kingdom. Either way, the effort had at least partly failed, but it still struck a powerful blow to Sarket and the tenuous peace between the two kingdoms. More rebel groups popped up on both sides, emboldened by the incident, and began harrying merchants and other travelers, some even attacking a few smaller towns and watchtowers along the western borders of the Crimson Break.

Despite assurances from Sarket that Jaysen had recovered from his injuries, Veyl received no response from him to that first letter, or the next several she sent. It wasn't until nearly eight months later, when—primarily through the diligence of the Vanrian military—the region grew quiet again, that a reply finally came.

Her parents were involving her more and more in political affairs. As a result, she was with them in a large council chamber with framed maps of different regions hung along the walls when three missives arrived. Several of the core members of her father's unit had gathered to discuss the state of things and see what news the messenger brought from Sarket's capital.

The twins and their tehnaaks were also there, seated near the end of the table with her to wait on Kince and Darro, who were planning to take the four out with them on patrol and start teaching them the routes. She watched her father pull the sealed missives from a satchel and place them on the table. He hesitated for a moment, staring at one, then his gaze lifted to her.

Picking up the missive, he held it out and said, "This one appears to be for you, Veyl."

It was all she could do not to run to the opposite end of the table, trying to contain the anxious excitement bubbling up within her. Tears stung her eyes when her mother took it from him and passed it to her. She stepped to one side, quickly broke the seal, and started reading.

*Khesran Veyl Markanis,*

*I remember well the day I arrived in Vanris. I was terrified. I felt lost, alone, and out of my depth. Then I met you. You were mourning your recently deceased tehnaak. I recall thinking that you looked even more miserable than I was. Still, when your parents introduced us, you put on a brave smile and asked me if I wanted to learn how to play Feral's Folly. Do you recall how I told you the beasts on the cards looked terrifying, and you responded by making your father promise to take us out to meet the tethdraks and his kanodrak the very next day? I don't remember a day without you in it after that until these last several months.*

*I feel now as I did when I first arrived in Vanris, only there is no you here. With my mother gone, I have no allies. Everyone treats me with suspicion, especially given the Vanrian attack on our return trip and other incidents that have occurred since then. Even King Regent Thrasser, the man who acted as a father figure to me before I went to Vanris, handles me as if I am a spy in his household. They have been cruel in their treatment of me. I am unsure how to prove myself to them. I am not certain I can hope to do so knowing that I miss you more than I miss my own mother, Havaad keep her.*

*In light of these things, though it breaks my heart to write these words, I feel we must limit our communication. If you received this letter, it is only because I was able to sneak it in with the others. Please do not write to me again. If a time comes that I feel it is safe to resume doing so, I will reach out to you. Words cannot express how truly sorry I am.*

*Yours in perpetuity,*
*Crown Prince Jaysen Lodmund*

Veyl let the letter fall to the floor. She felt isolated, as if everyone else in the room stood on the other side of a wall, their voices muffled in her ears. The four youths at one end of the table were watching her. Ahrin half-stood as though he might come to her, but something seemed to hold him back. She looked at her parents at the other end, two missives laying open on the table before them while they discussed whatever messages were within with Darro, Kince, Merrin, and Avris. Yserra was there too, an Evoker who acted as one of her father's elite personal guards, along with her tehnaak, Dampener Minera.

"I want to go out with the others and learn the patrol routes," Veyl said, distantly aware that she had spoken over someone else.

Heavy silence filled the room. Her mother walked

to her and picked up the letter. After skimming the contents, she reached out, unwanted sympathy in her eyes, but Veyl sidestepped away from her hand. That contact would bring tears, and she didn't want to cry in front of them all.

Her father met her mother's eyes as he stepped away from the table, then turned a gentle gaze on her. "You are a khesran of Vanris, Veyl. It may be peaceful again right now, but that doesn't mean there are no more threats out there waiting for a chance to strike a crushing blow to Vanris."

"I don't care. You have another heir if something happens to me, one that's probably a mind-crafter. I want to learn the patrol routes. You raised me as a soldier. Let me use that for something."

His expression darkened.

Before he could speak, Merrin stepped forward. "Kince and Darro have their hands full, but Avris and I could take her out."

Avris stepped up to support her tehnaak. "We'll keep her safe, country boy," she said, falling back on an old nickname that hearkened to his upbringing in a remote village in Fallend.

The resistance didn't fade in her father's eyes. "No."

"Please." A tremble crept into Veyl's voice then, and she drew a deep breath, fighting not to feel her sorrow.

Not one to let her father's status as khemron intimidate her, Avris walked over and smiled at Veyl, brushing a tear she hadn't even realized was falling from her cheek. "If she keeps her sun hood up, no one will know it's her." She glanced over at Kince and Darro. "You can make sure your group does the same."

The two men nodded.

"You know we'll protect her with our lives," Merrin added.

Her parents' eyes met again, then her father looked

at her and nodded. "All right, but you will do every-thing Merrin and Avris tell you out there. Agreed?"

"Agreed." Veyl offered a slight bow. "I'll go get changed."

She sent a summons for Lanis as she exited the meeting chamber. The woman arrived at her rooms a few minutes after she did and helped her change into simple leather armor with dark metal plates protecting some of the more vulnerable areas. She had finished changing and was standing staring at the dagger and sheath Jaysen had given her where it sat on the sitting room mantle when her mother walked in.

Lanis excused herself and left them.

"Veyl, have you considered that it might be time to sever the tehnaak bond between you?"

She blinked a few times against the fresh sting of tears and picked up the sheath, adding it to her belt. "I don't think it is yet. His mother hasn't been dead a year, and he's surrounded by wolves, waiting for him to mess up so they can tear him apart. Severing the bond would only make him more vulnerable at a time when he can't afford to be." She took the dagger and sheathed it before facing her mother. "Besides, we don't even know if he still has the vial Father gave him. He could have lost it in the attack."

Her mother walked over and set the folded message from Jaysen on the mantle where the dagger had been. Then she looked at Veyl, a solemn, proud smile curving her lips. "When did you become such a wise young woman? You make sensible arguments. We will wait." She reached out to check a buckle on Veyl's armor, adjusting it slightly. "Be careful."

"It's not as if Father won't have Akyla or one of his sandhawks following us."

Her mother laughed. "You're probably right."

## CHAPTER EIGHT

Veyl sat on her favorite horse, a gelding named Kivast, outside the main gate into Etrion, staring west. That odd feeling that something drew her in that direction had grown stronger in recent years. A foolish fancy that contributed to her chronic restlessness, considering there was little in that direction beyond military bases, watchtowers, a few small towns, and the ocean.

What had Gannon called it? Her fish sense.

She breathed a soft laugh.

Ahrin waited next to her, with Iyvalin on his far side. Since that first scouting adventure a couple of years ago, she had discovered a passion she could focus on to help her cope with missing and worrying about Jaysen. Most of her time she invested in academic studies, training as a soldier, and political meetings, all to prepare her for her future as ruler of Vanris. The rest she put into working patrols around the area and aiding the city watch, activities her parents were marginally less resistant toward now that things had quieted down in the region.

They were heading in from a patrol route now, waiting on a large Delaphinian merchant wagon departing through the main city entrance. While there was adequate space for them to maneuver past it, none of them were that eager to come in off the day's adventure yet. One of the gate guards offered them a nod and a wave. They passed through often enough, heading out on routine patrols, that the guards knew them well. It didn't hurt that Veyl and the others had worked directly with several of them while assisting the city watch. These were the things she was good at. They gave her purpose.

"Don't let him through!"

The shout came a second too late. A rider leaning low over his mount went racing past the wagon out of the city at full speed. Veyl spun Kivast, kicking him to a run before he had fully finished the turn, and gave chase.

"Veyl!"

Ignoring Ahrin's shout, she embraced the surge of exhilaration that made her feel more alive and urged the gelding faster in pursuit of the fleeing rider before letting go of the reins to draw the horse bow she carried. Holding on tight with her legs, she nocked an arrow and aimed.

"Stop!" She shouted the order, giving him a mere second to respond before loosing the arrow.

It grazed his arm, tearing the fabric of his shirt and opening a gash in his shoulder. A warning. He grabbed for the wound with his other hand and viciously kicked his horse, demanding more speed from the animal. His response convinced her not to give him a second chance. Changing her target, she fired the next arrow into his thigh. His torso jerked with the sudden pain, the violence of the movement making his fast-moving mount stumble. The distressed animal skidded to an abrupt stop and bucked, apparently through with its rider's antics, and the man slammed forward onto its neck. He clung there for a second, unable to find his balance again with the injured leg, and slowly fell off the side.

Kivast stopped and Veyl swung down, storming toward him with another arrow nocked and ready to release. She was aware of other riders racing up around them. The man rolled onto his back and sat up, pressing a hand to his thigh next to where the arrow shaft protruded. He had drying blood on his clothes, a spattering of it on his face that, combined with his pained grimace, made him look wild and dangerous.

"Khesran Veyl!" His gaze locked on her, eyes widening with surprise and what looked disconcertingly like hope. "You're the ruler Vanris needs. We can help you free us from the mind-crafters in your family. We've been preparing the way for you."

Veyl retreated a step, lowering her bow as several guards rushed past her to grab the man. She knew there were activists in Vanris who believed mind-crafters received unfair advantages and that their existence inspired conflict with other countries. While the first point could be debated, the latter had a basis in history. The long war with the now-disbanded Pandrean Alliance started because the southern kingdoms didn't trust Vanrian mind-crafters, but for this man to believe that she would ever harm her own family...

"My father stopped the war," she shouted at him, fingers tightening on the bowstring again. "You owe this peace to him!"

A hand came to rest on her shoulder. "Don't let him get to you."

She glanced at the man next to her, his long blond hair woven into a series of braids along his scalp. Dhomen Tarik, head of the city guard in Etrion, and one of her regular mentors over the last couple of years. "Why is he covered in blood?"

Tarik ignored her for a moment, calling out orders. "Take him to the prison and have his wounds seen to. We want him healthy enough for a chat with an Evoker."

A chat they all knew would involve a Frightener too, though Tarik didn't say as much. He turned back to her, his brow furrowing. "According to a witness, it appears he disapproved when his son invited a friend with a newly awakened Enkindler ability over after classes. He stabbed the boy to death and discarded him in the alley behind his house. Fortunately, the son slipped away while his father was getting rid of the body and came for us, or he might have escaped."

Veyl's gut twisted as she watched them dragging the struggling man back toward the gate. How could he hate his own people that much? Enough to kill a child. "Newly awakened. Then the boy was only—"

"Thirteen." Tarik's jaw clenched. He shook his head and drew a breath. "Excellent shooting, by the way. You apprehended him without compromising our ability to get information out of him. It was well done."

"I wish I had shot to kill," she hissed.

"I understand the desire, but it's good that you didn't. Someone like that may know more like-minded individuals. A few rounds of interrogation could help us save others from the same fate as that poor boy." He squeezed her shoulder before taking his hand away. "Let's get back inside the city."

Veyl mounted Kivast and rode through the gate with the dhomen. Ahrin and Iyvalin were waiting inside.

"That was amazing." Iyvalin's pale eyes shone with admiration. "I wish I had half your skill on a horse."

"I wish I had half your skill with a bow," Ahrin added, grinning at her.

*I wish I had my tehnaak.*

Veyl couldn't bring herself to appreciate their praise. The man had been covered in the blood of a child. She glanced behind them to see the guards leading the man through the gate and her stomach clenched.

"Is everything all right?" Iyvalin asked.

Veyl looked at her friends. Should she tell them what the man had done?

"Khesran Veyl." An attendant came trotting up to them on a horse from the palace stables. "Khemron Kasiel wishes to speak with you right away."

It was too fast for her father to have heard about this incident, wasn't it? Unless he had been keeping watch through the eyes of one of his birds again. If that were the case, he might have already summoned someone from the watch as well.

"Thank you." She glanced at the other two, swallowing against the ill feeling in her gut. "I'll see you both later."

"Good luck," Ahrin said, his blue eyes full of genuine concern.

It always surprised her how different he was from his brother, despite how similar they looked. Ahrin's kindness made the features he shared with Gannon softer somehow, giving the sharp jaw and pronounced cheekbones a beauty his brother would never possess.

Veyl forced a smile for him and Iyvalin before following the attendant back to the palace, where they left the horses with a groom at the stables outside the main entrance. When she reached her father's study, a city guard was there ahead of her, giving a report on the incident with the murderer she had apprehended. Her father's hair hung loose today, hiding his cut ears from view, though the way it laid over them made it obvious his ears didn't taper to points like everyone else's. Sometimes, his hair being down merely signaled that he was in the mood for a relaxed day, other times it warned of a melancholy state of mind. She hoped today was the former.

Shoulders knotted and nerves dancing, she waited to one side, dreading what would come next.

Her father finally dismissed the guard, waiting until

he was gone to arch a brow at her. "We have discussed the risks you take a hundred times, Veyl."

She went to stand in front of his desk. "From what I saw today, I'm in less danger out there than the rest of my family." While she was speaking, Irith came up and pressed his head against her hip, looking for affection. She scratched behind his ears, reassured by his presence.

Her father let her actions sidetrack him, watching his companion lean contentedly into her hand. "Animals have always loved you. You would have made a great Feral."

Her chest tightened and the aging cliff cat's ears flattened back in response to the tension that rose between her and her father. "But I'm not a Feral, Father. I'm not anything. I'm just a girl. This, running patrols and working with the guards, this is how I help my country."

He came around the desk and reached for her chin. Veyl jerked back, irritated when her avoidance didn't lessen the gentle fondness in his regard. Given how often she evaded the gesture, it was a little surprising he hadn't stopped trying.

"You will never be *just a girl*, Veyl. All your instructors tell us you excel at everything you put your mind to. You will be a remarkable khevarin one day. Not being a mind-crafter might just make you the most popular khevarin Vanris has ever had."

Before she could respond, her mother entered the room holding a couple of unopened missives. "There's my fearless daughter." Her gaze went to Kasiel. "You know she gets her recklessness from you."

"Reckless!" Veyl snapped, her self-control disintegrating. "If Ahrin or Iyvalin had been the one to bring that murdering bastard down, they would get nothing but praise. Why can't you treat me the same?"

"Language, Veyl," her mother cautioned. "Because

you are not the same. You are the future ruler of Vanris. If we are going to allow these activities to continue, you need to demonstrate that you can act with some degree of caution."

"Your mother is right. You are very good at what you do, but you can't rush in without thinking. Trust me, I know how disastrous that can be." He walked over to give her mother a light kiss before he looked down at the missives she carried.

"This came for you." Her mother held one of them out to Veyl.

Veyl hesitated for a moment, staring at the unbroken wax seal bearing the mark of the crown prince of Sarket. Her heart stuttered as she took it and moved away from them, breaking the wax to read the disappointingly brief message within.

*Khesran Veyl Markanis,*

*There will be a council next month between our kingdoms in Balarus, near the coast. Afterward, King Regent Thrasser is allowing my companions and I to stay a few extra nights away in the integrated town of Deepwater, less than half a day's ride to the northwest of Balarus in the Break. My last few nights of relative freedom before my birthday and coronation, if you will. The ocean town is a popular destination for people from both our kingdoms. With peace restored in the Break, it is a place you might convince your parents to allow you a little freedom of your own before the greater burdens of adulthood fall upon your shoulders.*

*A coastal retreat seems the perfect place to celebrate birthdays recently passed and those soon to come. I hope this opportunity will not pass us by.*
*Crown Prince Jaysen Lodmund*

That was it? No apology for the long silence. No

warm greeting or closing words of friendship or affection.

She flipped it over a few times, then held it up to the light, searching for anything more, but there was nothing.

This was only the second time she had heard from him in nearly three years since he left Vanris. His reference to birthdays obviously referred to her coming seventeenth, and his eighteenth, soon after which he would be coronated as king of Sarket. With no explanations and no niceties, he expected her to go to the trouble of trying to convince her parents to allow her to visit Deepwater without them before returning to Etrion after the council in Balarus. And who were these companions he mentioned? If he had friends in Andaro, why did he need to see her?

Besides, there was hardly a point to revisiting the connection they had once shared when he would be king soon. Their tehnaak bond had been severed a few months before she turned sixteen. Even then, she received no word from him. From that painful moment on, she had buried herself deeper in her lessons and combat training to hide her misery. She avoided dealing with the aching emptiness within by spending her free hours working herself to exhaustion helping the city watch and running different patrol routes in and around Etrion, activities that led to arguments with her parents about acceptable risks and how far into the Crimson Break they would permit her to travel. The compromise had been that she never went out alone, either patrolling with a tehnaak pair or a couple of palace guards, sometimes both, depending on the route.

Their former tehnaak bond aside, Jaysen was also betrothed now. That news had come as a brief note in a missive from King Thrasser three months ago. Ongoing trust issues between the people of Vanris and Sarket were reason enough for them to avoid each other. His engagement merely added one more to the mountain of arguments stacked up against partaking in any clandestine reunion in Deepwater.

She stared at the page in her hand.

And yet…

Deepwater was as far west of Etrion as one could travel on Pandrea. It could be an opportunity to follow that inner call and see if there was anything to it. She was already attending the council. Her parents involved her in nearly all kingdom affairs these days, preparing her for her role as khevarin. She sat in on smaller political meetings with just her mother. Since Tavin's Trial, her father dedicated considerable time to working with him. Like him, her little brother was a Feral, though his ability hadn't manifested as strongly. His testing earned him a companion hunting hound, though he was trying to train up to working with cliff cats. His tehnaak, Ellaris, Jethan and his wife's second daughter, turned out to be an Enkindler. Although Veyl tried not to resent the two for something they had no control over, part of her did. She stayed away as much as she could, spending time with people like the twins and their tehnaaks who also had no mind-crafter abilities.

She skimmed the brief note again. Maybe… But she couldn't ask right now, immediately after getting the missive. This required a little finesse.

Veyl went to her chambers and burned the letter, not willing to risk someone else reading it. Choosing her moment, she waited until after dinner to slip off to the reading room where Sylaryth's claw was on display, knowing her father frequently visited there prior to retiring for the night. She carefully staged the scene before he arrived, ensuring he would find her sitting on the couch by the fireplace, looking dutifully through a book on the region surrounding Balarus. The coastal town of Deepwater in particular.

About twenty minutes later, her father came in alone, having apparently sent Irith off to bed with her mother. "It's getting a little late to be up reading, isn't it?"

Veyl didn't look up from the pages. "Oh, is it? I guess I lost track of time."

"What has you so engrossed?" He wandered over to sit beside her as she had expected he would.

"I was reading about the area around Balarus, since we'll be visiting soon. This town," she said, pointing to it on a map on one page, "Deepwater. It was abandoned during the war, wasn't it? I think I remember one of my instructors telling us it's now the most successful example of peaceful integration between Sarket and Vanris. I'd love to see that."

"Itching for an escape, are you?" He smiled and reached across to turn the page, revealing an illustration of the town in its destroyed state before the end of the war.

"I was just thinking—"

"That's concerning."

She elbowed him playfully. "Father, I'm serious."

He chuckled. "Of course. What were you thinking, favorite daughter of mine?"

She rolled her eyes at him and flipped back several pages to a map of the western half of the Crimson Break that showed the many watchtowers lining the borders of Vanris and Sarket. "Deepwater is supposed to be incredibly beautiful and very safe now, and it's not that far north to the Vanrian border from there. It'd be a straightforward journey back to Etrion if we traveled along the watchtowers."

"It would be a lovely respite, but there have been reports of unrest in northern Vanris. More anti-mindcrafter groups. I don't think your mother and I can afford to be away from the city any longer than necessary this time around."

If only he knew how perfectly his words set up the desired outcome. "That's just it. I was hoping maybe the twins and their tehnaaks could come, and just the five of us could spend a couple of days in Deepwater after the council." She saw an argument rising with the furrowing of his brow and rushed to intercept it. "Not alone, of course. We would obviously take guards with us."

He regarded her in thoughtful silence.

"Please. It would be safer than many of the patrols I ride."

"I'm not sure that's your strongest argument." He took the book and closed it, then kissed her forehead. "I won't promise anything, but I'll discuss the idea with your mother. Now go to bed."

Two things helped Veyl win her parents over. The first was how excited the twins and their tehnaaks were about the idea. Enough so that they immediately went to work on their parents to gain their support. The other was the fact that her parents discussed the idea with her trainers and mentors, all of whom had nothing but praise for her skills in combat and navigation. All five of them had extensive weapons training and patrol experience. With watchtower guards keeping an eye out for them on the return trip, all she needed to do was ensure they checked in on time at each one. Regardless of how things went with Jaysen, it presented a perfect opportunity to earn more trust and freedom.

Now, as their entourage approached Balarus, crushing apprehension pressed in with the realization that she would see Jaysen soon, and with no idea what to expect. All his brief missive told her was that he would be here with companions. Knowing she would have her own friends to stand with her made that a fraction less intimidating. But she hadn't disclosed to them her hidden motivation for asking to go to Deepwater. She couldn't risk them resisting the idea, particularly Gannon. Jaysen's brief letter suggested they might have an opportunity to connect in the coastal town. That would be a couple of days away, though.

What would happen before that, at the council? How was she supposed to act when she saw him for the first time in years?

Kivast, her gelding, jumped a foot to the side when a bird darted out of the trees, zipping past his ear. He didn't spook easily unless he was bored, which he was right then, and looking for ways to entertain himself. She couldn't blame him as she directed him back into line. The forest full of tall, skinny evergreens had looked precisely the same for at least the past two hours. That wasn't to suggest she didn't appreciate a change in scenery from the desert around Etrion, but riding along an endless dirt road amidst equally endless stands of nearly identical trees made it hard to imagine a beautiful coastal town waiting not that far away. It did nothing to distract her from her anxiety.

"Veyl."

She startled at Iyvalin's voice, unintentionally jerking Kivast's reins. The gelding snorted, giving a little half-hop kick combination in protest. She placed a hand on his neck to calm him.

Iyvalin's brows rose. "Are you all right?"

"Yes. I was just lost in thought." Veyl turned away to hide the warming in her cheeks.

Iyvalin nudged her horse closer and lowered her voice. "Were you thinking about him?"

"What? Who?" As if there were really any question who. "Why would I be?"

"Because you were best friends for a very long time," Iyvalin answered, absently tugging her silvery braid over her shoulder.

"*Were* being the relevant part of that sentence. That ended when he left Vanris." Had it? Would there be anything remaining of that friendship now? She wasn't sure whether it would be worse if there wasn't, or if there was. Either way, this would be a brief visit of a kind that would never happen again.

Iyvalin's indulgent smile said she wasn't convinced, but she was apparently willing to let it go for the time being.

The wall around Balarus looked like they constructed it using the tallest and skinniest of the trees simply limbed, topped off, and stuck in the ground as they were. It struck Veyl as one of the uglier walls she had ever seen. The view didn't improve when they went through the gates with her father's six tethdraks creating a protective buffer to either side of their column. The small village tucked in between the outer wood wall and the inner stone one around the keep looked run down and poor, the few people who dared to come out to watch their passage dressed in ragged clothes. A stink hung over it that hinted at a long history of chamber pots being dumped out of windows.

The keep that looked out over it all was a massive, uninspired stone structure with flat gray walls and square corners. Somehow, the village's stench didn't reach beyond the small moat and inner stone wall they passed through, the narrowness of that gate forcing her father to split his tethdraks up to the front and rear of the group. As they entered the courtyard, several servants hurried out into a line, ready to take mounts and move luggage. Not that the Vanrian contingent had much. This was to be a short council, so they opted to travel light with no carriages or wagons to slow them, bringing only what pack animals could carry.

The buildings within the wall were in far better condition than those without. It bothered her that Sarket's leaders weren't ashamed to hold a council in a place where such squalor was on open display. Did they care nothing for their citizens?

A procession of finely dressed individuals emerged from the main castle entrance. At the front, between two well-armed guards, was King Regent Wilkin Thrasser, cousin to former King Roald Lodmund, Jaysen's father. She had seen him in person a few times, on the rare occasions he visited Etrion over the years. The lines in his face had deepened and his hair turned more gray than brown now. He looked like he had sucked on a lemon when his gaze fell upon her father. Given that her father had routed Thrasser's forces twice toward the end of the war, she could see how the man might not be that fond of him. His fancy, multi-layered garments proudly displayed the silver and green colors of Sarket.

"Is that Jaysen?" Iyvalin whispered next to her. "He's gotten *really* handsome."

Veyl's gaze moved beyond Thrasser, and her chest tightened. Iyvalin wasn't wrong. She had always thought Jaysen attractive, but he had filled out in the years since she last saw him, growing into his height. A hint of stubble cast a shadow along his angular jaw. His swath of dark auburn hair, worn a little longer than the cut she had last seen him with, hung in slight disarray, as if he had passed through a bit of a breeze on his way here. He wore a partial set of mixed leather and plate armor that, while clean and attractive enough for a formal event, appeared more functional than ceremonial. A long dark cloak with an understated, thin trim of Sarket green and silver hung from his shoulders as if he were prepared to travel somewhere.

Suddenly, she was acutely aware of how many days they had been on the road. Her attire wasn't that different from his, with a less fine travel cloak over her Vanrian leather and dark metal armor, all of it dusty from days of riding. She had two braids worked closely along each side of her head, pulled together with the loose portion on top into a ponytail that hung over the rest of her blood-red hair. A few dark metal ear cuffs and a set of silver earrings in the shape of kanodrak claws adorned her exposed, pointed ears. She yearned for a chance to clean up first, but that wasn't an option, so she forced herself to sit tall in the saddle as they circled into the courtyard.

Veyl dismounted when her parents did and joined them at the front. The rest of the party followed suit a respectful second later and lined up behind them.

"King Regent Thrasser." Her mother matched the bow Thrasser offered as he greeted her.

Veyl noted her mother's approach. In Sarket, women didn't hold any actual power, and the accepted style of greeting would be a demure curtsy. That her mother bowed instead, greeting him in a manner appropriate for anyone in Vanris, but that would be considered masculine in his country, was interesting. Her father and Thrasser also bowed to each other, exchanging brief words before her parents moved on to Jaysen, who stood beside the King Regent now. Jaysen's greeting was equally formal, offering no hint of the fact that they had acted as his parents for nearly seven years.

Then it was Veyl's turn.

Drawing in a bracing breath, she stepped up before Thrasser and, taking guidance from her mother's approach, bowed to him. "King Regent Thrasser."

Thrasser offered the barest hint of a bow in return. "Khesran Veyl Cavenos," he greeted, choosing to use her father's surname, though either was technically appropriate in Vanris. "You have blossomed in the last few years, although," he paused, his disdainful gaze taking in her attire, "it is a shame you choose not to embrace more of your femininity."

A foul taste rose in her mouth, but she opted to ignore the comment, inclining her head slightly before forcing her leaden legs to move her over in front of Jaysen. His bright blue eyes met hers, his expression infuriatingly flat and unreadable.

"Khesran Veyl." He offered more of a bow than Thrasser had at least. "It has been a while."

"Crown Prince Jaysen." She wasn't sure if she wanted to embrace him or punch him until she broke through that stony expression to whatever he was hiding beneath it. She settled for bowing in return. "Has it? I barely noticed."

*

The council session grew tense within minutes of the two sides sitting at the meeting table. Thrasser and his advisors asked, somewhat forcefully, for substantial changes to the terms of the agreement with Vanris. In their surrender at the end of the war, they had sworn fealty to Vanris. Now they wanted to transform that into an alliance with a peace treaty similar to those established between Vanris and the other southern kingdoms of Delaphine and Fallend. It wasn't an unreasonable request, but they also wanted half of the Vanrian advisors and military forces stationed in the capital of Andaro and other key locations throughout Sarket to be called back to Vanris. The new treaty they proposed would also remove many of the restrictions on their development of alchemical weapons, which they said was necessary to ensure that Sarket could defend itself in case of attack from some theoretical ocean-faring threat.

Her parents, to their credit, expressed a willingness to bring the proposed changes before their council in Etrion, though they made it clear up front that some terms, such as the alchemical weapon development, would be extremely unlikely to get approval.

"We would prefer to have the new terms written out and signed before we conclude this council," Thrasser pressed.

"If you must have an answer now, it is more apt to be the one you do not want," her father countered. "We have reports from some of our people in Sarket that, on several occasions over recent months, our advisors were excluded from important meetings. That violation of the fealty agreement does not inspire confidence in your ability to adhere to the terms of a new treaty."

"Oversights, I assure you." Thrasser's tight smile struck Veyl as disingenuous, though she wasn't sure she had ever seen him look sincere. "Is it not absurd to continue leashing Sarket like some dog you cannot trust after nearly twenty years of peace?"

"With the coming coronation, perhaps it is not the best time for making significant changes," her mother suggested. "Besides, it has not been that long since we brought the substantial unrest caused by the queen's unfortunate death back under control."

Jaysen bowed his head at the mention of his mother. The first notable hint of emotion he had shown since they arrived.

"Prince Jaysen has faced unfortunate challenges securing the support of our people, but he has made notable progress in that area of late. Imagine how it would boost his popularity if the announcement of a freer Sarket accompanied his birthday and coronation?"

Clever trying to turn this into a show of support for the crown prince, though Veyl observed a distinct tightening of Jaysen's jaw and curling of his hands as if they wanted to make fists when Thrasser spoke of him. Not a reaction that suggested a warm relationship between him and the king regent.

Her father looked at Jaysen, a hint of paternal fondness softening his expression. "You make a reasonable argument there." He turned to her mother.

After a brief meeting of eyes, they each nodded and faced Thrasser again. This time, her mother spoke. "We will hear the details of your proposal. That is all we can promise you right now."

"Thank you, your majesties." Thrasser held a hand out to one of his advisors, who passed him a stack of pages.

Her parents never mentioned the unrest to the north in Vanris during the discussions that followed, which made Veyl wonder what information Sarket might also be withholding. It wasn't hard to see that a significant lack of trust still plagued the relationship between the two kingdoms. Perhaps that was a problem she and Jaysen could address, assuming any part of their childhood connection remained. There must be something. Why else would he have wanted to meet with her? She would have to wait until they could speak alone to find that out.

Over the two full days of the short council, it became clear Jaysen was avoiding her. If she saw him at all outside of the meetings, he was always with three young Sarketi men disappearing into a room or down an adjacent hall. The closest she got to him was at the noon break on the second day. She was strolling along an exterior walkway with Ahrin and Iyvalin when she overheard him talking to his companions around the corner. His group was crossing through a courtyard with a statue of a mounted Sarketi general at its center. Veyl held out a hand to stop her friends and moved up against the wall, inching toward the corner to hear better. The other two crept up close behind her.

"At least you've got something to look at during the council sessions," one of his companions was saying. "Khesran Veyl's would be a field worth plowing. Did you ever cultivate that soil when you were in Vanris, Jaysen?"

Veyl's fists clenched, and a barely audible gasp came from Iyvalin behind her. She held her breath, waiting for Jaysen to come to her defense.

"The khesran was barely fourteen when I left and I

wasn't fifteen yet," he answered in a flat tone, "so no."

She let herself breathe, trying to cool the flush of anger that heated her. Was that really all he had to say?

Iyvalin placed a supportive hand on her shoulder.

"Tell me you at least tried kissing her. You couldn't have lived with them that long and not stolen a little taste of the forbidden." This was someone else, his voice a fraction deeper than the first man's.

Her chest tightened in the brief pause. She never told anyone about that kiss, but Ahrin and Iyvalin might find out in a few seconds. What would they think of her then?

"You've seen her father's beasts, right? I had no interest in being fed to a kanodrak. You don't mess with the daughter of a man like that when you're in his city."

Veyl let out a slow breath, struggling to force out some of the tension and anger with it. At least he had kept their secret.

"You should have tried it. They might have sent you home sooner."

Jaysen's chuckle caused a prickling along the back of her neck where he had touched her ke'hanoath the night before he left Vanris. "Shit. Why didn't I think of that?"

Ahrin leaned close and whispered, "Do you want to talk to him?"

Veyl shook her head. If she spoke to him right now, it would be in front of his friends, if that's what they were, and she might give in to the temptation to punch him just to make herself feel better.

The youth who had spoken first, a young man Veyl already despised, was talking again. "Probably a good thing you didn't go there. Stick a good Sarketi cock in even the finest Vanrian soil and it will probably rot off afterward."

Their laughter—Jaysen's laughter—faded as they rounded a corner on the far side of the courtyard. Her stomach twisted, pain lancing through her chest, but she wouldn't let herself cry, not for him.

Was it too late to change her mind about Deepwater?

By the time the last council session ended, the two sides had not come even close to establishing a new agreement. The only concession her parents agreed to make was that Vanris would gradually reduce some of its military presence in Sarket over the next three years, so long as Thrasser ensured that Vanrian representatives in Andaro attended all his political proceedings. Given how much he asked for going in, Thrasser appeared understandably unimpressed by the concession. Jaysen remained unreadable throughout, providing no hint of what he might want from all of this or why he had reached out to her.

Their departure late the next morning played out as a reversal of their arrival, with little emotion and substantial tension. Veyl felt a weight lift from her the moment they were outside the main gates of Balarus, at least until she considered what might await her in Deepwater. Perhaps, if she avoided Jaysen and his companions, she could still enjoy a stay in the coastal town with her friends.

They reached a fork in the road around midday the next day, one branch heading northwest to Deepwater, and the other continuing north to Vanris. Her parents had taken the small entourage several miles off track to stay with them until they were safely past the Sarketi border watchtowers. The forests around Balarus had fallen away behind them by the end of the previous day, and they could see the expanse of blue ocean stretching along the horizon far to the west. The landscape here was more desert-like, with areas of low, hardy plants and rock in places mixed with patches of sandy dunes. They lingered at the parting point for an embarrassing amount of time while her parents fretted over her.

"I wish I could leave some of my tethdraks with you," her father said.

Veyl blew out a breath, flipping up a strand of hair that had fallen into her face. She hadn't braided it today, leaving most of it down in a softer, less militaristic style for their arrival in Deepwater. "Father, I'll be fine. I'm 17 now. You were fighting in the war at my age."

"Technically, when I was exactly your age, I was being dragged across the hostile Sarketi countryside by a band of strange Vanrian soldiers, so I guess it could be worse." He gave Jethan a teasing grin.

"If we'd have known how much trouble you were going to be, we'd have left you in Fallend," Jethan countered with a wink.

His wife, her mother's tehnaak, had stayed behind with Tavin and Ellaris. Plenty of other people could have filled that role, but they all sympathized with her reluctance to be away from her second daughter after losing Minya. Veyl understood a portion of the sorrow that still hung over Jethan and his wife. At the same time, she didn't envy Ellaris how hard it was going to be for her to earn any freedom from her obsessively watchful parents. At least they weren't in a time of war when Tavin, as a Feral, would be too valuable a military resource to keep out of the fighting. In that situation, Ellaris, as his tehnaak, would deploy with him. She wasn't sure the girl's parents could handle that.

"Come on, Veyl. It'll be midnight before we get there at this speed." Gannon's horse stomped one foot in response to its rider's impatience.

Her mother scowled at him. "I suggest you find your manners, Gannon, or you'll be riding home with the khemron and I."

Gannon colored. His tehnaak, Lorek, chuckled, ducking behind the curtain of his long red hair and transforming the reaction to a cough into his hand when Gannon cast the scowl he didn't dare give her parents at him instead.

"Apologies, your majesties." Gannon sounded as meek as Veyl had ever heard him. A testament to how much he apparently wanted to visit Deepwater.

Seeing him put in his place was worth the delay.

Veyl turned her attention back to her parents. "We'll be careful. I promise."

They each gave her a hug and placed a kiss on her forehead. Then, finally, they allowed the small group to head off, two of the guards breaking away to accompany them. That she had talked them down to sending only two was a small miracle. Slipping out to meet Jaysen would be a challenge, but not impossible, though it surprised her to realize she was still considering doing so after what she had overheard in Balarus.

It wasn't long before they spotted Deepwater on the horizon. The buildings were constructed in tiers down the gradual slope toward the water, designed to blend with the desert in dusty reds and tans, most of them with flat rooftop terraces. The feature that made many of them stand out was the tiny oases of greenery cultivated on those rooftops. With the tiered hillside, it almost made the town itself look like a lush garden.

Excitement at the prospect of discovering this new place pushed away the dread that had risen in Veyl over the course of the council. The two guards, who her parents had chosen because they were familiar with the town, led them to an inn that catered to elite clientele, helping them board their horses, secure rooms, and move their packs inside. They got two rooms, both tastefully decorated using simple, but well-made furniture in desert colors. One for the three boys to share and another for Veyl and Iyvalin.

After cleaning up from the road and changing into more casual attire, they hurried out, heading for the market near the beach. The guards had agreed to dress down and keep a bit of distance while walking the streets to avoid drawing attention to the fact their group was being supervised.

Compared to Etrion, Deepwater's streets weren't crowded, though they were more diverse, with plenty of people of various nationalities wandering through the town. She saw Sarketi, Vanrians, and even some darker-skinned Delaphinians making their way around in pairs or groups, most paying scant attention to anyone not in their immediate company. After Balarus, it was hard not to be impressed with how clean the streets were, most paved with stones partially obscured by a light layer of sand. The number of streets and alleys that did not allow equine traffic played a role in that. Visitors had to board their mounts in local stables and settle for exploring on foot, which seemed a better way to experience the area anyhow. The crisp scents of salt and sea dominated the air, suggesting a more aggressive management of human waste in the small town as well.

Ahrin moved up beside her. "Thank you."

"For what?"

He grinned. "For suggesting this."

The slightest twinge of guilt in her chest reminded her she had done all of this to enable a meeting with Jaysen. Now that she was here, however, she was glad she had her friends to experience the adventure with her, even if Gannon could be a bit of a pest.

"I'm glad it worked out." The genuine smile that

curved her lips felt nice.

Standing on her other side, Gannon slid his arm around her shoulders and leaned in. "I know you just wanted to spend more time with me."

"You're insufferable." She chuckled at his expression of mock offense when she shrugged his arm off, then turned the group down a side street toward the sounds of the ocean and vendors calling out to people.

Ahrin and Iyvalin stayed beside her while Gannon and Lorek fell in a few strides behind, whispering and laughing. They eventually emerged out in a large open area full of vendor stalls on the waterfront. Deepwater got its name because of the steep drop-off mere feet beyond the edge of the waterline along much of the shore that allowed larger ships to enter the shelter of the bay for loading and unloading cargo.

Veyl stopped, her attention captured not by the shops, but by the ocean beyond the inward curving spits of land that created the bay. The distinct salt smell of the air and water, the faint mist in the breeze, the roar of the waves outside that sheltered area, they all called to her, beckoning her away from the tame world of the coastal town. Farther down to their right, past the end of the market area, there was a stretch of sandy beach with the curved wall of the cliffs beyond protecting it from exposure to the wider ocean.

"This place is fantastic!" Lorek grabbed his tehnaak by the arm and pulled him toward a vendor stall selling odd-shaped pastries.

It *was* fantastic, though it wasn't the collection of colorful wares and the diverse populace working the stalls or shopping at them that Veyl longed to explore. That magnificent body of water rumbling beyond the bay filled her with vibrant energy, unlike anything she could recall feeling before. Could it have always been the ocean that drew her to the west? The ocean surrounded all of Pandrea, though it was certainly closest to Etrion here. Or was it something in or beyond that vast expanse of water? If so, she might never have her answer.

But the ocean and her curious attraction to it would have to wait. Ahrin and Iyvalin had also dashed off to a shop displaying delicate jewelry made from various shells and polished stones. Veyl followed them, knowing the guards wouldn't appreciate them splitting up into more than two groups. Perhaps tomorrow, when they had the whole day, she could try convincing the others to hike around the outer edge of the cove to a beach she had seen on a map of the area.

When early evening crept in, they started back toward the inn to get dinner, laden with the various treasures they had acquired. Veyl was licking sticky sugar off her fingertips from another of the fabulous fluffy pastries Lorek and Gannon bought. She wasn't sure she could consume anything else after how many of those she had eaten, but it seemed wise to try balancing the sugar out with some healthier, more robust fare.

She spotted Jaysen and his companions a block away as they stepped into a crossing street. His group had also dressed down, though their casual attire still had that finer look of nobility about it.

Ahrin also spotted them. "Isn't that—"

"Shh." She put a hand over his mouth. "I don't think they've seen us. We should avoid them."

Gannon looked taken aback, then a faintly pleased smirk curved his lips. "We can go around a different way," he offered.

When she nodded, the others ducked back down the alley. Veyl hesitated, glancing over her shoulder to find Jaysen looking at her. His companions were heading up the street away from him. His expression told her nothing, but he pointed to the alley next to him, then casually tapped the light post beside him with two fingers. She answered with a subtle nod, lightning crackling through her nerves as he responded in kind before following his companions.

After a pleasant meal, Veyl and the others relaxed for a time, taking advantage of some decks of cards in the common room to create their own small tournament. As it grew closer to the end of that two-hour window, butterflies of excitement in Veyl's chest started waging war against the roiling pit of dread-snakes in her gut. It was now or never.

"I'm a little tired. I think I'm going to head off to bed so I can have more energy for tomorrow." When she stood, they all got up with her. She breathed a laugh. "You can stay out here for a while if you like. I think I can handle sleeping by myself. I've done it before. Although..." She glanced at Iyvalin. They were sharing a room. She was going to notice if Veyl wasn't there when she came to bed. "Could you come help me with something? It will only take a moment."

The other three wished her goodnight, already refocusing on the game as Iyvalin accompanied her to their room. One guard followed them in, inspecting the space for any potential risks before leaving them to themselves. The minute they were alone, Veyl hurried to the window, making certain it would open in such a way that she could climb out through it. The guards had insisted on rooms with only interior doors, but there were other ways to get around that.

"What are you up to?" Iyvalin stood watching her with her arms crossed over her chest and her nose scrunched in a manner that Veyl always thought was rather cute, though she only did it when she was suspicious or caught a whiff of something unpleasant.

Veyl faced her, trying to infuse her tone with the earnestness of her request. "If I'm not in here when you come to the room later, I need you to promise not to tell anyone. I swear I will be back before morning. Probably a lot sooner."

"You're going to meet *him*, aren't you?" An edge of disapproval sharpened her tone.

"Please." Veyl took her shoulders, peering into her pale gray eyes. "Please, don't say anything about this to anyone."

"Are you sure this is safe? If something happens to you because I kept my mouth shut…"

She patted the sword and dagger at her belt. "I'm taking precautions. It'll be fine. Deepwater is one of the safest towns in all three kingdoms right now. I researched it."

Iyvalin's smile was too compassionate. "I don't mean that. I mean, are you sure you can still trust him? You heard him with his friends in Balarus."

The dread-snakes ate the butterflies. Veyl forced a smile. "I can. I know I can. Please, Iyvy. He was my best friend growing up. This will be our last chance to just be friends before his marriage and coronation."

Iyvalin drew a deep breath and let it out. "I hope I don't regret this."

"You won't." Veyl leaned in and placed a light kiss on her cheek. "Thank you."

Slipping out the window once she was alone was simple enough, and her dark cloak made moving through the nighttime streets easier still. When she got to the place she had seen Jaysen from earlier, she lingered at the corner, peering warily around it until she spotted him lurking in the shadows of the alley behind the light post.

Could she still trust him?

For a few seconds, she watched, making sure no one else was with him. When she was confident he was alone, she snuck over to where he waited. Their eyes met for an instant before he backed up into the deeper darkness of the alley. Her hand sank closer to her sword hilt. How much had he changed in the last three years? He had maintained a convincing distance between them in Balarus, but then, she had followed his example just as convincingly. Was it all merely for show?

Lightning flashed along her nerves when she stepped into the darkness after him.

"Jaysen?"

Peering into the hood of his cloak, she searched for some clue as to his intentions. She almost took hold of her sword when he grabbed her shoulders and pulled her into his arms. He smothered her in a desperate embrace, pressing her to him and drawing in a shaking breath. The fear broke before a wave of relief and long-suppressed sorrow. A single sob escaped her when she put her arms around him, clinging to him. The distance between them that had tormented her in Balarus melted away. For the first time in years, she was whole again.

"I thought that Break-blasted council would never end," he murmured into her hair, his voice raw as if he were on the verge of tears.

"I know," was all she could choke out.

She leaned into him, relishing the intensity of his embrace, feeling the slight tremble that moved through him. How could their connection still be this strong? The tehnaak bond had been severed, and yet it felt like he was a piece of her that had been torn away. One she could never be complete without.

After several long seconds, he let go and took her hand. "Come with me."

Jaysen led her to the opposite end of the alley, pressing back against the wall to peer out. After a few seconds, he nodded and hurried into the street, keeping a brisk pace while cutting across it toward an inn there. He led her around the side and up some stairs to an elevated walkway, and along that to a locked gate at the end. This he opened with a key he pulled from his pocket. Once he had locked it again behind them, he led her up more stairs to a private rooftop terrace. There was a cozy sitting area with a fire crackling in a round brazier in the center, and what looked like a bed with a raised head to allow reclined occupants a comfortable view of the ocean and the sky.

"I slipped away from the others earlier to come rent this place. You have always had an affinity for rooftops."

The teasing grin he gave her when he faced her almost brought tears to her eyes again. He placed his hands on her cheeks, a fond smile curving his lips, a dramatic change from the stone-faced young man of the last few days. This was her best friend.

"Look at you. I never would have believed that you could get even more beautiful." He leaned in and placed a soft kiss on her forehead. "Crack a stone with me?" He gestured to a small side table where a stoneglass bottle sat between two mugs.

She took a step back, giving him a stern look. "I don't know. A handsome young man leads me to a rooftop with a bed on it and offers me a bottle of mead. I think my parents have warned me about you."

Jaysen grinned and held his hands up. "I promise, my intentions are pure."

"Pure as mud, I'm certain." She arched a brow at him.

He breathed a laugh. "Havaad's mercy, I've missed you."

He pulled her into his arms again, and lifted her off her feet, spinning her around before setting her down. One thing was certain: he had gotten a lot stronger in the last few years.

## CHAPTER ELEVEN

Veyl wanted to bask in the joy of finally getting the reunion she hoped for, but she couldn't cast aside three years of feeling abandoned by him. She pulled away, her smile faltering. "You never wrote to me. You never explained. Was it truly so awful that you couldn't manage one letter?"

His expression sobered. "I'm so sorry, Veyl. Going back to Sarket was never going to be easy, but you know a Vanrian rebel group killed my mother before we even got there. It would have been better if I had died with her." He held up a hand to stop the objection she opened her mouth to make, then walked to the table, continuing while he worked the cork out of the stoneglass bottle with the edge of a dagger. "People blamed me. They said I helped orchestrate it somehow. That I was just a Vanrian thrall bent on further destroying Sarket. They whispered I wasn't fit to be king. In fact, many didn't even bother whispering it. They shouted it in the streets. A few even screamed it in my face if I dared to leave my rooms."

He started filling the two mugs. "Do you have any idea how hard it has been to get them to trust me? Especially when what I really wanted through it all wasn't their trust. It was to be back in Vanris with you?"

He took off his cloak and sword belt, tossed them

on a chair, and untucked his shirt. Lifting one side, he showed her a thick scar below his ribs. "This happened in the attack that killed my mother." He dropped the shirt and lifted his chin, turning toward the light of a lantern hanging in one corner to reveal a scar that stretched halfway across his neck. "This was the first assassination attempt."

He took her left hand, turning it over to reveal the scar on her palm, and held his right hand up next to it, displaying a longer one that cut diagonally across from the pad of his thumb to the base of his pinky finger. Letting go of her, he unbuttoned the top button of his shirt and pulled it to the side to show a scar above his collarbone. She thought she glimpsed the end of yet another thick scar below that, but he shifted the shirt back into place too quickly for her to be sure.

"Those I got fighting the second would-be assassin who turned out to be a concerned citizen trying to protect his country from Vanris's puppet. I escaped a third with no additional scars. That was all in my first year back."

Hot tears spilled down her cheeks. "Jaysen," she paused, swallowing against the painful lump in her throat. "I had no idea." Had anyone from Sarket told her parents about these incidents? If so, they hadn't bothered passing that information on to her.

Moving closer, he brushed away her tears with his thumbs. "I'm not telling you this to make you feel bad. I just want you to understand why I couldn't risk anyone finding out how much of me belongs to you. The slightest hint that someone in Vanris held sway over me in any way would have turned even more of my people against me."

She stepped abruptly back from him. "Then you shouldn't be here. If anyone finds out—"

He stopped her with a finger over her lips. "I will

be king soon and married as well. I will try to be the best king I can, but there is nothing in that life that I am looking forward to. All I want is one last chance to spend an evening with you, sitting together, drinking mead, and talking like we used to. That is the coronation gift I long for more than anything else."

A thousand arguments against it rested on the tip of her tongue, but standing there gazing into her best friend's warm blue eyes, she found she couldn't refuse. "All right. A couple of hours."

He smiled and picked up the two mugs, handing one to her. After she took it, he held his up between them. "To best friends."

Veyl smiled. "To best friends." She clicked her mug against his, then took a large swallow to try quieting the anxiety his revelations had sparked.

Once they had both taken a drink, he gestured to the two different seating options. "Where shall we sit?"

Veyl pointed to the bed, her pulse quickening when the memory of that one kiss in his room all those years ago raced to the fore. Before she could reconsider her selection, Jaysen went to sit on it, reclining against the raised back, and gestured to the spot next to him. She took off her cloak and weapons and sat cross-legged, facing him.

"Are you disappointed that my parents didn't agree to the changes Thrasser was proposing?"

"Back to politics already?" He smirked. "No. Thrasser was hoping to pressure them into it by leveraging their connection to me and my coming coronation. That's part of why he waited until so close to my birthday to request the council. I told him it wouldn't work. I honestly would have been disappointed if it had. Your parents are too intelligent to be manipulated by him."

"Is it what you want?"

He took a sip of the mead before answering. "I

would like to see the relationship with Vanris change to an alliance, but not the way Thrasser wants it. He sees it as an opportunity to get out from under Vanris's heel. I see it as an opportunity to build a stronger connection between the two countries. Think of everything we could accomplish if we acted as partners. I hope to invest some productive time in negotiations with Vanrian representatives to discuss these things in the future. I will have to be careful how I go about it, though. If I move in that direction too quickly, my people will turn against me again. It's been painful enough gaining their trust up to now." He flexed the hand with the scar, the motion reminding her how literally true his words were.

"You've made friends though," she prompted, curious to see what he would say regarding his companions who had spoken so crudely about her.

"I don't know if I would call them friends. They're not completely awful all the time, but there is little respect for women in Sarket, and those three are prime examples of that mindset. They put too much effort into trying to bed any woman they can charm into believing they care just so they can boast about their conquests later, as if each one were a hunting trophy to hang on their walls. Unfortunately, they come from some of the most influential families in Andaro. Working my way into their favor has opened doors to gaining considerable approval among the nobility."

"And what did you have to do to get admission to their elite group?" Unease woke the serpents of dread in her gut again, and she took a long swallow of the mead to try silencing them.

He shook his head, his gaze sinking to the mug in his hand. "Please don't ask." He was silent for a moment, then he rallied, looking up and giving her a playful smile she could tell was at least partly forced. "I have to know, who was your second kiss, and was it as pleasurable as our first?"

Her cheeks flushed hot, and she took another quick swallow of the mead. How could she tell him that was her only kiss? In truth, she simply hadn't had the desire to be intimate with anyone since then. The mere idea of engaging in that kind of intimacy with someone she had no genuine interest in felt like an insult to the sweet, innocent moment they had shared.

"You haven't had one?" The surprise in his expression slowly faded and a pleased smile curved his lips. "First one was too good, huh?"

She rolled her eyes at him. "I just haven't had time for such things. But you have kissed other girls, haven't you?"

He cleared his throat and gazed back down at his mead. "A few."

She didn't honestly need to know more, but the question burst forth in defiance of her better judgment. "How far have you gone with them?"

"I... Maybe we should talk about something else." His brow furrowed, a hint of desperation in his eyes when he looked at her.

"You've slept with someone, haven't you? More than once, I'm guessing." She hated how abandoned and naïve that certainty made her feel.

He placed a hand on her arm. "You don't understand. To gain the support of the courtiers and nobles my age, I've had to be more like them. Even Thrasser seemed to feel I wasn't a suitable prince until I had experienced bedding women. I have only ever loved you, Veyl, but I have had intimate relations with more than a few women."

Her jaw clenched, and she shifted her arm out from under his hand. "Did you boast about them like hunting trophies when you were done?" She shouldn't be angry with him. This was part of how he earned his place in Sarket after his years in Vanris turned him into an outcast. Perhaps it was her parents she should be upset with for putting him in this position. Either way, she was angry, and it didn't feel good.

"Veyl."

She held her mead in both hands to hide the slight shake in them and stared down into the mug. Uncomfortable silence stretched between them.

"The view from here is incredible," he prompted.

Veyl looked toward the ocean. A dark night sky full of stars and a three-quarter moon reflected brightly on the calmer water in the bay. She could hear the crash of waves on rocks beyond the shelter of the bay, the voice of the ocean calling to her, powerful and persistent. A few larger ships, trading vessels perhaps, were entering the protected area, and she envied them their ability to sail those waters. If only she could be out there now. What would it be like to feel the salty spray of the ocean upon her skin and a wooden deck beneath her feet, rising and falling with the waves?

"You came with the twins and their tehnaaks. I take it you still haven't found a tehnaak of your own?"

Her throat tightened, and she took another drink to soothe it. "I don't want one," she murmured.

He took her mug and got up to refill both. Then he set them on the table by the bed and dug into his pocket, pulling something out before he sat back down. He held up a delicate chain from which dangled a perfect half of a small scallop shell. The chain ran through a set of holes in the narrow top and a little polished stone of a pale gray-green hung framed within the curve of the shell.

"The stone reminded me of your eyes. I forget what it's called, but it's supposed to bring good fortune."

Joy blossomed in her chest. He had found her a stone the color of her eyes in the setting of a shell from the ocean she was so relentlessly drawn to. A giddy delight danced through her at the way his cheeks colored when he held it out to her. Turning around on the bed, she lifted her hair to let him fasten it on her. The light brush of his fingers against her neck reminded her of that last night before he left, and reckless curiosity flared hot within her, pushing her to try that kiss again. She let her hair fall and lifted the delicate pendant, admiring it for a moment while she waited for her racing pulse to slow.

"Do you like it?"

When she turned around, he was leaning against the raised back of the bed again, watching her, a hint of color still warming his cheeks.

"It's perfect." She moved to sit next to him, letting him wrap one arm around her shoulders and pull her close, as he had so many times in their rooms growing up.

He kissed her head, then handed her mug back to her. "You should have someone to support you. You deserve that."

She settled against him, leaning her head on his shoulder as she gazed at the ocean beyond the bay. A few hours. They would get no more than that, likely for the rest of their lives. The next time they met, it would be at some political council. He would be king and married as well.

"What's she like? Your betrothed?"

"I don't know her. She had a gracious smile the one time we met, though her eyes were sad. But we've talked enough about me. What have you been doing for the last few years?"

Maybe there was no point in asking those questions. It was obviously an arranged marriage, and the hesitation in his voice when he spoke of it told her he wasn't comfortable with the situation. She went along with his change of subject, talking for a while about working on patrols inside and outside the city. He seemed amused by how she had taken it upon herself to become involved in protecting her home in such a direct way.

"That must make your poor parents crazy."

"It does, but we find compromises. My father tries hard to help me be happy. I think he still has guilt over his kanodrak deciding to make us tehnaak and all the trouble that caused."

They both chuckled at that, though Jaysen's arm around her shoulders tightened a little. "Do you think… When we embraced earlier, it felt like I became… Never mind."

"Whole again," Veyl finished for him. "Me too. It should take a lot more time around each other for the bond to reform, but maybe it did somehow." She took his hand, twining her fingers through his. "Maybe we're supposed to be connected. We could just give in to fate and run away together."

"I've thought about that. I even came up with a few plans. Where we might go from here. How we might travel."

She had been joking, but the seriousness in tone sent a chill through her, and she pulled away enough to look at him.

He shrugged. "I know it's a ridiculous idea, but I'm tired, Veyl. At every turn, Thrasser works to make this harder for me. In Royal Council meetings, he is constantly trying to weaken my position. I'll suggest something, and he'll come back with, 'We must remember what happened when,' and mention some incident or another that undermines my idea. Then he'll follow it with, 'Apologies, Prince Jaysen. I forgot you were living in Vanris then.' I keep waiting for him to make a public play to keep me off the throne or privately send a few more assassins my way. I'm sick of playing these games. Every minute of every day, I must fight for the right to keep the station I was born into, when I don't even want it."

An ache spread through her chest. She turned the rest of the way around and leaned across him to set her mug on the table, then met his eyes. "I wish I could make it better for you. Maybe my parents could alert the Vanrian representatives to your concerns. They might be able to help you without being obvious about it."

"Maybe, though, they would need to be *very* discreet." He set his mug next to hers and smiled then, the expression chasing away some of her earlier chill. "I love your sincerity, Veyl. It's incredibly refreshing."

"You're my best friend, Jaysen. I want you to be happy."

He stared into her eyes a moment, then his gaze drifted to her lips.

Without considering what she was doing or why, Veyl leaned in and touched her lips to his in a light, quick kiss. When she went to draw away, he placed one hand against her cheek, not stopping her with force, but achieving the same result with his touch. His eyes searched hers for a heartbeat, then he slid his fingers into her hair and leaned in to kiss her again. It started soft and tentative. Then his mouth opened, and his tongue brushed her lips. She responded instinctively, parting her lips for him and letting him deepen the kiss. A warm flush swept through her, her heart pounding in her ears like the drums in a parade. His other hand moved to her waist, and he shifted them both until she reclined on the bed half under him, her thoughts fragmenting with the unexpected intensity of the moment.

A woman's voice coming from down by the gate broke them apart. "Your friend rented the room and terrace earlier today." Her words accompanied the metallic clink of a key being turned in the gate lock.

"Thank you for your assistance." Veyl recognized the voice of one of Jaysen's companions from the council.

"Of course, my lords."

Jaysen was on his feet as quickly as she was, both grabbing for their sword belts.

"Is there another way down from here?" She scanned the terrace while they buckled on their weapons.

"I don't think so. Not a practical one, anyhow."

He handed her cloak to her before grabbing his own, and she put it on, yanking the hood up. Heart racing for an entirely different reason now, she hurried to the edge of the rooftop, leaning over to search for an escape.

"Doing a little whoring on your own, eh, Jaysen?"

Veyl turned at the man's words, her gut twisting when her eyes met those of a young man with short-cropped dark-blond hair. The other two stood behind him, and all three looked understandably surprised when they saw who their prince was dallying with.

"The khesran," one of them said, his mouth dropping slightly open.

The blond grinned. "So, you were plowing those Vanrian fields? Well done. I think I might enjoy planting a few seeds there myself."

He took a step toward her, and she started drawing her sword, casting a quick glance at the street below. If she jumped for the top of the half wall between this building and the next, she should be able to get to the bottom without hurting herself.

Jaysen, who had moved protectively closer to her, reached for his own weapon.

"Don't," she hissed, speaking in Vanrian to block them out even if they overheard. "I can get away. Play along with them. You have to."

He paused a mere heartbeat before his hand moved away from the sword. "I was just getting her warmed up." He let out a sharp laugh.

Even knowing he didn't mean it, hearing him say

those words was crushing. Veyl sheathed her sword. The blond licked his lips, eyes lighting with anticipation at her apparent capitulation. Jaysen turned, reaching out as if to grab her. She had an instant to see the distress twisting his features before she spun and vaulted over the railing that ran around the terrace. Her aim was a fraction off, but she landed with one foot solidly on the thick wall and sank into a crouch, grabbing on with her hands to steady herself. From there, she hopped off to the ground and looked up to see Jaysen staring down at her.

"Vanrian whore," one of the others shouted. "Get her!"

*Run*, Jaysen mouthed.

Veyl hesitated. This couldn't be the way their last time together ended.

Something large crashed into the next building and its side wall exploded, sending debris flying in all directions. Jaysen, his eyes widening, vaulted over the railing the way she had gone. He fumbled his landing on the wall and fell the rest of the way to the ground, winding up on his rear in the street.

Veyl hurried to him, offering her hand. "Are you all right?"

He nodded, scrambling up with her help. "What was that?"

The struck building was burning, a gaping hole in its side. More explosions broke through the previously peaceful night from elsewhere in the town, smoke billowing up into the sky. She could hear screaming between the explosions. Another large, burning ball came hurtling through the air, crashing into a building farther along the street.

"The town's being attacked from the ocean side." As she said it, Veyl recalled the ships she had seen entering the bay. Not trading vessels, after all. If only she had known.

Jaysen grabbed her hand. "We need to head inland, then."

Five figures carrying axes and wide, curved swords came running out of an alley on the bay side a few blocks ahead, their features hidden in the shadows of their hoods. A glance in the opposite direction revealed three more coming up from a crossing street down that way. Jaysen's companions burst out of an alley on the inland side.

"Prince Jaysen," one shouted, spotting them.

Veyl's gut clenched at the sight of them, but they all had bigger problems now, and the twins and their tehnaaks were still at the other inn closer to the bay. "I have to help my friends."

Jaysen let go of her hand and drew his sword. "I hate to disagree, but I think we need to help ourselves first. If we group with my companions, we stand a better chance. We can deal with any problems that may lead to later."

As wary as she was of the three, he was right. She nodded and drew her sword.

The trio of armed invaders spotted them and turned their way, breaking into a jog. The five off in the other direction had noticed them as well, but hadn't started advancing yet. A whistling sound above provided warning and the enemy figures heading toward them ducked behind a cart as another burning projectile hit the wall of the building next to Jaysen's companions. She watched the blast send the three Sarketi youths flying, a chunk of debris striking one in the head hard enough to crush part of his skull. Then Jaysen grabbed her, pulling her to the ground with him and shielding her with his body. He grunted when something hit him, but the second the debris settled, they were up again, weapons ready. They could do little about any injuries he might have sustained while they still were in danger.

They could see far enough through the billowing dust and smoke to spot two of his companions lying unmoving amidst the debris. The last one was on his hands and knees, struggling to stand, when one of the three enemy fighters rushed out of the cloud of dust and ran him through with their sword.

Jaysen made a distressed noise, freezing in place. A quick glance in the opposite direction showed Veyl that two of the other five were now coming their way as well. Not the greatest odds, but either enemies or debris currently blocked all their escape routes.

She touched Jaysen's arm, getting a small startle from him. "I need you with me," she said when he looked at her.

"I'm always with you," he answered.

"If we go for the three, we can probably break through before the others get here. Then we run up the first open alley we see. Agreed?"

He nodded.

She couldn't imagine what he was going through, having just watched his companions die in front of him, even if he hadn't been that fond of them. Trying not to think of the friends she had left at the inn, she drew a deep breath and raced forward to meet the approaching trio, Jaysen keeping pace with her. Veyl ran in with a right-handed swing that her chosen opponent blocked. Then she flipped the sword to her left in the middle of the next attack. Their reaction, calculated to counter another right-handed attack, missed completely. She cut into their ribs and spun, kicking them in the knee to take them down. That move shifted her out of the path of someone else's swing through sheer luck. The individual dropped their weapon when Jaysen's blade sliced into their arm from behind, and Veyl kicked them in the chest as Jaysen side-stepped out of the way, sending them staggering back. The third fighter was struggling to stand, blood streaming from a wound in their leg.

None of the three enemies were dead, but that wasn't what they were fighting for. They just needed to buy enough time to get out of there, so they turned and ran.

The minute they broke through the cloud of smoke and dust, they spotted more hooded enemies ahead. Veyl groaned and looked to their left and right. They were at the junction the three fighters they just escaped had come from. On the inland side, the direction they wanted to go, more burning debris blocked the way. In the other direction, toward the bay and the inn she was staying at, it was clear at least as far as she could see, which was only to the next street, but it would get them closer to where she had left her friends.

"This way," she shouted.

She bolted down the side street as more whistling sounded overhead. The noise sent a flash of fear through her. She started turning back to see where Jaysen was when a portion of the wall next to her exploded. The blast threw her hard enough that she hit the ground and skidded up against the side of the opposite building, her hand reflexively tightening on the hilt of her sword to avoid losing it. A stinging barrage of debris struck her, though nothing substantial enough to do serious damage.

She surged to her feet, peering through the dust. "Jay–"

Something hit the side of her head so hard it sent her staggering into the wall next to her. The blow dazed her for an instant, long enough for her attacker to strike her across the back of the knees. Her legs buckled, knees slamming into the hard stone that paved the streets. Someone grabbed her arms, twisting them painfully up behind her as another individual relieved her of her sword. She tasted blood.

"She's Vanrian." The woman spoke in Vanrian, though her accent was strange, putting emphasis in places Veyl's ears didn't expect to hear it. "You four, take her to Ahnkreth Kyril. The rest of you, come look for the other one with me."

Veyl shook her head, trying to clear it as they hauled her roughly to her feet. An ahnkreth was a mind-crafter leader of a fleet of anywhere from five to ten ships. These people were Vanrian. What was happening here? If she understood the situation from what little the woman said, they were taking her to their ahnkreth *because* she was Vanrian, but what did that mean for Jaysen?

"Wait!" She struggled against the ones holding her. "Let me go!"

Something struck behind her legs again, dropping her to her bruised knees a second time. One of them grabbed a handful of her hair and yanked her head back, forcing her to look up at him.

"We're happy to drag you there," he snapped, his accent the same as the woman's, "conscious or otherwise."

She ignored the threat, staring into light green eyes not that different from her own. "Please, my companion, don't hurt him."

The man hesitated, his painful grip on her hair easing a fraction.

"Please," she repeated.

His gaze shifted to the blood-red hair in his fist. He cursed under his breath, letting go. "Get her to Kyril. I'll catch up."

Veyl didn't fight when they pulled her up again, the rawest glimmer of hope in her chest. They escorted her none-too-gently to the inn she was staying at, continuing inside. The common room was full of the wounded and dead, though she didn't see more than a couple of Vanrians among the latter. Of the injured, none were familiar beyond that she might have seen them in passing as guests or as workers in the inn. They marched her past the rooms her group had been staying in. The door to the one the boys shared was closed, the other stood open. One of her guards lay dead on the floor. Iyvalin sat upon the bed, a minor cut above one eye. Her hands were bound, and an individual dressed like Veyl's captors stood leaning against the wall with a crossbow trained on her as if waiting for something.

"Iyvy!" Veyl shouted.

Iyvalin looked up, her eyes widening. "Veyl! You're alive."

The two holding Veyl shoved her past, forcing her on to the end of the hallway. They took her inside the room there, while the third left them, vanishing into the room across the hall. Rather than allow her to sit, they bound her hands and positioned her with her back to the wall before moving a few feet away to watch her, hoods still up and weapons ready. One, a woman, threw Veyl's sword into the corner behind the bed, putting it out of easy reach. The other, distinctly masculine in build, leaned against the fireplace.

"Who are you?" Veyl demanded.

Neither spoke.

She didn't have to wait long before the third returned on the heels of another man. With no hood obscuring his features, she could see that he had the tan of someone who spent a great deal of time in the sun, more even than she did. His hair was night-black, with streaks of dark blue painted into it. Several braids woven through it had small shells and bones bound onto them. Eyes of a pale silver-blue took her in dispassionately. His ears were his most disconcerting feature. He had pointed Vanrian ears, decorated with a few cuffs and earrings, but that black hair wasn't Vanrian. Her hair was unusually dark for her people. Black was unheard of. He also bore no visible ke'hanoath, though that didn't mean he had none. Plenty of canvas remained hidden beneath the dark leather armor and clothing he wore.

"She's good with a sword," the man behind him said, stopping in the doorway. "She was fighting in the streets with a young Sarketi male. They took down three of ours."

The black-haired man paused, eyes narrowing with a hint of distress or anger. "Killed?"

"No, but wounded enough to be out of the fighting."

He nodded and resumed his advance.

Veyl lifted her chin, hoping her trembling didn't show as much as it felt like it did.

He disregarded her attempt at defiance, reaching up to take a lock of her hair, and gazing at it thoughtfully as he rubbed it between his thumb and fingers as though inspecting each strand. "This is an unusual color for a Vanrian."

His voice was deep, and he spoke with the same peculiar accent as the others had. Standing this close, she could see that his features were unmarked, aside from a small scar on the right side of his jaw. He looked young to be an ahnkreth, assuming he was the individual they had been taking her to, though not, she suspected, as young as her.

"It's not unusual in my family." She could hear the shake of fear in her voice, which meant he would as well. Not the courageous first impression she had hoped to give. "I don't understand. Why are you attacking here? You're Vanrian, aren't you?"

"Yes, and no. And right now, I'm the one asking the questions." He dropped the lock of her hair. "Are you a mind-crafter?"

His expression gave her no clue as to the answer he might want to hear. Being a mind-crafter would make her more dangerous, however, so she opted for the truth. "I'm not. I want to see my friends."

"Are these Vanrian friends or something else?"

Her chest squeezed as Jaysen jumped to the fore of her mind. Under the circumstances, asking about her Vanrian companions first might gain her more favor. One thing at a time. "Vanrian."

"If they survived the initial assault, they are awaiting evaluation here or already on their way to one of my ships."

"Evaluation for what?"

His brows pinched. Those pale eyes giving off no hint of kindness. "You're used to getting your way, aren't you? Still, if you're a good fighter and can set aside your pride, I may have use for you on my crew."

"Excuse me, Ahnkreth Kyril," the man in the doorway began, "they've got the Sarketi youth who was with her."

Veyl's heart jumped into her throat. Jaysen. That meant he had survived the explosion at least, though his situation may not have improved if these people were looking specifically for Vanrians.

The black-haired man, Kyril, lifted his lip in a faintly animalistic snarl. "You didn't kill him?"

"We thought it might be prudent to keep him around, given..." the man trailed off, nodding toward Veyl.

Kyril considered her again, not breaking eye contact when he spoke. "You could be right. Bring him in."

She tried to hold his gaze, but her courage faltered when three more of the strange Vanrians entered with Jaysen bound and walking at spear point ahead of them. Dust covered him from head to toe, and he had a bloody nose and a bruise rising around one eye with a cut through that eyebrow. His eyes widened a fraction when he saw her, though he was clearly trying to avoid any powerful reactions while he assessed their situation. He spit blood that had trickled down from his slowly bleeding nose. One woman scowled and shoved him at the side wall. Twisting, he took the impact with his shoulder, and rolled to his back to lean against it, looking as exhausted as Veyl felt.

Kyril never looked away from Veyl. "Nalika, see what you can get out of him. No need to be gentle."

An Evoker?

Veyl's stomach clenched as the woman sheathed her sword and walked up to Jaysen, taking his chin in one hand to look into his eyes. "All right, pet, let's see what we can learn from you."

"Leave him alone," Veyl growled. Would they kill him if they found out who he was? Take him hostage?

Kyril narrowed his eyes at her. Then he turned and considered Jaysen. "They were fighting together. See if you can learn anything about her while you're in there. Strip his mind if you need to."

Veyl's stomach turned.

Jaysen looked at her. "It'll be all right."

She wasn't so sure.

Kyril was watching her intently again, the faintest calculating smirk on his lips. "Change that. Just kill him. We can get what we want from her. We have no need for the earless bastard."

Veyl's breath caught as Nalika stepped aside and another woman came forward, raising her spear to aim at Jaysen's chest.

"Don't. Please." Veyl met Kyril's eyes, fully prepared to set aside that pride he had noted a moment ago and beg.

Panic exploded through her when he only smiled,

and the woman drew the weapon back. This man was going to make her watch as they killed her best friend, her tehnaak. She couldn't breathe. Darkness threatened at the edges of her vision. The woman's muscles twitched as she began her strike, everything suddenly moving in slow motion.

"No!" Veyl screamed. The darkness swept in across her vision, rendering her blind for an instant.

The spear clattered to the stone floor. When Veyl's vision cleared, the woman who wielded the weapon was standing perfectly still, arms hanging at her sides. Jaysen pressed back against the wall, pale as a ghost, slowly lowering his hands that he had thrown up in front of him as if to protect himself from the attack. Kyril strode to the woman, his expression souring when he stepped around in front of her, putting his back to Jaysen. She didn't react to him. A trickle of blood ran from her ear.

"Illis?" He searched the woman's face, whatever he saw deepening the furrows in his brow. "Illis?" He pulled off a glove and snapped his fingers in front of her eyes, still getting no reaction. Then he wiped her cheek as though brushing away a tear, but his thumb came away smeared with red.

Kyril turned on Veyl, his chin lowering, a fury in his eyes that reminded her of her father's kanodrak when the beast saw someone as a threat to her bonded rider. She swallowed, shrinking from him. In a few lunging strides, he was in front of her, his hand clamping around her neck. He slammed her back against the stone behind her hard enough to knock the wind out of her. Before she could catch her breath, his hand tightened, and he slid her up the wall, bringing her feet off the floor. This man was all muscle and fury. With her wrists bound and the point of a dagger he had pulled from somewhere pressed to that soft place below her sternum, she could do little to fight back.

"You lied! You *are* a mind-crafter. A dangerous one." His hand squeezed harder as he spat the accusations in her face.

Veyl wanted to tell him she hadn't lied, but she couldn't do more than make a few pathetic choking sounds with his hand crushing her throat. Blood pounded in her head. She kicked against the wall, trying to push off and disrupt his hold, but he didn't budge, and the sharp pain of his blade point breaking the skin discouraged a second attempt.

"She wasn't lying!" Jaysen shouted.

The Evoker approached Kyril. "I don't know if it matters, sir, but I can get enough to know they both believe she is telling the truth."

His brow smoothed some, the rage fading enough to let in a hint of wary curiosity. "Stay out of her head until we know what she is," he ordered, still holding Veyl there as if they had all the time in the world to discuss the matter. As if a different darkness weren't closing around the edges of her vision now.

He eased her to the floor. The care with which he returned her to her feet prior to letting go allowed her the chance to lean against the wall before her legs gave out and slide down it in a slightly more dignified manner. A fit of coughing consumed her for a few seconds, then she rested her head back against the stone and closed her eyes.

"Here." She opened her eyes to find Kyril crouched in front of her, offering her a water skin he had pulled from his belt. When she made no move to take it, he arched a brow at her. "You torture only yourself by refusing."

She wished he was wrong, but her throat hurt. The water wouldn't fix that, but it might ease the urge to cough again. It might also spare her his wrath for a little longer, a possibility worth considering. When she reached out, he removed the cap for her and handed it over. She watched him uneasily as she brought it to her mouth, trying not to think about how many times his lips had probably touched that opening before hers.

"What's your name?" he asked when she handed the skin back.

Three more armed fighters entered the room as he spoke. They stopped by the door, waiting in silence. The woman who had almost stabbed Jaysen still stood motionless, staring at him, or more accurately, at nothing, blood drying in a line down the side of her neck and smeared upon her cheek.

Where were these people from? Would they recognize her name if she gave it to them?

"The young woman down the hall called her Veyl when we were bringing her here," one of his soldiers commented.

So much for coming up with a false name. "Who are you?"

"Ahnkreth Kyril," he answered, as though he expected that to be adequate.

Veyl looked around at them. Many of those who didn't still have their hoods up had darker hair with odd colors painted in, and braids with shells and bones in them like his. Not one of them had a tattoo that she could see. She faced him again. "I can't be a mind-crafter."

"Why not?"

"Because my little brother is one."

"Which makes you that much more interesting." Kyril's eyes narrowed a fraction before he capped the water skin and stood, turning to his fighters. He gestured to the Evoker. "Nalika, take Illis to your ship and keep an eye on her. Let me know if there are any changes in her condition." He glanced between Veyl and Jaysen. "And someone find me the Bondmaker."

The three recent arrivals by the door left, perhaps to search for the Bondmaker. Two more of them escorted

Illis out. When they turned the woman, Veyl could see a trail of blood coming from her other ear, and, though she went with them, her movement was strange, like that of someone walking in their sleep. She couldn't have done that to the woman, although she had no alternative explanation for it.

"Before I go," the Evoker Nalika said, stepping closer to Kyril, "might I have a word, Ahnkreth?"

He glanced at Veyl again, then nodded and gestured toward the door, following the woman out. A chill swept through Veyl. If the Evoker had gotten something from their thoughts that was worth discussing in private, it couldn't be good for them.

She brought her bound hands up to gingerly touch the side of her face where one of them had struck her earlier. It throbbed and her careful exploration found painful swelling along her cheekbone and ear. At least they didn't seem to have broken anything.

"Are you all right?" Jaysen asked.

The three strange Vanrians remaining in the room watched them, not demanding silence as she had expected them to. Perhaps they hoped to learn something by allowing them to talk.

"I'll live. Did they hurt you?"

He spit more blood from the trickle still running from his nose. "Most of this is from the explosion."

If she hadn't taken off down that street hoping to help her friends, they might both still be free right now. Maybe they could have found a way out of Deepwater. "I'm sorry, I–"

"Did nothing wrong," he interrupted. "They've already taken the whole town. We were never going to make it out of here. At least you're alive."

At least *she* was alive. He suspected the same thing she did. They didn't want Sarketi or Delaphinian prisoners. Whatever their goal was, they appeared to only want Vanrians. Would they let the other survivors go, or did they mean to kill them all?

She met Jaysen's eyes for a moment. If she never made it back to Vanris, her parents and her brother would still be there to see to their country and its people. Jaysen, however, was Sarket's greatest chance for a better future, at least as far as she could see. He could bring peace and partnership with Vanris and the other two kingdoms. Thrasser seemed unlikely to embrace those things.

Her throat tightened, and she stared at the floor, not wanting him to see the tears rising in her eyes. She could think of nothing more wonderful than to be home with her family right now, but that wasn't how this was going to end.

"Don't give up. You can survive this, Veyl." The concern tightening Jaysen's voice suggested he had guessed at least part of the direction of her thoughts.

She couldn't look at him. Instead, she stared at the spot of blood on her shirt where Kyril's dagger had broken the skin beneath.

The ahnkreth came back into the room at that moment. An older man with the milky white eyes of a Bondmaker followed him in, but it was the lean canine trotting alongside him that caught her attention. The animal looked similar to wolves she had seen in some of her lesson books. It was narrow of build and tall, up to Kyril's ribs at the shoulders, with long slender legs. Fishlike, gleaming black scales showed over its forehead, across the front of its shoulders, and along the back of its hips. Its coat of odd fur was long and black, with a shine about it that made it appear wet. The black ears had a partial transparency to them like a bat's wings and fine ridges at intervals in the membrane, giving them the appearance of fins. Its paws were broad and scaled, with webbing between the toes as if designed for swimming.

Embracing the distraction of this strange new creature, she sank into a crouch and met its sea-green eyes; eyes that seemed to carry the waves within them. It approached her, and she held her bound hands out for it to sniff, its long narrow snout reaching out warily. After a moment, it licked her fingers, then stepped back beside Kyril.

She looked up at the ahnkreth. "You're a Feral?"

He set a hand on the beast's shoulder and nodded, his brow furrowing as if he couldn't decide what to make of the interaction. Then he turned to the man who had followed him in. "Well?"

"Such a destructive reaction under duress isn't unheard of for someone with a powerful enough ability," the man answered. "Incidents like this, while exceedingly rare, are one of many reasons we try to awaken people in a controlled fashion, so they are less likely to harm those around them. In such a situation, a strong mind-crafter might try working with the individual to see if they could gain control of their ability. If not, they would be culled." He glanced between her and Jaysen, his lips pressing into a tight line for a moment. "As for these two, they are tehnaak, as you suspected."

Veyl stood, panic sparking in her chest again.

Kyril drew a deep breath and shook his head. "Sever it."

Energy crackled in Veyl, a storm bursting to life inside her and spreading through the room with a sensation like lightning about to strike. The odd wolf-like dog growled.

"Hold." Kyril held a hand up, eyes narrowing a fraction when he faced her. "Perhaps we should move him to another room and sever the link from there, since she seems unable to contain her ability."

"I am not a mind-crafter," she snapped. Another flicker of energy moved through the room.

Kyril arched a brow at her and stepped closer, staring

down into her eyes. "I know very little about you, but two things I know for certain. The first is that you *are* a mind-crafter, and the second is that your ability awakened a moment ago when we threatened to kill your tehnaak. I would like to unravel some of the other mysteries here, such as how you can be a mind-crafter if your brother truly is one, and why the tehnaak bond was used to connect you to this *earless* foreigner in a land where that is *apparently* never done." He put a vaguely bitter emphasis on the words earless and apparently that drew her curiosity. "Now, unless we can control your ability, you are a threat to my fleet. If you are going to leave this room alive, it will be bound to me as zenyal. That can only happen if your tehnaak bond is severed."

Veyl struggled not to look away from that intense gaze. Whether everything he said was true, he admitted to curiosity about her, and that could prove useful. "What's a zenyal?"

His brows pinched, and he cocked his head slightly in the way of an inquisitive animal, a mannerism all Ferals seemed to pick up with time. "Do they teach you nothing? It's a kind of bond. It will give me at least a moderate amount of control over you until you can manage your ability reliably on your own."

She looked at Jaysen. To lose their connection when it had only just reformed. The very thought was devastating. How were they supposed to survive that again? It would be the third time in her life she had lost her tehnaak. Then, to be bound to this man in a manner granting him control of her in any way… The thought made her stomach turn. And yet, Jaysen had to get out of this.

"You've had a moment to consider the situation. Are you going to try controlling your ability, or do we need to remove him from the room for this?"

She could see the challenge in Kyril's eyes. He wanted to push her, to see if she could do it. "Neither." She lifted her chin, emboldened by a glimmer of pride she suspected was coming through her bond with Jaysen, an experience that would only last until their link was severed.

Kyril's jaw clenched.

"I have a different proposal," she said before he could speak.

"This isn't a negotiation."

The wolf-creature echoed the growl in his voice.

"Promise me you will let him leave this place unharmed once the bond is severed, and I will do whatever you ask."

"Veyl, no."

The desperation in Jaysen's voice threatened her tenuous resolve, but she kept her attention on the ahn-kreth, letting her swiftly expanding hatred of him help her hold back the tears she was fighting.

"Agreed. No interference this time."

She forced a nod, swallowing against a powerful burst of sorrow.

Kyril nodded to the Bondmaker.

Veyl closed her eyes and willed herself to be calm, recalling the moment Jaysen had pulled her into that first embrace only a few hours ago now. Then her world shattered. A crushing blow that had no physical source knocked her to her knees as the bond was severed with brutal precision. A bottomless chasm of heartache spread through her chest. She glanced over to see Jaysen on his knees as well, teeth clenched, his eyes squeezed shut to try stopping tears that broke free despite his efforts. A sob escaped her, and she curled on the floor, unable to stem the tide of anguish that came. The wolf-creature took a step closer to her, head and tail lowered, whining softly.

"That's sufficient for now. Get him out of here,"

Kyril ordered. "We have what we want."

"Veyl." Jaysen's voice cracked as three soldiers dragged him from the room.

She pressed her hands over her ears, trying not to hear his fading calls as they took him farther away. At least he would go free now. That was all that mattered.

Veyl wasn't sure how long she lay there. The ahnkreth and his Bondmaker left for a time. Two guards and the wolf-creature stayed with her, watching her cry until the tears were simply gone, leaving behind the aching sense of absence where some essential part of her had been, once again, ripped away.

Judging from occasional glimpses of the night sky through the smoke outside the window, it was not long after midnight when Kyril returned, the Bondmaker still with him. They spoke in hushed voices by the door for a few minutes, and she felt something change within her. It was subtle. The bleak emptiness inside became a little less empty, if no less bleak, and she was suddenly more aware of Kyril's presence. Interestingly, her awareness of the wolf-creature increased as well.

"You two, take her to the ship and secure her in my quarters."

Veyl stared at his feet as he approached her.

The Bondmaker stepped closer to him. "Ahnkreth, she's dangerous. You shouldn't–"

"I what?" A disconcerting growl accompanied his words.

The man lowered his gaze. "It is inadvisable to engage with her alone and unprotected."

"I will not be alone or without protection." He bent

down and grabbed the rope between Veyl's wrists, pulling her to her feet.

As strong as he was, she saw little point in resisting him. Instead, she let him do most of the work. Crying had sapped what energy she had left after the running and fighting and fear. When she was up, he stepped back, letting his soldiers move in to take hold of her arms.

"Don't let her get her hands on your weapons and do not interact with her beyond getting her there and secured." The ahnkreth folded his arms in front of his chest as he watched them. "Ceris will guard her until I get there."

She balked when they tried to move her, looking up at him. "You set him free?"

He met her eyes, his unwavering gaze giving her hope. "As agreed."

She let them take her out then, with the wolf-creature, Ceris, accompanying them. It was still dark outside, though several burning buildings cast a reddish light over the town. More of the strange Vanrians were escorting others like her to dinghies waiting at the docks. She didn't see Gannon or Lorek, but she spotted Iyvalin being put in one boat and Ahrin being taken to another. Both were bound and going along quietly with their captors. Given that they were all being placed in different boats, she saw little reason to call out to them. Perhaps it was just her sorrow weighing on her, but she didn't think it wise to risk stirring up trouble by drawing their attention to her. Nor did she want her friends to see how thoroughly they had broken her.

Veyl knew little about ships. Under different circumstances, the size of the one they took her to might have impressed her. As it was, with Kyril's crew watching them escort her to his cabin, she barely looked up from the planks under her feet. They slapped shackles around her wrists and attached those to a chain secured to the wall before removing the ropes and leaving her there. Veyl sank down on the floor next to a cot, rested her arms across her knees, and let her head fall on the table they made.

She had been there only a few seconds when a cool nose tried to push up under her arm. Veyl shifted away from the beast. *His* beast. The creature crept closer and sat, leaning in to lick her cheek. She looked at him, trying not to let those brilliant green eyes draw her in.

"Ceris. Is that your name?"

The wolf-creature let out a soft whine and nosed her arm.

She scooted a few inches away again, and Ceris followed, leaning his weight against her as he sank to the wood floor. Tentatively, she moved her hands over to feel that strange fur. The strands were thick and silky beneath her fingers. Ceris looked up at the contact, a shocking sympathy in his beautiful eyes that pulled tears from hers again. When she started crying, the wolf-creature sat up and pushed his nose up under her arm. This time, she let him do so, ending up with her arms around his shoulders. She buried her face in that long, peculiar fur and wept.

*

The door opening and the creak of footsteps crossing the room woke her. She had fallen asleep on the wood floor with Ceris stretched alongside her, keeping her warm.

"Not what I had in mind when I sent you to guard her."

Ceris got up and circled around Kyril to stand at his side, looking up at his companion with a large canine grin, as if he felt he had done well. Kyril picked up a blanket from the cot next to her, then took hold of her arm and helped her up. Without looking at him or his beast, she turned her back to them and curled down onto the cot. After a moment, he put the blanket over her and exited the cabin with Ceris, leaving her alone this time.

When she woke again, the ahnkreth was sitting at a table toward the rear of the large cabin, his feet resting on it as he looked over some papers in the ambient daylight streaming around closed curtains along the back wall. It took her several seconds to realize that the disconcerting rocking motion was the ship moving on the water. Ceris lay on the floor next to Kyril's chair, peering at her as she sat up on the side of the cot. Veyl's stomach turned, threatening to deposit her last meal on the floor. She gripped the edge of the cot, pulling the chain between her shackles tight across her thighs. Her eyes squeezed closed while she tried to will away the nausea. Ceris, seeming to sense her distress, let out a soft whine and came over to set one large, webbed paw on her knee.

"He rarely takes to people like this. You must have an affinity for beasts."

"I grew up among them. My father is a Feral." She looked into the sea-green eyes of the wolf-creature, not interested in visually acknowledging the man she was speaking to. "What is he?"

"A wave dancer. Sey'yaluth ayon." Kyril walked over to stand in front of her.

She started looking up, but the movement made her stomach worse, so she continued staring at Ceris, sliding one hand into the sleek fur around his neck. "That's not Vanrian."

"No."

A flash of irritation at his unwillingness to expand upon his replies also caused her stomach to protest more violently, so she tried to let it go. "Were all the mind-crafters you took made zenyal?"

"No. The Vanrian mind-crafters and fighters who proved most dangerous during the attack we placed in the brig on this ship, and they will remain there until they express a willingness to cooperate. The rest are on the other ships, either locked up or being trained to work with the crews if they are agreeable to doing so."

She swallowed saliva, trying not to think of waves, or Jaysen, or how much she wanted to run this man through with her sword, or any sword really, given that hers was gone. All things that triggered a tempest of emotion, making her feel sicker. "And if the ones you locked up agree to cooperate?"

"They will be welcome among us as equals. I made you zenyal because your case is unique. Right now, you have the potential to cause damage without meaning to. You will continue to pose a threat until we figure out what your ability is and bring it under control. Until that time, you will remain my zenyal."

"And if I can't get it under control, will you cull me like your Bondmaker suggested?" A small spasm in her stomach warned her to stop talking.

"I don't intend to let that happen."

Her head throbbed, joining the protest now too. She rubbed her temples, hissing with pain when she bumped the tender part of her cheek. Iyvalin sitting on the bed at the inn with a cut on her forehead came into her mind then. "Did you separate all the tehnaak pairings onto different ships?"

"Yes."

"Why?"

"Why do you think, Veyl?"

She hated her name on his lips. "Control. Leverage." She dared to look up at him then. It was a mistake.

He nodded.

She threw up on his boots.

To her surprise, his first reaction was to hand her his water skin to rinse the taste from her mouth, then he slipped off the boots and carried them out the door. A few seconds later, he returned bootless with one of his crew behind him, a lad of about thirteen who went to work mopping up the mess she had made. While the boy busied himself with that task, Kyril strode to a cabinet in one corner and pulled something out. He came back and held what looked like a dried white carrot out to her.

Veyl shrank away from it.

"Chew on it," he said, a glimmer of frustration sharpening his tone. "It will help with the seasickness."

"What is it?" Her stomach was turning again, making the offering infinitely more compelling.

"It's a type of woody vine," the boy answered for him. "We peel the bark and dry it. It's kind of bland, but it really works."

Something in the boy's open smile inclined her to trust him more than the ahnkreth. "Bland sounds perfect right about now." She cringed when her fingers brushed Kyril's as she took it.

He arched a brow at her reaction before going to pull another pair of tall, black boots from under a bed at the far side of the cabin. He carried them to the table and sat while she bit off a piece of the root and chewed it. It was bland, as the boy had said, but the fibrous texture was satisfying somehow.

"I take it you've never been on the ocean?" Kyril began pulling on the boots as he spoke.

"This trip is only the third time I've even seen…" she trailed off. Her first two experiences visiting the ocean were on the opposite coast in the city of Trenath. Adventures she had gone on with her family and Jaysen at the ages of ten and twelve. This trip had also been with Jaysen in a way, and now she might never see him or her family again. A steep price to pay for such a brief adventure.

She slid back on the cot until she bumped into the wall, then pulled her knees to her chest, the vine hanging forgotten in her hand. Closing her eyes, she let her head rest against the wooden side, fighting the bleak emptiness that threatened to consume her.

"Thank you, Fen." Kyril's voice was softer now, coming from directly in front of her. "You can go."

"Yes, sir." The boy, Fen, followed his example, keeping his voice soft.

Kyril and the wave dancer left a few minutes later. Veyl sat alone in the ahnkreth's cabin. When the crush of sorrow eased, she started looking around. Bright daylight crept in at the edges of the curtains over the windows. Perhaps he kept them closed to allow her to sleep, or maybe there was some other reason for it. If not for the chains, she could open them to see the world outside, and inside given how dim the cabin currently was, but she wasn't sure she would care enough to do so.

A slight turning in her stomach reminded her of the woody vine, and she started chewing on it again.

The furniture was nicer than she would have expected, though she had never taken time to consider what the interior of an ahnkreth's cabin might look like. It hadn't been something she ever thought to experience firsthand. Vanris never went to great lengths to develop a naval force beyond what was necessary to ensure safety for their fishing vessels. When at sea, the crew lived on the ship. This cabin was much nicer, she imagined, than the quarters most of the rest of his crew shared, but being the ranking officer usually came with some benefits. Several polished cabinets and a wardrobe stood along the walls, presumably fastened into place, given how much the ship was bound to move in rougher weather. Kyril kept everything tidy, with little, if anything, left lying about. Although, someone like Fen might also handle the cleaning for him as far as she knew.

She didn't sit there much longer before Kyril returned, Ceris padding along beside him with his long tail swinging gently to-and-fro. The ahnkreth stopped and considered her for a moment, then came and unlocked the wrist shackles from the chain that connected them to the wall. When he reached down as though intending to pull her up, she jerked away, hurrying to her feet on her own.

"Is your stomach calmer?"

She nodded.

"Follow me then." Without waiting for a response, he started back toward the door.

Veyl glanced around once, looking to see if any weapons might be lying in the open. When she turned his way, he was standing at the door, staring at her with a flat expression that said he suspected what she was thinking and was neither surprised nor particularly concerned. Ceris was watching her as well, and she realized then that, even if she had a weapon, she would never get to him before the wave dancer got to her. With a sharp exhale of frustration, she followed him from the cabin.

The ship was large. At least thirty people were on deck, going about their duties in the shadows of the towering masts. The sails were furled, and they were moving very little beyond the rocking from the waves. Many of those closest to the end they were near—the stern, if she recalled correctly from her studies—turned to watch them, their gazes lingering on her. She stood before them bruised, wearing dirty, tattered clothes, with her hair a mess and her hands shackled. Another time, she might have had the resolve to face them with defiance, but the aching hollow that made up the core of her being now denied her that. Instead, she avoided their eyes.

"Come over here." Kyril held one hand out to her, stopping a few inches shy of touching her arm, and gestured toward the starboard side of the ship with the other.

Veyl waved him away with her shackled hands and waited for him to go ahead of her, following with her eyes focused on his back to avoid looking at anyone. He stopped at the railing, encouraging her up beside him where a cool, salty mist hit her face, carried on the steady breeze. The unexpected sensation drew a soft gasp from her, and she looked out at the vast, blue expanse before her. A flicker of that yearning she had felt in Deepwater returned, the sense of wonder struggling to get past her sorrow. A few tears slipped warm down her cheeks.

Kyril was watching her intently now, as if she had, once again, become that much more interesting. "You feel it, don't you? The ocean calls to you."

Veyl didn't answer him. In the distance, she could see land. "Is that..." Her throat tightened before she could get the words out.

"The western coast of Pandrea? Yes."

Everything she knew and loved was already so far away. The hollow expanded, nearly big enough to swallow her now.

"Look alongside the ship," Kyril prompted, leaning on the railing to peer down.

Following his example, she saw what appeared to be a group of massive snakes twining about each other in the water next to the hull. There were at least three of them, easily a foot around at the widest point. Their constant movement—coiling and twisting together—made it impossible to determine how big they were. Their scales shimmered in a stunning blend of lavender, pink, silver, and pearlescent white, with a translucent dorsal fin running along their substantial length.

"They're beautiful," she murmured.

"They're a type of eel. Extremely venomous, but, yes, beautiful... and delicious."

Veyl continued watching them, mesmerized by the rippling, coiling, endless motion. "Venomous?"

"Yes. They have a painful bite, but the real danger is the stinger at the end of their tails. The toxin can paralyze prey in seconds. For air-breathing creatures like us, it's probably a good thing. It means we typically drown before they start eating us. But they are lovely from a distance."

That didn't sound so awful at the moment. She was already drowning. How much worse could it be?

"Ahnkreth Kyril." The woman who called out on her way over to them was one of those who had helped capture Jaysen. Her hard gaze flicked past Veyl dismissively before settling on Kyril. The dourness of her expression said she wasn't bringing good news. "I received word from Evoker Nalika's Speaker."

It made sense they would use Speakers. Who better to manage communication at a distance than mind-crafters with the ability to speak directly into the minds of anyone within visible range or to other Speakers at a greater distance.

He stepped away from the rail to speak with her, leaving Veyl there. "What is it?"

"She wanted you to know there's been no change in Illis's condition." The woman cast Veyl a scathing look before continuing. "She remains unresponsive and won't eat or drink anything."

Kyril cursed under his breath. "She won't last long that way."

A twisting sensation in Veyl's gut opened the way for the hollow to expand still more. Crushing weight on her chest made it hard to breathe. She had destroyed the woman with whatever ability had awoken in that room. An ability she couldn't control. An ability she shouldn't even have.

"Veyl!"

She startled, turning to see Gannon rushing toward her. He had a bruise along his jaw, but looked otherwise unharmed, and wasn't bound. Someone drew a sword and swept it into his path, bringing his approach to an abrupt halt. Gannon cast a glare at the man who had blocked him, but he didn't push to go any farther.

"She's a friend," he snapped.

Kyril glanced at Veyl and shook his head, a hint of pity in his regard. Then he gestured to the man blocking Gannon. "Move that one to another ship immediately."

Gannon looked like he might object until one of the strange Vanrians set a hand on his shoulder and whispered something in his ear. Gannon avoided Veyl's eyes, the muscles in his jaw jumping as he let them lead him away.

Kyril looked at Veyl again, a storm of frustration in his silver-blue eyes.

She glared back at him, that brief contact with one of her friends leaving her feeling more alone than ever. "Will you let me have nothing?"

Ignoring her question, he frowned and turned back to the woman he had been speaking with prior to the interruption. His voice was strained when he spoke. "We'll have to let Illis go if this doesn't resolve quickly. Tell Nalika to let me know if there's still no change by tonight."

His lack of answer was answer enough. He would allow her nothing.

Veyl grabbed the rail and jumped over.

She barely stopped herself from inhaling with the sudden shock of the cold water when she went under beside the coil of serpents. Something brushed along her arm as she surfaced, one of the snake-like creatures already moving around her. This close to it, she could see it was more than three times her height in length. She reached out to touch the smooth, shimmering scales, watching as they slipped past under her fingertips.

Sharp pain shot through the side of her calf at the same moment two large objects splashed into the water near her. It was hard enough to swim with the shackles, but that pain spread quickly through her leg and the muscles stopped responding. The paralytic venom wasted no time in going to work in her body, the fear that made her heart race undoubtedly aiding the process.

As she slipped below the surface again, one eel turned to face her, showing off a mouth full of tightly packed, needle-sharp teeth. An instant of panic flashed in her at the thought that she might not drown before they started eating her after all. Then a piercing noise blasted through the water. The eels twisted about and raced away. Ceris swam past in pursuit, shockingly elegant and agile beneath the waves. Veyl's ability to hold her breath gave out a heartbeat before arms clamped around her from behind and lifted her through the water.

Moments later, she was lying on the deck, helpless to do anything. Someone cut open the side of her pants, then sliced into her calf. She assumed they were attempting to drain venom from the wound itself, but the pain of the process was excruciating. Kyril, water still streaming from his hair, knelt next to her and lifted her torso. Someone else helped him force her mouth open and pour a bitter liquid into it. Then he pressed under her jaw, holding her mouth closed.

"Swallow."

She couldn't force herself to do so, nor could she stop the liquid from starting to trickle down her throat. That reflex kicked in sluggishly, finally taking the substance into her system. It was hard to breathe, and her heartbeat felt much too calm for the situation. Veyl closed her eyes, exhausted, and let herself drift on the edge of consciousness. She was vaguely aware of someone lifting her.

"You should've let her drown," a woman muttered.

The thud of a door shutting preceded his murmured words. "She deserves better."

That was the last thing she heard.

## CHAPTER FOURTEEN

Veyl crawled to consciousness sometime later, her head pounding violently enough that she expected to find someone hitting it with a hammer. With a groan, she put a hand over her eyes, reluctant to open them out of fear that even the least amount of light might make the situation worse.

"Perhaps you would have been more circumspect if I had also mentioned that the antidote gives you a severe headache."

She groaned again. Everything that had compelled her to jump into that water came rushing to the fore with the sound of his voice. Opening her eyes, she rolled onto her side and threw up in a wooden bucket someone had placed on the floor, presumably for that purpose, then she curled around her aching stomach.

"Here." Kyril moved the bucket out of the way. He picked up a mug from the side table near her head and offered it to her. "This will ease the headache and the nausea."

The last time she had seen him, he was leaning over her dripping wet, having apparently jumped in after her, along with Ceris, who had chased after the serpents. A quick glance around found the wave dancer stretched out asleep a few feet away. Relieved to see the beast unharmed, she closed her eyes again.

"No, you don't."

Veyl glared at him as he set the mug back on the side table and took hold of her arm. He released it when she tried to pull weakly away and let her struggle upright on her own. Pressure around her leg when she moved told her someone had secured a bandage over the stinging cut. It wasn't until she was situated that she registered she was on his bed, not the cot now on the opposite side of the room. The clothes she wore weren't hers either, though they fit relatively well.

"Don't look so offended. You're the one who jumped into the ocean. I let two of the women on my crew handle finding you dry clothes and getting you changed."

He didn't say whether he was there when they did it, but perhaps it was better not to know all the details. The last thing she noticed was that the shackles were missing. She drew a sharp breath of surprise and rubbed at her wrists.

"If you try something that foolish again, they will go back on and never come off. How long you get to be free of them is entirely up to you."

He put a blanket around her shoulders, the thoughtful action contrasting the bluntness of his words, and gestured to the mug on the table. Once she picked it up, he nodded and carried the soiled bucket out of the cabin. Veyl tried a tentative drink, swallowing more when it proved palatable enough. It was warm, easing some of the persistent chill of the ocean from her bones. When Kyril returned, he brought a plate of food. Ceris got up and met him at the bed, eyeing the meal optimistically.

"Don't get your hopes up," he told the beast. Turning to her, he said, "I'm guessing it's been close to a full day since you last ate. Try not to spill it all over my bed."

She took the offered plate, made of a thin and light but sturdy wood-like substance. The roasted vegetables it held looked familiar enough. The slab of pale meat had an odd lavender color to it, unlike anything she had ever eaten. "What is this?"

"One of your swimming companions from earlier."

Veyl stared at it. It wasn't as if the meal didn't look or smell appetizing. The problem came with finding the desire to eat at all. The ache of hunger that should cramp her stomach had become lost within the emptiness of having everything that mattered to her taken away.

"Those serpents... eels... They fled from Ceris in the water. Why?"

Kyril took the fork off the plate, speared a bite of the tender meat with it, then held the handle out to her. "I would prefer to be civil about this."

The threat behind his words made her want to hit him, but in her current state, she didn't have the strength to follow through beyond that. She took the fork. When she merely sat staring at it for a few seconds, he raised his brows at her. With a sigh, she put it in her mouth and chewed. The meat was delicate, with a hint of sweetness and an underlying earthiness that worked unexpectedly well together. That first morsel awoke a ravenous hunger, as if her system had been waiting dormant for some sign of life, though she did her best to hide it, making herself pause a second before going for another piece.

He watched her work through several more deliberate bites before answering her question. "Ceris is immune to their toxin. He's one of their natural predators."

Kyril stood and strode to the back of the cabin to brush aside a curtain. He lingered there, gazing out for a few minutes while Veyl continued eating. Ceris sat in front of her, his bright eyes watching every forkful pass between her lips. As hungry as she was, she couldn't resist offering him a morsel, which he took delicately from her fingers, his long tail whispering across the wood.

"Don't spoil him."

She opened her mouth to ask how he knew with his back to them, stopping herself when she remembered he was a Feral, and this creature his companion. Ceris's excitement at the treat would have been enough to alert him. At least Kyril was unlikely to share her father's ability to see through the beast's eyes. That skill was extremely rare. Still, it might be wise to practice caution around the wave dancer going forward.

Ceris cocked his head to the side, watching the next bite travel to her lips. Kyril busied himself at his table, looking over a nautical map he had spread out there. When she was done with the food, she set the wooden plate on the side table and drank the last swallow from her mug.

"I could use…"

Without looking up, he pointed to a tiny area in one corner of the cabin that was walled off from the rest with a little door in the front. "Leave the bucket in there when you finish. I'll have Fen remove it."

Veyl slid to the edge of the bed, tentatively putting pressure on the injured leg. Before she could try to stand, Kyril strode swiftly over to intercept her. "Hold on. It might be better if you didn't use that any more than necessary yet." He picked her up with an unsettling lack of effort.

Warmth suffused her cheeks that she attributed to anger when she found herself cradled in his arms. "I've had injuries before. I can manage," she growled.

"I'm certain that's true, but this time, you have also been drugged to help you get some healing sleep. I'd rather not risk you falling."

Fury burned through her, but her attempt to twist free of him resulted in her being held more securely against his solid chest. A fog was sinking over her thoughts, backing up his claim of having drugged her. Kyril carried her to the small partition and carefully set her on her feet, at which point she attempted to punch him, but her movement was sluggish and uncoordinated, the effects of the drug rapidly taking hold. He easily caught her wrist and turned her to face the narrow door.

"I suggest seeing to your needs before it puts you to sleep. I'd hate having to drag you out of there with your pants down."

"Sheyvyosk," she growled under her breath.

Kyril chuckled. Not the reaction she expected to casting a crude Vanrian insult at him, calling him stinky smegma. "Try to watch your language. This is a civilized ship."

"Slave ship," she grumbled under her breath as she shuffled into the tiny room.

When she emerged, there was a brief standoff as she tried to avoid letting him lift her again, but she was having trouble balancing now, the pull of sedation from the drug growing more insistent. In seconds, he had her back in his arms.

"If you're this determined to fight me," he said, setting her on the bed, "consider that you might have better luck if you were healthy."

Veyl's head found the pillow, and she rolled on her side to put her back to him, her heavy eyelids sinking closed. "I will always fight you," she muttered as he placed a blanket over her.

She drifted into a bottomless darkness under the influence of whatever he had given her, sinking too far down to react to his next words.

"For your sake, I hope that isn't true. I will win, one way or another."

*

Veyl woke alone. The curtains at the back of the cabin were open now, letting in the fading light of evening. She felt stronger. Like it or not, Kyril had been right about the value of food and rest. He had also been right about the fact that she would need to take better care of herself if she wanted to resist them. She vaguely remembered him saying something regarding how he would win as she fell asleep. That would never happen if she could find any way to stop it. The battle ahead was going to be a difficult one, and she had no clue how to fight it yet, but she had to overcome her sorrow somehow and turn her energy to finding a way out of this. For herself, and for everyone else they had taken.

Sliding out of bed, she limped to the windows and peered outside. They were moving, the ship's wake suggesting they were doing so at a good clip. She could see three other ships traveling along with them. Were any of her companions on those ships? Or were there more she couldn't see from here that carried the friends she had dragged into this mess with her need to meet Jaysen in Deepwater?

Staring out at that open water, no land in sight, sent a fresh surge of hopelessness through her. Was there a point in trying to fight these people? They were trapped on a ship full of enemies somewhere out in the ocean. Even if they could escape, there was nowhere to run away to beyond another suicidal dip in those cold, dangerous waters.

As she stood gazing at that endless expanse, she started trying to pull her fingers through her hair. After her plunge into the ocean, it was a tangled mess. Oddly, it didn't feel salty, almost as if they had rinsed her off before they put her in clean clothes. She hated to imagine being so completely at their mercy for that long, but they appeared not to have done her any harm beyond the wrongs already committed against her.

With her head clearer, she could sense Kyril coming before he entered the cabin. A sensation like the slight itch she got between her shoulder blades when she believed she was being watched. Only this itch was in her mind. She glanced back as he walked in, Ceris padding along beside him. He strode to a cabinet near the rear and rummaged through it, pulling out a brush and bringing it to her.

"Feeling better?"

"Physically." She snatched away the brush and started carefully working out the tangles.

Kyril turned to gaze out the windows, his eyes lighting with an inner fire as he watched the wake churning behind them. Ceris padded over to sit between them.

"You want me away from your crew to protect them. Why aren't you concerned about my ability hurting you?"

He set a hand on the wave dancer's shoulder, a gesture that reminded her enough of her father that she couldn't breathe for a few seconds past the painful twisting in her chest. "Because Ceris will keep you out of my head, and the zenyal bond also affords me some protection."

Veyl glanced down at the beast to find him calmly watching her. Through force of will, she drew in a breath and pushed her memories to the back of her mind. "He can defend you the way a kanodrak can. Is he as intelligent as they are?"

Ceris reached over to nudge her hand with his nose as if to say he was.

"Possibly. I've never been around a kanodrak, though I've read about them in our histories. They seem extraordinary. As for Ceris, I'm confident he is smarter than I am at times."

"That doesn't seem so difficult."

Kyril smirked at the insult and went to open another

cabinet. As he pulled out two mugs and a bottle, the boy, Fen, entered the cabin carrying two wooden bowls full of food and set them on the table.

"Thank you, Fen." Kyril nodded to the boy and placed the items he had gathered between the bowls.

Fen offered him a smile and a slight bow. "My pleasure, Ahnkreth." The boy glanced at Veyl, lingering for a moment as though he wanted to say or ask something before dashing back out.

"Eat with me." Kyril gestured to the table. "Tell me about yourself."

"No." Veyl used her fingers to undo the last significant tangle, then ran the brush through her hair one more time.

"Fine." He sat in front of one bowl. "Eat with me, and I'll tell you about us."

That caught her attention. She wanted that information. When he nodded encouragingly, she limped around the table to the chair across from him and settled into it.

"What do you want to know?"

With such an opportunity set before her, a flurry of questions ran through her mind. She blurted one at random. "How old are you?"

He gave her a curious look before turning his attention to filling their mugs from the bottle, the distinct aroma of mead reaching her. "That's not the first question I expected."

Her cheeks warmed. How old he was didn't matter, but there was a legitimate reason for her curiosity. "It's just that you seem young to be leading a fleet of..." she trailed off, sniffing warily at the contents of her mug.

He chuckled. "It's not drugged this time." Once she had taken a drink, he answered. "Seven ships. I'm twenty, as of three days ago, not that my age should make a difference. I've trained to lead a fleet my whole life. This voyage is my first significant mission as an ahn-kreth, and it has been quite a successful one."

She had been right about him being young for this level of military responsibility. Although, he was older than her father had been when he helped end the war between Vanris and the southern kingdoms of Pandrea. Somehow, the idea of leadership on the ocean struck her as more complicated. She ate quietly for a time, giving him the chance to do so as well. This meal was stew made with the same eel meat they had used earlier. The creatures had been big, but she suspected that more than one of them had lost their lives to his crew. She had nearly finished with her food and was starting a second mug of mead before she asked another question she craved an answer to.

"What is your mission?"

"That will take time to explain." He pushed his empty bowl away and settled deeper into his chair.

"Do you have somewhere to be?"

"As we recently discussed, I am in charge of this fleet. Though my second is capable of handling matters for a time. She's had to do a fair bit of that since we brought you aboard."

"I hope you don't expect me to feel sorry for her." Veyl eyed the remains of her meal, aware of him watching her. "Besides, I assume she knows where to find you."

"There it is again, that attitude that says you're accustomed to getting what you want. Are you?" He took a drink from his mug, providing her an opportunity to respond.

"I thought you were answering my questions," she countered, taking another drink. She'd already had more of the strong mead than she should, but she appreciated the calm confidence it brought.

He came back at her with yet another question, albeit

one that had the potential to lead somewhere interesting. "You're Vanrian. I assume you know how our ancestors fled their original homeland?"

"I do. A series of severe volcanic eruptions made the island uninhabitable. You *are* Vanrian then?"

Ceris sank to the floor next to Kyril and inched his way under the table until he was curled up between their feet. The ahnkreth looked down at the wave dancer, his brow furrowing. After a moment, he shook his head at the beast and turned his attention to her again, leaning over to refill her mug before filling his own. She picked hers up, sipping at it as he spoke to avoid watching him.

"As I said before, yes and no. The ships that fled Vanris didn't leave all at once, nor did they all head in the same direction. A faction from the district of Thaelis had come into frequent conflict with Vanrian leadership over how they were managing certain things well before the eruptions that drove us all away. Because of those clashes, when the island's volcanoes became more and more active, that faction recruited others of like mind and formed their own fleet to go in search of a new place to call home. So, I am Vanrian in part of my heritage, but my ancestors founded the country of Thaelis on a new group of islands, so we are now Thaelian."

Veyl remembered the district of Thaelis from her studies, along with dozens of other districts that existed in the original homeland. That a faction from there had gone off on their own, however, was information not included in the histories she had grown up with. "But if you are Vanrian by blood, why is your hair black?"

His somber regard held a glimmer of regret. "My ancestors integrated with the natives inhabiting the islands we settled, and a considerable amount of mixing between our races occurred. The pointed ears turn out to be a dominant trait much of the time, but lighter hair is not. The other thing that turns out not to be dominant is mind-crafting. We discovered after a few generations that introducing non-Thaelian bloodlines reduced the frequency of children with abilities being born to families with only one mind-crafter parent. Our leadership put an end to interbreeding for anyone with mind-crafter lineages when they realized what was happening, but the damage was done." He rotated his mug on the table, a hint of a bitter smile pulling at his lips. "It appears your ancestors were able to keep the bloodlines pure."

"Not necessarily by design. A few years after we first encountered the southern kingdoms on Pandrea, there were incidents involving mind-crafters that led to a breakdown of developing trust and, eventually, to war. Our pure lineage can be contributed primarily to the fact that we remained at war with the other races until about eighteen years ago."

"That makes sense." As he spoke, he went to get a second bottle and returned to his seat. "We were fortunate because the natives where we ended up were far behind us in development. With our advancements and abilities, they were in awe of us. We had a more difficult time convincing them not to try making gods of us."

She set her nearly empty mug on the table across from his and watched as he filled them both. Had that been her third refill? The warmth from the mead moving through her was soothing, helping her compartmentalize her hatred and fear, and making it easier to hold a conversation with him, though she was starting to feel mildly drowsy and less focused. "So, your line and those of most of your crew members aren't pure Vanrian. That's where the darker hair comes from."

"Yes."

"But you are a mind-crafter."

"Interbreeding reduces the chances of the trait passing to the offspring, but doesn't eliminate it entirely. My father was half Thaelian, my mother three-quarters and an Enkindler. The odds of a child from their line having an ability were decent."

She took a long swallow of the mead. The boat was rocking less, though her own equilibrium was a little off now. The seas outside the windows under a darkening sky had grown calmer, the waves much smaller than earlier. "None of that tells me why you attacked Deepwater and took my people captive."

He drank some of his mead and watched her in silence for a moment. He was too relaxed, too confident in his control of the situation. It rekindled her unease around him. She took another long drink.

"You seem to be faring better this evening."

The simple observation unlocked a bombardment of memories. Her parents fussing over her before they parted ways outside Deepwater, Iyvalin promising to keep her secret when she snuck out, Jaysen pulling her into his arms with such love and desperation, the two of them on their knees crushed by the severing of their tehnaak bond yet again. Tears stung her eyes. "I'm just…" Her throat tightened, and she trailed off, afraid she wouldn't be able to keep from crying if she continued.

Ceris moved closer to her and rested his head on her knee.

"You refocused your pain and anger, putting that energy into gathering information about your perceived enemy. Not everyone has that level of self-control. It's an admirable skill."

"Perceived!" She surged to her feet, setting them wide to compensate for the slight spinning of the room, and grabbed the fork she had eaten with as if it were a dagger. "You stole my life from me and my people's lives from them. You replaced a sacred tehnaak bond with this abomination binding me to you." Her voice lowered, picking up an edge of threat. "You *are* my enemy, and somehow, I will make you suffer for everything you've done."

"Not with a fork." He took a calm drink of his mead.

She threw the utensil at him and he snatched it from the air. Frustration flared and a flicker of that strange energy crackled through her. Turning her back on him, she tried to bring her rage and the heartache that fed it under control. Behind her, she heard him push his chair out. He walked around the table to where she could see him, watching her with a wariness that she found somewhat gratifying.

"Come. I want to show you something."

He waited for her to rein in her emotions. When she gave a curt nod, he led them out of the cabin and up on deck to the stern of the ship. Going up the stairs was slow between the stinging wound in her leg and the fuzziness from the alcohol, but she jerked away from him when he tried to help her. The waves were gentle now, almost comforting, and the nearly nonexistent breeze barely moved them. When they reached the railing at the top, he pointed out to the water.

Veyl could hardly miss what he was trying to show her. They were whales. Seven of the massive beasts moving among the boats as if the fleet were their playground. They started emitting odd, musical noises, as though talking to each other. Ceris, who had stepped up to the rail between them and was watching with his ears perked far forward, made an eerily similar sound, as if trying to communicate with them. Two of the whales drew near, responding to the wave dancer. When they vocalized, a bright blue luminescence rippled along a trail of V-shaped markings that started on their heads and got smaller toward their tails. It made for a mesmerizing light show when the two enormous beasts swam closer still and began what seemed to be an enthusiastic conversation with Ceris. The wave dancer bounced from one paw to the other at the railing, excited by the exchange.

Veyl stared at the magnificent beasts, wonder stirring in her, drawing a faint, reluctant smile to her lips. A third whale breached alongside the ship, catching her by surprise and eliciting a gasp of awe as it hit the surface again. The resulting wave rocked them hard enough she had to grab the railing to keep her balance. She was still a long way from being at home with the constant, often unpredictable motion of the water, and the influence of the mead wasn't helping.

Next to her, Kyril also watched the whales. A soft smile curved his lips that she found difficult to reconcile with the awful man who had destroyed her life. A serenity had come over him, his strong features enhanced by moonlight as he stood on the deck of his ship, looking every bit like he was born to be there. She yearned to feel that kind of certainty and belonging. Now, more than ever, she also wanted to understand why he and his people were doing this.

"You never answered my question."

His smile faded, his hands tightening on the railing. "A sickness swept through the Thaelian islands. It killed around fifty percent of our population. We called it the Devastation. About a year after the last case, the council began sending fleets like mine out to look for more survivors from the Vanrian homeland, if there were any. We had no way of knowing if others had escaped, since our ancestors were the first to leave, but we lost too many people to the sickness. We need to grow our population, and we need more bloodlines. Mind-crafters, in particular, if we are to continue efforts to restore the purity and strength of our lines."

Articulation was becoming something of a challenge now, the mead making its cumulative presence known, so she spoke a little more slowly. "Then why not approach our rulers and open peaceful communication? Why take people by force?"

He drew a deep breath, staring at the frolicking whales. "Our ancestors left Vanris separately because they disagreed with how the leadership of the time was managing things. Everything from the selection of tehnaak to the handling of Trials and the hierarchy between mind-crafters and people without abilities. That rift led to fighting and an attempt by Vanrian leadership to eliminate those dissenting voices through violent means. In other words," he said, meeting her eyes, "your ancestors are the antithesis to the way of life we chose. When the council sent us out here, the mission they gave us was to locate Vanrians from our homeland. If we succeeded, we were to take who we could and return them to our country to see if they might successfully integrate into our culture. An experiment to discover if this would prove a viable solution to our population loss. If we approached your people to ask for help, what would stop them from trying to force us to integrate back into their version of Vanrian society?"

"The same way you plan to integrate us forcefully into yours?" He looked away, making no attempt to respond to that, so she pressed him. "Have you considered that we might not be the same after so many years? Those rifts that existed long ago might not be as wide now. Maybe some of our people would have even volunteered to travel to your land to help you. I'm sure my fa—" She cut herself off, shaking her head to try clearing the fog from her thoughts as she watched the strange luminescence ripple along the top of the nearest whale. No good could come from him knowing he had a khesran of Vanris in his possession so long as he considered her people as his enemies. "My people aren't what you think they are."

"I'm following orders, Veyl. It's not personal."

"That doesn't make it all right, but I have a feeling you know that." He continued staring out at the water, and she found she missed his enchanting smile from a few moments ago. She turned her attention back to the whales, drawing a few slow, deep breaths to calm herself and gather her wandering thoughts before speaking again. "They are extraordinary."

A shadow of his earlier smile returned, the moonlight reflecting brightly in those silver-blue eyes. "They are."

## CHAPTER FIFTEEN

The boat rocked hard, and Ceris bounced with excitement as Veyl grabbed the rail to keep from falling, her heart jumping into her throat, the alcohol undermining her ability to regain her balance. Kyril caught hold of her arm to help steady her.

"What was that?"

He chuckled, taking away his hand. "The whales like to push the ships around sometimes. Don't worry, I've never seen them damage one, but perhaps we should go back inside. I get the impression you don't normally indulge in so much drink."

Veyl's cheeks burned as she turned silently to go with him, pausing when she noticed Ceris lingering at the railing, talking down to the whales again in that strange, musical voice.

Kyril's gaze followed hers back to the wave dancer, his gentler smile returning in full now, exposing the affection he held for his companion. "He'll come down when he's done playing with them."

Veyl went with him more reluctantly now. The wave dancer's presence made her feel a little safer around him, even knowing the beast was his companion. At the stairs, she hesitated, the cut in her leg hurting more from use and the mead making everything less steady. Kyril took her arm, his other hand coming to rest at her waist to help support her going down. She nearly pulled away, her pulse quickening with that contact in a way that she wanted to believe was from fear and hatred. And yet, something about that gentle contact was immensely comforting, no matter the source. Maybe it was acceptable to let him help her this time, purely to avoid further injury. At the bottom of the steps, his hand lingered a moment longer than necessary at her waist, cool air rushing into that warm spot when he took it away. He opened the door and followed her inside, a heavy silence hanging over him now.

Veyl walked to the table, about to sit, when the ship rocked again, harder this time. She moved to step wide, going for a more stable stance, and her wounded leg struck the chair. A hiss of pain escaped her as she jerked the leg back, dizziness leaving her flailing for balance. Kyril caught hold of her, pulling her against him, his body providing a solid, stabilizing element. As the ship settled, she found herself in his arms, her pulse running wild. Something flared to life in her chest, encouraging her closer, the sensation reassuringly familiar, like that tugging feeling that had always called her west.

"Are you all right?"

The hesitation in his voice captured her attention. She twisted to look up at him, his supportive embrace intensifying her desperate longing for the comfort of human connection. His silver-blue eyes gleamed in the moonlight coming through the windows and she sank into them, drawn helplessly by the insistent tugging within. Her gaze drifted to his mouth, a wild recklessness rushing through her. What would it be like to kiss him? To taste the mead on his lips and feel his muscular arms pull her closer, supporting her, wanting her. To relent to the force urging her to him.

His hand slid to the small of her back, his gaze sinking to her lips. Desire sparked in his eyes and a pleasant warmth spread through her, heightening that from the mead. Forgetting for a moment who he was, she let herself become lost in sweet, intoxicating longing and the strange sense of security and rightness that came with being held in that firm embrace. The tremble of wanting in his touch granted her power, even as her actions put her more at his mercy. Unexpected longing melted away some of her agonizing aloneness.

She started to give in to that inner fire and the inexplicable sensation that drew her to him, leaning closer. Then Jaysen slipped to the front of her mind. The only person she had ever kissed before this moment. The tehnaak this man had taken from her.

Veyl jerked away, as if startled awake from a dream, bumping back into the table with the force of her extraction. She gripped the sides of it to brace herself, trembling with a tempest of confused anger and nearly unbearable longing. Kissing Jaysen had never brought her body to life the way merely being held by Kyril had. Her cheeks burned with humiliation. She stared at the floor, unable to look at him as the tugging sensation faded. An illusion born of desperate loneliness and too much mead, perhaps.

Without a word, Kyril spun and strode from the cabin. The instant the door clicked shut, she hurried unsteadily to the nearest cabinet and began digging through it. A surprising number of doors and drawers on the pieces of furniture throughout the room had locks on them. Those she could open held maps, navigational tools, clothing, a collection of shells and attractive stones with holes in them, and several bottles of mead, none made of the familiar, durable stoneglass they used at home for their Vanrian Black Mead. The keys that unlocked the rest were nowhere to be found. The one thing she hoped to come upon, an actual weapon, eluded her.

What she did find was the necklace Jaysen had given

her, tucked in the drawer with the other shells and stones. Struggling with clumsy fingers, she fastened it around her neck and crawled onto the cot, feeling confused, ashamed, and exhausted. Sometime in the night, Kyril came back and carefully pulled her blanket up over her shoulders. Veyl feigned sleep, not ready to face him after what had almost happened between them.

"Dream well, Khesran," he murmured.

Khesran? Her heart skipped a beat. He knew what she was. How long had he known? How had he found out?

*

Veyl slept very little after that, her mind racing with the implications of what it meant that he knew who she was. At some point, the influence of the alcohol pulled her into a restless slumber. She woke in the morning to the sound of him walking out. Despite a mild headache and some nausea, she hurried up and took advantage of his absence to use what passed for a privy chamber, then managed a hasty sponge bath using the basin set out on a cabinet near that tiny partition. When he returned, he held a bowl of something that he set on the table.

"If you're hungry," he offered, not looking at her. "It might help settle your stomach."

Veyl approached the table. She was hungry, and it vexed her that she had let herself drink more than she should have. The mere notion that she had some connection to this man beyond the forced zenyal bond was absurd, but she could berate herself for that later. For now, she had more pressing matters to address. "You knew what I was this whole time?"

He did look at her now, a hint of that predatory Feral nature in his calculating gaze. "Yes. My soldiers wondered at your lineage when they saw your hair. It is an uncommon color for anyone, especially a pure-blooded Vanrian, but its like is noted to have occurred in our distant history in a few elite bloodlines. We suspected you might be of noble blood, at the very least. Evoker Nalika confirmed those suspicions from your tehnaak's thoughts in the room in Deepwater."

Veyl recalled the Evoker asking to speak with him alone. That must have been when she told him. "Then you must have known who he was, too." A sense of dreadful certainty caused a sinking in her gut. "You didn't let him go."

He tapped a finger on the table, a hint of irritation in the sharp movement. "I couldn't let him go." Ceris came to stand beside him, continuing to watch her when Kyril turned his back to her to gaze out the window. "Our first encounter near Pandrea was with a Sarketi military ship. They were unfamiliar to us, but a few of them spoke rather poor Vanrian. That they assumed we must be Vanrian made it clear we had found where at least some people from our original homeland ended up. They invited us to a small port further south where Sarket's King Thrasser met with us. When he learned who we were and our purpose, he proposed a deal. He offered some of their alchemical weaponry and all the information about Vanrians living on the continent that we could wish for. His only ask in return was that we make at least one of our initial assaults on the town of Deepwater while the crown prince would be there and ensure that he did not survive the attack. The political conflicts of Pandrea were meaningless to us, so we agreed."

Veyl grabbed for a chair and sank into it. "Thrasser wanted you to kill Jaysen so he could keep the throne. He must have bigger plans." She looked up at him, feeling her world spinning further out of control around her. "I have to let my parents know."

"You can't."

"They'll come looking for me." She tried to make it a threat, but it came out sounding more like a desperate plea.

"Your people don't know we exist. No one is coming for you. Out here, you are merely another Vanrian on a Thaelian ship. Get used to it."

She closed her eyes for a second. He was right, and she hated him even more for it. How could she have almost kissed this man? Granted, she had been slightly drunk and suffering a magnitude of loneliness she hadn't known possible, but those were no excuses. "Did you do it? Did you… kill him?"

"No."

Hope sparked in her. She watched him carefully, searching for anything that might tell her if he was speaking the truth. "If you didn't, where is he?"

"In the brig."

He had been under her feet this whole time. "But our tehnaak bond—"

"Cannot reform so long as you are my zenyal. That's one of many reasons I did it."

Nausea swept through her as she tried to find focus among her racing thoughts. She finally latched on to the one thing she could act on, her hatred for him. "You make me sick."

He strode past her, heading for the door, Ceris trotting after him.

Veyl jumped to her feet. "Don't you walk away!"

"Stop me." He stormed out of the cabin.

She raced after him, bursting through the door with no coherent plan. A member of his crew was bent over outside the door with his back to her, picking something up. As he started to straighten, she reached around him, grabbing his sword and dagger, then she lunged after Kyril. Ceris leapt into her path, and she checked her attack. Several people called out to alert the ahnkreth, but he was already spinning and drawing his blade, undoubtedly reacting to a faster warning from his companion. Others around them drew their weapons.

"Stay out of this," Kyril commanded.

They backed away on his order. Even Ceris retreated a few steps, though his flattened ears and silent snarl told her that, no matter how much he might like her, he would do whatever was necessary to protect his bonded.

An invigorating rush swept through Veyl, all her misery and anger coalescing into her focus on him. The crackle of energy from her untamed ability didn't rise as she hoped it would, but it was exhilarating to have weapons in her hands again. Those simple lengths of steel carried with them an infusion of confidence that allowed her to block out the pain in her leg and narrowed her world to the two of them. No matter how this ended, she meant to make him pay for as much as she could before she met her own death.

She rushed in, using her dual-wielding skill to put him on the defensive. This unexpected development changed his bearing as well. Hunger and intensity rose in his eyes that told her to be wary, no matter what advantage she might have. Kyril blocked or dodged clear of her strikes, but she provided him with no opportunity to counter for the first few seconds. She had trained with her father when he had his kanodrak assisting him. Few opponents were more challenging than the two of them working together. This was Kyril's territory, though. He avoided hazards like rigging for the sails, with no need to watch for them the way she did and was far more accustomed to the movement of the waves. It turned the advantage back some, giving him an edge that balanced out her dual blades.

The ability to fight well with either hand, along with her speed and agility, were her greatest assets. The Feral ahnkreth was skilled, however, his instinctive reactions and speed reminding her of engaging with her father. Every attack met with his blade or empty air, as if he saw them coming before she even committed to them. If Ceris could protect his mind the way Niskenya could her father's, perhaps the wave dancer could also supplement Kyril's fighting ability the way the kanodrak could for her father. That would explain her inability to land a strike with either weapon. Most people misjudged at least one reaction by now.

Something flashed in his eyes, satisfaction and a vibrancy that made her wonder if he was toying with her. The rest of the crew stayed out of the way, adhering to their ahnkreth's orders, though several still had weapons drawn.

Veyl spotted an opening and swung for Kyril's throat. This time, he made no attempt to parry or move out of the way. The instant before the strike would have landed, pain lanced through her skull, dropping her to her knees with a cry, the dagger and sword clattering to the deck. She clutched at her head in a useless effort to block out the assault. Anguish left her unable to function for a few seconds, more than enough time for a couple of his people to rush in and seize the weapons. As the pain faded, Kyril grabbed her by the arm and hauled her to her feet, his fingers biting into the muscle.

"You are my zenyal," he growled. "You are welcome to try killing me anytime you want to experience that pain again."

Veyl jerked her arm away from him, breathing hard and struggling to leash the fury that turned the edges of her vision red. She couldn't fight him. She couldn't escape him. Letting out an incoherent scream of rage, she spun from the source of her misery and bolted for the stairs leading to the lower decks. Jaysen was down there somewhere.

"Ahnkreth, should we—"

"Let her go."

The first thing she encountered when she got below deck was more dark-haired Vanrians—Thaelians—going about their daily duties or conversing and relaxing. A long hall extended along the length of the boat, with several doorways on either side of it. It was darker down here, not surprisingly, but occasional lanterns kept it light enough to navigate comfortably. No one challenged her. They moved warily out of her way when she stalked through, limping on the injured leg and still breathing hard from the fight. Ceris padded up alongside her, pushing his nose into her hand, his presence no doubt meant to reassure the crew that their ahnkreth was aware of her wandering.

She wanted to be angry with the wave dancer, but he had only done that which it was in his nature to do. He would protect Kyril the same way Irith or Niskenya would protect her father. Once she acknowledged him with a scratch on the head, he trotted out in front of her, leading the way down the hall past some communal quarters for the crew. She focused on Ceris, trying not to look at anyone.

"He should get rid of her. She's been nothing but trouble," one man said loudly enough that it was clear he meant her to hear.

The words stung more than she wanted them to, driving home the fact that she truly was a Vanrian prisoner on an enemy ship. Her life as khesran, her time spent helping patrols and guards in Etrion, all the years dedicated to learning about the world she was part of— none of it mattered here. To these people, she was nothing more than a difficult prisoner they viewed as a burden on their ahnkreth.

Ceris slowed, dropping back alongside her again and pressed in close to her leg as if trying to offer his support. The gesture reminded her too much of Irith, and she swallowed hard against the tightening in her throat.

At the end of this level, she found a storage area full of sacks, crates, and barrels. Supplies for their journey, she assumed. Among them was a set of crates with a simplified version of the Sarketi seal painted on them in green. The alchemical weapons Thrasser had traded to buy Jaysen's death.

Ceris led her down a set of stairs to the bottom level, where several barred cells were built into the hull. It didn't stink, as she had feared it might, and it was as well-lit as the deck above. The cells were all relatively clean, with cots and blankets as functional as what she had in Kyril's cabin, though it was cooler down here. The thought of being below the waterline, the might of the ocean pressing in on all sides, gave her an urge to run back up the stairs, but she resisted it, following Ceris along the center.

Every cell held at least one Vanrian captive, including the lone survivor of her two guards, who rushed to the front of her cage.

"Khesran Veyl," she breathed, "I'm glad to see you alive, but I hoped you had escaped."

Some of the other prisoners looked their way with interest, perhaps hoping their khesran had come bearing the promise of rescue.

Veyl reached through the bars and took the woman's hand, ignoring their observers. "I'm sorry to see you here, but I'm happy you survived as well."

"Veyl!"

She spun at the sound of that familiar voice and rushed to a cell near the end. Jaysen looked disheveled and weary, but otherwise unharmed. They both reached through the bars, managing an awkward embrace, clasping hands when they stepped apart to prolong the contact.

"I'm so sorry. I tried to get them to let you go, but

I was a fool to believe they would do so." A few tears spilled down her cheeks. "I didn't know you were here."

He glanced at the wave dancer who sat behind her, watching calmly. "Have they hurt you?"

She shook her head. "I'm all right."

He reached up without releasing her hand and brushed his knuckles lightly across her damp cheek. "Don't cry. This isn't your fault."

"Jaysen, they made a deal with Thrasser. He wanted them to kill you in Deepwater. His actions are in serious violation of the fealty agreement. He must be planning something bigger."

"Bastard!" His hands tightened reflexively, almost painfully, on hers. "But if he made a bargain for my death, why am I still alive?"

"Because we thought you might be useful for controlling her."

They both looked behind her at Kyril's words, and Veyl extracted her hands from Jaysen's. With the sounds of the ship and ocean around them, neither had noticed the Feral joining them. He had four of his crew members waiting on the stairs behind him.

He met Veyl's eyes when she faced him. "We will transfer the former prince to another ship."

"You calloch," Veyl hissed, a charge of crackling energy moving through her, sparking through the air around them.

Kyril waved his people back and met her eyes. "Don't force me to hurt you again. That isn't what I want."

"Again?" Anger tightened Jaysen's voice, though he was helpless to do much from behind the bars.

Veyl shifted her balance to move with the ship as it started slowing. "Isn't it? I'm having a hard time believing that at this point."

"If you work with me on figuring out your ability over the next few days, and if you cooperate with me in general, I will allow you to speak with him again."

Veyl could see the spark of displeasure in the eyes of three of the four crew members with him. They appeared to agree with the man who had said she was more trouble than she was worth. If too many of them supported that assessment, might they convince Kyril of the same? If they did, Jaysen would die with her. They were only keeping him alive for his potential as a tool to control her.

"At least give him better quarters, please." She hated being polite to him, but he was right about another thing; keeping Jaysen alive gave him leverage over her. The other Vanrian prisoners were watching her, and an aching spread through her chest. They deserved her help too, but how much could she ask for before she pushed the ahnkreth's patience too far? She drew a few deep breaths, calming the surge of untamed energy.

Kyril arched a brow. "We aren't negotiating."

"Yes, we are." Veyl forced herself to hold to his gaze, an effort made more difficult by the memory of that unexpectedly intense moment of apparent madness in which she had almost kissed him.

Kyril drew a breath and gave an almost imperceptible shake of his head. "Very well. We will move him to another ship, where I will allow him the opportunity to earn better quarters and treatment by working with the crew. That is as much as I will give you. In return, Khesran, you will cease fighting me and work with me to manage your ability."

One of the female crew members, her dark brunette hair streaked with a red stain, smirked as if she found the exchange amusing. The other three seemed to find it less so.

This was undoubtedly the best offer she would receive under the circumstances. Veyl turned to Jaysen. "Will you work with them?"

He eyed Kyril past her. "Do I have a choice?"

"No, Crown Prince Jaysen," she answered, infusing a hint of their childhood teasing into her tone despite the tightening in her throat, "you don't."

His attention moved to her, a fleeting, wistful smile touching his lips. "Well, Khesran Veyl, I guess that means I'll work with them." He reached out and brushed his thumb along her cheek. "As long as they don't hurt you."

"We are through here, Veyl." Kyril infused command into his tone, clearly grown tired of entertaining her antics. He handed a set of keys to one of the others, then gestured to the stairs. The four with him moved down and out of her path, waiting to take Jaysen from his cell.

"Couldn't I…" She trailed off at Kyril's scowl. When he said that was as much as he would give her, he apparently meant it. Veyl turned to Jaysen, putting her hands through the bars to take his. "Stay alive for me. I *will* see you again soon."

"You do the same." He kissed the back of one hand before releasing it.

Turning away from him hurt. Not glaring at Kyril as she walked past him was nearly as difficult, but she kept her eyes on the stairs and on Ceris padding along with her. When they reached the main deck, the sails were furled, and the ship was slowing. The rest of the six ships had moved in closer. She paused, tempted to try lingering until Jaysen and the others came up. Kyril shook his head and gestured firmly to the main cabin. Reluctantly, she entered ahead of him. Once inside, she stopped a few feet away from the table at the back, and he continued past her.

"You fight very well."

Veyl wasn't about to thank him for the praise, especially now that she knew he never had anything to fear in that encounter. She was nothing but a nuisance to him. Although, he had been attentive to her injured state. And hadn't she heard him say she deserved better when he carried her inside after the incident with the serpents? Could she have imagined that? "Why are you determined to keep me alive? Your crew would support you if you chose to be rid of me. In fact, I get the impression they would gladly help you do so."

Kyril spread out a map on the table and considered it for a moment in silence, his shoulders rising and falling with a few deep breaths. "You come from royalty and exceptional mind-crafter bloodlines, given what Thrasser's people told us about your parents and their lineage. Your mother comes from a royal line with strong abilities." A hint of admiration crept into his tone as he went on. "Your father is the son of an unrivaled Frightener and is one of the most powerful Ferals either of our countries has ever seen from the sounds of it."

"So, I'm desirable breeding stock," she snapped.

He drew another deep breath, the muscles in his jaw jumping. His gaze flickered to the necklace she had taken from the drawer. "None of you are breeding stock. We hope to integrate you into our society and make Thaelis your home. Ideally, you will build new families and lives there. No one is going to force you to choose a partner or have children, though they will encourage it. We do not mean to keep you like livestock to breed." He met her eyes. "You could make all of this easier."

Veyl took a half-step back. "What do you mean?"

"I mean, you are a khesran of Vanris. You were born to lead them. Someone they could turn to in a time of uncertainty to help them make this transition. I believe they would listen to you if you offered them guidance. They need that. They're afraid."

"Whose fault is that?"

"Is this your idea of cooperation?" He stared at her

for a second. When she said nothing, he continued. "They don't need to like me. Once I deliver you to my homeland, the council will almost certainly send my fleet out on another mission. I won't be dealing with most of you after that. But you are an icon of your people. Help them. Guide them."

"Convince them to give up, you mean. Don't try making it sound like I would be doing something beneficial for them."

"It is what you just did for your prince, isn't it? To keep him safe and alive. What do you think happens if they can't accept this as their future?"

A creeping sense of horror moved through her. This wasn't what she wanted, but he had her in a corner, at least for now. They couldn't run, and divided as they were, with his crew carefully managing them, they weren't in a powerful position to try fighting. Meanwhile, Thrasser could secure his place on Sarket's throne and move forward with whatever scheme he had come up with, which couldn't be good for Vanris.

"You know I'm right, Veyl. The more they cooperate now, the more freedom I can get them when we arrive in Thaelis."

If she could convince her people to follow her, that might also put her in a stronger position when they reached where they were going. Maybe there was an advantage to be had in that. And if she could gain Kyril's favor, perhaps she could make something useful out of that as well.

"All right. But if you want me to do this, you also need to be willing to work with me."

He nodded.

"Then where shall we start?"

irst, Kyril removed the bandage from Veyl's leg and checked the cut there to make certain she hadn't opened it in their fight. As much as she yearned to embrace a pure hatred for him, his gentle touch when he wiped on a light layer of salve and re-wrapped the wound recalled the more pleasurable aspects of the prior evening. His gentle support coming down the stairs from viewing the whales and the security of his arms around her when she stumbled into him in the cabin.

When he finished, he grabbed a blanket from the cabinet closest to his bed, spread it on the floor, and settled cross-legged on it, gesturing for her to sit across from him. Forcing back a surge of unease, she did as directed. She had agreed to work with him. That started now. Ceris joined them too, sitting to one side with his fin-like ears at attention, his presence easing her anxiety a little.

She gave the wave dancer a curious look. "He's here to protect you?"

Kyril nodded. "I'd prefer not to come out of this like Illis."

Veyl's chest squeezed unpleasantly. "Is she—"

"Dead?" The tightening around his eyes hinted at a deeper distress, an anger and sorrow he struggled to keep from her. "Yes."

Veyl swallowed. "I'm sorry."

He closed his eyes, drawing a deep breath. Trying, perhaps, to avoid lashing out at her for that loss. When he opened them again, those silver-blue depths pierced into her, as intense as the sea-green eyes of his wave dancer watching her.

"I've never done something like this before. Nalika had a few ideas for how to go about it, but I am the only one in the fleet who can do this with any measure of safety. It is up to you and I to figure this out together. How did you keep your ability under control when we severed your tehnaak bond?"

Mention of the incident rekindled her fury with him for destroying that pairing, lying about setting Jaysen free, and forcing her apart from him yet again. That dangerous energy rose within her, the feeling of lightning ready to strike moving through and around her.

Ceris flattened his ears back and whined softly.

"Veyl." Kyril's voice held a warning.

She closed her eyes and forced her breathing to steady, trying to forget the man sitting across from her. Memory took her back to the brief time on that rooftop in Deepwater when everything had been peaceful. The stars, the mead, her tehnaak next to her…

"That's it." Kyril's voice threatened her control.

Opening her eyes, she looked at Ceris, finding it easier to overcome the wild instability while gazing into those mesmerizing sea-green depths.

"It seems as if your ability is responding more readily to you. If you can rein it in reliably like that, you should be able to gain control of it. Nalika thinks you may be a Frightener or Dampener, given how it manifests in a way that convinces the minds of those affected that there is a visual and tactile element to it."

"Visual?" Curiosity pulled her attention fully to him.

"Your eyes. When the ability is manifesting, it makes it appear as if you have lightning crackling in your irises. It would honestly be quite beautiful if it didn't herald the possible breaking of someone's mind."

His words brought to mind her grandfather, Arhk. When he used his ability, black appeared to sweep in from the edges of his eyes. Did that mean she was a Frightener? There were no abilities she wanted less than that one. Frighteners had few uses in times of peace and tended to be feared and mistrusted even when they were needed. At thirteen, she still would have taken that over having no ability at all. But back then, she could have counted on having Arhk around to help her and sympathize with the related challenges. Now?

"What is it?" Kyril was watching her with open interest now.

She despised that he was the only one she had to share her insecurities with, but it was the unfortunate situation she was in. "If I am a Frightener, will they want me in Thaelis? It's not an ability that has more benign uses."

Sorrow added weight to his patient gaze. "You could have any ability under the sun, and they would be thrilled to have you. I don't think you quite comprehend how much we lost to the Devastation."

Devastation. The word by itself hinted at some of those losses. "I want to understand. I would also like to fathom how your people could harbor so much distrust and hatred for our shared ancestors that they believe this is the proper way to recover from that."

He regarded her in stony silence for a few uncomfortable seconds, then the expression gradually softened. "History classes for most of our early education go into considerable detail about the evils committed against our ancestors in the province of Thaelis because of their political dissent. We have statues in our streets devoted to people who lost their lives standing up to the Vanrian leadership back then. There are cautionary tales parents tell their children about those days that have been passed down through generations. I can't possibly explain it all to you in the time we have, but reminders of that rift are all around us in Thaelis."

His words struck a note of dread in her. "How much time do we have?"

"We should reach the islands in two to five more days, depending on the weather and winds."

"It's that variable?"

He chuckled. "Yes."

"I suppose we had best get to work then. What do we do now?"

He rested his hands on his knees, his shoulders visibly relaxing. "You seem to believe the Frightener option is likely, so let's start there. Try to draw upon your ability from a place of calm, rather than fear or anger. It might help to close your eyes and think of how it feels when it reacts to you."

Veyl did as he suggested. For the first few seconds in that darkness, her mind bombarded her with memories of Jaysen, her parents, and her friends, of her father's beasts, even Kivast, the gelding she had left behind in Deepwater. Then Arhk slipped into her mind and she latched on to his image. Many people had stories telling of the cold and brutal man he was. He had earned nicknames during the war that struck dread into their enemies. Beast of the Break. The Bane. The Waking Nightmare. Even her father had dark tales to share about him, but she had only ever known her grandfather to be patient, supportive, and loving, if firm when necessary.

If he were with her now, he would tell her to focus in that tone of voice that promised disappointment if she didn't. Disappointment that had never manifested, even when she failed terribly at something.

She focused on breathing, on pulling away from the darkness, anger, and pain into the memory of Arhk's embrace that heartbreaking morning of her Trial. Cradled in that safe space, she let herself recall the feeling of her ability crackling like a storm in her blood, the scent of lightning in the air.

"Exceptional," Kyril murmured from somewhere far beyond her carefully constructed refuge. "Now, see if you can find what I fear."

She let her awareness move toward his voice. For several agonizing seconds, she sensed nothing. Frustration started nagging at the back of her mind, so she leaned deeper into the memory of her grandfather's arms holding her while she cried. The frustration faded into the blackness, and she tried again, latching on to the faint sense of him through the zenyal bond this time.

An image gradually came clear in her head…

*Grassy dunes. The sea in the distance. She stumbled up to the edge of a huge depression filled with bodies, all of them covered with oozing sores, the flesh discolored to an unnatural grayish-green. The worst ones had sores on them so large and deep they exposed bone. Even the flies avoided this carnage.*

*As she stared at the grotesque scene, the bodies ignited, flames beginning to lick up around their discolored flesh, slowly crisping it black. She realized she was holding another body in her arms. A young woman with raven hair and pointed ears, a tiny mole under one eye the same silver color as her mother's, glazed over in death, her simple beauty lost to the sores upon her face. Tears spilled down Veyl's cheeks, the ache of a bottomless misery stretching within her. She wept as she tossed the young woman's lifeless corpse onto the burning pile, struggling with the impulse to leap in after her. Everything that mattered to her falling away with the body of the last person she loved.*

Veyl jerked as a presence cast her out of the scene and

back into herself. Her eyes snapped open, that crushing sorrow still clinging to her, trails of moisture on her cheeks. Kyril was on his feet at the cabinet where he kept several bottles. His back was to her, and he was pouring something that smelled much stronger than mead into a mug. Ceris stood beside him, whining softly.

He threw back the contents of the mug in one swallow and slammed it down. "I guess that answers the question of what you are." His voice sounded strained.

Veyl got up, warily taking a few steps closer. He rested his hands on the cabinet and bowed his head, his long hair hiding his face from her.

"I didn't mean to... I had no idea it would be like that." Could Arhk experience the fear of his victims in that way? If so, he had to have some method for shielding himself from it. How would he be able to stand it otherwise? If only she could ask him. "Was that woman—"

"I'd rather not talk about it."

"I'm sorry," she murmured.

He was silent for a few minutes. Long enough that she started wondering if she had done something to him. A sufficiently powerful Frightener could scar their victims' minds and drive them mad, but she couldn't imagine Ceris would have allowed her to get that far.

Kyril drew a deep breath and let it out. When he turned to face her, there was a haunted look in his eyes that she hadn't seen before. "You did exactly what I told you to, and you did it well. If you're up for it, perhaps we should visit some of your people. We have several ships to cover."

She got the sense his suggestion came from a desire to avoid engaging with her again right then. It stung like a rejection, though it shouldn't matter to her if he did reject her. As a Frightener, the sooner she grew accustomed to not being wanted, the better. Pushing away an irrational pang of loss, she took a deep breath, much the way he just had, and focused on the fact that visiting her people might mean seeing some of her friends.

"About that," she began tentatively.

"Speak your mind." Despite the encouragement of his words, she could hear the wariness in his tone.

"Let me tell them you will reunite them with their tehnaaks where possible if they agree to work together with you and your crew. I can think of no faster way to gain their cooperation."

Kyril's jaw tightened, that vulnerable, haunted look retreating behind a cooler regard.

"You know I'm right," she pressed. "You can have grudging partnership or hostile control, but not both."

He looked toward the back of the ship, at the windows and the vast expanse of blue beyond, as if seeking something. The wave dancer trotted to the windows and peered out. Somehow, she got the impression they were searching for the same thing. A sense of peace, perhaps. The ocean, as fearsome as it could be, held a boundless serenity within it, too.

"All right." He faced her, not looking especially pleased. "We will reunite the tehnaak pairings. But that will not include you and your prince. He is neither Vanrian nor Thaelian. As far as our council will be concerned, he is not an acceptable tehnaak for someone of your lineage. Many of my people lost their pairings to the Devastation, leaving plenty of opportunities to arrange a more suitable one. Until then, it's better if we don't allow the bond between you to reform, as it will only end in suffering for both of you. Keeping you as my zenyal should be sufficient to prevent that."

Veyl lowered her eyes, staring at the floor to hide her anger and the wave of fresh, raw heartache. Gaining his trust and support was her best option right now for improving the situation for herself and the others, at least until she could figure something else out. Fighting him at every turn was never going to get her there. Unfortunately, that meant she would have to swallow some bitter pills along the way.

"I am sorry, Veyl."

To her surprise, he sounded like he meant it. Drawing another deep breath, she raised her head and brushed away a few rogue tears. "Thank you."

Kyril unlocked a drawer and pulled some pages out, skimming them. Veyl crept a few steps closer and peered at them over his arm. They were lists of the people taken from Deepwater, with pairings noted where relevant and the names of the ships they were on. There were so many. Ten or more per ship. With seven ships, that meant they had captured over seventy Vanrians. She quickly spotted Gannon and Jaysen. They were two of three with initial ship assignments scratched out because they had been moved to different ones, to keep them away from her in both cases. She also spotted Iyvalin, Ahrin, and Lorek on the lists. All four of them were alive, at least. The knowledge filled a tiny corner of the hollow inside her with a spark of light.

Kyril tapped Iyvalin's name with one finger. "This is the young woman who called out to you in Deepwater. Why don't we start there?"

She knew what he was doing. Just as she was working to manipulate him into wanting to help her, he was attempting to manipulate her, trying to make her feel grateful to him for giving back tiny pieces of the life he had taken away. As much as she hated to admit it, it had the desired result. A surge of delight filled her at the idea of seeing her friend that translated into an almost irresistible urge to thank him for it.

Ceris trotted over, his tail and ears up, tongue lolling as he nosed her palm, responding to the glimmer of pleasure that she was trying to hide from Kyril. The ahnkreth put the pages away and placed a hand on the beast's head. The wave dancer stilled, letting out a soft whine when a hint of haunted sorrow rose in Kyril's striking eyes again. Jaw tightening, he turned and started for the door.

Veyl and Ceris followed.

She hadn't considered how they would move from ship to ship. It never occurred to her they might end up engaged in an interesting dance with the other vessels, using careful control of wheel and sails and whatever other mysterious methods to bring theirs and the one Iyvalin was on up alongside each other. Kyril and Ceris jumped across when they were nearly close enough for the hulls to touch. Then the ahnkreth turned and held a hand out to her.

"Be careful of your leg," he cautioned.

Veyl glanced down. She wasn't afraid of heights, or even of the churning waters below, despite her incident with the serpents she had ironically ended up dining upon after attempting to feed herself to them. What gave her pause was the awful possibility of being crushed between the hulls of the two ships if she missed. Still, this was not the moment to appear timid. She reached out, struggling to ignore the memory of his arm around her waist as his warm, firm grip closed on her hand. Eager to break that contact, she put most of the effort into her uninjured leg and hopped across, having the sense to at least keep hold of him until she was confident of her footing.

He placed a hand to the small of her back for a second, guiding her clear of the opening they had come across. Her pulse quickened, sending a warm flush through her. She hurriedly stepped away from him. Ceris cocked his head at her, and she got the feeling the keen mind behind those bright eyes sensed a little too much.

"Veyl!"

Iyvalin, her silver hair bound back in a simple tail, came sprinting across the ship. A few people moved in as if to intercept her, but an abrupt signal from Kyril stopped them. The tackle of her hug nearly knocked Veyl over. Bracing against it caused a sharp pain in her leg, but she didn't mind. She wrapped her arms around the other woman and closed her eyes, basking in the sensation of that glorious embrace.

"Iyvy," she murmured. For a few seconds, neither of them moved or spoke. Then Veyl eased her back and took hold of her hands, peering into her pale gray eyes. "Are you all right?"

Iyvalin nodded, though a few tears slid down her cheeks. "I guess. Other than… I mean, all of this." Her voice waved, and she swept out with one hand, nearly hitting Kyril as he moved around them. "I didn't know if you were alive, but you're too stubborn to die. I should have believed in that."

Veyl caught Kyril's smirk as he continued past, stopping not far away to talk to the woman who appeared to be in charge of this ship.

"I don't even know if Ahrin's alive," Iyvalin was saying, more tears falling freely.

Veyl gently wiped one away. "You're his tehnaak. You would know if he was not. Besides, I've convinced our gracious host," she allowed some bitterness to slip into her voice, receiving an arched brow from Kyril that confirmed his eavesdropping, "to reunite the pairings if we are all willing to cooperate with them."

"You did?"

Iyvalin's desperately hopeful smile tugged at the tears Veyl was holding back. She swallowed hard. "I did. It's the least I could do, since I got you all into this."

"No, Veyl, this isn't your fault. How could you have known something like this would happen? None of us could have imagined this."

She ducked her head, swallowing again and fighting to stay in control. It took a massive force of will, but she finally met Iyvalin's eyes again. "Have you spoken with any of the other Vanrians on this ship?"

Iyvalin nodded. "Yes. They sometimes give those of us who are working with them time to visit."

"Could you introduce me?" She met Kyril's eyes as she asked, receiving a subtle nod from him. Exactly how much freedom would he allow her if she continued this way?

Keeping hold of her hand, Iyvalin led her toward another Vanrian woman, who was being shown how to tie knots. It looked as if they really were letting those who cooperated work with the crews.

They continued that way through the rest of the afternoon. On each ship, Kyril spoke with the subordinate ahnkreth about the logistics of moving Vanrian tehnaak pairings back together while allowing Veyl to talk with her people relatively unsupervised, even those who hadn't behaved well enough to be released from the brigs yet. The captives warmed to her faster than she had expected, some crying and hugging her when she told them of the coming reunions with their tehnaaks, a development she didn't hesitate to take credit for. She spoke with Ahrin, receiving another almost violently enthusiastic embrace from him, and Gannon, who she was, for once, delighted to see.

On the fourth ship, she seized a moment to move off alone and take a brief rest, growing weary of all the activity and emotional conversations. One of the Thaelian crew members, a lean man with dark auburn hair and a set of nasty scars down one forearm, approached her. He was chewing on some of the dried vine Kyril had given her to settle her stomach after she threw up on his boots.

He followed her gaze to his scars. "Ji'ikyan caught

hold of my arm," he said around the piece of vine.

"I don't know what that is."

"I heard you tried swimming with some the other day." He came to stand beside her, his pointed gaze going to where Kyril was speaking with the ahnkreth of the ship.

"The eels?"

He nodded. "Kyril seems to have taken a liking to you."

A chill moved through her in response to the edge of displeasure in his tone. "I'm not certain that's true, but would it be so awful if it were?"

"I'm Rel." He offered her a painfully firm handshake, brows rising slightly when she matched the aggression in his grip. "And yes, it could be. You see, we all lost people in the Devastation. I'm guessing he's told you about that by now. But Kyril, well, he lost more than most. His tehnaak, his parents, his brother, and the woman he loved."

Veyl's chest tightened. She hated feeling pity for the man who had taken everyone from her, but hearing that, she couldn't help it. "Does he have anyone left?"

"He has us and his younger sister."

Everything came together abruptly. "Raven hair, silver eyes with a mole under one?"

His brows pinched. "He told you about her?"

"In a sense." That was what he feared the most, losing his sister the way he had lost everyone else. "That still doesn't explain why him taking a liking to me would be a bad thing."

"Well, *Khesran*," he said her title with a sneer, "you're a rare piece, aren't you? A mind-crafter. A royal. No way the council's going to allow a mere ahnkreth to be with the likes of you. He's lost enough. Maybe don't encourage him to get too attached. You get my meaning?"

Veyl watched Kyril for a moment, trying to see him as a stranger might. He was tall and lean, his long black hair streaked with that deep blue, the braids with their decorative shells and bones giving him a wildness complementary to the predatory demeanor that came naturally to Ferals. If she focused simply on him, and not the things he had done, he was fiercely handsome, especially with those striking silver-blue eyes that were looking their way now.

Rel gave a snort. "You appear to have missed my meaning by a few leagues."

Veyl startled. "I have no interest in—"

"Just know that we're his crew," he interrupted, "and we will protect him with as much devotion as that wave dancer does."

Veyl scowled at him. "You needn't protect him from me. I'd rather swim with another jikan than get closer to him."

"Ji'ikyan," he corrected, shaking his head at her as though he had decided she was a hopeless cause.

The subject of their conversation approached them, rescuing her from Rel. Kyril nodded to the man, who returned the gesture and wandered off to go about his business, whatever that was. Something other than trying to defend his ahnkreth from the woman they had taken prisoner, she assumed.

"It's getting late. We'll visit one more ship tonight. The last one we can do in the morning."

Veyl gestured for him to lead the way, too weary and bothered by the encounter with Rel to speak. After they boarded the next ship, Kyril made her wait by the rail while he had a hushed conversation with the subordinate ahnkreth there. The woman watched her as they spoke, eventually nodding, though some displeasure lingered in her eyes.

Kyril returned to Veyl, pointing toward the main

cabin. "There's someone inside who could use your help."

"All right." She didn't ask questions, figuring she would have the answers soon enough.

Kyril let her enter alone. The cabin was almost identical to his, if somewhat less tidy. On a cot against one wall, set up in the same position as the one she used on his ship, Lorek lay on his side with his eyes closed. His features appeared sunken and paler than normal, his light red hair lacking its usual healthy shine. The Thaelian woman sitting next to the cot glanced up when Veyl walked in and hurried to intercept her.

"You're the Vanrian khesran?" She kept her voice barely above a whisper.

Veyl nodded. "Is he sick?"

"Seasickness, but it's severe enough he hasn't been able to keep any food or water down since we set sail. He's just not made for the ocean, and I worry that he may have given up."

The genuine concern in her voice broke through something in Veyl. She gave the woman's arm a gentle squeeze. "Thank you for helping him. I'll see what I can do."

The woman nodded and retreated to the back of the cabin, giving them space. Veyl strode over and knelt on the hard wood floor in front of the cot, moving a bucket out of the way.

"Lorek." She brushed a lock of hair back behind his pointed ear.

His eyes fluttered open. "Veyl." Her name passed his lips like a sigh and his eyes drifted back closed. One hand moved up to cover hers, pressing it weakly to his cheek. "I missed you," he whispered.

"I missed you too." She waited until his eyes opened again to say more. "Gannon will be here soon."

A light sparked in those glazed depths. "He will?"

"Yes. Very soon. You need to hang in there for him."

"I hate this ship," he murmured.

Veyl breathed a soft laugh, blinking back the tears that stung her eyes. "We'll be on land again before you know it."

He nodded, letting out a soft groan as his eyes closed.

She leaned in and kissed his forehead before carefully extracting her hand. The Thaelian woman returned to her seat next to him when Veyl got up to leave. Outside, in the fading evening light, she spotted Kyril still talking to the other ahnkreth and hurried to them.

"Is there any way we could get Gannon, his tehnaak, over here tonight?"

Kyril glanced toward the cabin, then down at her. "I'll make certain of it."

Relief swept through her. "Thank you."

Exhaustion plunged in on the heels of that relief, and she wavered slightly with the movement of the waves.

Kyril turned to the ship's ahnkreth. "Can I trust you to work with Nichal to make that happen?"

"It will be done, Ahnkreth." She inclined her head to him.

"Thank you." He placed a stabilizing hand on Veyl's shoulder. "You need food and rest. Let's get you back to my flagship."

Veyl didn't pull away. She couldn't afford to heed Rel's warning. Doing so would undermine her efforts to win Kyril over, and, though she was loath to admit it to herself, there was something pleasant about his hand resting there.

The next morning, Veyl joined Kyril at his table for a breakfast of surprisingly warm and fragrant bread along with fish that tasted a little like dirt, though the light, spicy sauce they cooked it in somehow made the earthy flavor acceptable.

"How many crew members are on each ship?" she asked, picking a bone out of the flaky meat with her fork.

"Calculating your odds for a successful uprising?"

Veyl stared at her plate, trying to will away the sudden flush in her cheeks. That wasn't why she had asked. At least, it wasn't the sole reason. It had been partly pure curiosity.

Kyril sighed. "I'm not an idiot, Veyl. I know better than to believe you've truly stopped fighting me. You have merely changed tactics."

She poked at the fish. "As have you."

Ceris got up from under the table and came to her side, resting his head on her thigh. His big sea-green eyes stared up at her, pacifying her irritation with his bonded companion. She stroked his head, the odd textures of smooth scales and slick fur beneath her fingertips becoming more familiar. When she looked up, she found Kyril watching them with a solemn smile.

"A wave dancer will die before it will allow you to

break it, but you can befriend one with patience and kindness."

She wanted to take offense at being compared to an animal, but it was something her father might have said without meaning to insult. Besides, there were worse things to be likened to than the extraordinary creature now attempting to comfort her. Looking into those eyes, she wasn't sure she deserved the comparison. How was it fair that Kyril had such a magnificent companion there to help him lull her into a more amenable state of mind?

When her silence lengthened, he spoke again. "Our tumultuous start aside, you did important work yesterday. The level of cooperation on all the ships we visited has noticeably improved this morning."

Her appetite left her, and she set her fork down. "If only your praise didn't make me feel ashamed of myself."

"Would you feel less so if I told you I received word this morning that Lorek is already doing better? His tehnaak stayed awake at his side throughout the night last night to help him. You're the reason that happened."

She let out a soft, bitter chuckle. "I guess Gannon isn't always a calloch after all."

Kyril sat back in his chair and crossed his arms, his brow furrowing. "I got the impression he was one of your companions in Deepwater, but it sounds as if you don't like him that much?"

"I grew up with the twins and their tehnaaks." She picked up her fork and poked at the fish again. Anything to avoid looking at him. "Gannon and I clashed a lot, usually over the time I spent with Jaysen. It was Jaysen's theory that Gannon acted the way he did because he was jealous."

"I imagine you encounter problems like that with some frequency."

Veyl focused on her plate, trying not to acknowledge

the flutter in her chest that rose in response to the compliment hidden in his words.

"There's one ship we didn't make it to yesterday. If you are up for it, we can do that this morning before we get back to work on controlling your ability."

How easily he played her, and yet, she could do nothing to stop the glimmer of giddy hope that sparked in her chest. "Is…" She hesitated, drawing a breath to control the excited tremor in her voice.

His gaze flickered to her neck, and she realized that she had reached up to touch the necklace. "Yes, your prince is on that ship. You have shown that you can work with me. It would be ungrateful of me not to reciprocate."

She arched a brow at him. "I see you've developed some morals since lying to me about setting him free."

He chuckled and shook his head at her. "Don't push your luck, Khesran." Ceris bounded excitedly toward the door when he stood. "When you're through eating, come find me, and we'll go."

Veyl turned to finishing her meal as he walked out with the wave dancer. The desire to see Jaysen was far more compelling than any need for sustenance, but she had to stay healthy. Besides, appearing too impatient would emphasize to Kyril exactly how much power this one thing gave him over her. What she needed him to see was that she was in control of her emotions, her ability, and, in time, her situation.

When she finished eating, she checked the wound on her leg. It was healing well, though there was a dark circle on the skin around where the serpent's, the ji'ikyan's, stinger had sunk in. The cut that crossed through that spot was clean and well-stitched, the salve helping it heal faster.

She walked to the cabinet where Kyril kept some medicinal supplies and pulled out what she needed, pausing there with the items in her hands. A wave of despair slammed into her when she looked around. This place had already become not quite comfortable, but familiar. She knew what was in every unlocked drawer or cabinet. That she would sleep on the cot at the side of the room each night and eat at this table were things she had ceased questioning. A few simple days and she had accepted this place, this situation, as her new reality. Not a welcome one, but the one she was stuck with. How long would it take her to adapt to Thaelis after they arrived? How much time would have to pass before she started forgetting what daily life had been like at home and accepting the new existence they forced on her?

Fury and sorrow soared, pushing beyond her capacity to endure. Peering frantically around, she searched for a release, anything that might ease the pressure building inside. She could light his sheets on fire with a candle or use the privy and dump the contents on his maps. None of it would matter, though. It would only undermine the progress she had made and move her further away from regaining everything she had lost. Everything *he* had taken.

The tempest swirled, expanding that bleak inner hollow that had shrunk a little yesterday when she visited her friends. Wild energy crackled to life in her, filling that emptiness and growing until it flared out through the room. The door flew open and Kyril rushed in with Ceris, his abrupt arrival providing the storm inside her with a target. Veyl hurled the salve container at him, her Frightener ability lashing out with it. Another presence repelled her, slamming her power back into her at the same moment a familiar pain speared through her head. The combination crushed her, dropping her to her knees with a raw scream of agony and frustration.

The tempest fractured, and the pain immediately

stopped. Veyl curled over, clutching her head in her hands, and broke into heaving sobs.

"Is everything all right, Ahnkreth?" a woman's worried voiced asked from the entrance.

"Yes. Give us some privacy, please," Kyril answered.

The door clicked closed. A moment later, he knelt next to Veyl, gathering her into his arms. She was helpless to control her sobs, now so violent she could barely breathe through them.

"Easy," he murmured, settling on the floor beside the cabinet and holding her close.

He could have been anyone at that moment. It didn't matter. She curled in against his chest and wept. After a time, the tears abated, and she rested against him, trembling and exhausted, but finally able to breathe again. His strong arms still encircled her and the only thing she wanted more than to get away from him was to stay in that embrace where she could pretend she was safe, even if it was a lie.

"Maybe this isn't the right time to visit the last ship," he murmured.

Despair swelled again. She pulled back to look at him. "No, please, I…" Her voice cracked, and she swallowed hard against more tears. So much for showing him all the control she had.

He reached out and brushed beneath her eye with his thumb. It came away smeared with red. He frowned at it. "We need to get your ability under control."

"Please." It was all she could think to say.

He regarded her quietly for a moment, then gave a reluctant nod. "You can't go anywhere looking like that." He took her hands and lifted her to her feet with him. "Let's clean you up."

He carried a chair over by the washbasin and sat her down on it. Then he retrieved a second chair and sat in front of her, using a dampened cloth to wipe away the bloody tears. A shudder moved through her when she looked at the reddened fabric. The backlash of her ability had nearly broken her this time.

"Does that mean, if not for Ceris…"

He began wiping the other side. "Would I have met the same fate as Illis? Most likely."

"How are you not upset by that?"

He sat back, lowering the cloth. "I am, but there's no point in being angry with you. The strength of your ability isn't your fault, Veyl." Leaning in, he wiped at her face again, his touch disconcertingly gentle.

"I still hate you."

"I could tell by the way you threw the salve at me." A faint smirk tugged at his lips.

Veyl exhaled a small laugh, her face warming. "I did do that, didn't I."

His smirk turned into a smile. "For future reference, I think I prefer swords to projectile weapons."

A tremulous grin crept across her lips. "Perhaps we should spar again, then?"

"Again? I didn't get the feeling you were just sparring with me last time."

Veyl shrugged.

"Ask me when your leg has fully healed." He sat back and considered her. "Well, you look like you haven't had the best morning, but the blood is gone at least. Do you still want to go to the other ship?"

"Yes, please."

Kyril shook his head as if he thought she was making the wrong choice, but he stood, offering her a hand up that she accepted.

*

Jaysen was near the opposite railing, busy coiling a rope when they boarded the last ship, his dark auburn hair, still too short to tie back, falling repeatedly in his eyes. He kept tossing his head to get it out of his face, never looking up from his task. Veyl glanced at Kyril, irritation flaring when she realized she was seeking his permission. Although, considering that what she had done this morning could have killed him if not for Ceris, some extra deference might be appropriate to help smooth things over.

Kyril nodded. "Go ahead, but remember, you need to talk to the others too. You're not here solely to visit with your prince."

"He has a name. Why do you keep calling him *my prince?*"

Kyril grinned. "Because every time I do it, you get this cute little wrinkle of irritation between your brows."

Veyl rolled her eyes at him and walked away, trying to imagine the smile that tugged at her lips was for Jaysen.

Her former tehnaak didn't look up when she stopped next to him, either too focused on his task or simply assuming she was someone else. "Are you sure you're doing it right?"

Jaysen's head snapped up. He dropped the rope and surged to his feet, sweeping her up in an enthusiastic embrace. If his strength and energy were any indication, they were at least feeding him adequately. For the moment, she didn't care that the Thaelian crew and other Vanrians were watching them. She returned his embrace with equal exuberance, closing her eyes for a few seconds to imagine they were in a better place, though the gentle rocking of the waves quickly shattered that fantasy.

He set her down and held her at arm's length, his joyful expression clouding over. "You've been crying."

"Who among us hasn't been," she evaded.

"Veyl," he pressed.

His gaze moved from her, picking out Kyril on the quarterdeck, talking to Evoker Nalika. The ahnkreth wasn't watching them.

Veyl placed her fingers along Jaysen's jaw, applying pressure to get him to look at her. "It would appear that you're cooperating with them."

He let her pull his attention back. "For you, yes. I don't mind the work. It's better than wasting away in a cell."

She refrained from pointing out that none of them had much choice. Their Thaelian captors would be entirely unbothered by having to lock one of them back up in the brig.

"Good. Keep doing so. Kyril is—"

"Kyril? You're on a first name basis with that bastard?"

"Jaysen." She lowered her voice as one of the crew walking past gave him an icy glare. "Please don't provoke them. He's allowing me to talk to the Vanrians on the ships and reunite the tehnaak pairings." She shook her head at the brief flicker of hope in his eyes. "Not us. I'm sorry. But we need to make the best of our situation until I can figure out how to leverage the freedoms we're earning by working with them."

Jaysen cupped her jaw in one hand, and brushed his thumb lightly across her cheek, affection rising in his eyes. "I should have known your capitulation was just for show and that brilliant mind of yours was busy plotting a way out of this."

Ceris padded over and nudged her hand with his nose. She glanced up to see Kyril watching them now and moved away from Jaysen's touch. "I need to go talk to the others. I will come back and see you again before we leave the ship, I promise."

Jaysen glanced down at Ceris, his jaw tightening, but he said nothing as she walked away. The wave dancer accompanied her below deck. He wandered around sniffing at things as she talked with the Vanrian captives and shared the news about their tehnaaks. While she was doing so, a few of the ship's crew also came down to collect individuals they were moving to other ships and delivering three who had just arrived to reunite with their tehnaaks on this one. If any of her people had doubted her, they stopped doing so then. The three pairings cried and thanked her several times, each insisting on hugging her before she could extricate herself, the pleasure of seeing those joyful reunions overshadowed by the knowledge that she wouldn't get such a moment for herself. She was Kyril's zenyal. She couldn't have her tehnaak back.

Up on the main deck, she searched for Jaysen, spotting him being shown how to do something with one of the rigging lines. Before she could go to him, a horn blared out. Kyril leapt down from the quarterdeck and raced past her, going to the opposite end where one of his crew was pointing at something off the port side of the bow. Most of Kyril's fleet was currently behind or to the starboard side of this ship, his flagship being the closest. Another vessel was becoming visible in the glare of sunlight on the ocean waters in the direction they were looking, surprisingly close already.

Kyril snarled something in a language she didn't recognize, his tone making it clear it wasn't positive. Veyl moved within earshot, her attention on Kyril, watching the tension in his curt movements and the narrowing of his eyes. Whoever the approaching ship belonged to, he wasn't happy to see them.

"What do you want to do?" Nalika asked, joining him at the rail.

"We can't run. Their ship is faster, and we're already heading on an intercept course. It would take too long to change direction."

"This is outside their usual territory," Nalika remarked.

Ceris came up beside him, and he rested a hand on the wave dancer's head, his posture relaxing a fraction with that contact. "It looks like it's a single ship too. Maybe a rogue crew, which could be good or bad. We hold our heading and let them come to us. I'll stay here. There's no time to rearrange the ships. Have your Speaker spread word to the others that we need all our mind-crafters on alert and weapons discreetly made ready, but violence is our last option, understood?"

"Yes, sir."

Veyl backed up near the entrance to the ahnkreth's cabin, staying out of the way as a flurry of activity ensued. The approaching ship was smaller and moving fast. Its sails had full advantage of the wind and there appeared to be oars sticking out the sides. It would be upon them in a matter of minutes. They put Jaysen to work helping the crew subtly adjust some ballistae on the port side to have them ready for attack if it came to that.

Kyril took advantage of every second, helping his people complete their preparations. The strange ship, flying a flag with a sun that bled red upon a field, was slowing for its final approach when he noticed her and hurried over.

"Go inside the cabin and stay there until I come for you."

When she nodded, he left her again, apparently assuming she would do as directed. She intended to, for a second, but the charge of dreadful anticipation that flowed almost tangibly off his crew kept her glued to the spot.

The strange ship curved around, coming up beside them. Three individuals—she couldn't be sure if they were male or female under the disarray of mismatched hides, fabrics, and plants that they covered themselves with—jumped on board without awaiting an invitation to do so. Two of them used ropes they carried across to secure their ship to the Thaelian one. Their hair had bones, twigs, and what looked like seaweed bound into it, but not in the clean, attractive way the Thaelians added their embellishments. The newcomers' hair was also matted and tangled, clumped with dirt or some other matter, and they gave off a foul stench that wafted over from their ship as well. They had painted every spot of visible skin with clumpy substances in sickly shades of gray, brown, green, and red.

Curiosity drew her closer until someone from Kyril's crew stopped her with a hand on her arm. She didn't look to see who it was, wary of taking her eyes off these morbidly fascinating uninvited guests. Unease flickered through her when Kyril approached the lead stranger, a man as best she could tell, with an array of wood spikes attached to the shoulders and arms of his clothing.

He grinned at Kyril, showing off a set of sharpened brown teeth, and declared something in a language that sounded similar to the one she had heard Kyril using a moment ago.

"Who are they?" She asked softly, daring a glance at the brunette woman standing with her hand still on Veyl's arm.

"Ukhen'kya, the Unclean," she answered, a note of disgust in her voice.

That didn't sound reassuring. "What do they want?"

"Quiet," the woman hissed.

Kyril and the stranger continued their exchange, tension in their postures and rising voices.

"They demand that we give a tribute for their harvest feast if we wish to proceed unharmed," the brunette said in a low voice, removing her hand from Veyl's arm.

"Food? That shouldn't be a terrible price to pay."

The woman looked at Veyl, the dread in her pale green eyes carrying a warning. "Once a year, the Ukhen'kya hold a feast to ensure a bountiful harvest. Their gods demand that they consume human flesh and spread human blood upon their fields. They prefer not to use their own people for that."

Veyl's stomach turned. "Then why is Kyril even talking to them? Why not just attack?"

"Don't judge what you don't understand."

Veyl watched with a distant horror as the argument between Kyril and the strange man escalated, their voices rising, the stranger's much more than Kyril's, as though the ahnkreth were trying to keep things from spiraling out of control. The Unclean man stomped one foot, then pointed at Jaysen and shouted something.

Veyl grabbed the woman's arm. "What was that? What did he say?"

"He says that one is obviously not a man of Thaelis, so they will take him."

Her breath caught when Kyril's gaze settled on Jaysen.

"It's a fair compromise," the woman next to her said. "We lose none of our people, and you lose none of yours."

"Jaysen is one of mine," Veyl hissed. She stared at Kyril, willing him to care, willing him to have mercy on the Sarketi prince. Lightning crackled in her chest, but she fought it back. He couldn't let this happen. He wouldn't. But if he tried to, she would stop him.

Kyril met the stranger's eyes and shook his head, drawing his hand sharply across in front of him in a clear negation. Veyl let out the breath she had been holding, the terror releasing its stranglehold on her.

"Idiot," the woman next to her muttered.

The stranger shouted, and Veyl caught the glint of metal near his hand, something that looked like a set of claws dropping out of the hide hanging over that arm. Several crew members grabbed weapons at the same instant the man swiped out at Kyril. Panic clenched in her chest, and the tempest lashed out from within her.

## CHAPTER EIGHTEEN

The Unclean leader and his two companions abruptly stopped moving. Ceris already had one pinned on the deck, but the individual went limp, staring blankly at the sky and no longer trying to fend off the wave dancer. A heartbeat passed, everything frozen in time as Kyril, who had grabbed the leader's wrist, pulled the ends of the hooked blades out of his neck where the man had made contact before Veyl's ability broke him. All three Ukhen'kya on the Thaelian ship had blood running from their eyes, ears, and noses.

A sharp whistle from Kyril snapped everyone free of that instant of stunned inaction. Flaming arrows hit the Unclean ship's sails and two Sarketi firebombs, hurled from another ship, exploded on the deck, blasting into the Unclean crew. Kyril twisted clear of a spear that flew at him from the enemy vessel, catching the haft as it shot past. His gaze flickered to her, blood streaming freely from the three fresh wounds on his neck. Then he flipped the spear and turned, leaping across to the other ship along with several of his crew to wreak havoc upon the Unclean not taken out by the firebombs.

Veyl started forward, reaching for the sword that wasn't at her waist.

The woman next to her caught her arm again. "Stay back, hyeralisk."

Without a weapon, Veyl remained where she was, watching as the woman drew her blade and ran to join the others. The battle was over in minutes. When Kyril came back across, a crushing tension lifted from around her. Obviously, concern for Ceris explained that, since the wave dancer had also crossed over, fighting close by his companion throughout the brief battle. The Feral ahnkreth came aboard shouting orders. He stormed past Jaysen without a glance at the prince whose life he had spared.

"Throw the bodies on their ship and burn it! Take *nothing* off that ship. Everything goes to the flames. Then we're setting full sail out of here. I don't care if we need to tack a few leagues off course. Whatever's necessary to put some distance between us and that ship."

There were shouts of 'yes, sir' or 'yes, Ahnkreth' following in his wake as he made his way directly to her. Blood was still running from the three wounds on his neck where the Unclean leader had nearly opened his throat. He gestured toward his flagship with a jerk of his head, taking hold of her arm above the elbow.

"Back to my ship."

Veyl didn't argue. She caught Jaysen's gaze for an instant before she let Kyril steer her to the opening, where they jumped across to the flagship. A man from his crew moved to intercept them on the other side. Kyril stepped around him, continuing toward the quarterdeck.

The man hurried after him. "Ahnkreth, those wounds need cleaning."

Kyril waved him off. "Later."

The man ran up beside the Feral and reached for the bleeding cuts with a cloth he held. "At least..." Kyril blocked his hand and continued past again. The man stopped, his dark brows pulling together as he watched his ahnkreth stride away, the rejected cloth now hanging at his side. "...put some pressure on them," he muttered.

Veyl took the cloth from him. "Let me try."

He nodded. "Thank you."

Before going after Kyril, she glanced at the man. "What does hyeralisk mean?"

His brow furrowed. "It's a Qwilki word for a severe hurricane that results in loss of life."

"Of course it is." Veyl blew out a heavy breath and hurried after Kyril. He was at the top of the deck, having a heated conversation with a woman who appeared to hold some rank, judging from the marks on her uniform. Veyl hung back at the foot of the steps, listening.

"She's dangerous! You should kill her and burn her with their ship!" the woman declared.

"I take it you object to how she just saved my life," Kyril snapped back.

"I appreciate that, Ahnkreth, but would you have given them the Sarketi youth if she hadn't been there?"

Kyril said nothing.

"She is your zenyal right now. That won't last." Her voice calmed, her tone turning earnest and persuasive. "Her ability is unpredictable and too powerful. We can't take her back home and put others at risk. We have eighty-three new people and four of them are mind-crafters. That's enough. We don't need her."

Kyril's voice lowered, an edge of restrained anger in it. "Let it go, Meyla. I'm taking responsibility for her."

Frustration raised Meyla's voice again. "Why? I don't understand."

"Because she's important," Kyril answered, suddenly sounding tired. "Not merely for her royal lineage or her mind-crafting ability. She can guide the others and help them transition. She's young, but there is a leader in her. The proper patient guidance is all she needs to manage her ability and draw that leadership out."

"They didn't ask us to bring back leaders, Kyril."

"Do you honestly believe I'm doing this for them

anymore? These people aren't that different from us, and we destroyed their lives. We took everything from them. The least they deserve is a voice to represent them in Thaelis."

"But she—"

"Let's focus on the current problem," he interrupted.

The sails were going up, and the ships were being turned. A roaring blaze was climbing up the masts and spreading across the deck of the Unclean vessel.

Meyla exhaled heavily. "You're bleeding like a butchered goat. You know that, right?"

Taking that as an ideal opportunity, Veyl continued up the steps, the two falling silent when she came into sight. She walked past Meyla, the brunette she had noticed once before with red streaks in her hair, and gently pressed the folded cloth to the cuts on Kyril's neck. They were deep, but nowhere near as damaging as they should have been. The Unclean leader had intended to kill him and would have done so if the blades had sunk in much farther.

She looked up at him, a surge of reckless courage spurring her on. "You almost sounded like you regret what you've done to us."

He met her eyes, resting his hand over the top of hers on his neck. Her heartbeat quickened, and she withdrew her hand, letting him take over the task of keeping the cloth in place. Meyla walked away, going to bark orders at some of the crew below.

"Who are you doing this for?" Veyl asked, holding his gaze.

"I'm trying to make a better future for my sister," he answered. "That was my purpose in coming out here. That, and to escape the memories that haunt my home."

Veyl swallowed against the tightening in her throat. He didn't deserve her sympathy, did he? "Do you truly believe I could be their voice in Thaelis?"

"I do."

Veyl averted her gaze. "You should let the healer clean that, assuming the man who was trying to chase you down is a healer."

"He is, and I will, once we're well on our way. Go to the cabin and—"

"No. It needs tending now. Those people were Unclean in more than just name. Don't pointlessly risk yourself. Your crew is capable, but they need you healthy. They want you healthy." She lowered her gaze, watching as Ceris nudged his hand and whined softly. "Others need you too." She included herself as one of them, because his crew would kill her without him, as surely as they would have given Jaysen to the Ukhen'kya for their harvest feast.

Kyril gestured toward the steps.

Not certain if he meant to come with her or not, Veyl turned and headed down, relieved when his footsteps followed her. The healer still waited at the bottom, a flicker of gratitude in his eyes when she walked past to head into the ahnkreth's cabin. At least one person on the crew seemed to not hate her now.

Kyril paused outside to exchange a few more words with Meyla before coming inside with the healer. He sat at the table and Veyl dug into the cabinet, handing the man items she assumed he would need. He accepted them, nodding approval at her selections.

"If you'd be willing to assist..." he trailed off when she nodded.

Kyril pulled his hair out of the way, leaning his head to the side to give the man better access to the wounds. Veyl winced inwardly when he moved the cloth away. The healer also grimaced. The three parallel gashes were at least smooth cuts. Those hooked claw-blades had been sharp. Plenty sharp enough to end him had the man wielding them survived to follow through with his attack.

"It might be easier to put you out for this," the healer said. "These need stitches."

"No. Not now. We don't know for certain yet that our friends were alone out here."

The healer nodded as if he had expected that answer and held a hand out to Veyl. Accepting her role as his assistant, she opened a couple of containers and sniffed at them. She gave him the one that smelled like the liquid they used to numb and clean wounds in the field in Vanris when it wasn't safe to render a patient unconscious. The healer glanced at what she had given him, thanked her, and applied some to the cuts. Kyril's sharp hiss earned a wince of sympathy from her. If it was like what her people used, the substance had a fierce sting before the numbness set in.

Ceris rested his head on his companion's leg, whining softly.

"The language you were speaking out there..." she trailed off, realizing now might not be the best time to ask.

"Qwilki," Kyril answered through gritted teeth. "The language of the natives who lived on the islands when our ancestors arrived."

When he finished cleaning the wounds, the healer turned to organizing items on the table for the stitching process, periodically wiping fresh blood from Kyril's neck while waiting for the numbing solution to take effect.

"But those people out there weren't Qwilki."

"No. About seven years ago, a couple of Qwilki fishing vessels washed ashore with their crews gone amidst signs of a struggle. We couldn't locate the missing people, so we started sending out military ships to protect Thaelian and Qwilki fishing boats. Nothing else happened until a year later. A strange vessel attacked a Thaelian fishing boat and one of our military ships came to its defense. We captured two of the assailants alive. They spoke broken Qwilki that they claimed they had learned from an individual they held hostage off the fishing boats they attacked the year before. They told us they needed fresh meat for their yearly harvest ceremonies, as if that were an entirely rational reason to attack our ships unprovoked. When we discovered what kind of meat they wanted, we executed them."

A visible shudder moved through the healer, who had turned his attention to threading a needle.

Kyril gave the man an unreadable look, then continued. "We searched for their home after that, hoping to eradicate them, but never found where they had come from. What we did find was more of their ships traveling in groups of no less than five. Coming upon one alone the way we did today is practically unheard of since that first encounter. We lost a couple of our military ships in engagements with them. After that, we began protecting our fishing vessels with full fleets like mine. The next year, we successfully kept them away from our boats during their harvest time, but they slipped in under our watch and took some people from one of the smaller outer islands. In return, they left four of their own people on the beach, all of whom turned out to be sick with an illness we had never seen before."

Veyl gasped, horror sweeping through her. "The Devastation. They intentionally infected you."

He nodded. "Retaliation for refusing to go along with the demands of their gods. We spent the next three years at war with an enemy we couldn't even see. We—" He cut himself off with a pained growl as the healer started stitching.

The man stopped immediately. "Apologies, Ahn-kreth, I should have waited longer."

"Just get it done," Kyril snapped.

Veyl moved around the table, positioning herself where she could clean away the fresh blood that flowed with the stitching, freeing the healer to focus on his task.

"Why engage with the Unclean at all, then? Why not just attack them on sight?"

It was the healer who answered. "Because we don't know where to find them or how great their numbers are. We don't know what other ways they might have of punishing us for our resistance. On the few occasions we have captured any of them, their minds were so fractured our Evokers couldn't collect usable information from them."

"We will find them once our population has recovered enough to hunt down and confront them," Kyril stated, a dark edge beneath the pain in his voice. "One day, we will destroy them."

The healer had barely finished covering the wounds when Kyril got up and started for the door. "Stay inside, Veyl. I'll be back soon."

She glanced at the healer, who gave a helpless shrug. "Wait."

Kyril stopped and faced her. He looked weary and angry. Was any of that anger directed at her? She had ignored his orders to go into the cabin and had killed the Unclean leader and his two companions, complicating the situation. But there couldn't have been a peaceful outcome. Not unless he had given them Jaysen, but she could not have stood by and let that happen. He had to understand that.

"That was a serious injury. Shouldn't you rest?"

He started turning back toward the door. "Later. I have responsibilities to see to."

"Maybe—" She hesitated when he faced her again, his silver-blue eyes flashing with a predatory ferocity. Drawing a deep breath, she forged ahead. "Maybe I could help. I'd like to understand what you do. I mean, I realize I can't learn to do everything in the time we have, but I'd like to know more about handling a ship."

"So you can try to take one?" A bitter edge crept into his tone.

"No, because…" She shook her head. They both knew better, but her desire to help, at least in this moment, had not been driven by escape. "Never mind."

He strode back to her, stopping less than a foot away. She looked up into his eyes, distantly aware of the healer exiting the cabin.

"Why?" Kyril asked.

Her pulse sped up. She forced herself not to look at his lips. "Because, when I was in Deepwater, the ocean beyond the bay… I felt drawn to it. As if it were another home that I had somehow never visited."

His expression softened, becoming almost sorrowful, though a hint of disconcerting fondness crept through. "I had a feeling. Come along. I'll show you a few things while I make my rounds."

*

The next few days raced past. Veyl helped Kyril tend the injury to his neck every morning, after which she cared for her leg, insisting on doing it herself to avoid the emotional confusion his gentle ministrations caused. Then they ate, and she followed him through his early rounds. The crew started willingly including her in their chores, showing her how to help raise or lower sails, tie assorted knots, and myriad other tasks. When those duties were done, Kyril allowed her to cross to different ships and talk with her people, many of whom had taken to calling her khesran now despite her attempts to discourage use of the title. Jaysen was typically busy when she boarded that ship, and the crew wouldn't allow him to ignore his duties for long to talk with her, something she suspected Kyril had a hand in. Ceris always accompanied her, his presence a reminder that she wasn't simply out to make social visits.

In the late afternoons, she helped with tasks around the ship again. Then they shared dinner in his cabin. Before going to bed at night, he had her practice trying to access the less potent surface fears he and some of his crew carried. An exercise in finesse, but also a limitation likely intended to keep her out of those deeper fears that might be more sensitive, such as that of losing his sister.

Winds weren't optimal, making for a slightly longer journey. By mid-morning of the fourth day of this new routine, they came within sight of land. Fishing vessels and military ships dotted the horizon, the closer ones hailing them as they approached. Thaelians or those of mixed blood crewed the military vessels, but tan-skinned people with darker hair and eyes and rounder features crewed some of the fishing boats. Kyril informed her these were the Qwilki.

Veyl retreated to the cabin as noon arrived and the city they were heading toward became more distinct on the horizon. To calm her nerves, she did the meditative work of adding two precise braids along the side of her head in the traditional Vanrian military style. Something familiar to protect her personal vision of who she was before these strangers. The crew may have grown more accustomed to her over the last several days, and she to them, but they were still her captors. She wasn't about to pretend differently.

Kyril entered as she was finishing the second braid. He stood watching her for a moment, then he walked up to her, carefully removing a small spiral shell from his hair along the way. Without a word, he stopped in front of her and held out a hand toward her nearly completed braid. She looked at the hand, then into his eyes, unable to ignore the quickening of her pulse when she did so. With a hesitant nod, she let him take it. Saying nothing, he wove the shell onto the end of it and fastened it in place. Instead of moving away when he was done, he lingered there, gazing at the braid resting in his hand while her heart beat like a hammer in her chest. Her attention drifted for an instant to his lips, recalling the brief embrace that remained seared in her memory. When she glanced up, she caught him looking down at her lips before he met her eyes. Was he remembering the same moment? Could he feel the tension that rippled between them? Was she only imagining it?

He drew a breath and let go of the braid. Retreating behind the barrier of the table, he stared unnecessarily down at the map he had left laying out that morning. "I need you to walk beside me when we go ashore. Thanks to your help on our voyage, none of your people should need to be bound when we present ourselves before the council. If you are willing, I would like to put forth a cooperative front. That should make it easier for me to convince them to grant you and the other Vanrians more freedom here from the start."

Veyl took a few even breaths while he was speaking, trying to slow her racing heartbeat and turn her focus to more important things. "Jaysen isn't Vanrian. What will happen to him?"

His jaw tightened. "I wish I could answer that to your satisfaction, but I'm honestly not sure."

Veyl approached the table, nervous energy prickling up and down her spine. "He seems to have shown an aptitude for sailing. Maybe he could help aboard some of the fishing or military vessels. Or..."

Kyril looked at her, his gaze drifting to her lips once again, then moving down to the necklace she wore. "Or what?"

She tapped her fingers on the table, uncomfortable

with the suggestion she was about to make. Was it a betrayal to her country to put such an idea in his head? "He fostered in Vanris with my family for a long time. He might have a great deal of insight to offer about our people and culture from a slightly less biased perspective."

"I wonder if he realizes how fortunate he is to have your affection?" His solemn regard discouraged her from responding. "Veyl, you should know that there may be other Vanrians in Thaelis. We came upon Pandrea in the company of a second fleet. They chose to investigate the continent further to the north. Some of their ships are in the harbor. I don't know how things went for them, but it may not have been as peaceful as our journey. The ahnkreth in charge of that fleet isn't the most compassionate woman."

Veyl braced her hands against the table. The ship was slowing considerably now, undoubtedly entering the harbor he mentioned. She drew a deep breath. His words opened the door for an array of possibilities. The most obvious being a potentially more hostile journey here for any captives the other fleet may have taken.

"What are you trying to say?"

"I'm saying it is critical that you follow my lead and set an example for your people. The only way you can help them now is by gaining the trust of the Thaelian council. Can you do that?"

The gravity in his tone reignited the fear she had worked so hard to hide over the last several days. She couldn't let it show now, however. "You know I can."

A hint of sorrow subdued his answering smile, and his gaze shifted to the shell he had put in her hair. "I do."

The Thaelian port city of Dagony looked like a substantially larger version of Deepwater, with an abundance of beige buildings that appeared almost to have risen from the sand itself. More than a few even had similar garden oases on their rooftops. A nearly debilitating surge of homesickness struck Veyl as she stepped up to the gangplank. She sucked in a tremulous breath, tears stinging her eyes.

Though he had been busily calling out orders to his crew, Kyril apparently caught the soft, distressed sound she made and placed a hand on her elbow. "Are you all right?"

"I will manage." She moved her arm away from his hand.

Kyril leaned a little closer. "A cooperative front," he whispered.

She ground her teeth and drew a deep breath of air heavy with the smells of salt and fish. "I will follow your lead."

Citizens working around the port stopped to watch as the ships disembarked, some pointing and conversing amongst themselves. They looked excited, almost happy. Were they truly so desperate to expand their population that they could find joy in the hostile abduction of her people? The notion left Veyl feeling even more disconnected from this place they had brought her to.

They descended to the docks and Kyril's crew directed them to gather in a long, wide column in the largest street leaving the port with her people in the center and his around them. Though the Thaelian crew was obviously acting as escort to the Vanrian captives, their weapons remained sheathed and most of them looked at ease. A few even chatted with her people. With her and Kyril both encouraging the two sides to work together, it appeared a few had reached almost friendly terms on the journey over. She wasn't sure whether to be proud that she had helped them make peace with their captors or ashamed of having pushed them to accept their fate. At least now they had a chance of building new lives here if she failed to get them home again. That sounded positive, and yet, the successful integration felt too much like a precursor to giving up.

Kyril's hand rested on her shoulder. "This is your victory, not your failure."

"Aren't you the perceptive one?" She spotted Jaysen watching her, his brow furrowing the moment Kyril touched her. "I don't belong here. None of us do."

"Try. Please. If not for yourself, then for the others. Let's at least find out what happened with the first fleet before deciding what your future will be."

Something in his tone drew her attention fully to him. "You're worried. Why?"

More Thaelians were coming up the street, these in uniforms and armed with spears.

Kyril leaned closer, his voice low. "Because if the experience on the other fleet was a negative one, it will have reinforced the perception of your people as enemies who won't be able to work with us. That could make the situation here far more difficult for you." He met her eyes for a moment before adding, "For all of you. We might have the power to overcome such an obstacle, but

I can't do it without you."

"*I'm* your secret weapon?"

His smile set loose an irritating fluttering in her chest. "You are."

He took his hand away and walked forward to meet the leader of the approaching guards. Ceris, unexpectedly, stayed by her side rather than accompanying his companion. Perhaps the wave dancer trusted him to handle himself or simply sensed how utterly lost she was. Or perhaps Kyril urged him to stay to help bolster her courage.

He spoke with the leader of the armed group for a few minutes. She wasn't close enough to hear what they were saying, but the tense postures and occasional curt gestures made it appear as though they were arguing for at least part of the exchange. Kyril didn't back down from whatever stance he had taken. The guard leader eventually nodded and directed his troop to move out around their group. As they did so, Kyril rejoined her at the head of the column and they all started moving on his signal.

"I take it you won," she remarked quietly.

Keeping his voice low, he said, "This fight."

"Which was?"

He glanced down at her, his unreadable look making her worry that he might choose not to elaborate, but it appeared they had moved beyond such evasiveness at some point in their unusual relationship. "They wanted your people bound. Their hands, at least."

"The first fleet didn't go well, then?"

"Not so it would seem."

They continued in silence, Ceris nudging up between them to request occasional attention from each as they strode along. The streets were paved in tan cobbles and, unlike southern Vanris, where water was less plentiful, there were park-like squares with decorative fountains at many of the intersections. Several of those fountains had aquatic themes. A breaching whale, a trio of fish, and in the square before a massive building fronted by tall columns, a fountain featuring a statue of a Thaelian woman with a wave dancer by her side. Ceris let out a peculiar, melodic bark as they walked past it up the broad steps.

She glanced discreetly at Kyril. "This is our destination?"

He nodded. "The Great Hall, to stand before the Thaelian council."

Though Kyril moved with the confidence of an apex predator, she sensed unease in him that discouraged her from asking more questions for now, to let him focus on preparing for whatever he expected to encounter in the towering building.

The gaping doorway opened into a massive hall lined with statues of men and women Veyl didn't recognize. These weren't the heroes that appeared in paintings and statues throughout Vanris, despite their peoples originating from the same homeland and sharing the same early history. It served as a reminder that she was not familiar with their ways and could assume nothing from that common ancestry.

They continued between two rows of soaring columns. At the back of the room, seven individuals sat behind a long table on an elevated platform. All of them looked unexpectedly Vanrian with lighter hair and eyes and pointed ears that signified pure Vanrian lineage. She didn't see visible ke'hanoath on any of them. Had they abandoned that custom, or did they simply not tattoo their faces, as was quite common in Vanris? The council members wore matching off-white robes with generous gold and black embroidery at the cuffs and collars. At least half of the guards and others standing to the sides of the room had darker hair, like Kyril and much of his crew. A fair number of Qwilki stood among the bystanders as well.

She couldn't stop herself from arching a brow at Kyril in question. Sometimes it bothered her that he seemed to have an uncanny insight into her thoughts, but it was useful now.

"The councilors all come from purer bloodlines," he confirmed softly.

She wanted to ask why, but the time for private conversation was over.

A woman with white-blond hair and fierce gray eyes, dressed in armor like Kyril's, glowered at them from where she stood at one end of the table as they stopped a few yards back from it. Several of the guards came to stand near the front, in a position to defend their leaders if necessary. The men and women of the council looked the group over, more than one staring at Veyl. Given how Kyril's people had initially reacted to her, she suspected it was the blood-red hair that caught their attention, though her position next to the ahnkreth likely also contributed to their interest.

"Ahnkreth Kyril, it appears you and your fleet have brought us a great number of prospects for expanding our population," the man in the center-most chair stated, lines of age etched deeply in his features. His white-blond hair and ice-blue eyes, along with his regal composure, reminded Veyl a little of her grandmother. "How many lives has your fleet transported to Thaelis?"

"We bring with us eighty-four Vanrians, five of them mind-crafters, Councilor." Kyril bowed his head in a gesture of respect.

From her position next to him, Veyl could see the tension in the Feral ahnkreth's jaw. He wasn't as happy as they probably expected him to be about his delivery, judging from their pleased expressions. Evoker Nalika walked past him and set a pile of seven books on the table. The ship logs. The central councilor nodded his approval, and she bowed before returning to her crew.

A man with the milky white eyes of a Bondmaker standing behind the councilors stepped up, whispering something in one female councilor's ear. The woman's gaze snapped to Veyl, and she leaned forward, her long, light red hair woven back in a complex set of braids with pearls attached to them.

"Ahnkreth Kyril, you have made the woman beside you zenyal. Why is that?"

"Her ability awoke when we captured her, Councilor. She comes from an exceptionally powerful mind-crafter bloodline, and it manifested uncontrolled. I worked with her on managing it during the voyage, and I believe we have made considerable progress."

Veyl wasn't sure how much progress they had truly made, but if it kept these people from putting additional restrictions on her, she would go along with his statement.

"The blood of her people rests upon her head." The woman spoke softly, as if reciting from something. Louder, she said, "She is from a noble line as well, is she not?"

"Veyl was a khesran of the new Vanris, Councilor," Kyril answered.

There were some soft murmurs from the onlookers, and covetous smiles crept across the faces of several of the individuals seated before them. A powerful surge of defiance rose in Veyl, demanding they recognize her still as a khesran of Vanris, a hint of lightning flickering through her chest and out to her fingers. She fought it back. This was not the time.

A male councilor left of the center gestured to the woman standing at the end of the table. "Ahnkreth Eavara delivered us fifty-six Vanrians two days ago, all of whom remain imprisoned at this time because of their… hostility towards us. How is it you bring us over eighty, and they stand before us unfettered, without open opposition?"

Fifty-six more of her people, stolen from their homes. Veyl could sense the growing restlessness of her fellow prisoners upon hearing that. For now, she had to maintain her facade of calm and trust that they would follow her lead, though they might not like it.

Kyril met the man's eyes. "My crew and I worked with the Vanrians to encourage a cooperative atmosphere. Many of them assisted us in managing the ships for the return trip. Veyl was instrumental in helping us build rapport between our peoples."

He had left out some significant details, such as how she had broken Illis and tried to kill him, but he clearly had an objective. For now, that appeared to be working in her favor. Still, they had mind-crafters here. An Evoker could draw out information about the problems she had presented him on their journey if the logs sitting on that table didn't provide those details.

The man nodded thoughtfully.

The woman who had questioned her bloodline pointed to someone behind them. "What of that one? He is not Vanrian."

Kyril barely hesitated, keeping his eyes on the table before them. "We brought him because he has a close bond with Veyl and the companions we collected along with her. He has shown himself to be a hard worker and possesses a considerable knowledge of the Pandrean continent that may prove useful to us."

Again, he skimmed the surface. Did he mean to provide them with a more detailed accounting at some later time? Was that how this worked? Wouldn't they be angry if they read the logs and discovered all the critical information he was leaving out? But then, these were his people. She had to trust that he knew how to handle them.

"You have done exceptionally well, Ahnkreth Kyril." The man in the center nodded, a subdued smile curving his lips. "Yes. Exceptionally well." As he was speaking, Veyl noticed Ahnkreth Eavara glaring at her as if she hoped to strike her down with the expression alone. "You might have to teach Ahnkreth Eavara a few things before we send you out again. For now, the guards will show your guests to pre-arranged lodgings, where they will remain until we have evaluated them individually. Given that you are more familiar with them, it would please us if you broke them into groups for us."

Veyl made a soft noise in her throat.

The barest hint of a smile touched the corner of Kyril's lips. "If I may?" He waited for a nod before continuing. "Allowing the tehnaak pairings to stay together has been extremely helpful in the integration process thus far. With your leave, I would like to continue adhering to that practice."

The councilors conversed amongst themselves briefly, then the man in the center nodded. "Given the apparent success of your approach, we will allow the pairings to be housed together."

Murmurs of relief from the Vanrian group brought a bittersweet satisfaction to Veyl. If only hers could be one of those pairings, but she knew better than to even ask.

"Thank you. Meyla and Veyl can handle dividing them up," Kyril said, keeping their attention on him. "There was an incident on our journey that the council needs to be made aware of."

The Unclean. She had wondered if he would bring that up. At a gesture from him, Veyl joined Meyla and, with all eyes following them, they walked back to the waiting Vanrians while Kyril recounted the confrontation with the Ukhen'kya.

A guard approached them, holding a collection of

pages. He considered Veyl a moment before looking down at the sheet. "I can take eight for the first group."

When Veyl turned to Meyla, the woman gestured for her to go ahead, then crossed her arms and waited. Drawing a steadying breath, Veyl began dividing up her people, keeping the pairings together and, where possible, trying to house them with others who had traveled on the same ship to preserve the supportive bonds they had developed during their journey. As she filled each group, the guards escorted them from the room. She put the twins and their tehnaaks together with Jaysen and her surviving guard, watching with an ache of longing as they left the room.

Kyril had finished telling the council how she saved him from the Unclean leader, and she heard a councilor request clarification regarding what type of mind-crafter she was. Veyl's gut twisted into a miserable knot.

"She is a Frightener, my lord."

The tension that rippled through the room drew her attention back to the seven at the front as the last group of Vanrians departed with their guards. The councilors considered her with a new wariness now.

"We have no one here who can train her," the woman who had asked about her bloodline finally said.

They had no Frighteners?

Veyl returned to her place beside Kyril. If ever she needed to call upon her years of lessons in diplomacy and attending meetings with her parents, this was the moment. "If I may address the council?" When the woman gave a curt nod, she continued. "My grandfather is an accomplished Frightener, so I am not unfamiliar with the ability." She saw no need to tell them her familiarity didn't extend to how it actually worked. Admitting that would amplify their discomfort with her and undoubtedly lead to more restrictions. This was the time for strategy, not outright honesty. She knew how to play an Evoker well enough to keep that truth from them. "With Kyril's guidance, I feel I have gained considerable control since my awakening. If you have a Dampener or Enkindler who might take over the process, I don't believe it will be a problem."

The councilors pulled together and engaged in hushed conversation for a few minutes. When they settled back into their seats, the man in the center stood, walking around the end of the table to approach her. His gaze caught on the shell in her hair, then jumped to the braid it had come from in Kyril's.

Just how much significance did those decorations have that he could identify its origin that easily?

He looked at her again. "Veyl, is it?"

She wanted to incline her head to him about as much as she would want to lick tethdrak dung from his boot, but she made herself do it. "Yes, Councilor."

"You are gracious. A credit to your people. In the coming days, we would like you to speak to those transported here before you and see if you can ease their transition here the way you have aided those brought by Ahnkreth Kyril's fleet."

"Are the tehnaak pairings in that group already together?"

His eyes narrowed a fraction, and she got the impression he hadn't expected her to question him, but after a moment he glanced at another of the councilors who shook her head. Facing Veyl, he said, "Not at this time."

Encouraged by his choice of words, she dared to press for more. "Yes, Councilor, I will speak with them for you, but I share Ahnkreth Kyril's belief that allowing the pairings to remain together has had a significant bearing on our success. If you will allow me to reunite them, I am certain gaining their cooperation will go much faster."

His gaze drifted to the bandages on Kyril's neck. "We do not know what to make of you. To be candid, that you saved the life of the ahnkreth who took you from your home is bewildering. But there will be time to dig deeper into these matters. For now," he paused, turning to Kyril, "you, Ahnkreth, will accompany the guards and our Bondmaker to escort the former khes-ran to her quarters. Once the zenyal bond is severed, you will return here. There is more we must discuss."

Unease raced through Veyl at the idea of that bond being taken away. What if she lost control of her ability again? It was fine to play down the significance of her difficulty managing it to try earning more freedom, but she could break people's minds without intending to. And what about the severing itself? Would there be any of the trauma that came with losing a tehnaak? She got the impression that they meant to house her by herself. Deprived of her tehnaak bond and her home and family, what would another loss, even that of a bond she never wanted to begin with, do to her? She also dreaded being separated from Kyril, though she wasn't comfortable trying to sort through the reasons for that, preferring to attribute it to the fact that he had become familiar in a world where little else was.

"Yes, Councilor." Kyril offered a partial bow.

If he shared any of her concerns, he didn't show it as he turned and dismissed his fleet. When that was done, he faced Veyl and gestured toward a side exit. Two guards and the Bondmaker joined them, following a few steps behind. Veyl wanted to ask him about the severing of the bond, but their company made her hesitant to question him openly.

They had barely gotten through the side entrance when a whirlwind of raven hair sprinted out from some-where and leapt into Kyril's arms, forcing him to catch her. He staggered back, laughing, and spun the woman around, a broad smile brightening his features. Ceris bounded about them happily. When Kyril set her down, Veyl recognized her immediately as the girl from his fear vision. His younger sister.

"Kit, I think you gained weight," he teased.

She smacked his arm. "Nice to see you too, calloch."

"Maybe you're weakened by your wounds," Veyl commented with a pointed look at his neck. "You know, the ones you're going to rip the stitches out of if you aren't careful."

The young woman's eyes, bright silver like Veyl's mother's, focused on her now, her expression slack for a moment. Then a slow smile curved her lips, and she held out one hand in an offer of greeting.

"I'm Kitria, this idiot's little sister."

"Veyl." She accepted the hand in a brief shake.

Kitria stepped closer, her eyes focusing on the shell in Veyl's hair. She looked at him, her gaze picking out the now empty braid, again with an ease that suggested it was a noteworthy change. "Is there something you want to tell me, brother?"

He glanced at Veyl, his expression unreadable. "No." His gaze moved to the guards, the momentary happiness at seeing his sister disappearing behind a stern mask. "I need to finish up here, Kit."

"All right, I'll see you at your place later." She looked at Veyl, her gaze drifting back to the spiral shell. "Nice to meet you, Veyl."

Veyl nodded, watching her stroll away. When Kyril started walking again, she followed, fighting the inclination to touch the object in her hair that was now a source of yet more questions.

"She's young," Veyl prompted, falling into step beside him.

"Sixteen." The abruptness of his response discouraged further conversation.

The house they took her to wasn't that far from the Great Hall amidst rows of similar homes. They were all two stories, not small, but not overly large either. Judging the quality and worth of the structure was hard for someone who grew up in a palace with personal chambers bigger than some houses. The differences in their society left her feeling ill-equipped to figure out the value of what they were offering her. It appeared comfortable enough inside. Clean and quaint, with an abundance of furnishings and simple decor, mostly in warm tans and rusty reds, with splashes of blue and yellow adding visual interest.

She suspected the homes they were using for their Vanrian abductees were those that had belonged to people who died in the Devastation. As she had guessed, they appeared to expect her to live here alone. Whether they were isolating her intentionally or not, she was growing tired of it. Kyril had separated her from the others until she started helping with integration, and even then he kept her apart the rest of the time. Why? Because of her ability, or was there more to it? An attempt at breaking or conditioning, perhaps?

Once they were inside the house, Kyril turned to the guards and the Bondmaker. "I'd like to speak with Veyl alone for a moment."

The three didn't question him. Whatever his rank and accomplishments earned him, it was apparently enough to give him adequate authority here, at least for now. As soon as they stepped outside, he turned to her.

"You did well back there. Thank you."

Veyl breathed a bitter laugh as she walked over to a pale wood sideboard and ran her fingers down its length. "No one back home would have ever called me gracious. Hot-headed, moody, stubborn maybe. Not gracious."

When she turned, she found him watching with a fond, if sorrowful, smile. He walked over to her. "I'm sorry, Veyl. I never thought they would sever the zenyal bond this fast."

She wanted to tell him it didn't matter to her, but she suspected he would see through the ruse. "What about my ability?" She hated that her voice trembled when she asked. "What if I—"

"You can control it. I'll ask them to send a Dampener to work with you. That's probably the closest we'll get to another Frightener. An Evoker might—"

"No. Don't have them send an Evoker. Please."

"You're right. No Evokers." He started to reach out to her, then stopped and let his hand fall to his side. "Severing the bond won't be the same as losing your tehnaak, but it will be a loss. Like meeting someone you might have wanted to get to know better but never having an opportunity to."

"Will I ever get that opportunity?" She regretted the words the moment they passed her lips, but it was too late to stop them.

Kyril looked away, his gaze sweeping the room. "I'll ask them to bring someone here to stay with you. You shouldn't have to be alone after..."

After everything they had taken from her.

"I'll be fine," she snapped, ignoring the voice in her head that called her a liar.

Ceris nosed her hand and Kyril gave her a look that made it seem as if he had heard that mental voice, but he said nothing. Instead, he walked to the door and invited the Bondmaker and guards back in.

The severing of the bond was as unceremonious as when Kyril's Bondmaker cut her tehnaak bond with Jaysen. Though far less painful, it tore the scab off the other unhealed wound. Veyl did her best to hide the sorrow that settled into that emptiness, latching on to the dark anger that came with it instead.

"If you need anything, you're welcome to ask for me

as long as I'm in the city," Kyril offered.

"Get out," she whispered.

With a resigned nod, he followed the Bondmaker from the house, Ceris at his side. The guards left as well, but when she walked to the window and looked out, she saw them taking up posts outside the door.

Veyl was about to turn away from the window when she spotted Ahnkreth Eavara storming up to intercept Kyril before he had gone more than a few strides from the house. Ceris's ears flattened, and the wave dancer bared his teeth at the woman's aggressive approach.

Eavara didn't stop until she was in Kyril's face, where she shouted, "What in the Seven Depths is wrong with you?"

Kyril maintained an admirable composure before her assault, and Veyl ducked out of sight to one side of the window when he glanced at the house. "Not here, Eavara."

"That Vanrian qwe'pi was wearing one of my tehnaak's tokens. Is that how you honor her fucking memory?"

Veyl peeked out again. Eavara was close enough that their noses were nearly touching now. She wasn't sure what a qwe'pi was, but the woman's tone and manner made it clear it wasn't a compliment.

Kyril didn't move. He held her gaze, his eyes narrowing. "Call her that again, and I'll send you to see your tehnaak."

His icy tone sent a chill up Veyl's spine, making her grateful not to be the recipient of his anger, though she wasn't sure what to read into his defense of her. Deep down, it sparked an undeniable pleasure that contradicted the resentment and hurt she had been nursing when she sent him away. Why was she giving this man so much power over her emotions?

Eavara reached for her sword. Energy crackled to life in Veyl's chest, but one of the two guards took a step toward the ahnkreths. The movement caught their attention, and Eavara raised her hands away from her weapon before spinning and storming off down the street.

Kitria emerged from somewhere to the left of the house and walked up beside her brother. She took his hand.

He glanced at his sister, a weary affection rising in his eyes that caused a sharp pang of longing in Veyl. "You said you were going to the house."

Kitria shrugged. "I had to follow when I saw her heading this way. I thought you might need backup."

"Backup? Is that what you call waiting until she was gone to show yourself?" he asked, the barest hint of teasing in his tone.

"Yes. I figured I could drag you to the healers if the confrontation went poorly." She grinned and bumped shoulders with him when they started walking.

Kyril chuckled as their voices faded out of range. Loneliness raced in to fill the silent space. Veyl stepped back from the window, one hand coming up to touch the shell—the token—in her hair. She felt a little wobbly on her feet, as if her legs believed she was still standing on the ship at sea, so she sat on the couch and practiced drawing on the Frightener ability for a time. With no one to practice on, there wasn't a great deal she could do with it. She considered testing her control on the guards, though, without their consent, any mistake would surely lead to problems for her.

A quiet Qwilki woman brought food at one point. A reasonably appetizing seafood dish using shellfish in a creamy sauce over some roasted vegetables Veyl didn't recognize. Growing up in the desert of southern Vanris, she rarely ate fish, but she could learn to appreciate it. The guards watched her eat and took away her utensils when she finished, as if they expected her to use them in some harmful way. Perhaps they feared she might attempt to hurt herself or them. Like it or not, her record on the ship set a precedent for either possibility.

After they left, she settled in a chair and gazed out the window, alternatively fiddling with the shell in her hair and the necklace Jaysen had given her while she watched the occasional passers-by. Some were Qwilki, with darker skin and rounder features, but most appeared to be of mixed blood. Very few looked pure Vanrian, with their pointed ears, more slender features, and lighter hair and eyes, the most notable being the councilwoman who came to the door with a trio of guards after Veyl's evening meal. It was the one who had inquired about her nobility earlier. That the woman didn't bother knocking before entering set their interaction off negatively from the start.

"How are you settling in, Veyl?"

"Is that why you came, to see if I'm enjoying my isolation?" she snapped.

The answering smug smile put Veyl's hackles up, but also served as something of a reminder of who had the upper hand.

"There it is. I knew you could not be as acquiescent as you pretended to be in the Great Hall. Not if you were truly Vanrian royalty." She closed the distance between them, her guards tensing visibly as she did so. "I am Councilor Shyall, or my lady, if you prefer."

"What I prefer is to know what you want with me, Councilor."

Her eyebrows rose a fraction at Veyl's sharp tone, but she chose not to comment on it again. "To begin with, we would like you to continue working to help your fellow Vanrians integrate with our society. We wish to reach a place where you are all as free here as you were in your country, but that will take time and effort. Part of that will require learning more about our culture and life here in Thaelis." She offered a patently false smile. "I understand the young… Sarketi," she paused, waiting until Veyl nodded. "That young man was your tehnaak before the bond was severed to allow Ahnkreth Kyril to make you his zenyal. Is that correct?"

Veyl walked further into the room, putting distance between them. "He was." She forcefully held back the selection of bitter embellishments she wanted to add.

"We would like to arrange a more appropriate tehnaak for you. There are many here in need, and such a pairing would be a compelling display of unity between our people."

"Can it wait a while?" Preferably long enough for her to figure out how to escape this place. "I've had little time to adjust to the loss of my former tehnaak."

"That is not an unreasonable request, I suppose." The woman sniffed as if the idea offended her, though her words offered hope for a reprieve. "I will bring it up to the rest of the council. Regarding your isolation, you may leave this house so long as your guards accompany you. There are places they have orders not to take you yet. That includes, for the moment, visiting your countryfolk. We will determine how that is to be handled tomorrow. All we ask for now is that you remember you are not a khesran here. You are no different from any other man or woman walking these streets." She gestured to a sack that one guard now set on a table near the door. "There is a selection of clothing in that bag. I am certain you will find something that fits well enough. Goodnight, Veyl."

Without waiting for a response, the councilor turned

and walked out, her guards close on her heels. Veyl set her hands on the back of the couch, memory putting the edge of the display case that held Sylaryth's claw under her fingers, her father's hand resting warm and reassuring on her shoulder. Quiet tears slipped down her cheeks. She pushed away from the couch and went to grab the sack they had left. Carrying it into the bedroom, she dumped its contents on the bed. Then she stripped out of her clothes and took the most thorough sponge bath she could manage. It wasn't half as satisfying as a soak in a tub would have been, but, as Shyall pointed out, she wasn't a khesran here. Such luxuries could no longer be assumed.

She chose a dress in an unfamiliar style. The fabric, a sea-green that reminded her of Ceris's eyes, hung in light, loose waves evocative of the ocean, with a fitted bodice. The skirt had three layers of airy, flowing material cut at an angle and trimmed with lace of the same color. On one side, the lower hem nearly touched the ground. On the other, it exposed her ankle and a bit of calf. She found a pair of simple sandals at the bottom of the bag that she slipped on. A decent enough fit, like the dress, though she wouldn't want to wear them for any longer walks. None of it was Vanrian in styling, or practical for combat, but she could worry about obtaining more suitable clothing later.

She put the necklace Jaysen had given her back on. The complementary colors almost made it look like it belonged with the ensemble. Then she redid the braids in her hair. Kyril standing close in front of her, his fin-gers carefully placing the spiral shell on her braid came unbidden into her mind. She eyed the delicate token where she had placed it on the dresser. After a few sec-onds, she picked it up and secured it on a braid again. If she adopted more local styles, it would be easier to convince them she was willing to become one of their people. That was a more sensible reason for wearing the token than the underlying desire to maintain a connection to the man who had taken her from her home.

If they wouldn't permit her to visit other Vanrians, what would they permit her to do?

Veyl walked to the front door and opened it, gaining the immediate attention of the guards. "I'd like to speak with Ahnkreth Kyril."

The man on the left furrowed his brow, glancing up at the darkening sky. "Can it wait until tomorrow?"

"It really is urgent."

He shrugged. "All right. No one said you couldn't go there."

"I'm Veyl," she introduced as she stepped out of the house. They almost certainly knew her name, but being friendly might put them more at ease.

"Quillon," the man offered.

"Mardi," the other guard, a more mature woman, offered with some reservation in her tone.

Both had the Vanrian—or Thaelian—pointed ears, but their darker hair and eyes and slightly rounded features suggested a solid helping of Qwilki blood in the mix. Veyl couldn't keep from wondering what race they considered themselves. Would they acknowledge both equally, or did they prefer to be recognized as one over the other? How peaceful had the blending of the two races remained after the Thaelians discovered it broke their mind-crafter lines?

Adjusting the shoulders of the dress, she met Mardi's eyes. "Am I wearing this right?" She didn't doubt she was, but that wasn't the point in asking.

The woman's tense posture relaxed a fraction as she gave Veyl an appraising once-over. "Yes. It looks quite nice on you."

"Thank you."

As they started their walk, the two fell in on either

side of Veyl. It came as something of a surprise that they considered so few guards sufficient, but maybe the council hadn't read the logs yet and learned exactly how dangerous her ability had proven to be, though she would have expected Kyril or Meyla to have shared that information by now. Perhaps they simply didn't know what to do with her. How thoroughly had they planned their abductions? It was unlikely they had accounted for a captive presenting the unique challenges she did.

Quillon pointed to the south of the Great Hall. "Dagony Port is to the southeast of here. Most of the nicer homes are in this area or to the west of the Great Hall. The palace and upper society residences are toward the northeast by the shoreline there."

"Probably more like what you're accustomed to," Mardi remarked in a flat tone.

The comment sent a flash of irritation through Veyl, though she couldn't tell if the woman intended it to be insulting, or if it had merely been an observation. Either way, it told her they at least knew who she had been in her country. Getting angry about it wouldn't avail her anything, so she leashed her temper. How proud would her parents be to see her managing that so effectively? Granted, it was largely out of fear of what her ability might do if she lost control, but it resulted in greater restraint regardless of her motivation.

By the Break, her parents didn't even know she was a mind-crafter. Wouldn't that shock them?

The thought brought a sting to her eyes, so she searched for a way to divert her attention. "Where would we find Ahnkreth Kyril at this hour?" she asked, catching the slight tightness of sorrow in her own voice.

"Most of the ahnkreths live closer to the port. It's more convenient for them, given how often the fleets go out to protect our fishing boats," Quillon answered.

What if Kyril wasn't home? What if he was? She

didn't have a plan. She had mostly just wanted to get out of the lonely house and escape the prison of her melancholy. Not that there weren't plenty of questions she could ask him to give her visit the illusion of purpose. "Where are the markets and taverns here?"

"There are a couple more lively taverns around the port," Mardi offered. "If you prefer a calmer atmosphere, the Wave Dancer's Rest a few blocks west of here is pleasant." She pointed down a wide, well-lit street.

"As for markets," Quillon said, taking over, "there's a permanent marketplace near the heart of town where the Wave Dancer's Rest is. Seasonal markets pop up in the main square outside the Great Hall, and there are always vendors selling goods down at the port market. Tomorrow, we can show you where to find the best fish if you like."

Mardi gave a snort. "Are you trying to give your brother's business a boost with the newcomers already?"

Newcomers? Was that what they called them to avoid acknowledging what they really were? Captives.

Veyl forced a smile as Quillon's cheeks darkened a shade. "The city's name, Dagony, that sounds Qwilki, but the council is Thaelian. How did that come about?" She turned with them onto a quieter, darker residential street.

Quillon, seeming to enjoy his role as guide, jumped in before Mardi could finish opening her mouth to speak. "The Qwilki are a benign and, frankly, tractable culture. When the ships from the Vanrian homeland arrived, they welcomed them and all but gave them the city. The Qwilki lived in grass huts then—in fact, many still do—and could throw together a whole batch of them in a few days. They had no interest in assuming a leadership role, and after the first Feral bonded with one of their sacred wave dancers, it was all our ancestors could do to keep the locals from worshiping them as gods. Taking charge of the city was a compromise of sorts, helping to appease the native populace without allowing them to make deities out of them."

The two stopped, and her nerves sparked to life when they gestured to a single-story house that looked like all the others in this part of town. Most along this street didn't have the attractive rooftop gardens, but if these homes were where the sailing crews lived, that made some sense. Being at sea most of the time would make it hard to care for such a garden.

The guards advanced toward the front door, but Veyl didn't follow. Dim candlelight flickered through the window. That meant Kyril was home, but what if he wasn't alone? What if he wasn't the same person now that he was off his ship, and she was no longer his responsibility? Would that be better or worse? What if he was relieved to be rid of her?

The guards had stopped and were frowning back at her when the front door opened and Kitria stepped out into the dark street. She startled when she saw them there, then her gaze settled on Veyl. Not looking away, she leaned back a fraction to call into the house. "You've got company."

"I thought my company was leaving." Kyril was smiling as he stepped into the doorway. When he spotted them, his expression sobered.

He had dressed down in simple black pants and a white shirt that hung partly unlaced at the top. Something about the glimpse of that well-muscled chest left Veyl a little breathless, but his hard look and furrowed brow sent snakes of dread coiling through her gut. Perhaps this had been a mistake.

Kitria bounced up on the balls of her feet and gave him a kiss on the cheek. "Have fun."

To Veyl's dismay, the young woman walked up, put an arm around her shoulders, and guided her to the door where he still stood. Then she faced the guards and said, "You two can wait outside." With that, she sauntered off down the street.

Mardi and Quillon looked at Kyril in question.

Silence stretched for a few heartbeats before he nodded to them and stepped aside to let Veyl in. Gathering her courage with a soft inhale of the cool night air, she walked past him into the house.

It was dim inside, lit only by a couple of candles. Two mugs and a nearly empty mead bottle sat on a table alongside the couch, setting the scene of an intimate conversation. The furniture around the main room reminded her of his cabin on the ship somehow, everything clean and functional, decorated in stained wood and deep blue fabric nearly as dark as the blue in his hair.

Kyril shut the door and strode past her to pick up one mug, which he carried into the next room. When he returned, he stopped in the doorway, a distinct sense of discomfort hanging between them. Ceris emerged from a room on the opposite side and sat in that doorway to watch them.

"Why are you here?"

His faintly hostile tone demanded the safety of emotional distance. "I was bored," she answered curtly.

"Lonely?"

"What do you care?" she snapped. This was off to an excellent start.

Oddly, her aggression seemed to disarm him. He drew a breath, suddenly looking more tired than anything else. "You shouldn't be here, Veyl."

"I shouldn't be in Thaelis," she countered.

He took a step closer, his focus moving to the shell in her hair. From there, his gaze slowly traveled over the rest of her, a spark of appreciation lighting his silver-blue eyes. "Maybe not, but the local style does look rather lovely on you."

Heat followed in the wake of his gaze and Veyl's composure faltered, her cheeks warming. "I'm not… I don't typically wear dresses like this."

"That doesn't surprise me." A faint smile curved his lips. "Do you still feel as though you're at sea?"

"I do." The change of subject let her breathe normally again. "Is that common?"

He nodded.

"I wondered if something was wrong with me, though it is finally fading." She touched the shell in her hair. "There's a meaning to these, isn't there?"

The smile faltered. "Every one represents a memory, an emotion, a person."

"And this one. What did it represent?"

"It's a token I once gave to the woman I loved, before the Devastation took her."

His answer sent a charge of conflicting pleasure and unease racing through her. "Why did you give it to me?"

He looked into her eyes, letting his silence stand like a shield between them.

Veyl took a few steps closer, a wild fluttering in her chest. "You were thinking of kissing me when you put it in my hair. What stopped you?"

"You were my zenyal," he murmured, reaching out to brush a lock of her hair behind her shoulder. "I didn't want that bond compelling you to do something you didn't truly want to do."

The zenyal bond. Was that what she had felt when she almost kissed him that night? If so, why did she still feel so inexorably drawn to him now that it was gone?

Her heart raced faster, a rush of light-headedness making the room spin out of focus around them. "I'm not your zenyal anymore," she whispered.

His fingers came to rest along her neck, his thumb gently tracing the line of her jaw as he leaned in. Veyl met him halfway, her lips touching his, a molten heat racing through her.

His hand moved back into her hair and she parted her lips, inviting him to deepen the kiss. She could taste the mead he had been drinking on his lips and tongue as he accepted. His other hand slid around her waist to the small of her back, his touch lighting sparks along her skin through the thin fabric of the dress as he pulled her closer. The solid strength of him was as reassuring as it was arousing when she pressed against him.

Veyl breathed him in, savoring the taste of him, the hardness of his body as she slid her hands around to his back. He pulled her in tighter, his touch awakening a desperate longing in her. Kissing him was nothing like kissing Jaysen had been. It was intoxicating. Her longtime familiarity with Jaysen had made it simple and safe. If anything, this was the opposite. Though an unexpected rapport had been building between them on the ship, Kyril was still mostly a stranger. Arguably an enemy who she had alternately hated and felt sympathy for over the course of their voyage. At this moment, whatever they were to each other, she wanted him to have her. All of her.

He ended the kiss, bringing his hand back along her jaw far enough to place his thumb lightly over her lips, as if to stop her from kissing him again. Or perhaps to stop himself. He touched his forehead to hers, his eyes closed, his breath coming a little faster than a few seconds ago.

"This can't work. They won't let me be with you, Veyl." He brushed his thumb slowly across her lips as if memorizing the shape of them before moving it away.

"Doesn't what you want matter?" She asked in a breathless whisper, yearning to experience more of him. "If this *is* what you want."

"It is." He kissed her again. A warm, sweet kiss that sent an ache spreading through her chest. It felt like a kiss goodbye. Then he shifted away, not quite enough to fully separate them. "I'm going back."

For a second, his words left her confused. Then their meaning sank in. Veyl pulled completely free of him, the intoxicating desire driven out by a rush of dread and anger. "To Pandrea? You can't. Haven't you destroyed enough lives?"

"It's not up to me. I have my orders."

No. She couldn't let this happen again, and not only because of the Vanrians who stood to suffer from it. "You caught us by surprise the first time. If you go back there, they will be ready for you. My people will destroy you."

He walked to the table and downed the last of the mead in his mug in one swallow. "We're not going to Vanris."

She shook her head. "I don't understand. Where then?"

"There was more to our agreement with Sarket than I told you." He filled the mug and took another long swallow before going on. "King Thrasser promised that, if we returned, he would give us the people stationed at one of the Vanrian military bases in southern Sarket, near the coast."

Panic and fury brought a different flush to her cheeks. "No! You'll be helping him with whatever plot he's hatching against my country. My family and friends. I will not let you do this."

"You can't stop it, Veyl. I need to do this for my people."

"Does telling yourself that give you a clear conscience? It isn't enough to steal my people from their homes. Now you're going to help Thrasser hurt the ones you haven't taken too." Energy crackled through her, spreading out into the room.

"Don't try it. You know Ceris will turn it back on

you. I don't want to see you hurt."

"What do you think will happen if you harm my people?" She yelled the question. He was right, though. The wave dancer would protect him and potentially hurt or even break her in the process. She fought back the ability, struggling to contain her rage. Maybe there was another way to deal with this.

"Don't you see? Thrasser is using you to do his dirty work. If my country wasn't as powerful as it is, he wouldn't be trying to hide behind Thaelis. This will never end well. If you genuinely don't want me or your people hurt, then you must not go to Sarket. Sail to the border where Vanris meets the Crimson Break. Tell my people what Thrasser is doing."

He arched a brow. "You just told me your people would destroy us if we went there again."

"Then take me with you. They won't attack you if I am there."

He exhaled heavily. "They would never allow me to leave the port with any Vanrians on my ship. You in particular."

His rational tone sparked more anger, but she pushed it back. He was at least hearing her words. Now if she could only get him to listen to them. "Take Jaysen then. Tell the council you want to use him as a guide. He has extensive knowledge of Sarket and Vanris. It's a reasonable request, and my people know him. He can protect you."

"Listen to yourself. You're asking me to betray my country."

"No." Her throat tightened, and she had to swallow before she could continue. "I'm begging you to help me protect mine. I am their khesran."

He closed his eyes for a second, giving a small shake of his head. When he opened them again, he said, "Not anymore."

Her voice trembled when she spoke this time. "You can keep me here until the day I die, but I will always be their khesran. Always. Please help me protect them."

The slightest softening in his silver-blue eyes offered a glimmer of hope until he turned his back to her. "I can't."

A low whine came from Ceris. Heartache filled the space that passion had occupied mere moments ago. Veyl untied the end of her braid and removed the spiral shell. After setting it on the table, she left the house. The two guards were talking when she emerged.

"Can we please go back now?" She dropped the words between them like stones too heavy to carry.

Seeming to sense the change in her mood, they escorted her to the house the council had assigned to her in silence.

It took Veyl a long time to fall asleep that night. Anger and hopelessness kept her awake. Whenever she started drifting off, their kiss slipped to the forefront of her mind, sending her into a new spiral of confused emotions. Eventually, exhaustion and a reasonably comfortable bed won out, and she succumbed to sleep.

Someone brought food again in the morning. A fresh pair of guards who had apparently replaced Mardi and Quillon in the night watched her eat and took away the utensils again when she finished. Around noon, another set of guards arrived and entered the house without knocking.

"We have orders to move you to a different location."

Veyl eyed them with open suspicion, a poor night's sleep and the constant replaying of her encounter with Kyril in her mind starting her off with her hackles up. "Why?"

The guard who had spoken gave a disinterested shrug. "The council didn't give us that information."

Veyl gathered the few articles of donated clothing she deemed worth holding onto and followed them into the streets. The morning was warm but overcast, the threat of rain fitting her mood. They escorted her to a home a few blocks away that appeared suitable for a larger family. When one guard knocked on the door,

Ahrin answered.

Veyl dropped the bundle of clothing and threw her arms around him, helpless to control the wave of tears that burst forth. His rough return embrace was painfully tight, and she loved it.

A moment later, Iyvalin's arms encircled them both. "You're finally with us," she choked out through her own tears. "I'm never letting go of you again."

Veyl didn't try speaking. She just reveled in the feeling of their arms around her. It was a little taste of coming home, one that amplified her desire for the family she had unwillingly left behind.

"Are they moving you in with us?" Gannon asked from somewhere next to them.

Extracting herself from Ahrin and Iyvalin, she turned to face him. Lorek was with him. The latter still looked paler than normal and a bit gaunt, but his smile had some energy behind it now. He stepped past Gannon and hugged her.

"I owe you my gratitude," he murmured in her ear. "If you hadn't gotten them to bring Gannon when you did, I'm not sure I'd have survived that journey."

Veyl kissed his cheek. "I'd never let that happen."

When she moved away, Gannon took Lorek's place, pulling her into a brief embrace. "Thank you," he blurted awkwardly.

They were making it particularly hard to stop her tears. She stepped back and glanced around at the four of them. Her guard from Etrion wasn't with them, though, as guilty as she felt about it, that wasn't what concerned her most. The guard was at least Vanrian.

"Where's Jaysen?"

Before any of them could answer, a familiar voice spoke up behind her. "I was told to let you know your prince left with Kyril's fleet this morning. My brother's choice of words, not mine."

Veyl turned to face Kitria, hope sparking to life in her chest. "Did he say anything else?"

Kitria considered her for a second, her silver eyes narrowing with a hint of wariness. Then she held out her hand, the spiral seashell resting on her palm. "He said you forgot this."

The spark became a flame. Could he have decided to do what she asked after all? The burning hope felt like a cruel tease, but he *had* taken Jaysen. It was at least possible.

Veyl took the shell and met Kitria's eyes, still uncertain. "Why are they moving me?"

"My brother argued for it with the council yesterday afternoon. He told them it would work out better for everyone this way. They didn't want you with your guard, however, given the former power differential in that relationship, so they moved her elsewhere."

Knowing that Kyril had advocated for her even before she visited him last night made the flame within flare brighter still. Veyl pulled the tie out of one braid and affixed the shell on it. "When is the council going to have me speak with the others?"

"He said not until tomorrow." A certain mistrust remained in Kitria's stance and gaze when she gestured to the house with her chin. "I asked for food and drink to be delivered. It should be here any minute. Go spend some time with your companions."

"Thank you, Kitria." Veyl inclined her head slightly, unsure how else to express her gratitude.

"I just hope he knows what he's doing," Kitria muttered before stalking away.

Two of the guards departed as well, leaving the remaining two to join the one who had been standing outside when they arrived. A single guard for a home that had four people in it and two guards for her. How she earned those extra guards, she wasn't sure. It wasn't as though more bodies would make a difference if she used her ability on them, but it didn't really matter at the moment. Whatever made it easier for the council to feel like they had some control would pass for now, especially if it meant she could be with her friends again.

Ahrin picked up the garments Veyl had dropped and Iyvalin took her hand, leading her into a comfortable, if modestly sized, living area. A couch and two chairs upholstered in gray and white brocade sat on either side of a simple, white-stained wood table. Iyvalin had barely settled on the couch, positioning Veyl between her and Ahrin, when a trio of Qwilki arrived with two baskets, one containing basic fare of roasted vegetables, bread, and cheese, and the other holding five mugs and two pitchers, one with mead and the other with what appeared to be a juice of some kind. The three were polite and apologized several times for the interruption before leaving them.

Once everyone had settled, Gannon pointed to the shell in Veyl's hair. "So, what is that about? Are you adopting their culture now?"

Veyl touched the token, trying hard not to sink into the memory of Kyril's embrace. What would happen to him if he tried to communicate with someone in Vanris? Would Jaysen be able to protect him? Would he even attempt to do so? If she had realized they would send the fleet out again this soon, she might have insisted on talking to Jaysen last night, though there was a distinct possibility that they wouldn't have allowed it.

"It's nothing."

"It was his," Ahrin said with too much confidence, eyeing the spiral shell. "The ahnkreth leading the fleet that brought us here. I saw it in his hair."

"You can't possibly remember a detail like that," Iyvalin objected.

Veyl drew a deep, bracing breath. She had lied to

them by omitting her real reason for wanting to go to Deepwater, an adventure that led to them getting into this mess. Did they all realize that now? Had Iyvalin or Jaysen told them? Regardless, she could see nothing to be gained from misleading them again.

"He's right," she said, earning all their stares.

"That seems like a rather intimate gift." Gannon's bold glower demanded an explanation.

She glanced around at them. They had spoken several times over the latter part of the journey to Dagony, but always with Thaelian eyes on them. Her interactions with all the other Vanrians had involved reuniting them with their tehnaaks, ensuring they had help if they were having problems like seasickness, explaining what she understood of why the Thaelians captured them, and encouraging cooperation, at least for the time being. The more personal matters she normally might have discussed with her friends she left out of those conversations, given the circumstances. That included the fact that she was a mind-crafter after all, though Jaysen had known, and might have shared that information during his time with them the previous day.

"Did Jaysen tell you what happened when they caught us in Deepwater?"

"Us?" Gannon's tone was sharp enough to startle her. "You two were together when they came?"

That wasn't a secret she expected Iyvalin to keep for her. Not after all that had occurred since that night. Apparently, she had been mistaken about that.

She subtly squeezed Iyvalin's hand to let her know she appreciated her discretion, even if it led to some awkwardness now. Then she told them everything, or almost everything. She began by explaining how Niskenya had created the tehnaak bond between her and Jaysen that was severed when she was sixteen—a revelation they seemed to feel clarified some of her temper around that time—and how it reformed sometime during the negotiations in Balarus or their meeting in Deepwater only to be severed again by Kyril's Bondmaker, who replaced it with the zenyal bond. She told them about the awakening of her ability, her efforts to fight Kyril before establishing an uneasy truce, and what she knew of the agreements he had made with Thrasser. As much as she aspired to be transparent with them, she deemed it prudent to leave out her intimate encounters with Jaysen and the Feral ahnkreth, as well as her attempt to feed herself to the ji'ikyan.

"I knew there was something more between you and Jaysen. I just always thought it was romantic." Gannon flopped back on the couch as if freed of a substantial burden.

Veyl wasn't about to correct him. Besides, her intimacy with Jaysen had been more a product of curiosity and familiarity than desire. She hadn't discovered until recently what it felt like to truly desire someone. Why couldn't her fickle heart yearn for someone rational, like Ahrin or Lorek, or... She considered Gannon a moment and tossed that option aside.

"Are you joking?" Iyvalin was staring at Gannon as if he had said the sun was green, her mouth slightly open as she shook her head. "Your lifelong goal of luring Veyl into your bed should be the last thing on your mind right now."

Gannon's face lit a rosy red. "I haven't—"

"Don't even try to deny it, brother," Ahrin interrupted. "You're about as subtle as a mace."

Lorek snorted a laugh. "What? It's true," he defended when Gannon turned his glare on him.

"You're lucky you're still recovering, calloch," Gannon grumbled.

Ahrin snapped his fingers to get their attention. "What we should focus on is whatever Thrasser is trying to achieve and how we're going to get word back home to warn them."

Iyvalin lifted her hands in a gesture of helplessness. "We can't, can we? It's not as if we can go borrow a ship and sail merrily back across the ocean."

Veyl cleared her throat, and they all turned to her. She absently twisted the shell in her hair. "I went to speak with Kyril last night. I asked him to go to the border of Vanris and the Break to warn our people about Thrasser."

"That bastard's never going to help us." Gannon punctuated his words by guzzling the rest of his mead and slamming the mug down on the table.

Veyl pushed back against her growing frustration with him. "That's what you might believe, but I told him to take Jaysen with him so he could help convince our people to listen. Kyril refused last night, but you heard what his sister said. He took Jaysen with him when he sailed this morning."

The spark of hope in Iyvalin's eyes matched the one that flickered cautiously in Veyl's chest. "You don't think he's going to try it, do you?"

"I can't be certain, but he convinced the council to move me here with you and gave me this." She lifted the spiral shell. "It must mean something. It feels impossible, but there's a chance."

Gannon's eyes narrowed. "What were you doing with him last night that made him so eager to earn your favor?"

"Gannon!" Iyvalin shouted. "We're all in this mess together. If you can't rein in your Break-blasted jealousy for a few hours, you can go to your room."

Ahrin spit out his drink.

Gannon popped to his feet. "The company might be better there."

"Sit down," Lorek demanded, grabbing his teh-naak's arm.

Veyl hoped no one noticed the burning in her cheeks. "The council wants me to speak with the other Vanrians that were brought in before us," she said, eager to move away from talk of Jaysen and Kyril. "They want me to convince them to cooperate the way our group has."

"That could end up working in our favor. If you can get us all united," Ahrin said, "we might stand a chance of fighting this later, but we need to be patient and careful. They have Evokers, although they don't appear to have a lot of them."

"Can we afford to be patient?" Lorek let go of Gannon's arm once his tehnaak sat down again. "If King Thrasser is planning something, we might not have much time to head him off."

"We have no way to know if he's been plotting for a while, and the Thaelians just fit nicely into his plan, or if their arrival provided an opportunity he couldn't pass up, and he's still figuring the rest out." Veyl struggled to keep her voice steady, trying not to let her own fear slip out as she spoke. "Regardless, we will do the best we can here for now. Given the crossing time, it could be two weeks or more before we know if Kyril tried to reach out to Vanris or not. Until then, we build connections, encourage the illusion of cooperation, and learn everything we can about their naval complex and how to sail their ships. A lot of the people they captured lived in those coastal towns. Some will know their way around a ship. We need to find out who they are and help them gain the trust of our hosts."

"So, you are making a plan to escape this place?"

She met Lorek's eyes. "I *will* find a way, but I want to get all our people home if I can, and I could use your help."

Iyvalin gave her hand a squeeze. "You can count on us."

A brief silence fell between them, the weight of all that had happened and the enormous task they were assigning themselves hanging over them. Ahrin shifted to the edge of his seat on the couch, turning to look at Veyl. He picked up a slice of sticky yellow fruit, but didn't eat it.

"You're really a Frightener?" His tone made it more of a statement than a question, a touch of hesitation in his cadence.

"I am." A chill crept up her spine. Few people were comfortable around Frighteners. "Like Arhk." She tried hard to sound proud of it, but she couldn't fool herself enough to have any hope of fooling them.

"For all the terrifying stories I've heard of your grandfather, I can't recall any about him breaking a person's mind with a single attack," Gannon remarked unhelpfully.

Veyl lowered her gaze. She hadn't meant to break anyone. All she had been trying to do was protect Jaysen from Kyril's people and Kyril from the Unclean leader, as ironic as that progression was.

"Do your eyes turn black like his do?" Iyvalin asked.

"Not exactly." Veyl looked at them and cautiously drew on her ability, letting a touch of that storm crackle through her. It responded instantly this time, as easy to draw upon intentionally in the moment as it usually was to bring out without meaning to. If only she could keep it from reacting to her emotional state in such a violent way, especially considering that the road ahead promised to be a difficult one.

Gannon and Iyvalin both drew in sharp breaths.

"By the Break," Ahrin murmured, "your eyes. That's—"

"Terrifying," Lorek finished for him.

A crushing sensation pressed the air from her lungs. She clenched her teeth against that pain. Why was the one person who saw any beauty in her ability a man she should despise? She released the storm and got up, going to the window to peer out into the street.

Somehow, despite what he had done and how volatile many of their interactions were, she had connected with the Feral ahnkreth. As perplexing as it was, she missed the zenyal bond that tied her to him and to Ceris through him. But he and the wave dancer were gone, put out to sea with Jaysen and heading into a situation that would be dangerous at best if he attempted to do what she requested. If he didn't, if he helped Thrasser instead, she would hate him for it. But how could she expect him to aid Vanris when his culture raised him to see them as the enemy, and doing so would require betraying his own council? She was a Break-blasted fool for asking.

"Veyl?" She startled at Ahrin's hand on her shoulder. "You know we don't care what you are, right? We love you, and we will fight with you."

"Fight who?" She watched a Qwilki woman walk by with three children chasing each other around her and laughing. The woman smiled and shook her head at the trio.

Ahrin's brow furrowed, his head tilting to the side, as if her question puzzled him.

Veyl turned to face the other three. "Come with me to the market."

"Will they let us go?" Gannon asked, his words barely understandable around a mouthful of bread.

Veyl breathed a laugh, glancing at Ahrin. "I have a hard time believing that you two are from the same family sometimes, let alone twins. But yes, to answer your garbled question, Gannon, I think they'll let us go so long as the guards accompany us."

Iyvalin gestured to the tray. "You've barely eaten, Veyl."

A fist of sorrow squeezed her stomach. "I'm not hungry. Maybe a stroll will help me find my appetite."

Gannon grabbed another piece of bread as they got up. Veyl opened the door, pleased to find that Quillon and Mardi had replaced the previous shift, and without a third. Was that because she had behaved herself, or did they simply not have enough guards to manage all the "newcomers" they had?

"How can we help you?" Quillon asked, his cheery demeanor lifting her mood a little.

"Could we visit the market?"

"Of course." Mardi stepped away from the door to let them out. "Town center or port?"

Veyl almost looked over her shoulder to ask the others, then thought better of it. This was another small opportunity to build connections. "What would you two recommend?"

Quillon didn't hesitate. "The port. It's got a positive, casual energy I'm sure you'll enjoy."

"And your brother's shop," Mardi teased. "Come on. We'll take you there."

When they arrived, the port market was bursting with activity. Crews from a couple of fishing boats were bringing in their catches, which kept them away from Quillon's brother's shop for the time being, much to his disappointment. Several individuals in uniform, from the fleets that guarded the fishing boats according to Mardi, were helping with the work, joking and laughing with their civilian counterparts. Most of the larger, permanent shops on the waterfront handled seafood or provided supplies for ships. Across from those shops, two rows of smaller, freestanding booths offered everything from clothing and jewelry, or the raw materials for making such things, to food prepared fresh on the spot.

People stared as they wandered out into the market. That didn't come as a surprise. Given their guard escorts and the fact that they were all pure-blooded Vanrian, it was readily obvious that they weren't locals. A cautious hope peeked through in response to the many tentative smiles they received. The suspicion blossomed in Veyl that most of these people didn't know what awful crimes the two fleets committed to bring them here. How could they look at them this way if they did?

They were passing a booth displaying a selection of sweet and savory pastries. The scent woke up the hunger that had eluded Veyl earlier, making her mouth water. She stopped, taking a step closer before remembering that they had no currency to purchase with. This wasn't a real shopping adventure, merely a chance to leave the house and discover the city.

The older Qwilki woman behind the counter had graying dark hair and eyes that crinkled into slits when she smiled, the moderate points of her ears suggesting at least a little Vanrian blood somewhere in her lineage. "Try one," she offered with an accent so thick it took a second to understand what she had said.

Veyl held up her hands and took a step back. "Oh, thank you, but we haven't anything to pay with."

"Unfortunately," Ahrin muttered behind her. "Those smell amazing."

"Please." She gestured to the selection, her warm smile encompassing all of them. "We can never repay the gift you bring us simply by coming here. Have one. Each of you."

"I'd take one if I were you," Mardi encouraged. "Hila makes the best pastries in all Thaelis."

The older woman colored at the compliment and waved a dismissive hand at the guard. "Flatterer. You can both have one too if you like."

More certain than ever that these people didn't understand what the council had done to bring them here, Veyl accepted a pastry and inclined her head to the woman. "Thank you, Hila."

The other four followed her example. Then Mardi and Quillon each took one, though Quillon tossed some uniform chips of what looked like polished gray stone on the counter before they walked away. A very different currency from what they used in Pandrea, assuming that's what it was. Veyl was still savoring the first bite of the delicate pastry, delighting in the way it melted on her tongue, when another shopkeeper stepped into their path and bowed. He had dark blond hair and more refined features that suggested a stronger helping of Vanrian lineage.

"Pardon me for interrupting your day, but I wished to offer you each a token." He opened his hand to reveal five little shells worked together with beads in different delicate configurations. With his other hand, he picked one up and held it out to Veyl. "This one matches your eyes and the necklace you wear. They are designed to be worn in your hair, but you could place them on a bracelet or pendant if you prefer."

Unease prickled along the back of her neck. How awful must the traumatic events these people lived through have been for them to be this eager to have them here? Had they all lost that much? For a moment, she considered refusing, until Mardi moved around behind the man and made a gesture with one hand, encouraging her to accept the gift.

Veyl mustered a warm smile and took it from him. "It's beautiful, thank you."

She stepped back, letting him make his offerings to the other four. While they made their selections, she looked around and drew upon her ability, reaching out tentatively to the people in the market. For a second, nothing happened. Then images swept in, some of the pits of dead like she had seen in Kyril's fear, but also of people dying in beds, bodies burning in piles, homes once full of joy now standing empty. The images carried with them an overwhelming burden of sorrow. A gasp escaped her, tears spilling onto her cheeks as she tried to find her way back out of that whirlwind of death and loss.

A hand clamped on her arm hard enough to hurt, breaking her free of the rising storm. She met Mardi's eyes, startled by the anger in the woman's glare.

"What do you think you're doing?" she growled under her breath.

Veyl looked around. The mood throughout the market had changed, becoming subdued now, and several people wiped at fresh dampness on their cheeks. Some sniffles and a soft sob reached her in that unnerving silence. The sound of the docks creaking as the water moved them seemed louder than it had a moment ago.

"I'm sorry. I didn't mean to upset anyone. I just wanted to understand."

"That better be all it was," Mardi answered through gritted teeth. "This once, I will let it pass."

As if she could do otherwise. Veyl lowered her gaze, wiping at the tears on her own cheeks. "I truly am sorry."

Mardi released her arm. "Come on."

The two guards led them past the shopkeeper who had given them the tokens, who now stood staring into the distance, looking lost and crestfallen.

"What happened, Veyl?" Ahrin asked in a whisper.

She drew a breath, glancing around at the sorrow she had pulled to the surface with her careless actions. How raw they all were. How broken deep inside. Yet they were trying to move on with their lives. To smile and be greater than their losses.

"We can't hurt these people," she whispered back.

## CHAPTER TWENTY TWO

A general discomfort hung over their group for the remainder of that day. It was one thing to tell them she was a Frightener and show how it manifested in her eyes and with the hint of a coming storm in the air. It was something else for them to see her depress the mood of a market full of people with so little effort. The distance that lingered between her and the others throughout the evening forced Veyl's thoughts back to Kyril. To how impressed he would have been with the level of control she had shown, though he would have undoubtedly admonished her for using her ability on unsuspecting people that way.

But she couldn't do that. She couldn't turn to the Thaelian ahnkreth for comfort, and not just because he wasn't there. She couldn't allow herself to need him that way.

Mid-morning the next day, Councilor Shyall arrived with four guards to take her to the prison to meet with the "newcomers" from the other fleet. Mardi and Quillon, who had arrived earlier to take over the day shift again, came inside to stand with Veyl as if they were now there to guard her, as opposed to guarding the councilor from her. She recognized then that her captors were playing the same game she was, trying to build a connection and trust. Well-meaning or not, it was a form of manipulation. In her case, the goal was to gain more freedom and opportunities. For the two guards, they were acting most likely on the orders of the council to help bring her more under their control. All she could do was hope the two were a little like her, unable to fake friendship without at least some genuine feeling seeping in.

One of Shyall's guards carried in a bag with additional clothing options for them. This time, Veyl was happy to find some black pants and an ivory shirt of reasonable quality in the selection that fit her relatively well. The idea of going to speak with the other Vanrians in a Qwilki style dress didn't strike her as the best way to earn their trust. She was a khesran in Vanris, but she was also a soldier and scout. The new outfit let her draw confidence from that training at a time when what she was being asked to do left her shaken and uneasy, a state that wouldn't help her convince the other captives to integrate with this society.

Veyl talked Shyall into letting her companions come to assist in the effort, using the argument that one lone Vanrian, even if she had been their khesran, would be less compelling than five sharing the same message.

When they walked out into the street, Veyl moved up almost beside the councilor, staying a half-step behind to at least give the illusion of deference.

"Might I ask you something, Councilor?"

"Feel free." Shyall's weary tone didn't match her sentiment.

"Why are you going about it this way? Why not try asking for my country's help?" It was a question Kyril had attempted to answer, but the reasons he had given were unsatisfactory at best.

"We do not want our country flooded with your armies and leaders trying to make us part of your civilization. We prefer to remain hidden and rebuild the society we fought so hard for in the past without Vanris forcing its ways upon us."

"But taking people from their homes like this is wrong." The way Shyall lifted her chin and stared hard ahead told Veyl that the morality approach was going to gain her nothing. Fortunately, that wasn't the only direction she could take the conversation. "You must realize what you risk by sending Ahnkreth Kyril back to Pandrea. My people will be watching for their return. They could easily seize his ships, take his navigational charts, and come to Thaelis in force. I don't think you understand how great our population is, and how many mind-crafters we can throw at this problem. Vanris will not sit passively by and let you take our people."

"It is fortunate then that Ahnkreth Kyril is approaching well south of your former country, isn't it? The Sarketi king promised him more Vanrians and, most importantly, more mind-crafters if he returned. If we are to build our society up again after the Devastation and restore our bloodlines, we need those people. If the Vanrians on Pandrea are as numerous as you say, they should recover rapidly from these losses."

A storm started crackling through Veyl, and she hastily forced it down. If anyone deserved to have their mind broken, this woman did for her blatant lack of compassion, if nothing else, but she had to be smart about this. "I'm not certain you understand exactly what you've done. You took the only daughter of the khevarin and khemron of Vanris. Do you honestly believe they'll let that go without a fight?"

The woman stumbled a step, unnecessarily smoothing out her robes after she caught herself. "King Thrasser assured Ahnkreth Kyril that Vanris's primary military weakness is their lack of naval power. I doubt they have the ships necessary to search the oceans blindly for you for long."

Veyl smirked, forcing confidence and a hint of smugness into the expression. "Thrasser isn't wrong about that, but he left out some pertinent information. Vanris may not have a large naval presence, but our Delaphinian allies do. I promise you my parents will call upon those allies."

"And how much will they dare commit to the sea if Sarket moves against them on land?" The councilor struck the heart of Veyl's fears with those words as they stopped outside a long, low building that took up the space of three blocks. The woman faced her. "Now, will you and your companions work with us to get the rest of your countryfolk free of their imprisonment, or should I have the guards lock you in with them?"

Veyl drew a deep breath, finding it increasingly difficult to hold her ability in check. The woman was unfortunately right. If Sarket made their move soon, her parents would have to focus on protecting their country. She hoped Thrasser wasn't ready for that yet. "We will work with you. I have no desire to see my people suffer here. I am only offering you these insights because I don't want to see yours suffer, either."

"How charitable of you." Shyall gestured to the double doors leading into the building. "Shall we?"

The first detail that struck Veyl when they entered the prison was that it was unexpectedly bright inside. Large skylights installed throughout the halls supplemented the many lit sconces with natural light. None were in the cells themselves, as they would provide a tempting route for escape attempts, but the curve of the roofs and the angles of the architecture around those openings brightened the halls considerably, even on a partly overcast day like this one. That, at least, made it marginally better than the prison below the palace in Etrion.

They had housed the Vanrian captives four to a cell,

none in their pairings. The first order of business, with Shyall's reluctant agreement, was to gather everyone's name and those of their tehnaaks. Once that was done, the guards began rearranging cell assignments to put them together, assuming both halves of the pairing had ended up in Thaelis. The effort earned Veyl and her companions the immediate gratitude of those involved. It improved Shyall's reception as well when she presented herself as a vocal proponent of the process, though she waited until after it became clear the reunions were going to have the desired effect to do so.

As people were being moved to new cells, Veyl and the other four were permitted to speak with them in small groups. She had discussed with the twins and their tehnaaks in advance that they would not mention the possibility of future resistance today. This was entirely about introducing themselves and developing a sense of who these people were. Even amongst their own countryfolk, there could be some who would expose any subversive plotting to the Thaelians to better their personal situation. They had come up with careful questions and conversational topics to help them pick out anyone who might fall into that category.

Watching the reunions of separated tehnaak pairings, occasions full of smiles and tears, made it hard to focus on being shrewd and calculating. They had little choice, however, if they wanted to bring people together in the task of finding a way home. A lot of the "newcomers" in the prison were so exhausted and disheartened that having their tehnaaks back and seeing their former khesran walking unfettered among them was enough to make them more tractable. Although it made a few angrier.

"You've joined them!" a woman screamed at Veyl early in the day. "It's a good thing they captured you. You'd have been a lousy ruler!"

A short time later, a man had called her a Thaelian whore for working with their captors. Unfortunately, he had been a sailor back on Pandrea. They needed people with his expertise. Maybe if she let one of her companions talk to him next time, they would have a better outcome. But, if the day's efforts had shown her anything, it was that the game they were playing, hoping to unite the Vanrians in trying to escape Thaelis, would be slow and difficult, with a high risk of discovery. The kind of coordinated effort that could take months of careful planning and fall apart at the whim of a single malcontent. She hoped Kyril had gone to warn Vanris, because they would never make it home in time this way.

When they left the prison, Veyl was tired. Not physically as much as mentally and emotionally. Every reunited pairing was a victory of sorts, but the overwhelming, almost suffocating fear and rage they all shared left her resenting the time she spent urging them to cooperate. On the next visit, she hoped a few whispered words at opportune moments, hinting that this was not the end of the fight, would alleviate some of that. What if she was wrong, though? What if they never escaped this place? Or what if they simply grew accustomed to their new lives here and stopped trying?

Outside, Shyall left them in the hands of the two guards after a few words of praise and headed back to the Great Hall. A sound caught Veyl's attention as they moved away from the prison complex. The distinct clack of practice swords striking against each other. She turned toward the noise, the twins and their tehnaaks pausing with her. Mardi and Quillon stopped the instant they realized their wards weren't following them anymore.

"The barracks aren't far from here," Quillon offered in explanation.

"Can we go look?" The eagerness in Iyvalin's voice

expressed a longing they shared for the normalcy of the education and daily training they had left behind.

He shared a glance with Mardi, who shrugged. "No harm in it, I suppose."

They walked another block into the midst of three long low structures similar in outside appearance to the prison they had just left. In the middle of the buildings, a large group stood gathered around one of several fenced practice rings where two individuals were moving through a series of fighting forms, exhibiting various combat techniques. As they approached the ring, Veyl noticed familiar elements in some of the forms. They were strikingly similar to those she had learned while growing up, the original Vanrian foundations still evident in them. She also recognized Ahnkreth Eavara as one of the two providing the demonstration. Maybe they shouldn't be poking around there after all.

The two engaged in mock combat stopped as Veyl was about to encourage her group to leave.

"Veyl!"

She cringed inwardly and faced the ring again.

"That is your name, right?" Eavara's tone demanded a response as all eyes turned to them.

"It is."

"Why don't you demonstrate your country's techniques for us? I'm happy to be your opponent for that purpose."

All too happy, it seemed. The audience looked on with honest curiosity in their regard. Only Eavara appeared to harbor any open hostility toward them, or rather, toward her specifically.

Before Veyl could answer, Mardi stepped forward. "That is ill-advised, Ahnkreth Eavara. The councilors want no competition between locals and newcomers until things are more settled. Besides, Veyl is not wearing the proper armor for such activities."

"What competition?" Eavara took the practice sword from the other combatant. "This will merely be a demonstration." She held the blade out toward Veyl, hilt first. "Armor isn't necessary."

"Don't," Ahrin whispered in her ear.

Veyl walked forward, ducked through the slats of the fence, and reached for the proffered practice blade.

When her hand closed on the hilt, the other woman held onto it and leaned in. "Let's see if you're more than a pretty face, *Khesran*," she hissed before releasing the weapon.

So much for any hope that she meant to play nice. "I prefer sword and dagger," Veyl said, calmly checking the balance of the training weapon.

Eavara gestured to the man she had been doing her demonstration with. He collected two practice daggers from a table full of weapons and brought one to each of them before ducking out of the ring.

This was unquestionably a bad idea, but she suspected Eavara would seek more opportunities to confront her because of the token Kyril had given her and because she was instrumental in helping him make a better impression before the council. At least this was a somewhat controlled environment, and she had seen enough to know the ahnkreth wasn't as skilled as some people she had trained with. Merrin, Darro, her grandfather, and her father, especially when he had Niskenya engaged, were some of the best fighters in all Vanris. This woman was capable, but she didn't have that level of skill.

They moved out into the center of the ring. Veyl settled her sword in her right hand and the dagger in her left, letting Eavara make the natural assumption about which one she would be most adept with. Aside from the quality of her mentors and her ability to fight equally well with either hand, Veyl had a third advantage. An emotional one. While she had a general, though admittedly potent, dislike for the ahnkreth as one of those who had wronged her country, this was deeply personal for Eavara. All it took to verify that was touching the spiral shell in her hair before she sank into a fighting stance. The tightening of the other woman's jaw and the flare of hatred in her eyes in response to the gesture confirmed exactly how personal it was. Still, Veyl had one significant disadvantage she needed to stay mindful of. If she got hit, even with a practice blade, having no protection meant it was going to be painful and possibly do damage.

The initial engagements were tentative strikes, meant to test each other out. Veyl didn't try landing a hit in those first few minutes. Whether or not Eavara put forth genuine effort, Veyl never let her get close enough to make contact.

The intensity changed abruptly when Eavara lunged in with a flurry of alternating dagger and sword attacks, trying to unbalance Veyl before making a swift feint and thrust. Veyl was ready for it. She expected a burst of aggression to come eventually, and the deception was predictable on the tail of that overwhelming assault, given how much the other woman disliked her. Lessons with her mentors raced through her mind while she danced through a series of parries, blocks, and evasions, countering only when a clean opportunity presented itself.

Eavara was fast, comfortable with her weapons, and angry. Each failed strike fed into that emotion, making her attacks increasingly powerful and dangerous, but also more reckless. Veyl miscalculated on a block, and the other woman caught her dagger just right to twist it out of her hand, sending a sharp pain through her wrist.

"That's enough," Mardi shouted from the sidelines.

Eavara ignored the guard, eyes glinting with satisfaction as she went for a thrust into the resulting opening. Keeping the sword in her right hand, Veyl narrowly evaded the blade. She grabbed the ahnkreth's forearm with her left hand, twisting it behind her as she spun around her and rammed one knee into the back of her near leg. When Eavara's knee buckled, Veyl wrenched the arm up hard before releasing it, throwing the other woman further off balance. The ahnkreth stumbled, struggling to catch herself. Veyl stepped back and kicked her in the side under one flailing arm, sending her to the ground hard enough that her sword went flying.

Before she could get up, Veyl moved in, settling the point of her practice blade at the woman's throat. Someone ran up beside Veyl and yanked the weapon from her hand, tossing it aside.

"Let's go." Kitria pointed forcefully toward where the others still waited at the edge of the ring. "Now!"

Veyl took a couple of steps in that direction, then she stopped and turned back to Eavara, ignoring Kitria's hiss of frustration. The ahnkreth was sitting up. Undoing the end of one braid, Veyl pulled the shell off and held it out to her. Anger faltering before confusion, Eavara hesitantly accepted the offered token.

"You have more right to this than I do. All you had to do was ask for it."

With everyone's eyes on her, Veyl let Kitria lead her out of the ring. The young woman walked hastily away, gesturing for the others to follow them. When they were out of sight of the training grounds, she turned on Veyl.

"I actually thought my brother was exaggerating when he asked me to watch out for you because he feared you would get into trouble within the week."

Veyl pointed back toward the barracks. "I didn't start that. Ahnkreth Eavara called me into the ring."

"And you were quick to oblige her." Kitria shook her head. "Do you not realize the council is afraid of you? If not for your lineage and our need for more mind-crafters, they would have eliminated you already."

What she said might be true, but it didn't make sense given how they were treating her. "If they're so blasted afraid, why are they letting me have this much freedom?"

Kitria glanced at the two guards. Seeming to take their silence as permission, she lowered her voice and said, "They are giving you the illusion of freedom to keep you from turning your ability against us. You haven't stepped outside a residence once without at least two of our best archers and a Dampener tailing you, ready to end you if you do anything to prove that you're too great a threat to keep around. Defeating Eavara like that was not the cleverest way to put their minds at ease."

A shiver moved through Veyl. Did that little stand between her and the fatal point of an arrow? "Then why haven't they made me zenyal to someone the way your brother did?"

The others were watching in curious and, judging by their expressions, concerned silence. Iyvalin placed a supportive hand on Veyl's shoulder.

"Kyril is our strongest Feral, and Ceris protects him in ways another type of beast could not. We don't have anyone else with that kind of built-in defense in Dagony right now. A zenyal bond may allow someone to inflict pain to control you, but if you attacked them with your ability, you could still potentially damage their mind or break them the way Kyril said you broke Illis and the Unclean. Without a wave dancer to block you, a hidden assassin is more effective than a zenyal bond. I got the impression from my brother that the council is hoping to find you an appropriate tehnaak to see if that pairing can help keep you in line. They—"

"That's enough, Kit," Mardi said, the gentle firmness in her words hinting at a longtime familiarity between them. "You've already told them too much."

"Veyl?" Iyvalin squeezed her shoulder.

Her heart still beating hard from the exertion in the ring, Veyl made a slow circle, moving away from Iyvalin's hand. She scanned the people in the area, all of whom seemed intent on their own business. Were any of them the assassins waiting for her to make that one wrong move? Her gaze shifted to the buildings. Or were the ones watching her hidden away, ready to shoot her through an open door or from a rooftop garden?

"Veyl." It was Gannon this time. He took her hand, drawing her attention to him. "They're not going to hurt you. We won't let them."

She met his blue eyes, seeing, for a moment, a glimmer of the kindness that made his brother typically the more pleasant of the two. Offering a sad smile, she touched her fingertips lightly to his cheek. He drew back, his lips parting in surprise at the contact.

"I appreciate the sentiment, but you won't be able to stop them." She pulled away from him and started walking.

After a few seconds, she heard the others following. Even the guards didn't try walking with her, choosing instead to stay a few feet behind as she wove her way through the streets toward the call of the ocean. It beckoned her, teasing her with its strength and beauty, its freedom, and with the two men it had taken from her, carrying them back to the home she longed for. She hadn't noticed before now how much she could hear it if she listened for those waves crashing in the distance. The salt tang was ever-present on the breeze here, the hint of cool mist in the air becoming more prevalent as she sought it out.

The street she ended up on came up over a low rise, the cobbles gradually giving way to a sandy path that cut between two low bluffs covered in tufts of long, coarse grass. Ahead, beyond a stretch of smooth beach, curling waves swept in toward the shore, racing up the sand with a hissing sound. The constant roar of water moving in unfathomable quantities, rolling and crashing upon itself and the beach, filled the air. A light wind caught at her hair, bringing the side without braids forward into her face.

Every Vanrian she had seen in the prison survived many of the same awful experiences she had. They lost families and homes, and a few even lost their tehnaaks in the fighting before being taken. She didn't have it any worse than anyone else, did she? But if that were true, why did she feel so desperately alone and detached from them? Was it because everyone was afraid of her now, including her friends? The council feared her enough that her life hung in a delicate balance, its thread waiting to be cut at the slightest provocation. That knowledge brought a sense of hopelessness with it.

Kyril had known about the assassins and Dampener when she spoke to him. If his sister did, he must have.

Veyl continued down the slope out onto the beach, walking until the edge of the surf came up over her shoes, lapping at the ankles of her pants. Standing there, she raised her chin, opening her arms to embrace the wind. The salty dampness on her cheeks now wasn't entirely from the spray carried off the top of the waves.

She had lost before. More than once, her tehnaak had been taken from her, but these people had stripped her of everything. The endless expanse of water sending its cool caress around her feet made it possible for them to do so. Its rolling waves were the walls of her prison. The uncrossable gulf between her and all that her heart ached for.

And yet, even knowing that, as she stared out at that awesome expanse, drawn to its mystery and power, she loved it.

## CHAPTER TWENTY THREE

A heavy mist hung in the air when they visited the market at the docks the next morning. Veyl had encouraged the adventure. She didn't want to make any purchases, and without funds, there was little point in spending time there, particularly since their needs were being provided for them. Her primary goal was to get the others to stop brainstorming ways to improve her situation. They couldn't make the council fear her less, nor could they teach her how to control her ability better. They might be able to help her earn the council's trust through working with the prisoners, but that wouldn't change what she was or stop them from trying to choose a tehnaak for her.

Would they even give her a say in the selection?

She had a tehnaak. Yes, the bond had been severed again, but there was a reason she hadn't taken another pairing after Jaysen left Vanris. He was her tehnaak and would continue to be for as long as they were both alive. Almost getting into a romantic entanglement with him had been misguided, something made more apparent by whatever it was she felt for Kyril, but Jaysen was still her best friend and the only tehnaak she wanted.

At Quillon's recommendation, they stopped by the fish market that belonged to his brother. While the others wandered around within, Veyl found herself stalled at the entrance staring into a water-filled tub with live fish swimming in it, listening to the guard and his brother talking. It wasn't their words as much as the ease of their banter and the underlying affection that captured her attention. It was like listening to her father converse with Jethan or other members of his tehsheyn. She had often wondered if the strength of their bonds made her mother jealous, though she always insisted she was happy he had that close group of companions in his life. If only Kyril had something like that.

Not Kyril.

"Jaysen," she murmured, amending her wayward thoughts.

"What?" Ahrin walked up beside her, poking curiously at an odd, shelled creature trying to escape a crate full of others like it.

"Nothing."

His brow furrowed when he looked at her. "Do you want to go back to the house? You seem tired."

"I—"

The blare of a horn from out in the port cut her off, followed immediately by a second and third blast answering it from somewhere on shore. Veyl and her companions hurried after Mardi, Quillon, and his brother as they raced outside.

"What is it?" Gannon asked.

"Ukhen'kya, the Unclean," Mardi replied, thick dread tightening her voice.

Veyl's gut twisted. As they stood there, Thaelians, most in uniform, sprinted across the docks, heading for some of the smaller ships. She watched for a second, until she spotted Eavara coming up one street, shouting orders as she ran toward the docks. Glancing around them, Veyl saw panic in the eyes of merchants now hurrying inland from their booths. These people were terrified.

She ran after Eavara, ignoring the guards and Iyvalin

who shouted after her loudly enough that it pulled the ahnkreth's attention their way. The woman's scowl could have spoiled milk. She didn't slow her pace as Veyl raced up beside her.

"What do you want?" she demanded.

"Take me out with you."

Eavara scoffed and kept running.

Veyl grabbed her arm. "I'm a Frightener, let me help."

Eavara stopped and faced her. "Why would you want to?"

"Because I don't want to see these people hurt. And if you find that hard to believe, remember that some of my people are here now too."

Eavara hesitated a second, glancing at the two guards and her four companions as they came rushing up behind her. "All right." She held a hand up in front of Mardi when the woman moved a step closer and shook her head. "Only you, Khesran, and you had best not make me regret it."

She broke into a run toward one of the smaller ships. Dodging Gannon when he reached for her arm, Veyl bolted after her. Memories of the Unclean she had seen and what she had been told about them set off a chill that moved through her shoulders and chest, but she wasn't about to sit back and let those monsters hurt anyone here. Not Vanrian, Thaelian, or Qwilki. Not if she could do anything to prevent it. Besides, Frighteners had little purpose outside of battle. This was her chance to see if she could turn a burden into an asset.

Veyl lifted the skirt of the sea-green Qwilki dress she had put on that morning, silently cursing her choice of garments and the sandals that made her footing less sure on the docks. Somehow, she sprinted up the gangplank without falling into the dark water below.

"What kind of mind-crafter are you?" she asked,

following the ahnkreth aboard.

*Shut up and stay out of the way!*

At least that answered the question. She was a Speaker.

Obeying the orders Eavara had shouted into her head, Veyl moved up by the port side railing near the bow and tucked herself out of the way, watching the chaos of activity. Except it wasn't really chaos. Every person had their purpose, and somehow, despite how they raced about the ship, they never got in each other's way. She didn't have to ask why they were using the smaller vessels. These would be faster and had banks of oars on the deck below to get them moving in the calm water. In a matter of minutes, several ships were clear of the docks and on their way.

"Where are they at?" a man called.

"Heading for Mukyeny," someone shouted back.

Mukyeny. Was that a town on this island? Another island? This might be an opportunity to learn more about the area, assuming it didn't all go terribly wrong. She knew next to nothing of combat at sea and, if she were to be honest, not a great deal more about fighting as a mind-crafter. Still, she had never made a habit of avoiding conflict. Was there any reason to change that now when she might be able to help?

She moved closer to the bow, peering ahead for any sight of their target as more ships left the docks to join them. A light breeze had come up, not strong enough yet to chase away the low clouds hanging over the water, obscuring their view. They swung out and south, speeding along within sight of land. Then the shoreline started falling away, becoming lost in the mist that dampened Veyl's hair and collected on her skin. The rowers on all the ships stopped rowing, letting the hulls glide through the water.

After a few minutes of eerie quiet, the mist began thinning out, giving them patches of greater visibility.

Then they broke out into a wide, clear swath. Up ahead, Veyl could see boats coming out of another low cloud bank, at least twenty of them heading perpendicular to their route toward land a distance off on the starboard side. Without a single command spoken, at least not out loud, the rowers started rowing again, and the boats surged forward. The Ukhen'kya spotted them, and she could hear shouting on the distant vessels as they changed course, turning with surprising agility to face the oncoming fleet. Though outnumbered by more than two to one, the Thaelian ships didn't slow.

The writhing serpents of dread in Veyl's gut slithered up into her throat, making it more difficult to breathe. Despite that, some questionably sane part of her rejoiced at being on the water again.

"How close do you need to be?"

Veyl startled. She had been so focused on the Ukhen'kya she hadn't noticed Eavara coming up beside her. "I'm... not sure." She tried drawing on her ability, but the storm didn't answer.

The ahnkreth scowled at her. "You have no idea what you're doing, do you?" Veyl bristled at her condescending tone, but Eavara gave her no time to respond. "You'd best figure it out fast."

The woman moved away, her focus jumping around to the other ships, each of their crews rushing to respond to her unspoken commands when she looked their way. It was unnerving how silently the fleet operated. Archers stood on each of the vessels, aiming as the first of the Ukhen'kya ships swept in. The Thaelians loosed their arrows, and the Unclean raised painted wooden shields they had set beside them on the decks, blocking most of the projectiles. A few made it through, finding homes in flesh. Unnervingly, there were no screams of pain, just answering silence as the lead boats came up alongside them at speed. A group of Unclean, no less than twenty at a glance, leapt across with axes and hand claws flying, and now they did make noise, a shrieking that sounded more animal than human as they lashed out at anyone they could get within range of.

*Now would be a great time to use that ability of yours.*

Standing a few feet away, Eavara cast a cutting glance at her and drew her sword.

Before Veyl could come up with some biting retort, she noticed more ships emerging from the mist behind the last of the smaller Ukhen'kya vessels that were racing their direction. These were the larger Thaelian ships.

"Is that—" The blare of a horn interrupted her.

Eavara's eyes widened. "Kyril's fleet!"

"But I thought they were heading to Pandrea."

"They were. All that matters is they're here now. We'd be fools to complain, but we'll have to take care of ourselves. Some of the Unclean are already bringing their ships around to engage them." She sneered at Veyl. "Can you do anything, or did you just come along for the ride?"

Veyl cast a glance around at the chaos. The Unclean were on Eavara's ships battling her crew, several of their agile vessels coming back around to drop more fighters while boats that hadn't reached them yet were now rushing toward Kyril's fleet. "With so many of them on the Thaelian ships, I don't want to—"

"Fuck this up? Yes, I'd strongly advise you not to hit the wrong fucking people. Your pretty Sarketi boy is over there with Ahnkreth Kyril. If you want him to live, I suggest you figure it out now." With that, she spun and raced into the fray, hacking open the back of the first hide-covered, painted Ukhen'kya she reached.

Veyl's gut twisted when clothing and flesh split before Eavara's brutal strike, baring muscle and bone. She wrenched her gaze away from the chaos behind her and peered at the other fleet. She could see Kyril's flagship.

He would be on that ship. Jaysen might be too. How did Arhk do it? How did he attack fields full of enemies without affecting his own people?

An Unclean warrior staggered past her, blood spurting from a wound in his neck as he fell over the railing. In the distance, one of their ships was racing up alongside Kyril's flagship. Heart pounding, Veyl called upon the storm. This time it responded, filling her with its lightning. Trying not to think about the fight behind her, she reached out, cautiously at first. Fear swept in and she suddenly understood. The fears of the Thaelians were almost universally the same, the trauma of the Devastation still fresh in their memories. The Ukhen'kya were different.

Chaos answered her touch upon their minds. Flashes of loved ones being slaughtered like cattle, of being butchered themselves, people being forced to consume their own limbs, confusing fears of rejection, of starvation, of blackened crops rotting upon the fields. Beneath the horror—the raw, unrestrained terror that responded to her touch—there was a single thread. A sense of sameness connected them all. She had thought it was the Devastation that gave unity to the presence of the people of Thaelis, but that wasn't it. It was their culture, their heredity, and who they were as a society that linked them. That had to be how Arhk managed it.

Veyl focused on the common threads uniting the Unclean. Her stomach turned, souring with the bombardment of monstrous imagery as she sought more and more of them, reaching as far as she could push her ability. At the same time, she embraced the storm, letting it expand within her. When she felt stretched as thin as a spider's web, she set it free.

All awareness of time and her place in it became lost as the tempest swept her up in its fury, drowning her in their deepest fears, even as it turned them into a weapon against her enemies. She was distantly aware of a chorus of wails and screaming that now filled the misty morning. Her knees hit the deck, pain lancing through her skull. Dropping forward into her hands, she threw up until there was nothing left. Her limbs trembling, she crawled away from the mess she had made before falling on her side and curling up on the hard deck, pressing her palms over her ears to block out the noise. Her head felt as if someone was smashing a mace into it repeatedly. Different voices rang out, then. These sounded more like they were making declarations of victory, but they were still too loud and painful.

"Look at them flee!" a voice shouted from only a few feet away.

Veyl squeezed her eyes shut, pressing her hands down harder over her ears.

Someone set a hand on her shoulder. "You glorious imbecile. You're lucky you didn't kill yourself."

Eavara?

"You! Help me get her up."

Hands took hold of her arms and pulled her to her feet. When Veyl tried to open her eyes, blackness swallowed her.

*

The pain in Veyl's head was gone when she awoke. An odd sense of mental fatigue had taken its place. Still a distinct improvement, no matter how she looked at it. Cautiously, she opened her eyes. She was in her bed back in the shared house and Lorek sat in a chair next to it, fiddling with some interlocked pieces of twisted metal that he appeared to be trying to disentangle.

"It's a puzzle." He caught her by surprise with the fact that he noticed she was awake despite his intense focus. "How are you feeling?" He set the object on a side table and faced her.

"Cautiously alive," she answered. "What happened?"

"None of us were there, but they say you blasted most of the Ukhen'kya fleet with your Frightener ability and sent them running like cats with their tails on fire. Those whose minds you didn't break outright, that is."

Veyl shuddered. "Is it bad to be afraid of yourself?"

He breathed a small, humorless laugh. "Under these circumstances, I think it might be healthy to have a solid dose of wariness for your ability, at the very least."

"I didn't..." Those dread-snakes squirmed back to life in her gut. "Did I hurt anyone I shouldn't have?"

His eyes narrowed, his manner growing more distant, guarded. "The answer to that is arguably subjective, but you only hurt Ukhen'kya, if that's what you're asking."

Would he have preferred it if she had broken the Thaelians too? Her companions hated them more than she did, but they hadn't seen what her ability had shown her. If they had, they might understand the empathy she felt for them, despite what they had done. They might see why she had been determined to protect the people of this place. Enough so that she had once again nearly broken herself doing so. Learning to manage her ability needed to become a priority.

"Apparently, the council wanted to isolate you after they heard what you had done. How's that for gratitude?" He was watching her intently now, as though searching for something. "The crews of the two fleets fought them on it. For the time being, you remain at least as free as you were before that performance."

As free as anyone being followed around by assassins could be. "Even Ahnkreth Eavara's crew?"

He nodded. "The woman still doesn't seem to like you, but she was willing to defend you for your efforts on their behalf."

"How do you know all this?"

"That young woman, Kitria, came by to check on you about an hour ago. She was in the Great Hall when they were arguing over you."

Veyl's pulse quickened as the next question crossed her lips. "And Ahnkreth Kyril's fleet joined the fight, didn't it?"

His brows rose a fraction. "Yes. As Kitria explained it, they were on their way back to Pandrea when they spotted the Ukhen'kya heading toward Thaelis in force and gave chase. They lost sight of them in a storm but caught up again as they were making their final approach."

"Is Jaysen with them?"

"Kitria said he was with the crew." Lorek stood. "You've been out about three hours. There's food if you're hungry."

The prospect of facing her friends after everything that had happened did nothing to help settle her gut. "I hate to ask, but could you bring me something in here and tell the others I need some time to myself?"

Lorek nodded. "While you're thinking things over, maybe consider who you are and who you're fighting for. Word will reach the other Vanrians that you helped defend our captors. It could make them more hesitant to work with you," he said before walking out.

True to his word, Lorek brought her food and left her alone. As she ate, she considered what he had said.

She could argue, not without basis, that she was looking out for the Vanrian captives by protecting the Thaelian islands. The Unclean presented an extreme danger to anyone they got hold of. What she had done might gain her the gratitude of their captors as well, which had the potential to give her greater influence with them going forward. And yet, it had made them more fearful of her too. Now her own people would suspect her motives and probably be wary of her ability as well. Ultimately, she had wanted to fight the Ukhen'kya for everyone in Thaelis. No one deserved to be butchered like livestock—sacrificed and consumed in the name of some twisted religion.

Veyl got up and changed into another Qwilki dress, this one a light gray without the spatters of someone else's blood dried on it. Drawing a deep, bracing breath, she walked out to the main room. The other four were sitting around the table, talking softly. They fell silent when she entered and watched her with varying degrees of unease. After a few uncomfortable seconds passed, Iyvalin got up and walked to her.

"Are you all right?" she asked.

"I haven't been all right in some time." Veyl stepped around her and strode toward the door. "I'm going for a walk. I need to clear my head."

Ahrin stood. "Would you like one of us to come with you?"

"No. Thank you. Not this time."

As she left the house, Mardi joined her, leaving Quillon to watch over the others. The woman didn't say a word, but simply strode along a half-step behind, letting Veyl keep her silence. With the guard following, she wandered to the side of town the port was on, continuing south past the market and docks, answering the call of the ocean. Or was it something else this time? Whatever it was, she felt compelled to come this way, and she was content to let that sensation guide her for now.

South of the harbor was a manmade breakwater of heavy stone that extended far out into the water, helping to further protect the docks from the ocean's temper. Continuing past that, she followed a curving path heading out onto the beach. A few other people, most of them in pairs, wandered the sandy stretch beyond the rocks, but it was the man who stood directly ahead with his back to her who captured her attention and made her heart beat faster. The steady breeze that had chased away the mist caught his blue-streaked black hair, blowing it back from his face.

Ceris came racing out of the surf and sprinted past his companion, heading straight for her. The wave dancer bounded up to her, spraying damp sand on the skirt of the dress in his enthusiasm. Water sheeted off his strange coat, leaving him surprisingly dry to the touch when she crouched down and sank her hands into the thick, silky strands. His joyful, full-body wagging brought a smile to her lips, the warm moisture of his tongue on her cheek drawing out a light laugh.

Kyril stayed where he was, though he had turned enough to watch them, his expression carefully neutral. The fluttering in her chest when she rose and walked toward him was at odds with the unease in her gut that made her faintly nauseous again. When she stopped beside him, Ceris racing past them both to charge back into the water, he faced out toward the ocean.

"You returned." Veyl silently chastised herself for stating the obvious.

He glanced at Mardi, who had followed her out. "You can leave. I'll escort her back to the house."

Mardi inclined her head. "Yes, Ahnkreth."

When she was gone, he stood silent for a moment, his gaze tracking the wave dancer as the beast frolicked exuberantly in the surf. He didn't look at her when he finally spoke.

"I had to try stopping the Ukhen'kya. We spotted them from a distance. Their heading made it clear where they were going and, in those numbers, I feared it would be a massacre if they made landfall."

She drew a breath, trying to ease the weight of her next question. "Was their attack a retaliation for the ship we encountered on the way here?"

His jaw tightened. "It seems likely."

All because he had refused to give them Jaysen, and the confrontation had turned violent. Veyl watched Ceris, trying not to let the distance in Kyril's manner unsettle her. "Are you going back out?"

"Yes." A few heartbeats passed in silence before he continued. "Thanks to you, my crew suffered few losses today."

Her chest tightened. "But you did have losses?"

"There's a reason we try not to engage with the Unclean, especially now, when we are still recovering from the Devastation. They fight like wounded animals. They are fast, unpredictable, and fierce. I've seen one throw himself upon an opponent's sword just to get close enough to rip into them with those claws they favor. Fighting them always has a price. That's why Thrasser's offers of alchemical weapons and more mind-crafters were so attractive. One of our primary goals is to restore our numbers so we might deal with the Ukhen'kya."

She drew a breath, smelling the salt of the sea. The wind cast her hair into her face, and she brushed it away. The distance he continued to hold between them expanded the ache of loneliness that had taken deeper root with the reserved reception from her companions when she woke up. Why had she let herself believe Kyril would be the one to see only the good in what she had done out there? Her ability was unpredictable and dangerous, like the Ukhen'kya. Few people could ignore that. Still, at least she had a chance now to learn what his intentions were. She couldn't let her misguided emotions stand in the way of that.

"Will you take Jaysen with you again?"

Kyril glanced up and down the beach, then he turned toward town. "We should talk somewhere else."

Ceris sprinted out of the water to join them as they headed inland. Veyl mirrored Kyril's silence along the walk to his house. When they got there, he opened the door for her, letting her in ahead of him. She stopped in the center of the front room, unsure whether she should take a seat or if this might be too brief a visit for getting comfortable. Remembering the kiss they had shared in that space expanded the loneliness that threatened to drown her.

The door shut, and she heard him coming up behind her.

"Do you have any idea how extraordinary you are, Khesran Veyl?"

## CHAPTER TWENTY FOUR

The unexpected admiration in Kyril's voice, a considerable transformation from the wary distance he had maintained on the beach, crashed through the careful walls Veyl was trying to establish around her emotions. She held her breath for a moment, afraid to look at him and risk discovering that she had imagined his words.

His hand came to rest on her arm, and a gentle pull encouraged her to face him. She gave in to it, turning to look at him. He reached up to caress her cheek. The desire in his eyes warmed her through, sparking an inappropriate, giddy pleasure that made her feel almost drunk.

Veyl touched the now empty braid in her hair, suddenly self-conscious of the missing token. "The shell…" she trailed off when he smiled.

"It's fine. I heard about your *demonstration* the other day with Eavara. I wish I could have seen her face when you defeated her." He chuckled, a soft, throaty sound that sent a shiver through her, then he leaned in and kissed her.

Veyl closed her eyes, savoring the sensation of his lips against hers, the touch of his hand as it slid around her waist to her back, and the way time seemed to slow even as her heart raced faster. When he drew away, she met his eyes, all too willing to fall into those stormy, silver-blue depths.

"Is this what you wanted to talk about?" She flushed a little at the breathlessness of her voice.

"There were other things." He lightly traced her lower lip with his thumb. "But I'm willing to continue this conversation if you are."

Veyl nodded, her thoughts spinning apart when he kissed her again. His hand pressed against her back, moving her closer. A molten heat swept through her. Passion set a fire inside her she had no idea how to quench, but she had a feeling he did. She helped him pull off his shirt, putting the strength she had only felt in him up to now on full physical display. It wasn't at all disappointing. The symbols of a ke'hanoath she had thought didn't exist wrapped around his sides in three rows, following the lines of his ribs and meeting in the center to taper down between his well-defined abs. The sight of those stylized symbols in a deep blue that matched the added color in his hair was reassuring somehow.

He took her hand and led her through a doorway into what turned out to be a simple bedroom, as neatly organized as the cabin on his flagship. Drawing her close, he claimed her mouth again in a deeper kiss, his hands sliding partway down her thighs to gather the material of her skirt. When he reached the hem, he lifted, pulling the dress over her head, leaving her with only her thin undergarments to provide coverage. His gaze moved over her, the heat and desire in it stirring a desperate yearning for his touch. She watched, lips parted, pulse racing, as he discarded his pants, every inch of him defined with lean muscle. Then he took her in his arms and lowered her to the bed.

A sudden flash of panic constricted her chest. She tensed, and he stilled in response, leaning on one arm half over her, his other hand resting at her hip.

"What is it?" he murmured.

"I've..." She met his eyes, embarrassment burning in her cheeks. "I've never done this."

"You don't have to now if you don't want to."

"But... I do," she whispered.

"You're sure?" He still didn't move.

"Yes." Her throat tightened around the word.

He leaned closer, a wicked grin curving his lips. "What was that?" He moved his hand from her waist, deftly sliding it beneath her undergarments. His questing fingers finding the join of her thighs, releasing a burst of pleasure with a few skilled strokes.

She gasped, the intensity of sensation his touch drew forth making her tremble. "Yes," she breathed.

With another throaty chuckle, he leaned in and kissed her again, taking control of her with his exquisite attentions. The world outside his walls disappeared as Veyl willingly gave herself to him.

*

Afterward, she lay pleasantly exhausted with her head on his chest, wishing she could pretend theirs was a normal, acceptable relationship. A mountain of problems piled up around them that needed to be addressed, but the moment she asked the first question, this comfort, this warm sense of belonging, would disappear.

His arm rested around her, his eyes closed, though she didn't think he was asleep. His profile was striking, a quiet power hanging about him even in repose. She reached up, tracing her fingertips along his neck near the healing wounds from the Unclean leader's claws.

Kyril opened his eyes and turned to look at her. "I can see by your expression that our peace is about to end."

She breathed a soft, sad laugh as he shifted onto his

side to face her, brushing a lock of hair away from her mouth. His careful touch ignited fresh longing, though it was less for physical coupling at that moment than for the simple, welcome warmth of his body pressed against hers.

She ran her fingers through one of the dark blue streaks in his black hair. "What is this?"

"It's a Qwilki sailor custom. They make the stains from components found in the ocean depths. The Qwilki believe that wearing them in this way tricks the ocean into welcoming and protecting you as one of its own creatures."

A smile crept across her lips. "Do you believe that?"

Pleasure sparked in his eyes in response to her smile. "I believe I've never lost a ship."

Her smile faded. "Will you take Jaysen with you when you head out again?"

"I will. The council doesn't want your tehnaak bond reforming. That, combined with his knowledge of Vanris and Sarket, made it easy for me to convince them to let me take him."

Veyl propped her head on her hand. "And what will you do when you get to Pandrea?"

His expression turned serious, and he drew a deep breath, rolling onto his back to stare up at the ceiling. "You're right about what we did to you being wrong. Before I met you, your people were little more than a folktale for me. For most of us. We didn't honestly expect to find you. When we did, our orders regarding how to handle it were clear. The council insisted that creating a link between our people would bring about the end of the Thaelian way of life. We were to take what we needed without establishing communication, as the most innocent of words might give your people hints on how to locate Thaelis." He paused, drawing a deep breath. "But you aren't a folktale. You are as real and warm and deserving of happiness as any of us."

He looked at her, sliding a hand along her cheek and back into her hair. "I will try to warn Vanris. I feel like I owe you, all of you, at least that."

At a loss for words, Veyl shifted closer and poured her gratitude into a deep, lingering kiss. When she drew back, he stared at her like he wanted to do much more, but he made no move to follow through.

"Does my being a Frightener bother you?"

"No," he answered immediately. "What you did out there this morning was incredible. Your ability is extraordinary, although using it the way you did could have killed you. Promise me you'll be careful. I convinced Eavara to offer her Dampener to help train you. He's one of our more powerful mind-crafters. It may be a different ability, but he should be able to work with you on control. Just remember that anyone you use it on won't have a wave dancer to protect them like I do. The council fears you, now more than ever. Please, don't give them a reason to believe they must eliminate that threat."

Fear constricted her chest at the idea of facing them after what she had done. "When will you leave?"

"Possibly as soon as tomorrow morning. My crew and I are on duty, awaiting orders."

Veyl lay down against him, resting her head on his chest again. "I wish I could go with you."

He was silent for a few seconds, then he moved out from under her and got up. "I wish you could too, though I suspect not for the same reasons."

Trying not to become distracted by the lean, muscular body displayed in full glory before her, Veyl reached out and caught his arm. "Why do you say that?"

He pulled away from her and picked up his pants. "Because I know better than to think you would have ever been with someone like me in your country. You are a khesran. Even my people believe you're too good for me."

Veyl got up from the bed and caught his arm again, stopping him before he could get dressed. "If you think for a minute that I slept with you to convince you to warn my people, you're wrong. I would never trade myself that way. I truly would love to sail the ocean with you, just to be out there on the waves by your side. If there were any way..." What? What would she do if there were a way?

He considered her, his head tilting slightly in a manner that reminded her of Ceris. "Do you mean that?"

"Yes, you idiot. I should hate you, but I don't. I feel..." She stopped herself and drew back from him.

This time he reached out to her, his hand coming to rest against her jaw, his thumb caressing her cheek, igniting sparks of longing in the wake of that gentle touch. "What do you feel?"

She looked up at him, the sting of tears threatening. "I feel more at home in your arms than I've ever felt anywhere."

Kyril stared at her for a moment, his eyes searching hers, then he pulled her in and kissed her. Veyl kissed him back, a desperate, demanding kiss that stirred an obvious physical response in him, given their lack of clothing. He broke the kiss, and she threw her arms around his neck with a cry of surprise when he picked her up.

"What are you doing?"

Mischief sparkled in his eyes as he laid her on the bed. "Taking you home."

*

Veyl sponged off the scent of their lovemaking before Kyril and Ceris walked her back to the house later. The sun was setting by then. They had spent most of the afternoon together. How she was going to explain that to the others, she wasn't sure. The separation being out in the open forced them to maintain left room for her to question her choices without the distraction of being immersed entirely in him. She walked alongside him, keeping at least a foot between them with the wave dancer's help, and reminded herself repeatedly not to reach for his hand, no matter how she longed for the re-assurance of that contact. Her thoughts raced through the potential repercussions of what they had done. What would happen to him if the council learned of their in-timacy? To her? If she discovered a way to escape this place, how was she supposed to leave him behind? How would her parents feel if they knew she had given herself to any man, let alone the one who had taken her from them?

What if she became pregnant?

"Kyril," she hissed, staring at the house she shared with the others, now only four buildings away. "What happens… What if I… You know." She gestured vaguely toward her lower abdomen.

Kyril chuckled. Not at all the response she expected. "It took you long enough to get there."

She gaped at him for a second. Was he really laughing about the prospect of her getting pregnant? "This isn't funny."

"Don't worry. I was merely curious to see how long it would take you to get there on your own. I planned to have something sent by the house discreetly in the morning, assuming you would welcome such."

"Yes. Please." She blew out a breath of relief.

"If by any chance it doesn't arrive, reach out to Kit, and she'll help you." His lips quirked up in an amused smile, and he chuckled again. "I didn't know I could captivate a woman thoroughly enough to make her forget how children are made."

"Calloch," Veyl grumbled under her breath, hoping she wouldn't have to ask Kitria for help. It was bad enough that *someone* would have to know she had been sexually intimate for him to arrange the delivery. Bringing it up with his sister would be torture.

He stopped walking, and she faced him, unnerved by how serious his expression became.

"Veyl, promise me you won't draw more attention to yourself. I can't protect you when I'm not here. Eavara grudgingly agreed to offer some assistance after what you did for us today, and you can always turn to Kitria, but there's not much they can do if the council decides you're too dangerous to keep around. Don't let that happen. I can't lose you too."

Too.

The way he had lost most of the people in his life. And yet he would. If she escaped, they would both lose someone again. Even if she remained, the council had plans for her that didn't involve him. Maybe right before he left on a risky mission wouldn't be the best time to point out how impossible this was.

"Worry about yourself. You're not exactly heading out for a stroll in the garden. What happens to me will matter little to you if you're dead."

He stared at her in stern silence, the expression reminding her how terrifying he had seemed when she first saw him in Deepwater. Fierce and dangerous, the accent she now found attractive feeding into her fear and confusion at the time. She brought her hand to her throat, remembering how he had turned his strength against her. But she had been a folktale made flesh then, one that had just broken the mind of someone close to him. How dramatically and unexpectedly their relationship had changed.

His gaze followed the movement of her hand, his

brow furrowing. The muscles in his jaw tightened. "I'm sorry—"

"Don't. There's no point now. What matters is where we go from here."

He reached into a pocket and drew out the spiral shell he had given her before. "I don't suppose you would consider wearing this again?"

Veyl drew back, confused. "I returned that to Eavara."

"While she may not like you, she appreciated how you risked yourself for Thaelis. She decided that you having it might not be such an insult to her sister's memory after all."

Though that pleased her, she didn't accept the token. "Is it wise for me to wear this, considering the council wouldn't approve of us?"

One corner of his mouth twitched up in a faint smirk. "They can't stop me from declaring my interest."

Veyl grinned and accepted the shell. She wanted to do more. To be exact, she longed to put her arms around him and kiss him again until someone dragged her bodily away, but she occupied herself with working the shell back onto one of her braids instead. They were pushing their luck with how long they had been standing there in the open. Could her companions see them from the house? The guards most certainly could.

"Veyl!"

Jaysen's voice made her pulse jump. She turned to see him walking up the street beyond the house in the company of two guards. Her first inclination was to run to him. The second was to stay with Kyril, knowing she might not see the Feral ahnkreth again if they sent him out in the morning. Although, she might not see Jaysen either, since he would go as well.

She met Kyril's eyes.

"Go. I can't imagine they'll let you speak to each other long, given their concerns around the tehnaak bond reforming. Just don't fight them when they say you're done."

"I won't." Unable to walk away without any contact, she reached out and touched his arm. "If you leave before I see you again, know that I will be awaiting your return. I promise."

She caught a brief glimpse of his smile as he turned to walk away. Ceris licked her hand, then followed Kyril. A pang of loss pierced through her when they parted. She spun and jogged to Jaysen, letting his enthusiastic embrace be a balm to that fresh wound. Wrapping her arms around his neck, she buried her face against his shoulder and clung to him for a moment, the comfort of familiarity enfolding her along with his arms.

"I didn't think they were ever going to let me see you," he murmured, keeping hold of her until one guard pointedly cleared her throat.

Veyl moved back from him, watching with a spark of unease as he looked her over, his gaze lingering on the necklace he had gifted to her before shifting to the shell she had just put in her hair. Had he been close enough to see Kyril give it to her?

"Do you want to come inside?"

"Want to? Yes, but they said I could only have a few minutes with you. Some nonsense about not letting—"

"Our bond reform. I know."

He scowled. "I guess I'm not approved tehnaak material."

Veyl countered his irritation with a fond smile. "You never were."

The scowl softened. "A fair point, I suppose. Was it really you who drove those Unclean bastards off?"

Veyl nodded, warily watching for any hint of fear in his regard.

"The overflow alone was terrifying. I almost felt sorry for them. You are a full-fledged mind-crafter now.

I guess that changes some things." Before she could ask what it changed, he glanced over her shoulder, his brows pinching. "What did Ahnkreth Kyril want with you?"

The question reminded her they had very little time, but they also had two guards standing too close for her to tell him the truth. "You're going back out with him, aren't you?"

"Unfortunately, yes."

She needed to tell him to help Kyril without exposing the Feral ahnkreth's intentions to the guards. That wouldn't be easy. "Cooperate with him, Jaysen, please. It will work out better in the end. I promise."

His gaze shifted to the spiral shell again. "Tell me you haven't given up," he whispered.

Matching his volume, she said, "I haven't. I need you to trust me."

He reached out and brushed the backs of his fingers along her cheek. "I do."

A flicker of disquiet ignited in her chest. Their relationship had nearly gone down a different path that night in Deepwater, but she had taken it upon herself to change that course. How would he feel if he knew that? If he learned who she followed that path with in his place, there was little chance he would react well.

"Time to move," the female guard stated.

Jaysen spun toward the woman and both of guards reached for their weapons. "You Break-blasted—"

"Jaysen!" Veyl grabbed his arm.

He faced her, frustration and exhaustion making him look older than he was. "I'm tired of being forced to leave you," he said in Pandrean Common.

Hope dared to peek through the dark worry in her chest. They could speak languages these people couldn't. Why hadn't she thought of that? She responded in kind. "I know, but I truly need you to trust me on this. Kyril is going to help us warn Vanris about King Thrasser's betrayal, but he needs your help to do it."

Jaysen shook his head, his nose wrinkling as if he had smelled something unpleasant. "Why would he—"

"Enough!" the male guard shouted, raising the curved blade he carried in threat.

The guards in front of the house were heading over now as well. Mardi and Quillon had been relieved during her absence. She didn't recognize these two.

Jaysen set a hand on her shoulder and placed a kiss on her forehead. "I trust you, Veyl." He stepped back from her and let the guards guide him away.

One of the house guards walked up beside her as she watched the others escort Jaysen down the darkening street. She was tired of being parted from him too, and of being afraid for her country and family. She was also sick to death of other people trying to run her life and tell her who she could and couldn't have in it.

"Is everything all right, Lady Veyl?"

The guard's chosen address sent a chill through her. The councilors wouldn't appreciate it if people started giving her a title of any kind. "Just Veyl, please. I'm a little tired and hungry."

"There's food inside. It might not be hot anymore, though. We can send for more."

"I'm certain it's fine, thank you."

She strode past him and went into the house. Ahrin, Iyvalin, and Lorek were sitting in the main room, watching as she entered. Gannon, standing behind a chair, hurried to intercept her as soon as she closed the door. With a deep breath, bracing herself for confrontation, she stood her ground and faced him.

"What was all of that?" He stopped a mere few inches in front of her and pointed toward the door. "Did you spend the entire afternoon with that Thaelian bastard? We saw you tie his shell in your hair again, and the way you touched his arm before you left him like he was a friend, or something else. And Jaysen! I saw him caress your cheek! That was more than a tehnaak bond on display."

Veyl was silent, exhaustion and frustration chewing away at what little self-control she had left. She couldn't tell him he was wrong, because he wasn't, but that didn't mean she had the patience to let him yell at her about it, either.

"Leave off, Gannon," Ahrin snapped, his weary tone suggesting they had already argued over this.

"No! I want to know if you're still fighting for our people, Veyl? Because if you've changed sides, we have a right to know."

She took his arm and drew him away from the door toward where the others were sitting. When she spoke, it was in Pandrean Common, in case the guards outside could hear them. "Yes, I'm still fighting for our people. I talked with Kyril, and he's agreed to take Jaysen to Vanris to warn them about Thrasser. You should be glad I got the chance to tell Jaysen that. I *am* doing all of this to help our people. And tomorrow we can continue meeting with the other captives to devise a plan for getting out of this mess."

Gannon leaned in close enough that she could see only his face, his blue eyes brimming with accusation and some deeper hurt. "How much of yourself did you give to that calloch to buy his help?"

Energy crackled through Veyl, riding on her explosion of anger. The storm swelled to the surface, sweeping her with it as it broke free.

*She was kneeling in a council chamber in the palace in Etrion, her parents standing at the edge of the curved dais staring down on her, fury burning in their eyes. Irith stood by her father's side, snarling. Several figures sat at the table behind them, all out of focus except for one. With a wave of disorientation, she realized she was that one. The dirt and blood covered hands bound trembling before her weren't hers. They were Gannon's. This was his fear.*

*"You failed them,"* her father accused, *his voice echoing in her ears.*

*"Abandoned them on the battlefield,"* her mother added, *shaking her head in disgust.*

*"Your brother, your tehnaak, everyone dead because you're a worthless coward,"* she heard her own voice saying.

Something hit Veyl hard, slamming her to the floor. She looked around to see Gannon cowering by the side wall, his cheeks damp with tears. The front door stood open, both guards now in the room. One held two throwing daggers in his hand, the other arm outstretched as if he had already released one. Iyvalin lay partly across Veyl's legs, a third dagger buried in the muscle over her collarbone close to her neck, her agonized cries the only sound for a heartbeat. Then Ahrin dropped to his knees next to her, one hand sliding under her head, staring in horror at the blood welling around the projectile.

"It'll be all right." His voice sounded strange, tight with concern for his tehnaak.

The other guard raised a crossbow, leveling it at Veyl.

"Don't shoot!" Lorek stepped into its path, replaying a similar scene to what must have occurred with Iyvalin mere seconds ago.

Veyl slid her legs out from under Iyvalin and stood. Her heart fragmented in her chest, broken by the wrong she had inflicted on her own friends. Not even Gannon deserved this. Her ability was a blight upon them all. She had wanted so desperately to be a mind-crafter once, now she wanted nothing more than to be rid of that hideous power. It was a death sentence here, with no one to help her control it.

*I'm sorry, Kyril. I lied.*

"No." She placed a hand on Lorek's shoulder and

stepped past him, tears streaming down her cheeks as she nodded to the guard. "It's better this way."

## CHAPTER TWENTY FIVE

Please, don't hurt her." Iyvalin's voice was a pained whimper, still trying to protect Veyl despite what she had done to them.

The guard waited, not firing the crossbow yet. Lorek hurried to Gannon, helping him up and pulling him into a tight embrace before casting a chilling glare back at Veyl. The guard holding the throwing daggers reached into his pocket and drew out a small vial. He tossed to Veyl, and she snatched it from the air reflexively.

"Drink that," the guard ordered. When she didn't move, he added, "It will put you to sleep so we can safely see to your companions. We handle it this way, and let the council decide what to do with you, or we kill you now. It's your choice."

Veyl sat in a chair and removed the stopper, downing the bitter liquid in one swallow. Lorek was whispering words she couldn't quite make out to Gannon. Closer to her, Ahrin was comforting Iyvalin while she alternated between groaning and cursing under her breath. Silent tears crept down Veyl's cheeks. She didn't look at anyone, staring at the window instead until the sedative dragged her into darkness.

*

She woke in a cramped stone cell across from a blank wall. Given the length of the hall, there couldn't be room for more than two cells next to hers that, judging from the silence, were empty. The lack of lighting was enough to tell her she wasn't being held with the Vanrians from the first fleet, though she could feasibly be in another area of that building. If there were guards, they waited outside the closed door halfway down the facing wall. The cell wasn't dirty, nor was it comfortable with nothing more than a hard cot and a chamber pot for furnishings.

With no other way to occupy her time, she sat on the cot and sank deep into regret. Would her ability have ever awakened if not for that night in Deepwater? She should never have gone to the coastal town. Although, if she hadn't, Jaysen and his companions still would have, and Kyril would have had no reason to let him live. But her friends wouldn't be in this mess now. What she had done to Gannon was unforgivable. It was hard to fathom why Lorek and Iyvalin had both tried to protect her after that. A last kindness to a former friend? Or perhaps habitual loyalty to their khesran? She wasn't foolish enough to assume their actions promised her welcome among them if the council allowed her to return.

Her ability seemed to control her more often than she controlled it. That wasn't how it was supposed to work, was it? Did everyone struggle like this? Could it have to do with the power of her ability, or was there something wrong with it, given that she shouldn't have had one to begin with? Two mind-crafter children in the same family was unheard of.

Whatever the truth, she had to figure out how to keep it contained before she hurt someone else. Although, that assumed they would decide to let her live after this incident, which was anything but certain. She had proven herself untrustworthy, even among people she cared about.

It had been evening when she returned to the house. There were no windows to help her determine how long the sedative had knocked her out for. Was it still night? Had morning come? It felt like night somehow, so she tried to sleep some more. Self-reproach, dread, and a nagging hunger kept her awake for a long time, but when no-one came to speak with or check on her, she eventually drifted off.

Two days passed, as best she could tell from scant meals brought by guards who refused to speak to or listen to her. Plenty of time to miss her home and family and fret about the potential fallout of her dalliance with Kyril, among other things. Aside from the guards, no one else entered her lonely prison block. A testament, perhaps, to how much the council feared her now. They appeared content to let her rot alone. Cowards.

The sound of the cell door squealing open startled her awake sometime early on the third morning. Veyl sat up, blinking in the light of the bright lantern the guard carried, expecting another less-than-appetizing bowl of slop to break her fast. Instead, he stepped aside to let a slight, raven-haired young woman in.

"Kitria?"

She stopped. "That is my name." She looked Veyl over before holding out a bundle of cloth. "It's chilly out this morning. You'll want this."

Veyl took the offered item and unfolded it to reveal a gray cloak a little darker than the dress she still wore. "Are we going somewhere?"

Kitria drew a deep breath, as if bracing herself for something before she answered. "I volunteered to be your keeper in Dagony. I'm not supposed to let you out of my sight, so you'll be staying with me now. It should be delightfully fun," she added, her flat tone suggesting otherwise.

"They're letting me live?"

She gestured to the cloak, and Veyl tossed it around her shoulders. "Don't get too excited. I had a hard time talking them into this. Fortunately, Mardi and Quillon spoke on your behalf as well. Having a few soldiers remind the council how effective you were against the Unclean also helped. They made it clear this is the last chance they're giving you."

A chill moved through her. She hadn't expected to get any more chances, but that didn't make it easier to have the fragility of her future confirmed. "Why are you doing this for me?"

Kitria silently helped her fasten the cloak and led her out of the building. The guards permitted them to pass without interrogation. Kitria didn't speak again until they were in the street outside the Great Hall, under which it turned out Veyl's cell had been located. Two guards joined them, following a few steps behind. Veyl got the sense Kitria wasn't so much ignoring the earlier question as waiting for the right time to answer it.

"You should know that they made you zenyal again while you were unconscious from the sedative."

Veyl's stomach turned. At least she hadn't eaten yet today, alleviating the concern that any meals would make unplanned evacuations. On the downside, she was beginning to feel shaky with hunger given the scant amount of food they had provided her during her imprisonment, which wasn't at all helpful for keeping her emotions on an even keel. "To whom?"

"One of the elite soldiers they've had tailing you. It provides them another way to neutralize you should they deem it necessary, and to track you if you were to sneak off somehow."

Veyl focused for a moment, struggling to put hunger and other distractions aside. After a few seconds, she caught that sense of a faint connection. A light tugging toward some place back and to the right. For now, she left it at that. Trying to locate their hidden soldier might not be the best way to put them at ease. "Do Kyril and Jaysen know what happened?"

"No. Kyril's fleet departed at dawn the day after you visited him. The council kept this quiet. I didn't know something was amiss until I went looking for you later that morning."

"You were…" Veyl trailed off, remembering the precaution someone was supposed to be delivering after her intimate afternoon with Kyril. "Oh."

"Yes. Don't worry. If you take it within four or five days of… you know, it should still be effective."

That was a minor comfort. "Is Iyvalin all right?"

"The dagger grazed the top of her collarbone, but the damage was mostly to soft tissue. It missed all the critical veins and arteries, though the injury is going to require some rehabilitation once it's healed. Lucky for her, she's a little shorter than you."

Veyl allowed herself a small sigh of relief. "What about Gannon?"

"I won't lie to make you feel better," Kitria said. "You scarred his mind with your ability. They had to have an Evoker extract his memory of what happened. He should be fine now. Unfortunately, they also found some fragmented thoughts about trying to escape that didn't please them a great deal."

"Fantastic." Veyl groaned and rubbed her temples, her head beginning to ache with all the problems and concerns stacking up. Several follow-up questions came to mind, none of which she was comfortable asking in front of the guards. Would those fragments of thought compel them to interrogate the others? It wasn't impossible to hide things from an Evoker if you knew how the ability worked, but the right leading questions could make it difficult not to slip up.

They continued northwest toward a corner of town where a series of moderate-sized, attractive homes stood along the beach, set far enough apart to offer the residents some privacy. Kitria led them to the third house down. The first thing Veyl noticed upon walking inside was an almost life-sized, exceptionally detailed driftwood sculpture of a wave dancer frolicking in the surf that took up a corner of the main room, currently lit by sunshine coming through a skylight. The rest of that room wasn't much different from other houses she had been in, though there was a simple elegance to the furniture and its arrangement that brought a sense of peace into the space.

She walked to the statue and ran a finger along the slender muzzle of the sculpted creature. "Ceris?"

Kitria closed the door, leaving the guards outside, and joined her. "Yes. It was a gift from the tribal Qwilki elders after Ceris bonded with Kyril. Our people may have convinced the Qwilki we weren't gods, but they see being befriended by a wave dancer as a sign that an individual has earned divine favor. To be bonded to one in the manner of a Feral companion is something even greater. They don't quite worship my brother, but they have a reverence for him that many people might consider excessive."

Veyl breathed a soft laugh. "And how does he feel about that?"

"He politely tries to discourage it, and they idolize him even more for that. They bring him offerings, and he attempts to pay them back by helping the elders with chores or diving with Ceris to collect materials for their crafts. Then they turn it around and gift him items they make, like the stain for his hair and tokens of protection for him and his ships and crew. It's a bit of a maze he can't seem to find his way clear of. I honestly think it works out well for everyone involved." Kitria moved away, pointing to a crossing hallway. "Kyril's old room is at the end on the right. He doesn't stay here much these days. I doubt he would mind you using it."

Pulling herself away from her examination of the statue, she faced Kitria. "This is your family home?"

"Yes. Though we haven't much family left now." Kitria lowered her gaze and walked into the kitchen area, running her fingers lightly along the edge of the counter. She picked up a mug sitting there and held it out to Veyl. "You'll want to drink this."

Veyl walked over and took the mug, downing the bitter contents in two quick swallows. She grimaced and handed it back. "Thank you."

"You asked me why I'm doing this," Kitria said, accepting the mug. "I'm doing it because I love my brother very much. We both lost everything in the Devastation."

Veyl's chest constricted. "Did you lose your tehnaak too?"

She nodded.

"I'm so sorry."

Kitria looked away and swallowed. "The point is, all we have is each other now. I would do anything for Kyril, and, unfortunately for him, he is rather taken with you."

"Unfortunately?"

"It's nothing against you, Veyl, but unless something changes dramatically, you won't be around by the time he gets back. If you're willing to work with me, however, maybe we can figure out a way to prevent that. Right now, there is extra suspicion cast on you since their questioning of Gannon revealed thoughts of escape. Apparently, the Evoker found no evidence of your participation in their fledgling plans for fleeing here. Gannon said that was because they didn't trust you after you put so much effort into convincing the Vanrian people to cooperate on the voyage over. Not being implicated in that should help you."

It impressed Veyl that Gannon successfully hid her involvement from an Evoker, though it came as a greater surprise that he would even try to protect her after what she had done to him. Maybe there was still a chance of earning their forgiveness if she made it through this. "Will the council punish them?"

Kitria started pulling out various implements for preparing food. "Not in any harmful way. They're being kept under heavier guard for a time and won't be allowed to interact with other Vanrians until the council is confident they aren't a risk."

It could be worse. No imprisonment, just greater restrictions for a time. "Does all this mean you have a plan for keeping me alive?"

Kitria shrugged. "It's still a work in progress, but we can start by helping some people around the port market this morning. Showing an interest in being useful and gaining favor with the locals can't hurt your position. Then we'll visit the prison and see if we can get anyone there to a point where the council is comfortable letting them move out into housing and closer to integration. But right now, we're going to make something to eat."

Veyl's stomach growled at the mention of food. "I'm extremely fond of the eating idea."

"Great. Let's teach you how to make your first local meal, then."

As someone who had grown up in a palace with her needs mostly provided for her, Veyl wasn't that excited about the idea of cooking. Once she relaxed into Kitria's company, however, the process became enjoyable. They put together a dish that featured a thin-sliced, salted raw fish in a light sauce with a chopped seaweed garnish that was apparently a Qwilki staple. The other woman even let her use the knife to try her hand at making some of the delicate slices, a skill that looked much easier than it turned out to be. When they had everything ready and arranged on the plates, Kitria brought out some flaky, lightly sweetened pastries to accompany the meal that she had picked up from the central market early that morning.

Eying the fish with suspicion, Veyl tried a cautious nibble, though only after Kitria had done so first with no apparent ill-effects. It was delicate, with a cool, subtle flavor. Combined with the sauce, it was smooth and slightly creamy on her tongue. She took a second bite, contemplating the taste and texture.

"Not bad, is it?" Kitria asked.

"Surprisingly, no."

"Father did it better than I do, but I keep practicing. He could slice it as thin as a flower petal." Her wistful smile came with the shine of unshed tears.

Veyl touched her hand. "Thank you, Kitria, for teaching me this, and for taking a chance on me."

The openness in Kitria's smile faded, and she moved her hand away. "Eat. We've got a busy day ahead."

After they finished and cleaned up, they left the house. Sometime while they were inside, Quillon and Mardi had taken the place of the other two guards. Together, the four of them walked to the port market. The ocean, not unexpectedly, was the primary source of food for the island's residents. The effort of keeping everyone fed made fishing and related trades the biggest sources of work for the people there, so the port was always busy.

Veyl spotted other Vanrians in the market, most in small groups with at least one guard accompanying them. They were all from Kyril's fleet, and several offered her discreet nods of recognition that she returned when she could do so without drawing attention. She had spoken with everyone on those ships. They all knew who she was, or at least who she had been in Vanris.

Their small group walked to Quillon's brother Cordin's shop, where Kitria offered their services for gutting and cleaning a fresh haul of fish. Not a task Veyl would have preferred to volunteer for, but under the circumstances, she couldn't afford to be choosy. Cordin and Kitria led her to a long table and walked her through the procedure a few times, then left her to it, Kitria moving down the table to work on her own. Veyl was struggling to process her second fish when Quillon came up and gave her a more detailed demonstration. Despite choosing to make his living as a guard, he was a deft hand at gutting fish. After watching him finish a couple and seeing the precision with which he wielded the knife, Veyl made a note to avoid ending up on the opposing side of his sword. He was a natural teacher, though, and she mimicked his technique when he handed the blade back.

Cordin and Quillon took up places at the table with them, the four of them making quick work of a barrel of fresh-caught fish, though Cordin stepped away several times to deal with customers. Mardi stood back, shaking her head at them periodically and wrinkling her nose. A sentiment Veyl didn't entirely disagree with, although, as slimy and smelly as the process was, once she slipped into a routine, she found she enjoyed the physical labor and the distraction from all her worries. She also appreciated the banter between the others. It reminded her a little of being around her father's tehsheyn. As much as they teased one another, an underlying affection colored all their interactions.

"You've got a knack for this. I'd be happy to have you help any time," Cordin remarked, returning to the table after completing a transaction.

A proud smile curved her lips as she finished another fish and moved it along.

"Veyl, try this one."

She turned to see Quillin tossing a large fish her way, a lumpy creature with a jaw full of horrifyingly long needle-like teeth. Snatching up the knife from the table with her left hand, she connected with the slippery thing with her right, not trying to grab it so much as redirect it onto the knife. The blade slipped into its belly and slid up until it caught on the edge of the jaw. Startled by the weight of the aquatic beast, she spun and slapped it down on the table before the knife could cut through any farther and let the fish fall to the floor or, worse yet, collide with her chest.

Quillon laughed. "Spectacular catch. You've half-gutted it already."

"You're hired," Cordin added, chuckling.

By noon, she was exhausted and as smelly as the fish she'd been gutting, but it was a good fatigue, if not the greatest smell. Kitria took her to a bathhouse near the center of town. When they finished soaking in the steaming water, she gave her one of two dresses she had brought along to change into. From there, they picked up fruit, cheese, and bread from vendors in the larger central market, and continued to the house.

As they sat relaxing in the pleasant weariness of work well done, the reality of the current situation crept back in.

Veyl swallowed a berry and considered the young woman sitting across from her. "What makes our cultures so different? What are these things the council fears my people would try to change about you?"

Kitria, who had been slowly sinking farther down on the couch as she nibbled at some cheese and bread, pushed herself upright again and folded her legs under her. "Let's see. As I understand it, in the original homeland, mind-crafters automatically ranked above their fellows because of what they are. In Thaelis, an ahnkreth and a kreth are the same rank, the title variation merely a way of noting their ability or lack thereof for military applications. No one gets treated like they're special merely for being born a mind-crafter."

"You say that, but your council seems highly focused on acquiring more mind-crafters. And why are the council members all pure-blooded Vanrians?"

Kitria shrugged. "We're Thaelian. They represent those who founded our country. It makes sense."

"Does it? Shouldn't your leaders represent the population they lead? Why are there no Qwilki or people of mixed blood on the council?"

Kitria set down the bread she'd been about to eat and put her feet on the floor, sitting forward. "You may have a point, but you're also proving theirs. Here you are already trying to show me that our way might not be the only, or even the best, way to do things."

Veyl sat back in her chair. "Fair enough, but you can't deny some validity to what I'm saying. In Vanris, I was heir to the throne, even though everyone believed I had no ability. All our people matter and have opportunity, but there is a slight advantage given to mind-crafters, particularly in our military. I have seen firsthand a little of the discontent that imbalance causes, but it is something we could fix with a few careful changes." She picked up a slice of a sweet, sticky fruit they didn't have in Vanris. "What else?"

"How about the tehnaak bond? Here, we allow those bonds to begin forming naturally before we involve a Bondmaker to make two individuals officially tehnaak. According to the histories, that choice used to be made for the child when they were too young to have a say in it. Do your people still force that bond on children?"

Veyl savored the sweet fruit, considering. When she finished, she licked the juice off her fingers and wiped them on a linen before responding. "We do create those bonds at a young age. You frame it as a bad thing, but I guarantee that almost any Vanrian you asked would say they couldn't imagine being without their tehnaak. Waiting would give them more of a choice, but leave them devoid of that valuable connection earlier in life. I believe growing up together is part of what makes the bond as powerful as it is."

She leaned forward and considered the selection of food as she continued. "I lost my first tehnaak when I was very young, though. My bond with Jaysen was always doomed and has been severed twice now. I can't claim to know from personal experience what it's like to have that lifelong tehnaak connection." She cut a piece of cheese and brought it to her lips, then hesitated, recalling a conversation with Kyril on his ship. "Your brother mentioned something different about how you handle the Trial."

Kitria grinned. "We definitely do that better."

Veyl smiled, intrigued by her certainty. "Tell me."

"There's a native plant that the Qwilki introduced us to when our people first came here. They use a drink made with its root to open their minds to the world around them during ceremonies. We discovered it can awaken a mind-crafter's ability without having to create a traumatic experience."

Veyl breathed a laugh. "All right, that *is* better, but you have a local advantage on that one."

Kitria smiled and stood. "Come on. We need to get to the prison. It's time to see if you can talk some of them out of there."

Veyl finished the last bite of bread and got up. "You'll be with me?"

"I'm afraid so. I'm not supposed to let you out of my sight, remember?"

Veyl considered Kitria for a moment and nodded to

herself. "That's fine. It could prove helpful."

That gut feeling turned out to be correct. Kitria was the perfect Thaelian ambassador. Naturally friendly and open, at least with everyone who hadn't played a hand in sending her brother into danger, she became instrumental in putting the Vanrian captives more at ease. A task also made easier by the more receptive moods of those reunited with their tehnaaks. By the time they left the prison, six pairings were being prepared to move out into houses. It felt like a successful day, at least as far as keeping the council from condemning her to death went.

After Kitria walked her through the preparation for another common Qwilki dish, they enjoyed a quiet dinner together. When dark had fallen, Veyl was ready to call an end to a long day, but Kitria negated the idea and led her out again, insisting they had one more task to complete.

This time, they walked up north to a rocky area along the coastline and climbed to the top of some high cliffs overlooking the ocean. Eavara's Dampener, an older gentleman with dark blond hair streaked through with a rusty red stain and woven into myriad decorated braids, waited for them at the top. The guards stopped several yards away, as though that distance might offer them some measure of safety from her ability. Another figure followed them up and sat on a rock facing away from them, staying far enough out to remain a mere silhouette in the moonlight. The faint inner tug in that direction and the fact that no one else acknowledged the individual told Veyl this was the elite soldier she was now zenyal to. She did her best to ignore them as the others did.

"Sit." The Dampener ordered, not offering his name or a greeting.

His gruff manner told her he would make it a

struggle to keep her temper reined in, given how tired she was already. She settled on the rough rock in front of him. Kitria sat to one side, and the Dampener sank down across from Veyl.

"Open yourself to your ability." He had a harsh, rasping voice, like sandstone scraping bare skin.

She did as the Dampener directed, letting a little of that energy crackle through her.

"Well done. Now keep it active within you and tell me about the night Ahnkreth Kyril took you captive."

Veyl sucked in a sharp breath, the energy surging. "This is a terrible idea." She moved to get up, but Kitria touched her arm, stalling her.

"You can do this, Veyl. If not for yourself, then for the people you care about."

Veyl drew a shuddering breath and made herself settle back down. As soon as she was in position, everything went black. The crackle of energy surged again, and she got a flash of imagery from someone's fear.

The man chuckled, a humorless sound. "Keep it contained, little Frightener, but keep it active."

He was using his Dampener ability on her, placing her in darkness where nothing could distract her from the intensity of her memories.

"You could have warned me," she snapped. But that was the point, wasn't it? To push her control. She listened to the sound of the waves crashing below and pulled the energy in close to her, letting the call of the ocean soothe her.

"Now," the Dampener rasped, "return to that night, and tell me what you remember."

The days that followed became a reflection of Veyl's first day with Kitria. Each morning, they went to help someone around the town, sometimes at the markets, sometimes at people's homes or other businesses like the taverns. Though the intent was to be charitable in their efforts, several people insisted on paying them with gifts. Veyl became the recipient of a variety of items, including tokens, a shawl, and a bracelet that was a near perfect match for the necklace Jaysen had given her. Each afternoon, they visited the shrinking number of Vanrians in the prison to try progressing more of them along the path to greater freedom. In the evenings, they ventured out after dark to meet Eavara's Dampener on the rocks to the north of the house. He never offered a greeting or introduced himself to Veyl, but Kitria said his name was Erkhan.

No matter how much she despised his gruff, unwelcoming manner, she had to admit his approach was helping her gain greater control of her ability, though it did nothing to teach her how to use it. Still, she hated his methods even more than she hated him. He locked her in darkness, then made her draw on her power and try to keep it contained while speaking of events that were likely to evoke sorrow and anger. It wasn't long before Kitria knew about her swim with the ji'ikyan—

an incident Erkhan had heard about from someone on Kyril's crew—along with precise details of the attack on Deepwater from Veyl's perspective, giving her knowledge of what her brother and his fleet had done to them that left her vacillating between sorrowful and furious most of the next day. Some of those retellings earned Veyl quiet hugs from Kitria before they parted to go to bed at night.

Forcing her to relive her misery wasn't always enough for Erkhan. Some evenings, he did the speaking, describing many of the awful things that had taken place when Eavara's fleet attacked the coastal town where they picked up their "Vanrian cargo," as he insultingly called them, and the suffering her countryfolk endured on their ships.

Whether his torturous methods were necessary, his objective was to give her the skills to prevent her ability from reacting so chaotically to her emotions. Beyond that, there wasn't much she could learn from him, but at least, with enough practice, the sessions might help prevent her from unintentionally harming anyone. To avoid another incident like what had happened with her friends, she would relive whatever trauma she had to.

Eleven days from the day Kitria led her out of the cell beneath the Great Hall, and thirteen days after Kyril and Jaysen embarked on their voyage, they spent a morning on the western side of the island helping a trio of Qwilki women collect mussels. The tide pools teemed with strange life the likes of which Veyl had never seen before. Whenever she spotted some new, intriguing creature within one of them, she forgot her task and stopped to inspect the discovery. Kitria and the other women patiently taught her about each one, giggling to themselves whenever she excitedly called them over to see what she had found.

"Stop poking the anemones," Nagi reprimanded

in her thick Qwilki accent, though there was a hint of restrained laughter behind her words. She gave Veyl a stern look that rapidly faltered, transforming into a smile when she shook her head and turned back to her work.

"They're just so fascinating."

"And you are trying to soak up the ocean with your dress," Anahela said, breaking into a laugh where she was working on Veyl's other side.

Veyl glanced down. She had pulled the skirt up between her legs and tied it around her waist the way they had shown her, but she had stretched over far enough to reach the anemone that one end of the tie dangled into a pool, rapidly absorbing saltwater. At that moment, a wave rolled over the rocks, splashing up her legs and getting the skirt substantially wetter.

"Blast it," she grumbled.

The other women chuckled.

"The tide's coming in. We should finish up here," Kitria called from where she was working a few yards away with another woman.

Veyl picked up her wooden bucket, her cheeks warming when she noticed how much fuller everyone else's buckets were. "I'm sorry. I wasn't that helpful, was I? More of a hinderance, really."

Anahela offered her a warm smile. "Nonsense. You made the hours race by. Seeing the tide pools through fresh eyes is a rare treat."

A larger wave crashed upon the rocks, and someone cried out. Veyl turned, dropping her bucket as a lizard-like beast the size of a juvenile whale swept up over the rocks with the water, catching Nagi's leg in its broad mouth. The gills on the side of its neck marked it as a creature of the ocean, its pale gray and blue mottled skin riddled with scars, perhaps from rugged shores like these.

The beast dragged Nagi, screaming and thrashing, toward the water. Veyl snatched up the knife she had been using to pry mussels from the rock and sprinted after it, struggling to find secure footing on the edges of the tide pools. Realizing she wouldn't reach the woman before the creature entered the water, Veyl threw the dagger. The blade found a home deep in the flesh below one of its eyes.

The beast reared back, dropping Nagi, and Veyl rushed in to try pulling her clear. Before she could secure a solid hold on the other woman, the creature's massive jaws clamped on her arm, and it yanked her off her feet. She slammed into the hard, jagged rocks of the tide pools on her back, the agonizing impact stunning her for a few critical seconds as it dragged her into the water, leaving her barely enough time to suck in a breath before it pulled her under. Veyl struggled violently, terror threatening to override rational thought. The storm rose within her, but that power only worked on people, so she pushed it back and twisted around, grabbing for the knife still sticking out of the beast's face.

Yanking the weapon free, she stabbed it again and again with frenzied desperation until the creature was bleeding from dozens of wounds. It released her, giving up on a meal that had proven too dangerous, and twisted away, vanishing into the deeper water with a cloud of red blossoming in its wake. Veyl struggled to the surface. Waves pummeled her, and blood ran from several wounds, pain flaring in the parts of her that had collided with the rocks. She struggled to draw a breath and orient herself in the rough water, still gripping the knife.

Something else grabbed hold of her arm. She twisted, prepared to fight through the pain and exhaustion, pausing when she saw a canine creature with long, thick black fur and fin-like ears, its jaws firmly but carefully clamped around her arm.

"Ceris?"

But it wasn't Kyril's companion. This one's eyes were a much deeper blue.

She adjusted her position, trying to make it easier for the wave dancer to pull her toward shore. Kitria and Anahela waded in to help drag her from the water. As they did so, the Qwilki women called out in their odd language with a chant-like cadence, even Nagi despite her injuries, though her voice shook. Once they were on the beach, the two uninjured women pulled Veyl clear of the surf and all three Qwilki knelt before the wave dancer, bowing their heads to the sand. Kitria hesitated for a moment before joining them.

The beast stepped warily forward and licked Veyl's ankle, then it spun and bounded back into the waves.

Kitria and the other two women turned to assessing injuries on Veyl and Nagi. Both were bleeding from an abundance of scrapes and cuts after their violent collisions with the rock. Veyl checked the arm the beast had grabbed, and, although it hurt something fierce and was darkening with bruises, there were no wounds on it.

"They don't have teeth," Kitria explained, as she tended to a gash on Veyl's thigh. "They drag their prey into the water, tenderize it by crushing it repeatedly between their jaws, and swallow it whole."

Veyl shuddered.

Nagi reached over and took her hand, tears streaming down her cheeks as Anahela continued checking her injuries and the third woman, Ferda, held pressure on a cut on Nagi's head.

"The ocean blesses you, child." Somehow, despite her wounds and the horror of what had just happened, Nagi was beaming.

Kitria helped Veyl stand, nodding to the other two women. "Come on, Nagi, we have to get you two to the healers."

Veyl was trembling hard enough that she struggled to get her feet solidly under her.

Kitria pried her hand open, taking the knife she still held in a death grip. "You can lean on me."

"What was that thing?"

"Kel'inuk," Kitria answered as they made their way up the sandy path toward town. "They rarely hunt this shoreline because of the rough terrain. Given the size of that one, I suspect it was an adolescent that got driven out of its territory."

Veyl's stomach turned, her voice shaking when she spoke. "An adolescent?"

Kitria nodded. "They can get very large."

Behind them, Nagi said something in Qwilki, and Kitria's jaw tightened.

"What did she say?"

Kitria lowered her voice to a whisper. "Nagi is saying the Daughter of the Ocean saved her life."

"The... She means me?"

Kitria didn't answer. Instead, she glanced over her shoulder and snapped something at the three women in their language. After a few rounds of what sounded like a heated exchange, they appeared to come to an agreement and Kitria turned her focus back to walking.

Once they reached the healer's building, Anahela and Ferda left to go collect the abandoned buckets of mussels. Kitria stayed with Veyl and Nagi. After the healers dealt with their injuries, they let Veyl leave with Kitria, sending someone to fetch Nagi's son so he might escort her home and care for her. The woman hugged Veyl and kissed her cheek before allowing her to go.

At the house, Kitria handled preparing a meal, giving Veyl time to rest. She had substantial scrapes and bruises on her back, arms, and legs, along with a few deeper cuts, though only one that required stitching.

Once she had finished picking at the food Kitria brought her, Veyl rested gingerly back in the soft chair, her heartbeat finally slowing to normal again. "Is it common for wave dancers to help people like that?"

Kitria licked a drip of sauce off one finger before reclining in her seat. "No. Not common at all. They have a peaceful relationship with the people of the islands, and the Qwilki leave them offerings when they know there are some around. They're reclusive creatures, though, so you don't see wild ones that often. On rare occasions, you might find pups playing with the children in some of the more remote villages. Adults have protected people from predators in the waters around here, but the wild ones almost never come into physical contact with humans. Aside from a couple that are bonded with Ferals on other islands."

"How many islands are there?"

"This one is the largest. There are six others in the chain. Villages on the two smallest outer ones had to be abandoned in recent years because population loss from the Devastation made it too hard to protect people from Ukhen'kya raids."

Someone knocked at the door and Kitria hurried over to answer it, returning a moment later with the eldest of the male councilors, the man with white-blond hair and ice-blue eyes.

Veyl moved to get up, but he raised a hand to stop her. "We can skip formalities given your injuries."

Veyl bowed her head, tight bands of tension squeezing her chest. "Thank you, Councilor."

"It occurs to me I have never properly introduced myself. I am Darith." He took a seat across from her, his two guards coming in to wait by the entrance to the room. "I understand you saved a woman's life today, nearly at the cost of your own."

"I did what needed to be done."

He regarded her with thoughtful scrutiny. "And you did not lose control of your ability as the kel'inuk was dragging you into the ocean?"

Kitria spoke up as she settled back in her chair. "I felt a brief flicker of her power, Councilor, but it vanished as quickly as it came."

"I knew it would be of no use to me against a beast," Veyl offered, "so I suppressed it."

Darith nodded. "I imagine that was an extremely emotionally charged moment for you. That you could stop it shows that you can be steady under pressure and suggests a substantial improvement in control. You have done well in other areas too, as I understand it. Making yourself useful in the community. Helping to get your countryfolk out of the prison. The council is pleased with your progress. In recognition of your efforts, we would like to propose removing the zenyal bond if you would consent to taking Erkhan as your tehnaak."

Anger flared, and Veyl had to push back the energy that crackled in her chest. Did he honestly expect her to be thrilled by the offer? "Thank you, Councilor, but no."

Darith frowned. "The Dampener has helped you control your ability, has he not?"

Veyl drew a breath, forcing a measured tone. "He has. I'd say the fact that I would love to punch his teeth in every time he opens his mouth and have not yet done so shows a dramatic overall improvement in self-control. But even if he weren't insufferable, he must be nearly twice my age."

Darith's brow furrowed. "I realize he is not especially charismatic, but age aside, he is one of few who has an ability that might complement and balance yours. If you feel that strongly about it, however, there may be a couple of other options."

"If I may, Councilor." Kitria folded her hands in

her lap, perhaps to stop the nervous fidgeting they had been engaged in while his eyes were on Veyl. "She did just experience a traumatic event and has several injuries to recover from. This might not be the best time for making life-altering decisions."

Veyl offered Kitria a brief smile of gratitude while his attention wasn't on her.

"Perhaps you are right." Darith stood, his gaze falling upon Veyl again. "Considering today's events, we suggest you take time to rest and recover. You may put off visits to the remaining prisoners and sessions with Dampener Erkhan for the next two days while you heal. We can revisit this topic when you are feeling better."

"Thank you, Councilor." Self-righteous calloch, she added in her head, finding it easier to offer him a respectful nod while silently cursing him. "Before you depart, I wanted to ask you about something. When we arrived, the council said Ahnkreth Eavara brought fifty-six people from Vanris, but there were only fifty-one when I first visited the prison. What happened to the other five?"

Darith frowned. "They didn't fare well on the journey over. Regretfully, we were unable to save them."

"They died? Five of my people died from seasickness?" She remembered Lorek, wasting away in the ship's cabin until they allowed her to intervene. "Didn't anyone try to help them?"

Darith glanced out the window. "As we stated before, things did not proceed as peacefully with Ahnkreth Eavara's fleet. I'll let you rest now." He offered a polite nod and hurried out.

She watched him leave, his avoidance stirring an uncomfortable feeling in her gut.

The next day was quiet. Kitria left to help some people in the port market around mid-morning, deciding that the guards and the person who controlled the zenyal bond lingering somewhere nearby would be sufficient supervision while Veyl was recovering. Left alone in the house, she tried resting only to find her body hurt too much for sleep once the elixir the healers sent with her to get her through the night had worn off. Bruises were rising in places she didn't recall being hit, but she had no desire to take more of the sedative without Kitria there. The people she met here had mostly welcomed her, but that didn't mean she was safe. She would never trust a leadership that considered it acceptable to steal people from their homes and force them to live in another land.

Being unable to sleep left too much time for reflection. She tried occupying herself with preparing food for later, but her mind wandered to Kyril and Jaysen, to her family, and to that awful night in Deepwater. She couldn't help thinking of the twins and their tehnaaks who must also miss their families. How she longed to see them. She would ask Kitria about them when she got home.

A knock came at the door a few hours after noon. Drawing a little of her ability, Veyl cautiously answered it. Mardi and Quillon were there as expected. Between them lay a collection of baskets full of clothing, food, and assorted other items.

Veyl gestured to the pile. "What is this?"

Quillon smirked. "Gifts for the, ah, *Daughter of the Ocean* who saved the people of Thaelis from the Ukhen'kya and rescued Nagi from the kel'inuk."

Mardi shook her head and stared out into the street, her jaw set.

"Oh. I didn't expect… What should I do with it all?"

"Burn it," Mardi grumbled.

Quillon rolled his eyes at the other guard. "Personally, I'd take it inside and see what you can make a meal out of. Some of the food smells incredible."

Quillon helped her move the baskets into the house. She sent him back out with a little sack of dried squid he had been eyeing covetously. By the time Kitria returned, Veyl had sorted through the contents, making a pile of scarves, skirts, shirts, and dresses along with various jewelry and tokens made mostly from shells and polished stone. Someone had gifted her a stain like those the fleet crew members used in their hair, this one a dark purple. The rest was all food, enough that she couldn't imagine how they were supposed to eat it all before it spoiled.

When Kitria walked in, she set down a shoulder bag full of food and stood staring at the collection for a second. "I see I shouldn't have bothered visiting the market." She ran a hand through her hair. "I told them not to tell anyone about the wave dancer."

"Is that why this is happening?"

"That and the Ukhen'kya harvest feast would have been yesterday. All the islands are reporting no losses this year. Many of the Qwilki and some others believe you driving them away with your Frightener ability deterred them from coming back for another try."

A chill crept up the back of Veyl's neck. Thaelis hadn't lost anyone, but Vanris had. "What if that's what happened to the five Vanrians from Eavara's fleet? What if the council gave them to the Ukhen'kya to keep them from taking your people?"

For a heartbeat, horror froze Kitria's features. Then she shook her head firmly and started picking more aggressively than necessary through the collection of food. "That's absurd. They would never *give* someone to the Unclean. Not under any circumstances."

Veyl wasn't so sure, but the frantic way the other woman snatched items from the pile for their evening meal convinced her not to push the issue. At least not right now.

While they ate, Kitria was quiet and distracted, her brow furrowed by the weight of thoughts she chose not to share. Afterward, she became obsessed with cleaning. When she revisited the same counter for the sixth time, Veyl walked over and placed a hand on her wrist to stop her from wiping it down yet again.

"What's wrong?"

"What if they did do something to your people? I never would have believed my brother could do the things he did when he abducted you from your country, and the council gave him those orders. I'm so furious with them I can barely think straight. With him too, and yet…" She looked at Veyl, those silver eyes, so much like Veyl's mother's, shining with worry. "I'm scared. I have a bad feeling that something happened to him. They shouldn't have sent him back there."

Veyl put an arm around her shoulders and Kitria leaned into her. "I'm sure he'll be back any day now. He's clever, and he has Ceris and an extremely devoted crew with him. They would all protect him with their lives."

"And he would do the same for them, which is what I'm afraid of."

Veyl said nothing. She knew it was true.

*

The next morning, the sound of someone pounding on the door dragged Veyl up from the grip of the sedative.

Kitria, awake and already preparing breakfast, judging from the aromas wafting through the house, called out, "Be right there."

Battling her way past pain and grogginess, Veyl stiffly pulled on her clothes from the previous evening, curious to discover what the noise was about. Kitria was opening the door when she came out into the front room. A young man rushed between the guards, pushing Kitria away from the door and shutting it behind him. He was breathing hard, as if he had been running.

"Kit, Nalika's ship just pulled into port."

The color drained from Kitria's face. "*Only* Nalika's ship?"

"I'm afraid so. She's on her way to the Great Hall now. I thought you'd want to know."

"Yes." She reached out and squeezed his hands, glancing around as if looking for something. "Thank you." Kitria let go of him and grabbed a jacket hanging by the door.

Veyl hurried over, gritting her teeth against the sting from the stitched cut in her thigh and various other aches. "I'm coming with you."

For a second, Kitria's lips pressed into a line as if she might argue. Then she met Veyl's eyes and nodded. "Fine. Let's go." She hesitated for a moment, glancing back toward the kitchen and whatever she had been making in there.

"I can handle it," the young man offered.

"Thank you again." Kitria moved around him, heading out with Veyl close behind her.

They hurried to the Great Hall, Kitria breaking into a jog that forced Veyl to push her injured body. Fear for Kyril warred against the hope that her people might have a chance of being rescued from this. That war was more balanced than it should have been. She was a khesran of Vanris, but even if she put aside her growing feelings for Kyril, this place was becoming familiar, and its beautiful aspects, in the land and the people, were things she was coming to appreciate. In a way, she could see how the Thaelian council's plans to integrate the Vanrians they had captured weren't as absurd as she had initially assumed them to be. Given enough time, there were aspects of this place that she could learn to love aside from just one Feral ahnkreth who might now be dead or in danger because of what she had asked him to do.

When the guards at the side entrance stopped them, Kitria didn't hesitate. "A messenger came requesting that I bring Veyl to the Great Hall at once."

Either because of the plausibility of her words or the confidence with which she spoke them, they stepped aside and let them in. Kitria moved up along the side of the massive room, staying behind guards standing along the columns. Nalika, looking haggard and distressed, was striding swiftly up the center with a few of her senior crew members flanking her. A fair number of townsfolk flooded in after her, moving off to the sides of the main hall or gathering just inside the doors. At the front, the councilors were filing in from a back room, claiming their seats.

Councilor Darith was still sitting when he demanded, "Where is the rest of Ahnkreth Kyril's fleet?"

Nalika stopped in front of the table, her chest rising and falling with a deep breath before she answered, her words striking like foreboding drumbeats in the sudden silence that filled the room. "Vanris has them."

Stillness swept along the council, their faces paling, everything from disbelief to fear in their eyes.

"How did Vanris get their hands on the fleet if you landed in Sarket?" The faint tremble in Councilor Shyall's voice could have been fear or rage, or both.

Nalika closed her eyes and took another deep breath, her jaw muscles tightening. Then she looked directly at Shyall. "We didn't go to Sarket."

## CHAPTER TWENTY SEVEN

Several councilors began shouting at once, but a shockingly forceful call for silence from Darith had the desired effect. When the others quieted, he pinned Nalika with his icy stare. "Explain."

She faced him with her back straight and her head held high, though her voice lacked the confidence of her posture. "We sailed to the northern edge of the region they call the Crimson Break, where it meets up with the border of Vanris, per Ahnkreth Kyril's orders."

For a few seconds, Darith looked ready to spit venom, his rage apparently overriding his ability to form words. The other councilors watched him warily, as though trying to decide if an explosion might be imminent that they should get clear of.

Finally, his lip curling with disgust, he asked, "Did your ahnkreth tell you why he gave you these orders?"

Nalika shook her head. "No, Councilor. He only said there had been a change in plans."

Veyl frowned.

Why would he have kept his intentions from his crew? Unless it was to give them deniability if something went wrong. Unfortunately, she could imagine him doing something like that, though she suspected his crew might not thank him for it. Or maybe they would. No matter how much they cared for him, what he had done fell into the realm of treason.

"What happened when you arrived there?"

"A few military ships were in the area. The young man from Sarket, Jaysen, spoke with them, and they gave us permission to anchor near the shore. From what I understand, Ahnkreth Kyril intended to let Jaysen disembark and leave him there, but a Vanrian officer at their base extended an invitation for him to come ashore and speak. Jaysen swore to him that our fleet would have his protection, and they would allow us to depart afterward. Kyril took Ceris and a small party to meet with them."

The councilors' expressions soured noticeably at this last revelation.

Nalika drew a breath, and it struck Veyl that the woman looked extremely tired and disheartened. "About twenty minutes after his group left the flagship, a substantial company of ships flying two flags, the Vanrian flag and another we hadn't encountered before, swept down from somewhere to the north of us. They must have had several Dampeners with them, or at least a few very powerful ones, because they rendered the entire fleet blind in seconds, putting us at their mercy. They swarmed us and seized everyone on board. After holding us for a day with no word of what was happening, they sent my crew and me back to our ship, demanding that we carry a message back to you."

Kitria looked like she was about to throw up. As much as Veyl wanted to offer support, guilt held her back. This was her doing, though she hadn't intended it to work out quite this way. She had hoped Jaysen's presence, along with the fact that they were bringing warning of the threat from Thrasser, would keep the situation from becoming too hostile, and ideally open a door for negotiations between the two countries.

Darith's face was slowly shading toward red. "What message?" he asked through gritted teeth.

"That they will return our ships and their crews to us unharmed the moment we do the same with the Vanrian citizens we took from Pandrea."

Murmuring drew Veyl's attention to the large number of people who had found their way into the building. She spotted a few other Vanrians standing among the locals, cautious hope rising in their eyes. A sizeable group of tribal Qwilki had gathered on the far side of the hall as well, a few of whom were watching her rather than the events unfolding at the front of the room, a heavy weight of expectation in their collective regard.

One of the other councilors was shaking her head. "Even if we wanted to send their people back, it would require a second fleet to transport that many. That would force us to leave our shores and fishing boats more vulnerable to the Ukhen'kya should they decide to launch another attack. We can't take that risk."

A charge of mixed excitement and anxiety raced through Veyl. She was crouched on the edge of the academy rooftop again, but it wasn't Tavin hanging below her this time. It was all the people who had been taken from Vanris with her. It was also Kyril and his fleet. Jaysen was once more poised on the roof above her. He hadn't done what she hoped he would, although she had no way to know if that was in any part his fault, but he hadn't let go either. He had left his hand extended to her, and she had but to take it to have a chance at saving her people. Yet, if she fell, it was going to be a very long way down, and she would fail all of them.

She placed a hand on Kitria's shoulder. "I'll fix this," she whispered.

"Veyl, no."

Ignoring Kitria's desperate objection, she strode out into the center. The councilors watched her walk up beside Nalika with expressions ranging from dread to resignation.

"If you would permit me to speak," she stated loudly. This wasn't the time for timidity.

Darith heaved a sigh. "If you have helpful information to add, then your voice is welcome. Otherwise, no."

She turned to Nalika first. "The unfamiliar flags on the other ships, did they have a white raptor flying on a light and dark blue background?"

Nalika glared at her, the resentment in her expression making Veyl wonder if she might know more than she was letting on about why Kyril had disobeyed his orders. If so, she played a dangerous game. "Yes," she answered sharply.

"Delaphine." Veyl faced the council. "I believe your best option is to send me back to Vanris with Ahnkreth Nalika's ship."

Several councilors shouted objections and people in the gathered crowd called out both for and against the idea.

"Silence," Darith roared. When everyone had quieted, he focused on her again. "While I recognize you are the daughter of the khevarin and khemron of your country, I doubt the recovery of one person is going to appease them."

They weren't having her dragged from the room for the suggestion. That meant they had few enough ideas of their own that they were at least willing to listen. She glanced up at a landscape etched in the white stone of the back wall. Though much was strange here, she recognized that view of the largest volcano on the original Vanrian homeland. There were paintings of that same setting around the palaces in Etrion and Doran. Bolstered by that familiarity, she faced the council.

"As do I, Councilor, but it would show a willingness to negotiate. Send me back so that I might speak to my people on behalf of Thaelis."

Blatant disbelief flattened his expression and that of most of the other men and women behind the table.

A few voices murmured elsewhere in the vast space, and she heard the title "Daughter of the Ocean" spoken by more than one person. The darkening looks of the council members made it clear they heard it as well. She stood before them with two token shells braided into her hair, one from Kyril and the other one of many gifts she had received from the people of Dagony. She wore a deep green Qwilki shirt and skirt that had been among yesterday's offerings, made of soft fabrics that didn't catch on the wounds from the kel'inuk attack. Had she planned to come before the council today, she would not have adorned herself in gifts given to her by people who had started treating her like a subject of worship. But then, it was possible that could work out in her favor. An opportunity to put distance between her and her growing number of admirers might hold some appeal for them.

"Close the Hall," Darith ordered.

The councilors gathered behind the table, conversing amongst themselves in low voices while guards began herding the people from the building.

"No!" Kitria's scream drew Veyl's attention to where two guards were trying to escort her out. One of them caught her arm, and she strained against him. "No! Nalika, where's my brother? Is he alive?" Her voice cracked with those last words, causing a painful squeezing sensation in Veyl's chest.

Next to Veyl, Nalika stood staring at the floor, hands clenched at her sides. When she didn't respond, Kitria's face fell, and she relented to the guards, turning away with a sob as they forced her out. Guilt was a twisting blade in Veyl's chest.

"Is he alive?" she asked in a low voice, dread coiling

in her gut.

"I honestly don't know. I never saw him again after he left his flagship."

When the guards had removed their audience and only Veyl, Nalika, and the council members remained, the council settled back in their seats and regarded her sternly.

"Why would you offer to negotiate on behalf of Thaelis?" Shyall sounded angry, as though she found the very suggestion offensive.

Veyl took a step forward, clasping her hands before her. "Because I have spent time among the populace here now. I have worked with them, I have laughed with them, I have even risked my life for them. They are good people. They didn't deserve what the Ukhen'kya did to them any more than my people deserve what you have done to us. I want to right the wrongs you committed against the people of Vanris, but no one should have to suffer through what the Ukhen'kya have done and continue to do to the citizens of Thaelis. I don't want to see them come to more harm, and I believe I can help prevent that."

"Assuming you could convince us you would negotiate fairly on our behalf, what would you expect to accomplish?" Darith asked.

"You took people from my country because your population is suffering. I imagine losing an entire fleet of skilled Thaelian citizens will not improve the situation." His expression and that of his fellow councilors darkened with growing anger, so she rushed ahead. "I'm certain I can convince them to release Ahnkreth Kyril and his crew and allow them to return first, so you won't have to risk another fleet when you can't afford to."

His brows rose. "Your suggestion assumes we intend to surrender to their demands."

"Please know I am not trying to be antagonistic

when I advise you to consider doing so." Veyl kept her hands at her sides now to keep from wringing them. This was a level of negotiation far beyond what she had observed in the time she spent watching her parents meet with dignitaries from the other kingdoms. With everything that was at stake, she mostly wanted to throw up, but she needed to appear confident. That was the only way they would take her seriously.

"What would you provide them in return for our fleet?" Shyall asked when Darith's contemplative silence dragged on.

"If I offer to let them come to Thaelis and retrieve our people themselves, I can spare you the costly effort of sending out more ships."

Shyall gave her a look that implied the woman thought she might be simpleminded or mad. Enunciating her words carefully as if explaining something to a child, she said, "We do not want them to take away the Vanrians we brought here. We did so at significant cost and returning them to Vanris would put us right back in the position that led us to this point. In fact, we do not want your ships to come here at all. Ever."

Veyl pushed back a crackle of energy that rose with her frustration. "It's too late for that. One way or another, they will come. If they have Ahnkreth Kyril's flagship, they have his navigational charts. Should you choose not to respond to their message, they will call upon the Delaphinian naval fleet and come here to take back our people by force if necessary. Vanris has an abundance of powerful mind-crafters and skilled soldiers to throw at this problem. You said yourself, you cannot spare another fleet right now. Nor can you afford to lose more people fighting a war with Vanris and her allies. Please, believe me when I say I don't want to see your people hurt, and resisting Vanris in this will be devastating for everyone here."

She chose her words deliberately to imply a tragedy as awful as the Devastation and, judging from the reflexive winces and uncomfortable shifting, it had the desired effect.

The councilors regarded her in stony, bitter silence. Nalika's report of how fast Kyril's fleet had been subdued lent credence to her words, and the council certainly looked concerned.

Darith glanced to one side, receiving nods from each of the councilors there. He got the same response when he looked the other way. Anger pinching his brows, he beckoned some guards forward. "Escort Veyl to her res-idence and see that she stays there until we send for her. Nalika, your crew may return to their homes, but be ready should we need to call on them. You will remain here for now to provide more details on your encounter in Vanris. The Great Hall is to remain closed to the public while we deliberate."

Veyl didn't protest. She had said her piece and could only hope her words had made an impression. As she walked out with the guards, a growing sense of unease moved through her at the idea of what might await her at the house. A concern that was justified when she en-tered to find Kitria sitting in a chair with an unsheathed shortsword resting across her lap, her hate-filled eyes rimmed with red from crying.

Veyl stopped in the entryway to the main room, keeping a sensible distance. She briefly considered call-ing for the guards to come inside, but that would do nothing to restore the peace between them. "Kit?"

Kitria looked up, her hand moving up to rest on the hilt of the weapon. "Is that why you slept with him? To convince him to go to Vanris for you and betray his people."

"It wasn't like that." Veyl lifted one foot to take a step toward her, but Kitria's hand closed around the grip, so she pulled it back. "Yes, I asked him to go to Vanris. I was afraid for my people after learning that King Thrasser was plotting something. I had to warn them. But I care about Kyril far more than I probably should. I would never intentionally bring him to harm. I believed Jaysen could and would protect him and his fleet."

"My brother is all I have left." Her voice broke, tears spilling down her cheeks.

Veyl moved cautiously into the room. "I promise you I will fix this. I will get him back for you."

"You don't even know if he's still alive," she shouted.

"He is." He had to be. If she had gotten him killed… No. She refused to humor the possibility.

"The council won't send you to Vanris, Veyl. Why would they? They don't trust you or your people."

Veyl came forward and sank to her knees before the chair. She gently pried the sword from Kitria's grasp and set it on the floor, then took hold of her hands. "They have no choice, Kit. They can't afford to lose Kyril's fleet, and they don't have anyone else to throw at the problem who possesses the knowledge needed to negotiate successfully with my country. I doubt they will send me alone, but they will send me. Besides, with all the trouble I've caused them, they may even welcome the chance to be rid of me."

Kitria met Veyl's eyes, a desperate hope shining in hers. "Do you truly believe you can get him back?"

"I do."

"And if you succeed, then what will you do? Stand aside and watch as your people destroy us for what we've done?"

Veyl shook her head. "I will not let that happen. I am nothing here, but there I am a khesran with considerable influence over the leadership of my country."

"Maybe." Her shrug suggested skepticism, though it wasn't clear whether that was regarding the magnitude of Veyl's influence or her willingness to use it in their favor. "You won't come back here when it's over, will you? You'll let him lose you like he's lost everyone else."

Veyl met those sorrowful silver eyes, an ache spreading through her chest. "I don't belong here."

"The Qwilki believe you do, and the wave dancers as well." When she spoke again, her voice was barely more than a broken whisper. "And my brother."

"Kit..."

"Come on." Kitria stood up abruptly, forcing Veyl to scramble back. "We should eat something."

Acting as if nothing unusual had occurred, she wandered out into the kitchen and showed Veyl how to make yet another of the seemingly endless array of traditional Qwilki seafood dishes. This one involved a selection of shellfish and boiled root vegetables. They didn't speak beyond what was necessary to prepare the meal. After they ate, Kitria left the house. Veyl couldn't go with her. She was under specific orders to stay put until the council called on her. Given what was at stake, she intended to follow those orders.

It was nearing evening when guards arrived to escort her back to the Great Hall. Kitria hadn't returned yet. Veyl took one of the token shells gifted to her, a lovely piece that had a delicate engraving of a wave in its diminutive surface, and left it on the other woman's pillow. A gift. A peace offering. A promise.

The council awaited her in their usual place, the Hall still closed to the public. Nalika stood in front of the table between two councilors with her back to them. Veyl was all too aware of the woman's roles as one of Kyril's subordinate ahnkreths and, more importantly, an Evoker capable of drawing out her truth before these people. She would have to keep her answers simple and her thoughts from straying.

"Once more, Veyl, please tell us why you would

want to negotiate for the release of our fleet." Shyall's gaze was penetrating, as if she intended to read Veyl's thoughts herself.

It occurred to her then that some, or possibly all, of the council members could be mind-crafters. They hadn't shown that they were, but that was no guarantee. Nothing called out most mind-crafters as different from anyone else when they weren't using their ability, or often when they were. The visual manifestations that accompanied the Frightener ability were unusual in that way.

"Because I care for the people here and recognize that they are not that unlike me and those I love back home in Vanris. Having learned some of what they suffered with the Devastation and the Ukhen'kya attacks, I would have to be a monster to consider inflicting any further hardship upon them." She paused, meeting Nalika's eyes. "I won't lie and tell you I don't long to return to my home in Vanris. I also want to do what is best for the Vanrians you brought here. What I do not want is to see the people of Thaelis harmed in the process."

"Nalika?" Darith drew the Evoker's attention to him. "Does she mean what she says?"

Nalika answered cautiously, not looking away from Veyl. "Her thoughts support her statement."

"We will accept your proposal and send you back to Vanris with a few other representatives to speak for us." Excitement flared bright and warm in Veyl's chest at Darith's words, though he raised a hand to hold off any response from her, making it clear he had more to say. "However, you will consent to negotiating within the terms detailed in this agreement." He tapped a finger on one of two documents sitting before him on the table. "You will read over this agreement and sign both copies, one of which shall remain with us. The other you will carry with you to present to Vanris in your official capacity as a Thaelian officer and ambassador. On the first two pages, we have stated that Vanris must agree to return the fleet and crew of Ahnkreth Kyril unharmed. We will permit them to accompany said fleet back here to collect their people following certain restrictions as dictated in this document. Any Vanrian natives who wish to remain in Thaelis are to be allowed to do so. These conditions are not negotiable."

He pinned her with a hard stare. "Additionally, you will return with them to provide testimony and bear witness to Ahnkreth Kyril's trial for treason committed against the country of Thaelis. Once those proceedings are concluded and all terms within the agreement are satisfied, we will rescind your titles and discuss your potential return to Vanris. The following two pages cover other terms we would like to have met, but that you may negotiate on. Two trusted officers of Thaelis will accompany and advise you throughout the negotiation process."

"You say I will act as an officer and ambassador of Thaelis, but I am not either of those things. You have made it quite clear I hold no rank here," she said, wary of trapping herself in the agreement they had drawn up.

"Once you sign these documents, you will be recognized as Ahninveth na sek Veyl, Ambassador for Thaelis. You may approach and read the agreement."

Veyl stepped up to the table and Darith turned one copy to face her, sliding it forward. She took several minutes to read carefully through each page, then looked up at him. "You want them to agree never to return to Thaelian shores after they have retrieved those Vanrians who wish to leave here?"

"Yes. They will, under no circumstances, ever set foot upon our land again once we have concluded these matters."

"But what if there is mutual benefit to be had? Trade or—"

"Those are the terms," he interrupted, fresh anger in his narrowed eyes and tight jaw.

The more she interacted with them, the more she wondered how much of the careful isolation they maintained was primarily to avoid anyone questioning their leadership here. The conditions of the agreement also dictated that the man holding Veyl's zenyal bond would travel with them, acting outwardly as an advisor and fellow negotiator, and that the bond would remain in place at least until after Kyril's trial in Thaelis. Another condition she suspected they had no interest in bending on. "What of me? If I am to be here to take part in Ahnkreth Kyril's trial, how do I return home afterward?"

"We will discuss that once you have fulfilled the terms of this agreement." Shyall gestured to the pages with an elegant wave of one slender hand.

If she signed this, she would get to go home, at least for a time. She could argue for the release of the Thaelians and discover what had become of Kyril. It would also provide her a chance to get her people back to their homes with minimal conflict, but at the cost of tying herself to Thaelis, potentially giving the council an opportunity to use her as leverage against her parents going forward. Still, this was only the opening of negotiations. The first step was to get them to send her to Vanris, which they wouldn't do if she didn't agree to their terms.

"I would like one addendum."

Darith's brows rose at that, as if her audacity surprised him even now. "And that is?"

"No one else is to be given to the Ukhen'kya while I am away."

Several councilors shifted in their seats, and someone coughed near the end of the table.

Darith held her gaze. "No one will be given to the

Ukhen'kya while you are away. An easy enough addition, considering we do not deal with the Unclean."

By dropping the word 'else' from his response, he removed any admission of prior guilt from the statement, but the reactions of some others at the table suggested she was not wrong in her suspicions. For an instant, she saw red, her ability crackling to life in her chest, but she suppressed it. The first step in this had to be returning to Vanris. The rest she could figure out when she had people she could trust around her.

Darith glanced up and down the table, receiving nods from the others. Then he dipped the quill sitting beside him in the ink and wrote out the requested addendum at the bottom of both sets. Next, he signed the last pages, then turned them to her and offered her the quill, sliding the ink closer.

Heart pounding in her chest, Veyl accepted it and regarded the document. She didn't have enough experience to be confident there weren't traps written into those words, but no one here was going to assist her with that. The best she could do was sign and trust in the people back in Vanris to help her navigate the process. People she would see again soon.

"Since I am not being permitted to remain in Vanris, perhaps sending a few of our citizens home with me and allowing them to stay would be a useful gesture to demonstrate your willingness to work through this peacefully."

"I assume you have someone in mind," one of the other councilors prompted.

A mix of anxiety and hope fluttered to life in her chest. "The twins, Gannon and Ahrin, are the sons of two members of Khemron Kasiel's tehsheyn. Returning them and their tehnaaks to Vanris would be a powerful gesture that might help put the khevarin and khemron in a more receptive state of mind." She deliberately avoided calling them her parents, hoping it would come across as a willingness to act as a Thaelian asset.

"We will take your suggestion under advisement. You depart in two days with Ahnkreth Nalika's ship. Until that time, you are to discuss the terms of this agreement and the coming voyage with no one. We will see to it you receive proper attire befitting a representative officer of Thaelis for your journey. You are dismissed, Ahninveth na sek Veyl."

"One last question." The jumping of muscles in Darith's jaw as he clenched his teeth told her he was ready to be done with her, but she pressed ahead. "What will happen to Ahnkreth Kyril if you find him guilty?"

"Treason has but one punishment, Ahninveth. I am confident a woman with your background is fully aware of what that is."

Veyl found it hard to draw a breath past the constriction in her throat and the tightening in her chest. Kyril had done this for her, and it would destroy Kitria if she lost him. What she hadn't expected was how deeply it would apparently affect her if something happened to him. She hadn't lied when she said she felt at home in his arms, but that was a complication she simply couldn't allow for. They belonged to different worlds. Worlds she was about to try reestablishing the separation between. Still, that didn't mean she would let him die. Perhaps that was a problem her parents might also help her with, though convincing them to save him, assuming he yet lived, wouldn't be easy. Especially if Jaysen told them everything Kyril had done.

## CHAPTER TWENTY EIGHT

A few days later, Veyl boarded Nalika's ship wearing the fitted black and deep green uniform of the Thaelian military. She appreciated the asymmetrical cut of the fitted jacket and the officer's cloak that draped forward more over her right shoulder, the clasp near the left bearing a wave dancer etched upon it. Under different circumstances, she might have been happy to wear such attractively styled garments.

A satchel hung on one shoulder containing the agreement she was to carry with her to Vanris—the document that bound her to Thaelis. A shackle she would gladly endure if it ultimately returned the other captives to their proper homes. She wore three different token shells braided into her hair now. The spiral one Kyril had given her along with another Nagi had presented her with the day before. The third was from Kitria, given to her that morning to protect her on her journey with explicit instructions to pass it to Kyril for the voyage home. Apparently, Kitria didn't care if Veyl made it back. After everything she had lost and the fact that her brother's current predicament was at least partly Veyl's fault, it was hard to hold that against her.

Two of Ahnkreth Eavara's ships were preparing to embark upon the journey with them. They would accompany Nalika's ship halfway to see them safely through waters the Ukhen'kya were more likely to be encountered in. It struck Veyl as odd to put the escort at risk, since her Frightener ability was probably the most effective weapon the trio of ships had for fighting the Unclean. Still, she wouldn't object to the added sense of security. Her ability might have been successful against them on two occasions, but she wasn't eager to test it again.

The man who held her zenyal bond watched her from the forecastle deck. He was a lean, rugged looking individual with coppery red hair and bright amber eyes that reminded her of a tethdrak somehow. When she approached him, intending to introduce herself properly, he narrowed his eyes and gave a subtle shake of his head. Something in those amber depths chilled her, so she changed course, walking up to Nalika instead where the ahnkreth stood near her cabin, overseeing preparations for departure.

"Do you prefer Ahnkreth Nalika or Evoker Nalika?"

Nalika glanced at her, a hint of a sneer pulling up her lip. "Either is fine, Ahninveth *na sek* Veyl." She put extra emphasis on the na sek portion that called it out as a temporary title. "On the water, I prefer Nalika. Titles and ranks are a waste of breath."

Veyl lowered her voice. "Kyril told you why he took the fleet to Vanris, didn't he?"

"You changed everything with your games. The fate of our country hangs in the balance because of you. Now it is on your shoulders to find a path to peace that serves us all, assuming you will even honor the agreement you signed your name to." She cast a disdainful glance at the satchel Veyl carried. "It would not surprise me to see you turn against us the same way your Sarketi friend did."

Despite the death grip she was trying to keep on her temper, some of Veyl's anger broke through. "It takes a lot of nerve to be angry with me about this when you're the ones who ripped us from our homes to begin with. Have you considered that he might have chosen this path because he knew what you did was wrong?"

"Veyl?"

The voice that spoke her name made her breath catch. She turned to see Iyvalin and Ahrin stepping off the gangplank onto the deck. Not sure yet where their feelings toward her stood after how she had wronged them, she moved a few tentative inches closer, aware of Nalika stalking away. They both looked well enough at least.

"Iyvy. Ahrin. They're letting you come with us?"

When Ahrin didn't speak or move, Iyvalin stepped forward and gave Veyl a reserved, one-armed hug. Over her shoulder, Veyl saw Ahrin glance at the arm Iyvalin kept back from that embrace, the one injured by the throwing dagger meant for Veyl, a slight frown tugging down his lips. Guilt heated her cheeks as they parted. Ahrin, following his tehnaak's example, gave her a hug as well, though his was stiff and devoid of warmth, the reluctance of the gesture causing a painful twisting in her chest that she did her best not to let show.

"Where are we going?" he asked as he moved back from her. "They told us you had requested us for a brief sailing trip."

"Is that all they said? I'm surprised you bothered to come." Veyl clenched her teeth in frustration and glanced behind them at the gangplank being taken down. "What about Gannon and Lorek?"

Ahrin shook his head. "Lorek is afraid to be on a boat again after he was so sick on the way here, and Gannon doesn't—"

Iyvalin interrupted him with a hand on his arm.

Veyl blinked against the sting of tears. "He doesn't want to be around me."

"I'm sorry, Veyl." Iyvalin's voice was soft with what sounded like genuine sympathy.

"I don't see how you can blame them," Ahrin stated, a harshness in his manner she had never seen from him.

Veyl lowered her voice. "They have to come. We're going back to Vanris. I encouraged the council to return the four of you as a gesture of goodwill."

Ahrin's eyes widened, and he spun around, taking a faltering step toward where the gangplank had been moments ago.

Veyl turned to Nalika, who was giving the order to move out. "Wait! We're missing two people."

Nalika answered with a curt shake of her head. "I was told they're not coming. We need to go."

"We haven't left the port yet, Ahnkreth," Veyl countered. "I outrank you here."

Nalika stared at her. The entire crew had stilled. Her zenyal bond-holder stood up from the crate he was sitting on, and Iyvalin's mouth dropped open.

"What do you mean you outrank—" Ahrin cut off when Veyl snapped out a hand up to silence him.

If Nalika could have killed someone with her eyes alone, Veyl was confident she would be dead now, but she hadn't wasted the last two days. She spent that time studying the agreement, looking for loopholes or traps, and learning everything about what power her temporary rank earned her. On shore, an ahninveth outranked an ahnkreth of the same level. By some technicality, the law stated that the port fell within the limits of the shore for this purpose. Once they were out on the ocean, Veyl had to answer to Nalika, but here, she could legitimately call rank.

"Put out the gangplank," Nalika snapped. "You have five minutes, Ahninveth, and you cannot tell them our purpose until they are on board this ship. Your fellow Vanrians will wait here."

Not having Iyvalin and Ahrin to help her convince them would make it harder, but Veyl didn't dare waste a second. The instant the gangplank was down, she was on it, hurrying off the ship. When she stepped onto the dock and broke into a jog, her zenyal bond-holder came up next to her. It was the closest he had ever come, but she supposed maintaining a distance between them mattered less now that she knew who he was.

"Since we're bonded, might I at least have your name?" she asked when he kept pace alongside her.

His long hair flipped back in the breeze, revealing a deep, thick scar on the right side of his neck and a missing earlobe.

"Jinau."

She had expected him to ignore her or simply say no. Since he chose instead to allow her to open the door, she would take advantage of the moment. Although chatting while jogging through the streets of Dagony wasn't ideal, she couldn't pass up an opportunity to learn something about this man they had tied her to. "That's a Qwilki name, isn't it?"

He nodded, apparently not intending to elaborate. Had the door closed already?

"But you look Thaelian." Why did her friends have to have a house on the west side of town? Five minutes wasn't much time. Of course, knowing Nalika couldn't depart without their ambassador made the limit somewhat arbitrary.

"I had a Thaelian name until the tribes gave me this one."

There must be relevance to the fact that he used his Qwilki name, though it could simply be because he hadn't liked his Thaelian one. Still, she itched to know if something else motivated that choice. She stayed silent for a few blocks, focusing on long, steady strides that would allow her to cover more distance with less effort, skills she had learned as part of her regular training in Vanris. When she was as comfortable with her pace as she could be, considering her still-healing injuries from the kel'inuk attack, she asked, "Does it bother you that there are no Qwilki members on the council here?"

He gave her a stony look. "Don't borrow trouble, Seh'hali."

"Seh'hali?" When he didn't respond, Veyl focused on the task at hand. Later, she could investigate what Seh'hali was. Almost certainly an insult of some kind, though the tone with which he had said it, one closer to respect, made her wonder. Right now, she needed to get Gannon and Lorek on their ship.

When they reached the house, the guards stepped up to stop her, but a sharp gesture from Jinau moved them aside. That they didn't hesitate to obey his signal gave her another question for later. What was his rank that he commanded such prompt compliance? The uniform he wore was simple, without insignia of any sort to answer the question for her.

She knocked.

Gannon opened the door, eyes narrowing when they met hers, and immediately moved to shut it again in her face. They didn't have time for delicacy. She shoved her way inside. Jinau followed, the two guards coming into the entry after him.

"I'm sorry about what happened, Gannon," she said, stung by how rapidly he retreated from her, to go stand next to his tehnaak. "I will figure out how to make it up to you, but right now, you need to board that ship with Iyvalin and your brother."

"No." Gannon crossed his arms and stood firm.

Lorek shook his head. "Veyl, I nearly died on—"

"And we won't let that happen again. I promise."

"It's still a no," Gannon declared. "We're not going anywhere with you."

She drew a deep breath and gave him a look she hoped would convey the importance of the moment. "You don't understand. Ahrin and Iyvalin want you there."

"I don't see them here asking," he countered.

"They have given their answer," Jinau said. She didn't have to look to know he was coming up beside her. She could feel him moving closer through the bond he held. "The time to leave is now, Seh'hali."

She caught herself before snapping at him, remembering the power he could have over her if he chose to use it. Frantic, she hurried to Lorek, opening her arms as if to hug him goodbye. Gannon reached out to stop her, but Lorek met her eyes and his widened a fraction. Something, perhaps the desperation in her expression, compelled him forward into the embrace.

She whispered in his ear in Pandrean Common, "We're returning to Vanris."

His shoulders tightened, and a new gleam of hope lit his eyes when she stepped back. He turned to Gannon. "Ahrin is your twin, tehnaak. We should at least go find out why he wants us there."

Jinau scowled and shook his head at her. He wasn't about to be fooled that easily, but he didn't do or say anything to correct her for breaking the one rule Nalika had given her.

Veyl shrugged.

Gannon glanced from Veyl to Lorek, the latter responding to his look with a nod of encouragement. "All right."

"Can we grab a couple of items?" Lorek asked.

"No."

She frowned at Jinau. "Yes."

The man's expression didn't change, but a warning flash of pain in her head made her wince.

Veyl met his eyes, refusing to be beaten into submission

that easily. "Yes."

Jinau muttered something under his breath in Qwilki as Lorek led Gannon to the next room. When they came back, they both held small packs and Gannon looked excited, making it clear Lorek had shared the truth with him.

"We grabbed a few things for Iyvy and Ahrin too," Lorek said.

Veyl nodded. "All right. We need to get moving."

When they reached the ship, Nalika was pacing, looking ready to tear someone's throat out with her teeth. Veyl, knowing well whose throat she would prefer it to be, hurried them on board. Once there, she moved them to one side to stay out of the way as the crew began freeing the ship from its moorings.

"How did you arrange this?" Iyvalin asked.

"And why are you wearing one of their uniforms?" Gannon looked from her to Nalika, who wore a similar ensemble, and back with a suspicious glower.

Jinau had returned to the crate he was sitting on earlier and settled to observe her with the casual threat of a hawk watching a squirrel that would soon be dinner. Waiting. Veyl turned her back to him, moving the group closer to the ahnkreth's cabin.

She kept her voice low, uncertain exactly how much, if anything, Kyril had shared with his crew. "Kyril took Jaysen to Vanris like I asked, but they seized him and most of his fleet. They've demanded the return of our people. Thaelis fears losing the protection of another fleet after the recent Ukhen'kya attack, so they can't send everyone. I convinced the council to allow me to act as a representative for them in Vanris, and to let me take the four of you as a gesture showing their willingness to negotiate."

"What does it mean to be acting as their representative?"

She met Ahrin's gaze, finding it less uncomfortable

than meeting Gannon's. "It means I signed an agreement to negotiate on behalf of Thaelis. I am, for as long as it takes to satisfy the terms of that agreement, an officer and ambassador of Thaelis. I am required to return here when we are through in Vanris."

Iyvalin took hold of her arm. "No, Veyl. We can't let that happen."

"It's too late, Iyvy. I signed the documents. The important thing is that the four of you are going home for good, and if all goes well, the rest of our people will soon join you."

Nalika strode over to them now that the ship was clear of the port. "You may consider my cabin yours to use, Ahninveth Veyl. You and your companions can spend time there during the daylight hours if it keeps you out of our way. At night, I arranged other accommodations for myself so that you and your controller may sleep there. Be aware that I may walk in without knocking if I need anything at any hour."

"Thank you, Ahnkreth."

Nalika gave a curt nod and stalked away.

"Controller?" Lorek asked.

Veyl drew a deep breath and blew it out. "Remember the zenyal bond I told you Kyril used on me?"

The other four all nodded or, in Gannon's case, made a sound of disgust that served the same purpose.

"I am now bonded as zenyal to that friendly looking man sitting on the crate over there." She nodded toward Jinau.

Gannon's lip rose in a slight sneer. "The one who came to the house with you. Why?"

Veyl glanced down at the deck, a familiar guilt twisting in her chest. "Of anyone, I would expect you to have the least amount of trouble figuring that out."

His expression darkened.

"Can we go inside?" Lorek asked, already looking

paler as the ship rocked on the water.

Veyl gestured to the door.

Gannon yanked it open and stormed through, the others following more calmly after him.

"This will help."

Veyl nearly leapt out of her skin when Jinau spoke next to her, holding out a stick of the woody vine they used for seasickness. She glanced at him. He was chewing on another piece. Apparently, not a fan of ocean traveling himself.

"How did you… Never mind." She snatched the root from him and handed it to Lorek once they were inside.

Jinau followed them in and went to recline in a chair near the back windows, placing his boots up on the sill and gazing out at the water while they talked. For a time, his presence impeded their conversation, but they eventually adjusted to his presence and spoke more openly, though still avoiding subjects he might consider treasonous. They slowly relaxed into each other's company, Gannon and Ahrin more reluctant to move past what had happened between them than Lorek and Iyvalin. Lorek, despite the root, relented to persistent nausea after a few hours and left to find a bed to rest in. The other three departed with him, leaving Veyl alone with Jinau.

She wandered to the windows and stared out at the waves, feeling that call again that had drawn her to it in Deepwater. Had it always been the ocean that drew her, even as a child? For all that the kel'inuk, ji'ikyan, and scores of other dangerous creatures made their homes within its depths, she still yearned to touch those waters. Waters that the wave dancers and whales also swam in. She placed her fingertips against the window.

"Seh'hali ne Kunua," Jinau murmured.

The way he said it this time made her realize she had heard those words before. "Daughter of the Ocean," she murmured.

"Yes."

What Nagi had called her after the kel'inuk attack, and others since. She looked at him, but he continued to stare out at the waves. "What does that mean to the Qwilki?"

"It means they believe the gods of the ocean favor you. You are a spirit sister to the wave dancers and other revered creatures of the water."

"That's ridiculous. I was born and raised in the desert."

He looked at her, an unnerving certainty in his amber eyes. "Then it is fortunate that you finally found your way home."

Bothered by his words and bold regard, Veyl left the cabin and went to the stern of the ship to stand at the railing, remembering too well the night she had stood watching the whales with Kyril on his ship. The memory brought a pang of guilt and longing. What would she find when she reached Vanris? Her parents weren't cruel, but to the man who had taken their people and their daughter away, she suspected they could be. And what about Ceris? The wave dancer would have protected his companion from mind-crafter attacks, forcing them to find another way to subdue him, unless they killed Ceris or Kyril outright.

The crew avoided Veyl, which didn't surprise her, particularly if they knew she had convinced Kyril to take the fleet to Vanris. That they also mostly avoided Jinau, where he now sat on another crate watching her, was little consolation. Something about the man's presence was inexplicably unsettling. When she wandered back to the cabin as dark fell, he followed her again.

"Could you give me a moment to myself?" she asked, stopping inside the door. "I'd like to put on some less formal clothes."

He walked past her into the cabin. "I will not stop you."

"Sheyvyosk," she growled under her breath, getting a chuckle in response. "At least do me the favor of looking the other way."

Jinau sat at the window with his back to her, putting his feet on the sill again.

Veyl hurriedly stripped out of her uniform. She had just finished pulling on a simpler set of pants when he spoke.

"You lost your first tehnaak."

She froze. The only way he could know that was by reading the ke'hanoath on her neck and back. Veyl glanced over one shoulder at him, unsurprised to find him looking her way. "By the Break, couldn't you at least pretend that you weren't watching?"

Jinau chuckled and turned away.

Veyl tugged on her shirt and slipped a light jacket over it. "I assume you're a mind-crafter, if they assigned you to me." She moved another chair close to the windows and sat.

He grunted assent. "Ahndhomen Charmer Jinau, if you fancy big titles."

Veyl snorted a laugh. "Charmer? At least we know the world has a sense of humor. That would make you the ranking officer here."

"Yes, but it is still Nalika's ship. Unless I feel she is acting against the council or putting us in danger, I defer to her on this vessel."

Veyl put her feet up on the sill. "You aren't that frightening after all."

He looked at her, all traces of humor vanishing from his eyes. "Don't pretend to know what I am, Seh'hali. The council compensates me well to be the darkness in our world."

A chill swept through her. She wasn't sure what he meant by that, or if she even wanted to know. "I think I'll turn in." She took her feet down and wandered over to crawl into the bed.

*

The violent rocking of the ship startled her awake some-time later. A flash of lightning outlined Jinau where he stood at the back windows, legs splayed wide and hands on the sill to balance against the wild motion. Wind howled outside and rain pounded loudly on the wood of the deck above. The world tilted as the bow of the ship climbed what felt like a mountain, giving her a view of the trough between two massive waves through the aft windows. Then it crashed down, jarring her as it cleared the crest of the wave. Her stomach turned, and her thoughts went to poor Lorek.

Veyl slid from the bed and hurried to the door, al-most falling when the bow rose again, climbing another wave. She pulled the door open, and the wind ripped it from her hand, slamming it against the outside wall of the cabin.

"Stop," Jinau shouted after her.

Veyl rushed out, the pummeling rain soaking her instantly. She could barely see ten feet with the wind blowing rain into her face and the spray from the waves crashing over the deck in the darkness. Several members of the crew were struggling to move around doing whatever they did on a ship at such a time. At least one appeared to be checking the bindings holding some crates and barrels in place, while a couple of others were attempting to retie a rope that secured part of one of the furled sails. She heard Nalika shouting something from farther along the deck, but she couldn't see her or make out her words.

Remembering well enough where the entrance to the area below and the crew's quarters was located, Veyl hurried that way. She had only gone a few yards from the cabin when the ship crested and came down hard again, throwing her off her feet. The force slammed her into the railing, the impact flaring pain in far too many places where injuries from the kel'inuk's attack were still healing. She started slipping overboard and grabbed frantically for purchase on the wet wood. A hand closed on her arm, pulling her down to crouch inside the rail. She froze, staring between them into the raging waters, petrified by what had nearly happened.

Jinau's fingers were like iron, digging into her jaw as he forced her to look at him. His other arm wrapped around her, pinning her against the rail. "You go over in this, you are lost. When I yelled stop, you should have done so. I will not be gentle or kind, Seh'hali, but I swear I will protect you. Deeps take you if you are too young and impulsive to recognize that for the gift it is."

Heart racing, she looked into his eyes. The coldness in them brought back the earlier chill, but there was something else in those bright amber depths. A fear like that she had seen in her parents' eyes the day she nearly fell from the academy rooftop. "You believe what the Qwilki say about me."

His jaw tightened. "I was watching when the sey'yaluth ayon helped you onto the beach. Wave dancers do not lie." Looking away, he waited until the ship had crested the next wave, then hauled her to her feet, dragging her back inside with a vice-like grip on her arm. "Stay here. I will check on your companions."

She stared after him as he laboriously forced the door shut behind him. Doing her best not to fall on her ass, she changed into dry clothes and went to sit on the bed that was solidly fixed to the floor. She curled back against the wall and closed her eyes, feeling the movement, the power, in each wave. It was both terrifying and awe-inspiring.

About the time she started worrying that she might have gotten Jinau tossed overboard with her folly, he came back. The storm was dying down, and water streamed from his hair and clothing.

"Your friends are well. Young Lorek suffers from the ocean's dislike for him, but they brought something stronger this time to help your delicate desert-born systems survive the voyage." He strode past, pulling off his sodden shirt as he did so.

Her gaze caught on a set of three thick scars that ran from his right shoulder and across his back at an angle to just above the waist of his pants on the left side. The scars destroyed much of a ke'hanoath tattoo done in three columns of symbols down the left side of his spine, making it illegible in places. Should she read anything into the fact that he had never asked a Heartsmith to fix it?

"Thank you, Jin." She turned away when he unfastened his pants. "I... I need them to make it through this all right. In Dagony–"

"I know what happened between you and your companions. It is why they gave you to me as zenyal."

She touched her jaw where it was still tender from his fierce grip. He had forced her to meet his eyes. "You didn't Charm me earlier, did you?"

He chuckled. "I told you I would not be gentle or kind, Seh'hali. Charming you would spare you the responsibility for your own actions. I will not do you that favor."

The storm, for all the misery it caused, at least pushed them in the right direction, speeding them on their way to Vanris. Veyl and Jinau conversed very little over the next several days. Nalika's crew remained reluctant to interact with her, though she found a few willing to let her follow them and teach her some of what they did on the ship, continuing her education from the journey to Thaelis. Outside of that, she spent a portion of each day at the stern railing, watching the ocean. During those times, Jinau often came to stand with her, rarely saying anything. Words didn't seem necessary. She felt as if they had come to an understanding the night of the storm.

She still had questions about the Charmer Ahndhomen. Why did he use his Qwilki name? Why did he let his ke'hanoath remain broken? How could he embrace tribal beliefs, yet serve the Thaelian council that did nothing to represent those people? How could he call her Seh'hali and believe her favored by the Qwilki gods while accepting ownership of her as zenyal? They were questions she wanted to ask, but something held her back. Perhaps she simply feared discovering what he meant about being the darkness in the world.

Being stuck on a ship together made it nearly impossible for the twins and their tehnaaks to avoid her. Lorek remained below deck most of the time, and Gannon rarely left him, but Ahrin and Iyvalin ventured out more, spending evenings in the ahnkreth's cabin, navigating the rift that had formed between them and gradually bridging it.

Iyvalin's arm was still healing. The blade had done substantial damage to the muscle over her collarbone. It would require months of rehabilitation to resume normal functionality. Being the kind person she was, she didn't hold it against Veyl, choosing to see it as an injury she sustained protecting her friend rather than focusing on why the guard felt compelled to attack Veyl in the first place.

Gannon, on the few occasions he and Lorek joined them, was more of a challenge. What she had done to him—unleashing her Frightener ability and turning his private fears into a weapon against him—wasn't something he appeared willing to work through, especially given his rather confrontational nature. That it had required a Thaelian Evoker meddling in his memories to fix it added insult to the injury she had caused. Still, he had concealed her involvement in their plans to escape their captors, despite how difficult keeping thoughts from an Evoker could be. That wasn't the type of effort a person went to on behalf of someone they hated, and it gave her hope that he would come around in time.

Tonight, Veyl stood at the back of Nalika's cabin, staring out at the calm nighttime waters, wondering if any of her relationships would ever be normal again when a heavy exhale from Jinau drew her attention.

"Eat." He gestured to the food she had brought in that was now growing cold on the table. "We should reach your country on the morrow."

Her stomach did a flip at his words. The thought of seeing her family and Jaysen again made her feel like she could fly, but remembering her commitment to Thaelis and obligation to return there instantly clipped those wings. That she had agreed to argue for the opposing side in negotiations would put a strain on her relationships with all of them, but the cost to her would be worth it if it helped save her people still trapped in Thaelis. With Nalika and Jinau looking on, her performance in those duties would be under constant scrutiny. And that wasn't all that had her gut tied in knots.

"It is Ahnkreth Kyril and his companion you fear for."

Veyl scoffed at him. "Why would you say that?"

"Because you wear a bracelet, a necklace, and three tokens in your hair, but it is always the same one you reach for when you become lost in thought."

Veyl jerked her hand away from the spiral shell, realizing when he smirked at her that her defensive reaction only reinforced his point. Warmth spread through her cheeks.

"It is admirable that you can see past his misdeeds enough to care for him, but balancing your loyalties will not be easy in the days ahead."

She caught herself reaching for the shell again and willed her hand to her side, then walked to the table to sit and poke at her meal. "He may not even be alive at this point."

"He is."

Veyl stared at him, wanting to believe him. "How can you sound so certain?"

"The ocean would have punished you by now had you sent him to his death."

She rolled her eyes. "I suppose you're going to tell me he is some divine child of the ocean too."

The hard look he gave her was devoid of humor and doubt.

She sighed and took two bites of the now-cold fish. The third she set back down on her plate, gazing into a sauce that might have been much more appetizing when it was still warm. "I wish I knew what to expect. I've never done something like this before."

"You've never held the futures of two societies in your hands?"

"You're not helping." She pushed the food away across the rough wood of the table. This cabin wasn't as nicely appointed as the one on Kyril's flagship, though the differences were subtle—the plain hardware on the cabinetry, the slightly less smooth finish on the wood surfaces.

And why couldn't she stop thinking about him? There was more at stake than the life of one man she had developed an inappropriate infatuation with.

"We all face uncertainty ahead, Seh'hali. Yours is not a path you walk alone, but those who travel it with you might not wish to make peace with each other. You must convince them to stand together or decide who you will stand beside in the end." Jinau pushed the food back in front of her, his face a mask of infuriating calm. "No matter the path, you will need strength to follow it."

"By the Break, I hate you," she growled under her breath, picking up the fork.

Jinau chuckled.

*

Mid-morning the next day, she stood on deck with Iyvalin and Ahrin, hoping for a view of Pandrea, but a dense cloud cover hung low over the water, reminding her of the day the Ukhen'kya attacked Thaelis. Not a comforting association. She wore the Thaelian uniform again, as prepared as she could be to start fulfilling the agreement she had signed her name to. Anticipation was electric in the air, making her jump at the smallest sounds on the deck behind them.

"Are you truly going to negotiate for them?" Ahrin stood beside her, staring down into the dark water, his hands gripping the rail a little too tightly.

The good people Veyl had met in Thaelis—Nagi, Quillon, Kitria, and many others—flashed through her thoughts. And Kyril. The man who led the fleet that stole them from their homes. The same man she had given herself to. Her cheeks grew hot with that memory. "Yes. Not for the council's benefit, but for the people of Thaelis. If we punish the country, we hurt them, and most of them don't deserve it."

"She's right." Iyvalin moved her shoulder in a careful circle. The sea was calm enough that she could stand without holding the rail, so she used her other hand to guide the injured arm. "All the ordinary people we met there were warm and welcoming. I wouldn't choose to harm them either, even if it means letting their leaders off easy."

Ahrin's hands loosened on the railing, a hint of the softer side she had always known peeking through. "I suppose you're right. I can't argue with both of you, anyhow."

"No, you can't. And don't forget it." Iyvalin poked him in the ribs, making him twist away with a light laugh.

That was a sound Veyl hadn't heard from any of them in too long, but she had a mere moment to appreciate it before another sound cut through the quiet morning. The blare of a horn. She recognized the alert from their encounter with the Unclean on the crossing to Thaelis and turned to scan the horizon, catching sight of three ships emerging from the low clouds off the starboard bow.

Jinau stood up from the crate he was sitting on as Nalika hurried over to them. "Those are Sarketi ships."

The ahnkreth pointed toward steps that would take them below deck. "Go to the crew's quarters and stay there until someone calls you up. They can't see Vanrians on board. They're already going to be suspicious because of our location."

Veyl nodded and hurried below with the other two, Jinau following close behind them. They joined Gannon and Lorek, the latter looking a little less pale today with the calmer waters, though he had visibly lost more weight during the crossing. If he had to do it again, she feared he would waste away to nothing. Jinau stopped near the stairs, perhaps to listen or be in position to act if something went wrong. Veyl considered staying with him, but it would increase the risk of her being spotted, so she accompanied the other two.

As Ahrin explained what was happening to Gannon and Lorek, Veyl wandered to a starboard porthole and pressed against the wall to peer discreetly out. A Sarketi ship was circling around the bow as the other two moved in on the starboard side. One slowed a short distance away while the third continued toward the stern as if they meant to surround the Thaelian vessel. Not an encouraging start to the encounter.

"Away from the portholes, Seh'hali," Jinau called sharply from the stairwell.

Though he couldn't possibly see her from where he was, he probably could see that she wasn't with the others. Scowling at the wall that hid him from view, she walked over to stand beside Iyvalin.

Gannon's brows pinched. "Seh'hali? Is that some Qwilki insult?"

"Everything he says sounds like an insult, but that isn't one." She didn't elaborate beyond that. Her body hummed with nervous energy, the faint lightning crackle of her ability rising with her nerves.

When she started pacing, Iyvalin set a hand on her

arm to still her.

Off the port side, a man's voice called out in passable Vanrian, marked by a distinctive Sarketi accent. "You're part of the fleet from Thaelis. We've been waiting for you in Sarket. Must have been a Havaad-cursed voyage for you to end up alone this far north."

"Greetings, Captain," Nalika shouted back. "We became separated from the rest of our fleet in a storm. An unfortunate setback, but nothing insurmountable."

Veyl held her breath. How close were they to shore? If the Sarketi captain wished to make trouble, he had the upper hand at three ships to one. Given recent incidents, there should be Delaphinian and Vanrian fleets patrolling the area, but the low cloud cover gave Sarket an advantage for the moment.

"Unfortunate, yes. What I find even more unfortunate for you is that we received word a few days ago that the rest of your fleet was spotted anchored in Vanrian waters. We came north to investigate those rumors. I'd say your presence here is confirmation enough, wouldn't you agree?"

The captain knew too much. Nalika needed to be exceedingly quick-witted to convince him there wasn't more to this, if it wasn't already too late for that.

"Seh'hali," Jinau called in a low voice, gesturing her closer.

Veyl hesitated, still listening to the conversation above.

"I told you we became separated. Storm damage may have forced them to turn toward shore sooner than planned," Nalika hedged.

"And their Vanrian hosts welcomed them in, did they? After you attacked two of their towns and abducted their people? How charitable of them." The Sarketi captain was playing with her. That much was clear now in his words and tone.

Nalika must have recognized it too, for she didn't bother to respond this time.

Veyl took a few steps toward Jinau.

A loud explosion broke the silence and Veyl fell against the wall when something smashed through the side of the ship. Jinau leaped between her and fragments of wood that sprayed across the quarters. Crew members who had been resting after working through the night woke with cries of alarm, except for a few directly in the path of larger projectiles who wouldn't be waking at all.

Jinau moved away from her, several splinters of wood sticking out of his back when he turned. Veyl looked for the others. Ahrin was leaning against the wall spitting blood, a long gash on the side of his jaw. Iyvalin sank down next to Lorek, who lay unmoving, blood streaming from a wound on his head.

"Lorek!" Gannon dropped to his knees next to his tehnaak. Red welled around several splinters in the arm he must have used to shield his face from flying debris.

The faint crackle of Veyl's ability swelled to a tempest, overpowering her emotions. She heard a crash elsewhere as another Sarketi bomb hit the ship.

Jinau grabbed her wrist. "Come with me. We will show them the ocean's fury."

Veyl didn't want to leave her friends, but she let him pull her to the upper deck. As she suspected, the Sarketi ships had surrounded them, putting themselves in a position to attack from multiple angles at once. The main mast was burning and Sarketi soldiers were firing more flaming arrows at the ship, lighting up the sails. One of Nalika's crew members staggered past them with an arrow in her chest and tumbled down the stairs.

Veyl didn't need direction. She focused her ability, sweeping out over the Sarketi ship on the starboard side. Imagery bombarded her, disparate fears creating swirling chaos in her mind. Falling, drowning, being torn apart by Vanrian beasts, burned in a fire, eaten by sharks—so many varied personal horrors rushed into her, feeding her ability. She stretched farther, unleashing her power as she went, and reached out to those on the ship on the port side now. Here and there, she touched a Thaelian mind and, feeling the difference in their fears and the flavor of their presence, pulled instantly back from them.

The surrounding chaos rapidly altered. People were still shouting and screaming on the Thaelian ship, but more screams came from the two vessels on either side of them now. Sarketi soldiers on the decks of those ships threw down their bows and ran below or cowered where they stood. Some even leapt overboard to escape the horrors her power manifested. What should have been a certain massacre of the Thaelian crew transformed into a desperate scramble by the Sarketi to escape the onslaught of her Frightener ability. Veyl reached out to the ship off the stern, drawing their nightmares into the mix.

Then her power touched on other minds. Neither Sarketi nor Thaelian. Not Vanrian either. She turned, struggling to see what was really in front of her and separate it from the terrors of hundreds of people racing through her mind. More ships approached, emerging from the low clouds. First one, then three, then five, all flying the flags of Delaphine and Vanris.

Veyl withdrew from them, holding the Sarketi crews locked in their individual nightmares, lightning crackling through her, searing her from within. The new ships spread out, sweeping in on the Sarketi vessels. She needed to hold them long enough to let the allied soldiers take control of the situation. Closing her eyes, she stopped trying to see and simply felt as the storm raged so fiercely within her it became impossible to hold on to her other senses.

She wasn't sure how long it continued. Someone caught her when her legs gave out and eased her down on the deck.

"It is enough, Seh'hali. You have won."

Jinau's voice floated in the distance. The storm had her fully locked in its embrace now. She wanted to end it, to escape all the fear spinning through her mind, but she couldn't get free.

"We need you here. You must stop, or you will break yourself."

A familiar darkness swept in around her, suffocating pressure closing in on all sides. She lost everything. Her friends, her family, her life. The darkness ripped it away, devouring it all.

Veyl screamed, her own fears wresting her from the storm. The darkness and pressure retreated instantly. She opened her eyes and looked up into eyes the same pale gray-green as her own.

Arhk's smile was strained. "I see you take after me in more ways than we realized."

Veyl sat up and threw her arms around his neck, trying vainly to hold back her tears. "I needed you," she sobbed, becoming the child again who had woken from her failed Trial to find him there.

"I am here now," he whispered, wrapping her in a secure embrace. When they parted, a rare hint of moisture shone in his eyes as he helped her to her feet.

Panic burst in her chest, spiking the headache that now pounded through her skull. "Lorek. He was injured. We need to help him."

"The twins are also here?"

Veyl nodded, taking in the surrounding scene. Two sails were burning along with some crates near the bow, and the ship was listing in the water. Arhk's three ever-present black-armor clad guards—an Evoker, a Speaker, and a Dampener—were standing close by, ready to act on his orders or in his defense. Other Delaphinian and Vanrian soldiers had boarded the ailing ship, moving in to take the Thaelian crew members prisoner. Jinau gave a look of warning to the two approaching him.

"Stop!" Veyl shouted. "These people are not to be arrested. They are part of a Thaelian contingent sent here to negotiate." She was still a khesran of Vanris, and they did stop, even the Delaphinian soldiers who looked to Arhk for confirmation.

His gaze took in her uniform and the shells in her hair, and he scowled. "These people abducted you and many other Vanrians. I will not suffer them to walk free on our soil."

"Dhomvalen, I return here as Ahninveth na sek Veyl, Ambassador of Thaelis. We can discuss the details of that later." Veyl glanced past him to where Nalika stood watching them, her eyes full of dreadful expectation. She was waiting for Veyl to betray them now that she was home, the same way it appeared Jaysen may have turned on Kyril. The two men who had taken hold of Nalika's arms let go. Veyl stood straighter. "If you will not respect that, then know that these people also come here under my protection as Khesran of Vanris. Beyond that, there isn't time to argue. Lorek may be dead or dying, and I am sure there are others who need our help. This ship is sinking. Let us address those problems first."

Arhk's eyes narrowed. "*Can* you be our khesran and their ambassador?"

She lifted her chin. "Give me a chance."

A hint of pride crept through in his stern regard, oddly mirrored in Jinau's expression.

rhk turned from her and called out, "Search this ship for anyone alive and move them to the flagship. The Thaelian crew is to be disarmed and kept under watch, but not bound or imprisoned. Anyone severely injured is to be stabilized as quickly as possible. Lock Sarket's soldiers up on our other ships. They will face trial for attacking a vessel carrying Vanrian citizens—" his unreadable gaze flickered to her "—and our khesran, in Vanrian waters." When they rushed to obey his orders, he shouted, "I also need a healer to follow me now!"

A Vanrian man ran over and Arhk faced Veyl. "Take us to Lorek, Ahninveth."

Veyl bowed briefly to him before hurrying to the stairs. Jinau went down ahead of her, watching for hazards as he led the way. Several splinters of wood still stuck out of his back, blood seeping around them. Veyl cringed inwardly, resisting the urge to pluck them out as she followed him into the crew quarters.

They had moved Lorek to a cot. Gannon knelt next to it with his face buried in the pillow alongside his tehnaak's head, his ragged sobs muffled, several splinters still protruding from his arm. Ahrin was beside him, one arm wrapped around his brother's shoulders and tears running down his cheeks while he pressed a cloth to the gash along his jaw. Iyvalin rushed to Veyl and grabbed onto her. She broke into sobs as the healer walked over to check Lorek's pulse, careful not to disturb the twins. He glanced back at Arhk and shook his head.

"No." Veyl choked on the word, tears breaking free. She wrapped her arms around Iyvalin, squeezing her eyes shut. Her chest seized, making it hurt to draw a breath.

"Seh'hali," Jinau spoke in a low, firm voice, "we cannot mourn here. I will help carry him to the other ship, but we must leave this one now."

"He is right," Arhk said. "This vessel is sinking."

When Jinau approached, Gannon broke free from Ahrin and surged to his feet. "Stay the fuck away from him, you Thaelian bastard!"

Veyl let go of Iyvalin and stepped forward. She met Ahrin's eyes for a second before facing Gannon, not bothering to wipe away the tears running down her cheeks. "Why don't you and Ahrin carry him? I imagine he would prefer that."

More tears spilled from Gannon's eyes as he nodded, glaring at Jinau as if the man had killed Lorek with his own hands. Turning silently, he slid his arms under Lorek's shoulders, a sob breaking from him when his tehnaak's head lolled to one side. Ahrin lifted Lorek's legs, and together they carried him toward the stairs, Iyvalin following.

Arhk ordered soldiers coming down to search for more survivors and sent the healer with them. Then he turned to Veyl, giving Jinau a wary look. "I am taking you to the flagship. They can handle the rest here."

She nodded, wiping at the tears that still slid quietly down her cheeks, and let him lead them up the stairs.

They had barely set foot on the deck of the Delaphinian flagship when a Vanrian soldier jogged up to Arhk.

"Dhomvalen." She offered a hasty bow. "There are

nearly forty Sarketi soldiers who are alive, but unresponsive. How would you like us to deal with them?"

"Was there blood coming from their eyes or ears?" he asked.

"Yes, Dhomvalen."

Arhk cast Veyl a thoughtful glance before answering, his gaze flickering briefly to Jinau still standing at her shoulder. "Their minds are broken. There is nothing we can do for them. Kill them."

"Yes, Dhomvalen." The woman bowed again before hurrying off.

The twinge of guilt in Veyl's chest vanished when she glanced at her companions carrying Lorek's body below deck. They had gotten no words of parting. He had been with them one second, then gone forever. Taken from them by Sarket. Gannon had lost his tehnaak. All of them deprived of a dear friend, and for what? Because Thrasser wanted to stay in power? None of them would have been here now if the Thaelian council hadn't tried to restore the population without sacrificing their power. Even fury at the senselessness of it all couldn't fill the hollow in her chest.

Arhk faced them, his icy gaze once again falling on Jinau. "Who is your shadow, Khesran... Ahninveth Veyl?"

"This is Ahndhomen Jinau." She hesitated, considering what else she might say about him, but somehow less information struck her as the best option for the moment.

"And what he called you earlier?"

Jinau saved her the trouble of figuring out how to answer that. "Some natives in Thaelis have grown fond of Ahninveth Veyl. Seh'hali is a title of respect they have given her."

Veyl wiped at the dampness on her cheeks. "Could we discuss this all later? Ahndhomen Jinau could use a healer's care, and I would like to be with my friends."

A hint of sympathy softened Arhk's regard. "You have until we reach the shore. Then there are matters we need to discuss."

"Thank you." She started turning away, pausing when Jinau didn't immediately follow.

The ahndhomen inclined his head slightly to Arhk. "Dhomvalen, how did you know to come when you did?"

Arhk took measure of the other man before answering. "A local fishing vessel spotted Sarket's ships moving through the low clouds south of here and came to alert us. They are permitted to sail in these waters, but the law requires them to announce their presence and purpose before doing so. We came out intending merely to intercept them and ascertain their reason for being here."

Jinau responded with a nod and grunt before turning to follow Veyl below.

As soon as they entered the crew quarters where the injured were being taken, Veyl spotted her companions. Gannon sat against the wall beside Lorek's body, his head hanging, one hand on his fallen tehnaak's arm. The splinters were gone, but blood still trickled from the wounds. He had probably chased the healer off before they finished tending the injuries. Ahrin sat next to his brother with a cloth still pressed to his jaw, Iyvalin leaning against his other side, her head on his shoulder.

Veyl beckoned a healer over to tend Jinau's injuries. It felt right to ensure he received proper care, given that he had taken those wounds shielding her from the blast. With that handled, she sank down by the wall on Lorek's other side.

Gannon looked up at her. "If not for you, I..." He closed his eyes and swallowed.

Veyl longed to comfort him, but without knowing whether he meant to curse her or something else, she wasn't sure how to respond.

He swallowed a second time, staring at his hand on Lorek's arm. "I might have lost him on the way to Thaelis if you hadn't convinced them to let me help him. Thank you for giving us more time. If I had known..." His voice cracked and he fell silent. He pulled his knees to his chest and dropped his head onto them as fresh sobs wracked him.

Ahrin got up, lifting Iyvalin by the hand. He gestured to his brother with his chin. Despite lingering uncertainty, Veyl stood and traded places with them. She sat next to Gannon, Iyvalin and Ahrin sinking down in her former spot on the other side of Lorek. Wary of a possible violent reaction, she cautiously moved her arm around Gannon's shoulders. Relief and heartache warred inside her when he curled against her, letting her hold him as he cried, far too grief-stricken to cling to his resentment for what she had done in Dagony. She stroked his hair and placed a kiss on his head, knowing nothing she could say would ease the pain of a loss this profound.

A short distance away, Jinau straddled a chair. He sat watching them, never flinching as the healer pulled splinters of wood from his flesh and cleaned his wounds.

It didn't take long to reach shore. Once the ships were as close as they could get without running aground, those going ashore transferred to tenders. Ahrin and Gannon rode the last stretch to the beach on a small boat with Lorek's body. Veyl rode in another with Iyvalin, Jinau, Arhk, and his three guards. Part of Nalika's crew stayed on the Delaphinian ship under watch since they had limited facilities for housing them all at the base. Nalika and the rest boarded boats heading ashore, relieved of their weapons, but not bound as the surviving Sarketi soldiers were.

Her parents had stationed Arhk with a modest com-pany at a military base on the edge of the southwestern

Vanrian border to coordinate with their Delaphinian allies and watch for foreign ships. Among those who came down to the beach to meet them, Veyl spotted Darro, Kince, Tath, and Nerith. Seeing members of her father's tehsheyn, people who had helped raise and train her, brought tears to her eyes.

Ahrin and Gannon's tender reached the shore first. Ahrin leapt out before it was all the way in, racing through the water and up the beach to his parents, Tath and Darro. He practically fell into their arms. Veyl envied him in a way. Not just for getting to have that reunion now, but for the simplicity of it and the fact that he would stay on Pandrea when the time came for her to depart for Thaelis again. Gannon didn't leave the boat until it slid up on the sand. Then he stumbled out and sank to his knees, not making it past the edge of the surf. Tath got to him first, kneeling next to her son and pulling him into a frantic embrace. A second later, Darro and Ahrin were there too, all four kneeling in the wet sand, holding onto each other.

The tender Veyl was on came ashore and Iyvalin jumped out, rushing to join the others. Veyl disembarked and walked far enough to escape the water, Jinau coming up to stand near her. She wanted to support Gannon, but he needed his family now, not the supposed friend who had lashed out at him with her ability.

Arhk walked up beside her. "You do not plan to join them?"

Veyl shook her head, swallowing against the sorrow that constricted her throat.

"There has been some conflict between the five of you?"

Veyl heaved a sigh full of regret. "Controlling my ability has been difficult. I unintentionally attacked Gannon with it. They had to use an Evoker to undo the damage."

"I did the same to your father when he first came to Etrion, and I had far more experience than you in dealing with my ability."

Veyl faced him. "You did? He never told me that."

Arhk grimaced. "I believe it is something he and I both prefer to forget." He looked at her. "That does not excuse it, but a Frightener ability as powerful as yours can be difficult to contain, especially when your emotions are running high. I can help you with that."

"You may never understand how desperately I've longed to hear you say that." Veyl moved closer, nudging her way under his arm until he relented and put it around her shoulders with a soft laugh.

"I am pleased to see some of the little girl I helped raise is still in there," he murmured.

She closed her eyes, letting everything else fall away. Standing with someone she loved, whom she had never expected to see again, was enough for the moment.

"Veyl!"

Opening her eyes, she spotted Nerith running over to them. She pulled away from Arhk and stepped into the healer's embrace. Nerith held her tightly, hugging her like they hadn't seen each other for years. It felt wonderful. Arhk was not one for large displays of affection. He expressed more with her than most, but the embrace he had given her on the ship was the maximum show of emotion she was likely to get from him. Nerith's enthusiastic hug eased some of the ache inside. Would it be like this to see her parents, Jaysen, and her brother? Even better, perhaps.

Nerith drew back, taking Veyl's face in her hands, tears streaming down her cheeks. "I feared we had lost you forever." She pulled Veyl into another hug, then let her go. She cast a brief glance at Jinau, her expression darkening a fraction. "Are you all right?"

Veyl looked past her to where the twins and their

family were now walking up the beach behind a stretcher carrying Lorek's body, Darro's arm around Gannon's shoulders, heading toward the black stone fort on the rocky hillside. Lorek had nearly made it home. Tears stung her eyes again. "That's a complicated question to answer."

"I imagine so." Nerith followed her gaze and took her hand, squeezing it gently.

Two Vanrian soldiers escorted Nalika over to them. Arhk's guards stepped closer to him at their approach. The Thaelian woman's gaze fell expectantly on Veyl, reminding her she had accepted certain responsibilities.

Intentionally changing her tone to something more formal, Veyl turned to Arhk. "Dhomvalen, where are the Thaelians from the fleet that arrived here before?"

The warmth in Arhk's regard faded. "Some we sent on to Etrion, the rest are imprisoned in the barracks here."

Fighting to keep her tone neutral, she asked, "And the Feral Ahnkreth who leads them?" She became more aware of Jinau standing next to her and Nalika watching her as butterflies fluttered wildly in her chest, their wings beating out a rhythm of hope and fear.

"Taken to Etrion along with his beast."

It was all she could do to hide the giddy relief that swept through her. He was alive. She drew a soft breath, calling upon some of the control she had gained sitting on the rocks with Erkhan in Dagony. "I signed an agreement with the council in Thaelis to represent them in negotiations with Vanris. I carry a copy of that document with me."

Arhk's eyes narrowed slightly, and he nodded. "Let us go to the fort. I would like to look over this agreement before we decide on our next actions."

Veyl hesitated when he started walking away, turning instead to face the ocean. The mighty expanse of water that could be as beautiful as it was deadly. She was in her country again. Nearly home. And yet, putting her back to the ocean felt wrong somehow, as if she were leaving some essential part of herself behind.

Coming home should have brought a sense of relief, but it felt more like the start of a larger battle. She touched the spiral shell and closed her eyes, letting the rising breeze brush across her face, depositing the taste of salt on her lips.

"Ahninveth Veyl." Arhk's tone was sharp, his displeasure with these new developments cracking his typically infallible composure.

She opened her eyes to find Jinau watching her with a discerning gaze. "Seh'hali," he murmured, gesturing inland, "the ocean will wait for you."

Arhk stared back at them, no doubt scrutinizing every interaction.

Veyl faced her grandfather, steeling herself. "Jaysen, did he stand up for the Thaelians?"

For a second, Arhk merely stared at her, a curious pinching between his brows. He shook his head. "No, he did not."

It appeared Jaysen had not been the ally in this that she had hoped he would be. Perhaps, if she talked to him, he would reconsider his position. She was eager to see him, but these developments would cast a shadow over that reunion.

Veyl drew another deep breath of the salty air, using it to counter the uncomfortable twisting in her chest, and walked up beside her grandfather, who resumed his trek toward the fort. Jinau and Nalika fell in on her other side, staying a step behind.

Arhk didn't look at her when he spoke. "I would like to tell you your ordeals are over now that you are back where you belong, but considering the circumstances around your return, I suspect you have traded one ordeal for another. I hope you are prepared for the challenges you will face."

She lifted her chin, a difficult feat with the body of a long-time friend being carried to the fort on a litter ahead of them. "I have to be." For the people here and those she had left behind. They all stood to suffer if she failed.

**THE END**

<u>Glossary</u>

*Terminology*

| | |
|---|---|
| **Calloch** | Rank ball of monkey shit. A favored insult in Vanris. |
| **Company (military)** | The units and unions under the command of a single dhomen or ahndhomen. |
| **Crack a stone** | Popular Vanrian phrase meaning to open and drink a stoneglass bottle of Vanrian Black Mead. |
| **Evalis** | Black fruit used to make Vanrian Black Mead. Imported from the original Vanrian homeland. |
| **Ke'hanoath** | Each Vanrian's or Thaelian's individual story represented in symbols tattooed somewhere on their person. |
| **Mindcraft** | Unusual abilities possessed by some Vanrians/Thaelians to manipulate the minds of humans or animals. |
| **Mind-crafter** | Someone with a mindcraft ability. |
| **...na sek** | Appended to an officer rank when a promotion is temporarily granted for a specific mission. |

**Sheyvyosk**

Stinky smegma.

**Stoneglass**

A Vanrian light metal alloy that looks like stone and is extremely durable. Primarily used to make bottles for Vanrian Black Mead… naturally.

**Tehanyehn**

A romantic spirit pairing connected by a Bondmaker (considered a deeper form of the marriage vows practiced in the southern kingdoms).

**Tehnaak**

Spirit siblings, bound to each other by a Bondmaker and raised together.

**Tehsheyn**

Spirit family, bound by a Bondmaker.

**The Deeps**

Vanrian solitary confinement in Etrion.

**Union (military)**

A grouping of three regular units combined under a third or fourth level ahninveth or inveth.

**Unit, Regular (military)**

A group of thirty-nine soldiers under a single inveth or ahninveth.

**Unit, Feral (military)**

A group of nine soldiers and up to twenty beasts under a single Feral ahninveth.

**Zenyal**

A type of unequal bond formed by a Bondmaker that gives one half of the pairing a measure of control over the other.

*Ranks & Titles:*

**Khevarin**

Ruler of Vanris – the rough equivalent of a king or queen.

**Khemron**

Spouse of the ruler of Vanris, shares some of the leadership.

**Khesran**

Child of the khevarin and khemron – basically a prince or princess.

**Dhomvalen**

Protector or warden. Top Vanrian military leader who answers only to the khevarin.

**Ahnvaris**

Dedicated elite guard to important personages.

**Dhomen**

A Vanrian or Thaelian officer – the rough equivalent of a general in the southern kingdoms. There are four levels.

**Ahndhomen**

A Dhomen who is also a mind-crafter (slightly outranks a dhomen). There are four levels.

**Ahnkreth**

A Vanrian or Thaelian officer – commander of a naval fleet.

| | |
|---|---|
| **Inveth** | A Vanrian or Thaelian officer – the rough equivalent of a captain in the southern kingdoms. There are four levels. |
| **Ahninveth** | An Inveth who is also a mind-crafter (slightly outranks an inveth). There are four levels. |
| **Inren** | A Vanrian or Thaelian common soldier. There are four levels. |
| **Omren** | A Vanrian or Thaelian mindcrafter common soldier. There are four levels. |
| **Idrek** | A Vanrian or Thaelian recruit – soldier in training. |
| **Odrek** | A Vanrian or Thaelian mindcrafter recruit – soldier in training. |

### Other Terminology

| | |
|---|---|
| **Havaad** | A god worshipped in parts of the southern kingdoms, particularly in Sarket. |
| **Pandrean Alliance** | An alliance formed between the three southern kingdoms of Delaphine, Sarket, and Fallend to fight Vanris. |
| **Hyeralisk** | Qwilki term for a deadly hurricane. |

| | |
|---|---|
| **Qwe'pi** | Crude Qwilki insult. |
| **Ket'ta** | The shell of a crustacean in Thaelis. Often used for making cups and small bowls. |
| **Eydarith** | Culture in Sarket that worships the Tempest, god of the sea. They have a unique language and consider themselves separate from the other citizens of Sarket. |
| **Itovanak** | Strong alcohol favored by the Eydarith. |
| **Ukhen'kya** | The Unclean. A cannibalistic culture in conflict with the residents of the Thaelian islands. |

### *Mindcrafting Disciplines*

| | |
|---|---|
| **Bondmaker** | **A mind-crafter who can cre-ate bonds between two or more individuals by using the life threads that exist within them.** |
| **Charmer** | A mind-crafter who can manipulate an individual or small number of individuals to go along with their suggestions. |
| **Dampener** | A mind-crafter who can interfere with the way people's minds perceive their senses, |

effectively taking away the sight, sound, smell, and/or touch of individuals or groups.

**Enkindler**

A mind-crafter who can inspire positive or negative emotions in individuals or groups.

**Evoker**

A mind-crafter who can see and sometimes alter a single individuals surface thoughts and memories.

**Feral**

A mind-crafter who can connect with, influence, and control the minds of animals or groups of animals.

**Frightener**

A mind-crafter who can access the fears of individuals or groups and cause them to see terrifying visions, sometimes permanently scarring their minds.

**Heartsmith**

A blind mind-crafter who can tap into people's deepest thoughts and emotions in an abstract way to read the story of who they are in order to tattoo it upon their skin.

**Speaker**

A mind-crafter who can speak into the minds of individuals or groups, limited somewhat by range and visibility (less so if their subject is also another Speaker).

### *Unique Creatures*

**Cliff Cat**

Large wildcats native to the mountains in Vanris. Some Ferals use them in combat. They have a deep blue-gray coat with darker blue stripes down the spine along either side of a ridge of longer hair. Their eyes are sapphire blue, and their tails end in a puff of hair the same blue as their stripes. Adults tend to be around waist high to a man at the shoulder.

**Kanodrak**

Impressive Vanrian predators brought to Pandrea from the original Vanrian homeland. Taller than a horse and used as mounts by a few Ferals. Vaguely feline with a silver-grey, scaled hide and milky white eyes. They have bone armor plating that starts at the nose and runs along the spine to the base of their long tail. Their massive front incisors extend below their lower jaw.

**Kednu**

Large deer on the Thaelian islands that are sometimes used
as pack animals and occasional
mounts.

**Kel'inuk**

Similar in appearance to a
salamander, but capable of
growing much larger than a
horse, these ocean-dwelling
amphibians have no teeth.
They crush prey repeatedly in
their powerful jaws and swallow it whole.

**Nightstar Eagle**

Large black eagle with gold
feathers sweeping back from
its eyes and along the lower
edge of its wings and tail. Revered by followers of Havaad
in the southern kingdoms.

**Sandhawk**

Desert hawks commonly seen
in southern Vanris and around
the Crimson Break.

**Tethdrak**

Vanrian predators brought
to Pandrea from the original
Vanrian homeland. Some
Ferals use them in combat.
Built a little like a hound, but
reptilian. Adults grow to rib
high to a man at the shoulder.
The thickly muscled limbs
and torso are covered in light
shades of red and brown
scaling with spiked plates
along the length of the spine
and thick tail. Two backswept
horns extend from the head

and their massive jaws bristle with sharp teeth.

**Wave Dancer**

Sey'yaluth ayon in Qwilki. Tall, amphibious canines. Narrow built with long slender legs, fishlike, gleaming black scales over the forehead, across the front of the shoulders, and along the back of the hips. They have odd, glossy black fur made up of long, thick strands. The black ears are partially transparent like a bat's wings and have fine ridges at intervals in the membrane, giving them the appearance of fins. They have broad scaled paws, with webbing between the toes designed for swimming. They tend to have eyes of some shade of blue or green.

*Places*

**Andaro**

Capital city of the kingdom of Sarket.

**Balarus**

Large town south of the Break in northeastern Sarket.

**Crimson Break**

War-devastated, desert region between Vanris and the southern kingdoms.

**Crimsondale**      Town where the incident that started the war happened. Now part of the Crimson Break.

**Dagony**      Port city on the main island in Thaelis.

**Deepwater**      Small integrated town on the western coast of the Crimson Break.

**Dekingham**      Main capital of Delaphine.

**Delaphine**      Eastern kingdom on Pandrea. Home to the Delaphinian people.

**Doran**      The northern capital of Vanris.

**Etrion**      The southern capital of Vanris.

**Fallend**      Southern kingdom on Pandrea. Home to the Fallenese people.

**Fernwallow**      Small village in Fallend.

**Hellaris**      Town in Sarket.

**Kilden Mountains**      Mountain range near the coast in Sarket.

**Mukyeny**      Town on one of the islands in Thaelis.

**Pandrea**      The continent.

| | |
|---|---|
| **Sarket** | Western kingdom on Pandrea. Home to the Sarketi people. |
| **Taro** | Coastal city in Sarket, mostly run by the Eydarith. |
| **Thaelis** | Island chain about a week west of Pandrea. |
| **Vanris** | Northernmost kingdom on Pandrea. New home to the Vanrian people after volcanic activity drove them from their original island home. |
| **Vareyl's Warning** | Black crags that create a natural border between northern and southern Vanris. Called Vareyl's Gift before the war. |

### *People*

| | |
|---|---|
| **Adnar** | Vanrian ahndhomen / Feral kanodrak rider / Nevias's tehnaak) |
| **Ahrin** | One of Darro and Tath's twin sons, named after his mother's deceased former tehnaak / Gannon's brother / Iyvalin's tehnaak |
| **Aitan** | Vanrian dhomen |
| **Anahela** | Qwilki woman |

| | |
|---|---|
| **Arhk Cavenos** | Dhomvalen of Vanris / Frightener / Veyl's grandfather |
| **Astrid Lodmund** | Queen of Sarket / Jaysen's mothert |
| **Avris** | Vanrian inveth and combat instructor / Merrin's tehnaak / part of Kasiel's tehsheyn |
| **Cordin** | Fish market owner / Quillon's brother |
| **Darith** | Thaelian councilor |
| **Darro** | Vanrian dhomen / Gannon and Ahrin's father / Kince's tehnaak / part of Kasiel's tehsheyn |
| **Eavara** | Thaelian ahnkreth (fleet com-mander) / Speaker |
| **Ellaris** | Jethan and Keyla's second daughter, named after Veyl's deceased grandmother / Tavin's tehnaak |
| **Erkhan** | Thaelian Dampener / part of Eavara's crew |
| **Fen** | Deck boy / part of Kyril's crew |
| **Ferda** | Qwilki woman |
| **Genyith** | Former khemron of Vanris / Veyl's grandfather |

| | |
|---|---|
| **Hila** | Qwilki pastry chef |
| **Illis** | Thaelian soldier / part of Kyril's crew |
| **Iyvalin** | Arin's tehnaak / Veyl's friend |
| **Jaysen Lodmund** | Crown prince of Sarket / son of Roald and Astrid / Veyl's best friend |
| **Jethan Markanis** | Vanrian ahninveth / Charmer / Kasiel's tehnaak and part of his tehsheyn / father of Ellaris and Veyl's former tehnaak, Minya / Velara's cousin |
| **Jinau** | Thaelian ahndhomen / Charmer |
| **Kasiel Cavanos** | Khemron of Vanris / Feral kanodrak rider / Vey's father |
| **Keyla** | Velara's tehnaak / mother of Ellaris and Veyl's former tehnaak, Minya |
| **Kince** | Vanrian inveth / Darro's tehnaak / part of Kasiel's tehsheyn |
| **Kitria** | Kyril's younger sister |
| **Kyril** | Thaelian ahnkreth (fleet commander) / Feral |
| **Lanis** | Vanrian attendant who helped raise Veyl |

| | |
|---|---|
| **Lorek** | Gannon's tehnaak / Veyl's friend |
| **Mardi** | Thaelian guard |
| **Merrin** | Vanrian dhomen and combat instructor /Avris's tehnaak / part of Kasiel's tehsheyn |
| **Meyla** | Thaelian officer / Kyril's second |
| **Minera** | Vanrian ahnvaris / Dampener |
| **Minya** | Jethan and Keyla's first daughter who died very young / Veyl's first tehnaak |
| **Nalika** | Vanrian subordinate ahnkreth / part of Kyril's crew |
| **Nerith** | Vanrian healer / Tath's tehnaak / part of Kasiel's tehsheyn |
| **Nichal** | |
| **Nevias** | Vanrian dhomen / Adnar's tehnaak |
| **Quillon** | Thaelian guard |
| **Rel** | Thaelian soldier / part of Kyril's crew |
| **Roald Lodmund** | King of Sarket / Jaysen's father |
| **Setera** | Vanrian ahndhomen / Evoker |

| | |
|---|---|
| **Seylin Markanis** | Former khevarin of Vanris / Enkindler / Veyl's grandmother |
| **Shyall** | Thaelian councilor |
| **Tarik** | Vanrian city guard |
| **Tavin** | A khesran of Vanris / Veyl's younger brother |
| **Tath** | Vanrian healer / Gannon and Ahrin's mother / Nerith's tehnaak / part of Kasiel's tehsheyn |
| **Velara Markanis** | Khevarin of Vanris / Charmer / Veyl's mother |
| **Veyl** | A khesran of Vanris / heir to the Vanrian throne / daughter of Kasiel and Velara |
| **Wilkin Thrasser** | King regent of Sarket |
| **Yserra** | Vanrian ahnvaris / Evoker |
| **Zafyr** | Vanrian ahnvaris / Evoker |

## ACKNOWLEDGEMENTS

Whether you started with the Warden's Son series or this is your first adventure in the tales of Vanris, thank you for joining me on this journey. I hope you enjoyed this book and will continue to follow Veyl's story in the next two books. There are a number of people I would like to offer my appreciation, so I will try to capture them all here.

To my mom, Linda, who has been my alpha reader through so many books and provided so much support and valuable feedback throughout the process. I can't imagine doing this without you.

As always, my best friends and beta readers, Rick and Ann, who somehow continue to stand by me regardless of where my crazy goes. You are now, and always will be, my tehsheyn.

To my additional beta readers, Patrick, Marla, and Lyra, your feedback was invaluable. You are greatly appreciated. And to all the ARC readers who have joined this journey, thank you!

As always, I want to acknowledge the fantastic team who helped me put together the finished book. Robert Crescenzio, my incredibly talented cover artist whose vision helps bring these books to life on the covers. Melissa Nash, the fantastic map designer who helped Kasiel's vision of the land come to life. Alexander Lockwood, my fantastic editor, fellow author, and now friend. Brian Short, my amazing formatter, whom I would also like to thank for your excellent company on many coffeeshop writing days. I love working with you all.

To my other friends and family, know that I love you and value your place in my life even if I don't call you out specifically here.

Last, but certainly not least, to my readers. To me, a book is a collaborative effort between the author and the reader. Without you, this world would only ever come to life in my head. I hope you enjoy experiencing it as much as I did and will continue along the journey as the rest of this series releases into the world.

# AUTHOR BIO

Outside of my career as an author, I am a professional technical and creative writer, spider wrangler, animal lover, and devoted cat mom. Writing fantasy and science fiction stories has been a lifelong passion for me. I love to draw upon my myriad life experiences for my books, doing everything from wild cave exploration and horseback endurance riding to practicing iaido and archery.

●

Thank you for taking time to read this novel. Please leave a review if you enjoyed it.

●

For more about me and my work visit me at http://elysiumpalace.com.

# OTHER NOVELS by NIKKI McCORMACK

CLOCKWORK ENTERPRISES
The Girl and the Clockwork Cat
The Girl and the Clockwork Conspiracy
The Girl and the Clockwork Crossfire

THE WARDEN'S SON
Child of Vanris
Blood of Vanris
Heart of Vanris
Throne of Vanris

FORBIDDEN THINGS
Dissident
Exile
Apostate

ELYSIUM'S FALL
Dark Hope of the Dragons
Dark Savior of the Dragons

SILVERBLOOD RAVEN
A Path of Blood and Amber
A Path of Secrets and Dreams
A Path of Storms and Reckonings

STANDALONE WORK
Golden Eyes
The Keeper
Making Monsters (short story)
In Silence Waiting (short story)
And they All Look Just the Same (short story)

## WAVE-TOUCHED

The fort overlooking the ocean at the southwestern corner of Vanris was built of the same black stone used in the border watchtowers and much of the city of Etrion. It was odd how just the sight of that stone made Veyl homesick for the black city even while she dreaded leaving the ocean behind. Weary after the voyage from Thaelis and heartsick from losing Lorek in the Sarketi attack on their ship, she followed Dhomvalen Arhk through the grounds and into the main keep. The two Thaelian officers, Jinau and Nalika, accompanied them.

The loss of Lorek hung heavy over a brief reunion with the Gannon and Ahrin's father, Darro, and his tehnaak, Kince. Despite the sorrow weighing on them all, their warm welcomes eased some of the feeling she had of no longer belonging in her own homeland, brought on at least in part by the role she had assumed as an ambassador for Thaelis. These people, members of her father's tehsheyn—his bonded spirit family—were as much her family in a way as her grandfather, Arhk. Still, the Thaelian uniform she wore created a distance between them, so she found comfort in an unexpected source. Whenever they passed an open window, the rumble of the nearby ocean soothed her, provided she didn't dwell too deeply on her connection to those untamable waters.

Ahrin, Gannon, and Iyvalin disappeared into a private room where they could grieve. Tath, the twins' mother, and Nerith, both healers who had firsthand experience losing a tehnaak, carried food and drink into the room to join them. Veyl watched them shut the door with an ache of longing. Her new role didn't afford her the opportunity to share in their mourning.

Instead, she followed Arhk to a large meeting room where some attendants were delivering food and drink. Kince, Darro, and the officer in charge of the fort, joined them. At Veyl's insistence, the two Thaelian officers, Jinau and Nalika, also sat at the table. She hoped to set a precedent for both sides by including them in proceedings from the start. Arhk's elite trio of guards took up positions along the wall behind him, their intimidating stares locked on the two Thaelians.

Arhk eyed her new companions. "What discipline of mind-crafters are you?"

"Charmer," Jinau stated in his concise, less-than-charming way, his amber eyes taking in their company and the stark, utilitarian surroundings.

Veyl caught the faintest hint of a smirk on Arhk's lips before he schooled it away and shifted his expectant gaze to Nalika.

"I am an Evoker, Dhomvalen."

Arhk's expression hardened, and he gestured to one of his guards. "Ahnvaris Zafyr is an Evoker as well. She will know if you use your ability here. Be warned that we will consider doing so a hostile act. I strongly advise against it."

Nalika's lips pressed into a tight line. The look she gave Zafyr when she nodded her understanding was far from friendly, but she wasn't foolish enough to believe she had a choice now that she was among the minority. Seeing the woman forced to rein in her temper wasn't nearly as satisfying as Veyl would have liked it to be.

Arhk's icy regard came to rest on her. "Let me see this agreement, Ahninveth."

She had an instant yearning to be anywhere else. How would he react to the demands the Thaelian council made in those pages? What would he think of the terms she had agreed to, such as returning to Thaelis when this was over or maintaining the zenyal bond with Jinau? Would he consider her a fool for having signed it? He might be her grandfather, but he would always be Dhomvalen, the military leader of Vanris, first. That was just his nature.

Drawing a shallow breath to brace herself, she reached into the satchel and pulled out the papers, handing them over to him. After neatly unfolding and smoothing them out on the table, he inclined his head to read, some of his long, white-blond hair falling forward, conveniently masking his reactions from the Thaelians sitting off to that side. Veyl followed his progress from across the table, remembering every line from the hours she had spent studying their contents. The others took advantage of the opportunity to drink and partake of the fruit and bread. Hungry though she might be, Veyl's roiling stomach and dancing nerves aggressively rejected that distraction.

Arhk's expression remained diplomatically neutral until the exact moment she expected it to change, then darkness crept in at the edges of his eyes and pressure increased in the room. A ripple of tension moved through the group, most of them fully aware of how his Frightener ability manifested.

Arhk's gaze rose to Jinau, his voice dangerously calm. "You have the audacity to assume such control over a khesran of Vanris?"

The other three Vanrians at the table looked between Arhk and Jinau now, unspoken questions on their lips, though none of them appeared willing to step in front of Arhk's anger and ask.

Jinau didn't flinch before the dhomvalen's fury or shrink from the darkening of his pale, gray-green eyes. "The Thaelian council ordered me to hold this bond solely as a method of protecting our people from her uncontrolled Frightener ability. I intend Ahninveth Veyl no harm, nor do I desire to demean her."

Trying to ignore how disconcerting it was to hear Jinau use her title and actual name for once, Veyl said, "I agreed to leave it this way." She had consented to those terms under duress because she believed she had little choice if she wanted to convince them to send her home, but the circumstances didn't matter now. She needed to keep the situation from falling apart before negotiations got underway or her role as ambassador would become meaningless. They hadn't even reached Etrion yet. "Please, Dhomvalen, Ahndhomen Jinau suffered injuries shielding me from the explosion when Sarket's ships attacked ours. I believe you can take him at his word when he says he means me no harm."

Arhk's nostrils flared as he drew a breath and he clenched his jaw, the black slowly retreating from his eyes.

"Pardon, Dhomvalen Arhk, but to what control are you referring?" Kince asked, absently brushing some of his long blond hair away from his face, exposing the symbols of the dark blue ke'hanoath tattoo on that cheek.

"They have tethered her to this man using a zenyal bond."

The three still looked lost.

"It is a type of nonreciprocal bond that allows the dominant half of the pairing the ability to, among other things, inflict debilitating mental pain on the submissive one." Arhk's voice was thick with disgust as he explained it. "A method of control that was outlawed soon after the first Vanrians set foot on Pandrea."

Arhk turned his attention back to the agreement and resumed reading. It was the thoughtfulness that had stolen over Jinau in response to his words that intrigued Veyl now. Intense calculations were working behind his amber eyes, and she itched for insight into what they were.

Arhk folded the document and handed it back to her. "You signed your name to these pages. For now, it seems, you must abide by the commitment you made to Thaelis. We can revisit that, and the other terms discussed therein, once we reach Etrion."

He turned his attention to Darro and the officer in charge of the fort, apparently not bothered by the scowls the implications behind his words drew from Nalika and Jinau. "Sarket's attack on any ship in Vanrian waters is a breach of their fealty agreement. Not that it is the first such infraction they have committed in recent months, but it was the most public and one that will necessitate a response sooner than we might have preferred."

"Is Jaysen here?" Veyl asked before either man could respond.

"The crown prince has gone into hiding in Etrion for now," Arhk answered. "Sarket is not yet aware that he lives."

"And he did not vouch for the Thaelians who brought him here?" She had asked him on the beach, but frustration with the situation compelled her to ask again, hoping that he might elaborate on his earlier answer.

Arhk shook his head, confusion furrowing his brow. "As I said before, he did not. In fact, he encouraged us to imprison them and use them as leverage against their country. Why would he have defended his captors?"

Jaysen had not merely ignored her request. He had done the exact opposite of what she requested of him. Granted, she was never able to explain the entire situation to him in Dagony, but she had asked him to work with Kyril. The Feral ahnkreth must have discussed his intentions with Jaysen on the crossing over. What convinced him to turn against them? Not that the Thaelian attack on Deepwater and their abduction wasn't reason enough for him to want to. Jaysen hadn't gotten to know people in Dagony the way she did. They never wanted him in Thaelis to begin with. But she had dared to hope he would trust her. The only way she might understand why he chose not to would be to talk to him.

"It doesn't matter right now. We need to continue to Etrion. We can straighten all of this out there. There are negotiations to be held, and I wish to see my parents and my brother." She stood. "We've wasted enough time."

Arhk rose, gesturing for the others to remain seated. "I would like to speak to my granddaughter alone for a moment. Stay and refresh yourselves."

Nalika shifted as if she meant to follow, but Jinau caught her arm and shook his head. When she settled, he met Veyl's eyes, and she nodded, offering him a look of gratitude. He answered with a slight nod of his own. She would grant him her trust, but she expected the same in return, and it appeared as though he would give it, for now.

Veyl followed Arhk through a door and up a narrow flight of stairs to a private study on the second floor. He strode to a window at the back of the room, looking over the outer fort wall toward the ocean. Walking up beside him, she gazed out at the water and the ships moving beyond the shore. The mighty expanse beckoned, and the prospect of leaving it behind sharpened the sorrow she was trying to keep buried.

"We have a Bondmaker here, Veyl."

She was silent for a moment, considering his words.

He was offering to remove the zenyal bond, but it would mean breaking the agreement with Thaelis before negotiations had even gotten underway. Not the most promising place to start from. "No. I will stand by the pages I signed as long doing so doesn't bring more harm to my people."

Arhk turned to consider her. "Why? The Thaelians cannot touch you here."

She faced him, a flush of determination warming her. "Because I want to protect the Vanrians who are still on Thaelis. And because the people of Thaelis are good people, even if their leaders leave something to be desired. I refuse to see any of them harmed by this conflict if I can prevent it. Besides, I know Ahndhomen Jinau will not abuse the power of the bond. Seh'hali ne Kunua means Daughter of the Ocean. The natives on Thaelis, the Qwilki, believe I am blessed by their ocean gods. He is, as best I can tell, more Qwilki at heart than Thaelian. He would not harm me unless he felt he had no other choice."

"He had best not," Arhk stated flatly. "It will not end well for him if he does."

Veyl removed the edge from his words with a fond smile. "I missed you."

He looked her over, his gaze taking in her garments and the decorations in her hair. "It is unsettling to see you in their uniform, wearing their trinkets on your Vanrian braids."

She touched the spiral shell, hearing the echo of Jinau's remark in her head, noting how the one Kyril had given her was always the one she reached for. "These tokens are a Qwilki tradition. As is the hair stain many of the Thaelian crew members use. There is much I could tell you about why I want to protect them, but perhaps it makes more sense to save all that for when my parents are also present."

Arhk drew a breath, sorrow pinching his brows as he considered her. "You are not the same young woman who left for Balarus with her parents. You have clearly grown and learned a great deal in a relatively short time. I hate to imagine what you must have suffered for the experience to have changed you this much."

Veyl looked out at the ocean again. Memories flashed through her mind. Of the attack in Deepwater and the severing of her renewed tehnaak bond with Jaysen, of the voyage to Thaelis and her struggles with Kyril and her ability, and that moment of despair when she had tried to kill herself. And of when she lashed out at Gannon with her power and shattered the trust of her dearest friends, one of whom she would never have the chance to make it up to.

But it wasn't all pain and misery. There was her newly discovered affinity for the ocean and the way Ceris had expressed a fondness for her from the start that left her feeling a little less alone. Many people in Thaelis had welcomed her warmly enough that she felt compelled her to protect them from the Ukhen'kya and to save Nagi from the kel'inuk. Through it all wove the thread of that strange and unexpected connection she had developed with the man who had taken her from her home. Her cheeks flushed at the memory of his touch, his kiss, of everything she had given him.

"It feels like years since I left here," she murmured.

"I am skeptical of your support for these people, Veyl," Arhk said, drawing her attention to him. "I will not pretend otherwise. And I do not envy you the task of convincing your parents to negotiate with them after what they did to you and so many others. You have grown stronger out of necessity, I fear. I will stand by you so long as I believe you are the one behind your convictions, and they are not the product of some outside influence."

She looked deep into those eyes that matched her own. The one person who could truly understand the challenges she faced with her ability. "Thank you."

He stepped close to place a kiss on her forehead, then gestured toward the door. "Let us rejoin the others. We have a few days of travel still ahead to return you to where you belong, and I am curious to see what your vision of the future regarding our relations with these people looks like."

Veyl glanced out the window once more. She was finally back in Vanris, ready to negotiate with her own parents on behalf of those who had taken her from them. She had no intention of letting the Thaelian council come out on top, but she hoped to find a way the people of both countries might win. Whether that was possible didn't matter. She intended to try.